## Dante regarded Min with dark fathomless eyes.

"I _____ my child, ine ... would be family."

"I...I suppose," she said.

"There will need to be photographs of us together, as I would not be a neglectful father."

"No indeed."

"Of course, you know that if Isabella were really my child there would be only one thing for us to do."

"Do I?"

"Yes." He began to pace, like a caged tiger trying to find a weak spot in his cage. And suddenly he stopped, and she had the terrible feeling that the tiger had found what he'd been looking for. "Yes. Of course, there is only one option."

"And that is?"

"You have to marry me."

**Millie Adams** has always loved books. She considers herself a mix of Anne Shirley (loquacious but charming and willing to break a slate over a boy's head if need be) and Charlotte Doyle (a lady at heart, but with the spirit to become a mutineer should the occasion arise).

Millie lives in a small house on the edge of the woods, which she finds allows her to escape in the way she loves best—in the pages of a book.

She loves intense alpha heroes and the women who dare to go toe-to-toe with them (or break a slate over their heads).

*This is Millie's stunning debut for Harlequin Presents—we hope you enjoy it!*

# *Millie Adams*

---

## THE SCANDAL BEHIND
## THE ITALIAN'S WEDDING

**⬦HARLEQUIN**
# PRESENTS

Recycling programs
for this product may
not exist in your area.

ISBN-13: 978-1-335-89355-0

The Scandal Behind the Italian's Wedding

Copyright © 2020 by Millie Adams

This edition published by arrangement with Harlequin Books S.A.

For questions and comments about the quality of this book,
please contact us at CustomerService@Harlequin.com.

Harlequin Enterprises ULC
22 Adelaide St. West, 40th Floor
Toronto, Ontario M5H 4E3, Canada
www.Harlequin.com

Printed in U.S.A.

# THE SCANDAL BEHIND
# THE ITALIAN'S WEDDING

For the book girls. Keep dreaming. Keep reading.

# CHAPTER ONE

IT WAS RUMORED that Dante Fiori could condemn a man to any level of hell he chose with the mere lift of his brow.

Powerful. Ruthless. Determined.

Dante was not a man to be trifled with or tested. He'd raised himself up from the slums with the aid of his mentor, Robert King, but then not only had he gone on to exceed the man's expectations, he'd increased his fortune, as well.

Dante was a force in the world. A man all other men looked to—save his best friend, Maximus King, who found him overrated in the extreme and was the only person who had the nerve to say so. A man all women wanted to be with.

A king in whichever kingdom he chose to rule, whether he was a King by blood or not.

So it was shocking, then, when the world

turned on its axis right in the middle of the King family's grand living room.

Dante was in town, and he'd been invited over, as he often was, to join the family for their rather loud and raucous get-togethers. They were celebrating the launch of their oldest daughter Violet's new makeup line, in a live video being broadcast from a nearby San Diego beach, to millions of viewers on her various media platforms.

Robert was lounging in his oversize chair, his wife, Elizabeth, sitting on the arm. Maximus was sitting back on the couch, one leg flung out in front of him, phone in one hand, a scotch in the other.

There was one family member missing. Two, actually. Minerva King, the youngest daughter and constant irritant, and her baby.

Dante had difficulty accepting the existence of the newest, smallest member of the King clan.

Min was nothing like Maximus or Violet. Maximus was a brilliant PR mind. A handler to the most difficult clients in the world. He did everything with a smile that the untrained eye might not be able to see was shot through with steel.

Violet was stunning. Keen and ambitious, she'd transformed her beauty into a multimillion-dollar enterprise. She was the driving force and face of her brand.

Then there was Min.

A little brown mouse who scurried about the grounds, always trailing about the place with animals dripping from her arms and a skinned knee. Her cheeks were always red, her hair always in a state.

And she talked. Constantly. About nothing.

She'd gone abroad to study nearly one year ago, and when she'd returned, it had been with a baby who was barely a month old. While initially shocked, over the past four months her family had accepted the existence of the little girl easily enough. The Kings weren't old-fashioned.

The shock hadn't come from the fact their daughter had broken with tradition and had a child out of wedlock—presumably with a foreign stranger—but that it had been Minerva and not Violet.

Dante did not feel accepting of it at all. He felt a strange burning in his chest when he looked at Min with the baby. This untamable, wild thing now tied down to earth by a child. By motherhood. She should be…out climbing trees. No matter that she was twenty-one, he couldn't wrap his mind around the fact that she was a woman now.

A *mother*.

The other urge he had was to find the man who had done it to her and send him back to dust.

Send him straight down to the ninth level where he could sit next to Lucifer himself.

It infuriated him perhaps because Minerva always seemed so hapless. Running around like a windmill, and falling down, often undented. Though she had been badly dented once at an event of her father's, and he remembered it well.

Some boy she liked publicly humiliating her on the dance floor.

Robert King had nearly had a stroke, and his anger had only embarrassed Min all the more.

She'd been seventeen or so. Dante had danced with her because she'd needed a partner.

*Don't let them see you cry.*

He'd said it sternly. More than he'd meant, but it had done the trick.

The idea that someone had harmed her now enraged him all over again.

He wasn't in the habit of questioning himself. He simply acted when he felt action needed to occur. And perhaps that was the issue here. There was no action to be taken.

It didn't matter. Minerva didn't matter. Neither did her current situation.

All eyes were on Violet and would be for the next fifteen minutes while she unveiled her next series of products. And then it would be time for Dante to speak to Robert about the joining of the two companies again.

He had been trying to tell Robert it was the best thing for everyone. And, of course, some of it was that Dante felt entitled to King Industries as he had helped to build it. He had gone off and made his own fortune, but his ultimate goal was a merger between the two.

Of course, Robert had feelings about keeping it all in the family.

But Maximus had no interest at all. Maximus was a billionaire, and his business methods were unorthodox. He had no interest in manufacturing.

Violet was much the same, and while she used King Industries to help make her products, she developed them on her own, and used her father's business simply for the manufacturing end, containing development and distribution within her own brand.

Only Minerva remained to take over the family business, and he knew that Minerva would have no interest in such a thing.

She was not... Ambitious.

Minerva was not brave.

If she were here now, it would be as if she weren't. She would simply be sitting in a corner, clutching her baby and looking around.

Unless she began to chatter.

But typically, she was quiet as her father commanded during times such as these.

Violet's beautiful, perfectly made-up face appeared on the screen, and the whole family paid heed. Dante looked up, sparing the screen only a glance before looking back down at his own phone.

But then, a moment later it wasn't Violet's voice he heard.

"I know you're watching to hear about my sister's products, and not to hear family gossip. But, as her new makeup line is called Rumors, I thought that I would put some rumors about me to rest."

He looked up and saw his brown mouse.

There was Minerva, her dark hair hanging loose and unstyled past her shoulders, not straight, not curled, somewhere in between. She was holding the baby, gripped tightly against her body.

"There has been much discussion in regards to the paternity of my baby girl. I'm used to being the King that no one has any interest in. And yet, the interest surrounding

Isabella's birth has been unprecedented for me. Well, it's time for the secret come out." Brilliant green eyes met the camera, Min's only stunning feature. And they were glowing now. "The father of my baby is Dante Fiori."

Whatever else was happening on the screen, not a single person in the family was watching now.

All eyes had turned to him.

He looked into his friend's eyes. And he saw only murder there.

She had done it. In a panic, she had done it, and Violet had been more than happy to allow her to step up and make the announcement because Violet loved nothing more than a spectacle.

Well, Min had promised her spectacle. She had delivered.

And now, in the limo, after the announcement was done, Violet had exploded.

*"Dante?"*

"Yes," Minerva said, lying through her teeth and feeling more and more terrified by the moment.

*"Dante? Dante slept with you?"*

She couldn't work out if Violet was shocked because Minerva was not the sort of woman

Dante typically went for, or if Violet was angry that Dante had touched her, or if Violet was angry because she was… Well, maybe a little bit jealous.

Violet was the great beauty in the family, there was no questioning that. Minerva wasn't much at all. She never had been.

Until she had returned from a trip overseas with a baby. And then speculation about her had begun to swirl. She should have known there would be no avoiding rumors. She should have known that avoiding the press would be impossible. She should have known that every jerk with a smartphone would try to take her and Isabella's picture, and that those pictures would be posted everywhere, for anyone in the world to see. And that Carlo would see them. And he would suspect.

And once she had gotten the threatening text, she knew that she had to act.

She was in danger. Isabella was in danger.

She didn't believe that Katie's overdose had been purely accidental, and she never would. Carlo was the kind of man who had access to all sorts of things, and her friend had been terrified during those last days of her life. Because he had found them.

It had been so simple for a while, to stay under the radar in Europe. Minerva wasn't a particularly famous face, in spite of her connection to the King family, and outside the United States nobody ever gave her a second glance. If she had been with Violet, everyone would have recognized them.

But on her own, she was just a university student. The same with her friend and roommate.

But clearly, Carlo had figured out who she was, and where she was.

And worse, where Isabella was.

She had no choice but to tell this lie. To throw him off the scent.

Because this baby could not be Carlo's baby. Not if it was hers. Not if it was Dante's.

There was a reason the deception about Isabella had been so paramount when she had first come home. That she insisted the child was hers.

Everyone had believed it. And she had thought it would be enough. It was one reason she hadn't worried over much when photographs of herself and Isabella had begun circulating.

She had never slept with Carlo. Therefore, any child of hers could not be a child of his. And besides, she was used to her superpower. Invisibility.

A wren among a gaggle of peacocks, Minerva was simply accustomed to being forgotten. She didn't imagine for a moment that Carlo would remember her face. He had only seen her a handful of times during the time she'd spent studying in Rome. And he had been entirely focused on Katie.

But clearly, he had begun to piece things together.

And so…

And so.

She had promised her sister a show. She had delivered.

But she did *not* seem pleased.

"Dad is going to *kill him*," Violet said.

"Do you think so?" Her father had responded to her return with a baby in an extremely sanguine manner. As far as Robert King was concerned, as long as none of his children were crack addicts he had done fine enough.

She had asked him if it bothered him. That she had a child without a partner.

He'd said: "Why would I mind? You're not a teenager, and you have the money to take care of her. It's not like the house isn't big enough."

And that had been the end of it.

She couldn't imagine he would be angry simply because the baby was Dante's.

Dante, on the other hand…

She could only hope that he was somewhere far afield. On the East Coast. In his New York office. Perhaps he would be in Frankfurt or Milan.

Just so long as he wasn't…

The limo pulled up to the front of the King family mansion, and all of Minerva's hopes and dreams were dashed when she saw him standing there.

Her heart nearly lurched up her throat and out of her mouth.

She had forgotten.

How imposing he was. How large.

How utterly, devastatingly handsome.

Which was ridiculous, because she had seen him only a month earlier.

She could still remember the awkward, horrible dance at one of her father's parties. Her biggest crush ever had only agreed to be her date for a dare. To see the inside of the infamous King mansion and to report back to friends at school.

Dante had taken hold of her after Bradley had embarrassed her, and held her close, shielding her from curious eyes. He'd been so strong and solid, and all the anguish and shame inside her had caught fire and burned hot. It had been so embarrassing but she'd also been unable to pull away from him.

But he'd been pity dancing with her. He'd added to the confusion of…everything.

And compared to Bradley's bony shoulders, Dante's had felt so broad and solid.

It had all been weird.

Even with that she could forget.

But she didn't think that the impact of a man like Dante Fiori could live in its genuine state inside a woman, or anyone. You would die of it.

It became clear only in person.

He had always made her feel small. Rattled.

She had the tendency to run at the mouth whenever he was around. He made her stomach feel like it was quivering.

She disliked it intensely. And yet, she had always felt drawn to him like he was a magnet. She had always felt compelled to get a response out of him. To go to him. And she could no more understand any of those tendencies then she could understand quantum physics.

Which was to say: not at all.

"He is unhappy," Violet said softly.

"Well… He'll just have to deal with it."

Minerva lifted her chin, affecting a posture of determination she did not feel. Her brother appeared behind Dante, and behind him was her father.

Everybody *did* look remarkably unhappy.

Min was not accustomed to being the source of people's unhappiness. She was used to being ignored, and when she'd shown up with her parents' first grandchild, they'd been happy.

No one looked happy now.

The car stopped, and Dante didn't wait. He marched over to the car and jerked the door open.

And she found herself face-to-face with his stormy black gaze.

It was fathomless. As if she could look all the way down into the depths of his soul. Into the depths of hell itself.

She knew the things they said about him. That when her father had encountered him in Rome when he was a boy, Dante had been attempting to rob Robert King at gunpoint. That something about the boy had made Robert pause. That he had given him his watch, but also his card, and told him that if he wanted to change his life, rather than just live to commit another robbery, he should contact him.

And that shockingly, Dante had.

But that he had been a man who had committed a great many atrocities prior to his salvation and education that had been financed by Robert King.

She had never believed the stories.

Mostly because her father loved a story, and it was one he did not tell. Which forced her to believe that the truth of it must be less dramatic, and far less interesting.

Now she wondered, though.

Because she felt like she was staring down the very devil.

"We have a lot to discuss, don't you think?"

Dante took hold of her hand, and lifted her from the limo, depositing her gently onto her feet. She looked past his shoulder, at Maximus and her father.

"And when you're done speaking to her," Maximus said, "I think you and I need to have a talk."

"I'm sure this will give you time to rally the firing squad," Dante said, his tone dry.

He was still holding her hand.

She could recall, with perfect ease, another time Dante had touched her hand. Not the dance, but earlier.

She had been a girl. All of twelve, and she had fallen out of a tree in the backyard.

Dante had found her lying pitifully on the ground, pondering her fate, and he had been afraid that she had broken her neck. He had yelled as much at her as he had lifted her up. His touch, hot and strong, had started to quiver low in her body.

She hadn't liked it. She had pulled away from him, then bent down to wipe the blood from her knee. "I'm fine."

"You are a menace," he'd said back.

She could imagine the exchange happening just that way now.

"I have to get Isabella," she protested.

"Go," he said.

She did, stumbling as she went. With shaking fingers, she undid the seat belt and lifted her baby girl up from the seat.

The thing was, it didn't matter who'd given birth to Isabella.

Minerva was her mother.

She'd cared for her from the time she was born while Katie shrank away in increasing fear, self-medicating away the terror of the possibility of Carlo finding them.

Min was not brave by nature. But she'd known someone had to be brave for Isabella. And since Katie couldn't, it had to be her.

They walked past her brother, who was looking at Dante as though he wanted to flay him alive, and her father, who looked stoic. Into the house. Up the stairs.

Totally silent.

Minerva clung to Isabella, thinking of her in some ways as a shield. Surely not even Dante would yell at her while she was holding a baby.

He opened up the door to her father's study, and ushered her inside, slamming it behind them. "Explain this, Minerva, because you and I both know that I am not the father of your baby."

Well, she was disappointed on that score. Dante was clearly fine yelling around an infant.

She cupped the back of Isabella's downy little head. "Did you tell them?"

"No, I didn't tell them. You're going to have to tell them, because if I tell them they're not going to believe me. In the hour it took you to get home from the press conference, I had to tell your brother about ten reasons he shouldn't kill me where I sat. And the leading one was that I might be the father of your child, and that you might need me in some capacity."

"I *do* need you," she said.

Silence settled between them as he waited for her to explain.

"I'm sorry," she said finally. "I panicked."

"Why did you panic? What is happening?"

"You were the only name I could think of. The only name that was big enough. I had to protect myself, Dante. I had to protect Isabella! And I thought seeing as you are so close with my family, it was believable enough that you and I…that we…"

"Yes, well. The problem is, *child*, that the idea I would touch you in that way is laughable in the extreme."

Minerva had never felt so small, or quite so dull.

Standing next to the brilliant Dante Fiori made her feel as plain and inadequate as she was.

He was right. The idea that he would touch her was laughable, though it seemed as if Maximus and her father were more than willing to believe it. So why wouldn't the rest of the world?

She knew he'd only ever danced with her four years ago because he'd pitied her. Everyone knew it.

Still, she held her head high.

"Men are renowned for touching women that don't make sense. It is common knowledge that the secret sexual fantasies of men are *unknowable*." She leaned in and did her best to seem confident when she was very much not.

"Is it?" he asked. "Well, mine are fairly knowable. Often plastered on the front page of newspapers here and there. *You* are plainly not my fantasy."

She thought of all the women he'd been seen with over the years. Sleek, polished and curvy. Brunette, blonde, pale or brown, didn't seem to matter to him, but there was a sophistication to the women he enjoyed.

Quite like her sister, and not at all like her.

"Well, that is good to know," she said.

"Why did you do it, Minerva?"

"I am sorry. I really didn't do it to cause you trouble. But I'm being threatened, and so is Isabella, and in order to protect us both I needed to come up with an alternative paternity story."

"An *alternative* paternity story?"

She winced. "Yes. Her father is after her."

He eyed her with great skepticism. "I didn't think you knew who her father was."

She didn't know whether to be shocked, offended or pleased that he thought her capable of having an anonymous interlude.

For heaven's sake, she'd only ever been kissed one time in her life. A regrettable evening out with Katie in Rome where she'd tried to enjoy the pulsing music in the club, but had instead felt overheated and on the verge of a seizure.

She'd danced with a man in a shiny shirt—

and she even knew his name because she wouldn't even dance with a man without an introduction—and he'd kissed her on the dance floor. It had been wet and he'd tasted of liquor and she'd feigned a headache after and taken a cab back to the hostel they'd been staying in.

The idea of hooking up with someone, in a circumstance like that, made her want to peel her own skin off.

"Of course I know who he is. Unfortunately… The full implications of who he is did not become clear until later."

"What does that mean?"

She could tell him the truth now, but something stopped her. Maybe it was admitting Isabella wasn't her daughter, which always caught her in the chest and made her feel small. Like she'd stolen her and like what they had was potentially fragile, temporary and shaky.

Or maybe it was trust. Dante was a good man. Going off the fact he had rescued her from a fall, and helped her up when her knee was skinned, and bailed her out after her terrible humiliation in high school.

But to trust him with the truth was something she simply wasn't brave enough to do.

Her life, Isabella's life, was at risk, and she'd lied on livestream in front of the world.

Her bravery was tapped out.

"Her father is part of an organized crime family. Obviously something unknown to me at the time of her...you know. And he's after her. He's after *us*."

"Are you telling me that you're in actual danger?"

"Yes. And really, the only hope I have is convincing him that he isn't actually the father."

"And you think that will work?"

"It's the only choice I have. I need your protection."

He regarded her with dark, fathomless eyes, and yet again, she felt like he was peering at her as though she were a girl, and not a woman at all. A naughty child, in point of fact. Then something in his expression shifted.

It shamed her a little that this was so like when he'd come to her rescue at the party. That she was manipulating his pity for her. Her own pathetic nature being what called to him, yet again.

But she would lay down any and all pride for Isabella and she'd do it willingly.

"If she were in fact my child, then we would be family."

"I... I suppose," she said.

"There will need to be photographs of us together, as I would not be a neglectful father."

"No indeed."

"Of course, you know that if Isabella were really my child there would be only one thing for us to do."

"Do I?"

"Yes." He began to pace, like a caged tiger trying to find a weak spot in his cage. And suddenly he stopped, and she had the terrible feeling that the tiger had found what he'd been looking for. "Yes. Of course, there is only one option."

"And that is?"

"You have to marry me."

# CHAPTER TWO

Two things had become clear to Dante as he'd stared down into Min's green eyes.

The first was that if Minerva and Isabella were in real danger then he would have to protect them. There was no choice.

He could not uncover her lies, because no matter how convoluted it might be, his protection was perhaps the only thing standing between her and this man she claimed wanted to do her harm. Dante was not so foolish as to think he could simply involve law enforcement and make an issue like a man connected to a crime family go away.

But he had resources. Men at his disposal. And more important, he had money. If her plan didn't work, he had other methods of being able to protect them.

And then, there was the second thing that occurred to him. Which was that if he wanted a stake in Robert King's company, then marrying his daughter, and being the father of his granddaughter, was likely the best way to accomplish that.

Dante had always known he would marry. It was a given. He had no plans to love his wife, as indeed he had no plans to love, much less the ability. But he had always thought that he might want a son. Someone to carry on what he had started.

He was a man from nothing. Nothing had been given to him. And he had much that he could pass on to an heir.

So yes, he had often thought that he would marry. Why not Minerva? Why not when it would benefit them so?

No, he would never be attracted to the skinny, dull little hen, but it didn't matter. They already had a child between them, as far as the world was concerned. And genetics meant nothing to Dante. The man who had fathered him had gone off God knows where and hadn't given a damn about him. While his mother...

She had cared the best she could. But she had been an old, tired whore—in a literal sense, not a euphemistic or insulting one—and in the end, the comfort of drugs was much more enticing than the grind of impoverished motherhood.

She had given up taking care of Dante when he was about eight years old. And she had given up living when he was ten.

He had been on his own ever since.

And while he was not sentimental, not really, on that score, he felt some measure of passion over the idea of protecting Isabella.

He did not need to become emotionally entangled in order to do this. It required legal paperwork and public trappings, and it was all the sort of thing he could engineer easily without needing to change diapers or rock her to sleep in private.

He also felt some grudging admiration for Minerva.

Minerva was protecting her child. She had come up with the solution that had seemed best to her in a moment of panic.

And he had the means to protect a child. He would not leave Isabella exposed. Not as he had been.

After all, he had been dependent upon the good graces of a man who had not been his father. Robert King was, in many ways, the closest thing he had to a father.

No, genetics were not required to make a family. Genetics, however, had been required for him to gain access to Robert King's company. And now…well. Now he'd have a link there, as well.

"Marriage?" She recoiled. "You have to be kidding me."

"I'm not."

Where did she get off looking horrified by the prospect of marrying him? He was the one who would be saddled to this plain little creature from now until eternity. *He* was the one who ought to be concerned.

"Yes, Min, marriage."

"You're *old*," she said.

He barked a laugh. "And you're a child. But you wanted my protection, and I am willing to give it. But you have to give me something in return."

"Marriage."

"Yes."

"What are your motives? Because I know it isn't to gain access to my bed."

"Indeed it is not. But what I would like is for your father to consider merging his company and mine, and barring a family connection, he is not interested." Her green eyes were jewel-bright and full of rage.

"So you're willing to help me, but only as it benefits you in a business sense?"

"Please, Minerva," he responded. "I don't need this. Make no mistake. Had I needed a family connection I would have pursued it on my own terms long ago. With Violet. Not you."

Her cheeks flooded with color. "Oh, really?"

"She is much more in keeping with my image."

"Your image!"

"Though, to be perfectly frank, little one, I could have seduced you at any point over the years if I'd wanted to. I did not need your little scheme. Had I wanted to marry you, I'd have done so."

She looked a second away from howling. "You could not seduce me, Dante Fiori," she spat. "I don't even like you. I never have."

"Oh, is that why you used to follow me around like a puppy?"

He did not know why he felt the urge to prod at her, only that he did. She was the one who had walked them into this situation, and now she was going to put up a fight because he had found a way to make it tenable for him. Well. He would not have it.

This little sprite did not own him, and she was not in charge here.

If it weren't for the fact that he was not quite the monster that the press made him out to be, he could destroy her farce easily. All it would take was a simple paternity test.

"You are using me to clean up for your bad choices, Minerva. All the better for you if you'd been seduced by me. Because at least I would have offered marriage, and I would have posed you no threat."

"You are a threat," she said darkly.

"A threat to what?"

"Common human decency."

The door to the study opened, and Robert King filled the space. "I think we need to have a talk," he said.

"Whatever you have to say to Dante you can say in front of me," Minerva said.

"I don't think that's true, Min," her father responded.

"It is," she said stubbornly.

"Fine," Robert responded. He slammed the door behind him. "How dare you use my hospitality so poorly. She's a child compared to you."

"You weren't angry when I came home with the baby!" she protested. "But now you're mad?"

"Why rail at you for your decisions?" Robert asked. "You were out in the world on your own, and you did not consult me on your choices. You came home and presented them, and what was the point in holding a postmortem on it? I'm not angry at you. I'm angry at him."

"That doesn't make sense," Minerva shouted.

But Dante knew that it did. Because Robert knew exactly where Dante was from. Not only that, he was thirteen years Minerva's senior. A man who had seen more and done more than Minerva ever would.

She had been cloistered, sheltered by her family connections, and Robert had extended the same to him.

Robert had always counted on Dante to take care of Minerva.

Oh, yes, the fact that he was treating it as a betrayal made perfect sense to Dante.

And it spoke volumes about Minerva's actual inexperience and age that she did not.

"Just tell me that you never took advantage of her when she was younger," Robert said, his voice like iron. *"Tell me."*

"I would not," Dante said, keeping his voice even. "I swear to you, I would never abuse what you gave to me."

"And yet," Robert said, "here is the evidence that you have."

"I seduced *him*," Minerva proclaimed.

Both of them turned to look at her. Dante wanted to laugh. There she was, looking as she ever did, a university student in a sweater that was overlarge and a slouchy pair of jeans.

He couldn't imagine her seducing a trembling virgin. Let alone a man of his vast experience and particular appetites.

"It was the night of my going-away party. Before I went to study overseas." She gave her father a conspiratorial look and lowered her voice. "He was very drunk."

*Madre de Dios...*

Dante remembered that night well. He was not drunk, and had in fact been in the company of a lush heiress who was much more age-appropriate to him.

"I've *always* had a crush on him," she continued as the color rose in her face. "Yes. You see, I've always wanted him, and I thought that before I left I would get what I wanted. So I crept into his room and I… Well, I'm afraid I took advantage of him."

"Min," he bit out. "Stop helping."

"It's true! You were reduced. Your senses. I apologize for my predatory behavior. And I was ashamed. That's why I didn't… That's why when I found out I was pregnant I hid it."

"And why did you decide to announce it on TV today?" Robert asked.

*"Well,"* Minerva said, clearly hunting around for an excuse.

And if Dante weren't so irritated he would be entertained watching her scrabble around for a reason why she'd chosen to reveal all today. And in public. She squinted. "I had been trying to talk to him. But he hasn't been returning my calls. I assumed because he was embarrassed."

"I was embarrassed?" Dante asked.

"Well, you were quite drunk," Minerva explained, like he was a child. "I don't know that you were up to your usual standards."

He could strangle her. Cheerfully. If she weren't holding a baby he might.

Her father, for his part, looked badly like he wanted to exit the conversation, and at least on that score he could give Minerva some points. She had successfully turned an uncomfortable situation into a horrific one, and Robert no longer looked angry so much as he looked utterly and completely appalled.

"You will, of course, do the right thing," Robert said, directing that at Dante.

"Of course," Dante returned.

"What's the right thing?" Minerva asked.

"Obviously he's going to marry you," Robert said.

"In fact, I informed her of this only a moment before you came in," Dante said. "She's being stubborn. She has no concept of the consequences of her actions."

"Well, then it will be up to you to ensure she does."

"Dad," Minerva said, her tone scolding, "stop playing the part of tyrant. It doesn't suit you."

"It does, however, suit me, *cara mia*," Dante said.

She shot him a fearsome look.

He would never have ascribed a word like *fearsome* to Minerva before. She had always seemed timid to him. But standing there, cradling her baby as she was, her posture defiant and defensive, he found that *fierce* and *fearsome* were words that described her extremely well.

As irritating as he found the situation he was in, he could only admire it.

That she was a woman willing to do whatever it took to protect her child.

Along with that came the discomforting thought of her being touched by a man who was involved in organized crime.

What had happened? Had the man seduced Minerva? Had she seduced him? Was it a piece of truth buried in the outrageous story she had made up about taking advantage of Dante while he was drunk?

Minerva was twenty-one, but he couldn't imagine that she had a very long or intense history with men. For as long as he'd known her she'd been unattached, and she had never seemed overly interested in that kind of thing.

He was basing that off her total lack of efforts when it came to making herself up. Her sister was a makeup mogul. If Min wanted to improve herself she could have easily done it.

But then, the fact that she had come back with a child, the fact that she had claimed for all the world that he was the child's father, and the fact that he had never guessed she would do any of those things made him acutely aware of the fact that he didn't actually know her that well at all.

"Your mother will want to speak with you," her father said.

"I imagine Maximus will want to speak with me," Dante said.

Robert gave him a long look. "Yes. I imagine. Though as you are marrying her…" He appraised him slowly. "You do know, I suppose, that this will put King Industries in your hands."

"It had occurred to me." There was no point pretending it hadn't. Robert knew him too well.

"Had the timing been different, I would've

suspected you of nefarious behavior, but you never inquired about the child, or made any effort to see if it was yours."

"It didn't occur to me the child could be mine," Dante said. "And no, I didn't plot this."

"No," Robert agreed. "A plot of yours would've been much neater."

Dante grinned ruefully. "Well, at least we both agree on that."

"I will leave you for the time being. But Dante, the wedding must be planned sooner rather than later. Now that it is revealed, you will move to make an honest woman of her. I do not want speculation to go on. Our official statement will be that fearing you wouldn't be receptive, Minerva kept it from you, and the moment you found out…"

"It's not a story," Dante said. "It's the truth."

Then Robert turned and walked out of the study, leaving the two of them alone again.

"You're a fool, Minerva. Did you not think that me marrying you was inevitable?"

"It never occurred to me that my father would force the issue. He was so… Lackadaisical about me being a single mother. About me returning with a stranger's baby."

"Yes, because he cannot force a man he's never met to act with honor and integrity. But he would expect it for me. Surely you must have known…"

"I didn't think about it," she snapped. "When Carlo texted me, I panicked. I did the only thing I could think to do. I jumped in front of the cameras. I don't regret it. Even now."

"Good. I'm glad to hear that you have committed to lying in the bed you've made."

"How long do you suppose we'll have to stay married? It seems to me that we should be able to have Carlo dealt with in a timely fashion, and even if we don't… Well, if we can keep up the facade for a long enough amount of time, then surely he'll fade into the background eventually."

He regarded her closely. "*Cara*, I'm Catholic. Divorce is out of the question."

# CHAPTER THREE

MINERVA HAD BEEN stewing on his sudden devoutness to his latent Catholicism for two weeks.

He couldn't be serious. He absolutely *couldn't* be serious.

Their marriage would have to have a term limit. She couldn't stay married to him *forever*. She wouldn't *need* to. And the idea of being shackled to Dante for her entire life…

It made her feel like her skin was too small.

She was the last woman on earth whom he wanted to marry, and surely at some point in her life Minerva deserved to be something other than last.

She didn't regret taking Isabella on. She could have allowed the police to take her into custody when she'd come home with Isabella and found out the news about Katie.

She hadn't had to claim that Isabella was hers. She could have come home with her and found her another home here in the United States, where she would maybe even be safer from Carlo.

But she… She felt like Isabella was her child.

She'd cared for her during Katie's depression.

Her stewing was productive ultimately. Because by the time the evening of their engagement party rolled around, she had realized the perfect solution.

He was *Catholic*.

Which meant that while divorce was complicated, there were ways around those complications. They would only need an annulment. Provided, of course, that the marriage wasn't consummated. And she was well aware that that would cause some slight issues with their ruse, but by the time they separated they wouldn't need it anyway. And neither she nor Dante was in any danger of temptation to consummate.

She was feeling borderline triumphant by the time she met with her sister to get her hair, makeup and wardrobe done for the event that she didn't even want.

But her family was under the impression that this was a real marriage, and not only was it a big deal because she was getting married, it was a big deal because Dante was getting married. The fact that they were getting married to each other was making it a whole King family spectacle.

"You need gold," Violet said authoritatively. "Gold eye shadow, gold bronzer, a gold dress."

"I'm going to look like an award," Minerva pointed out.

She was feeling out of sorts because she did not have Isabella with her. Her mother had Isabella for the time being, and then for the party itself she would be up in her room with a nanny attending.

"Well, that is exactly how you should look," Violet said. "Like a prize that Dante has won, right?"

She looked at her sister's sullen face. "Except, you think that *I've* won the award," Minerva said. "The award being Dante."

Violet's eyes locked with Minerva's. "I don't really. It's fine. I had a slight crush on him for a while, but I'm over it."

"I'm sorry," Minerva said. "I really didn't know."

"Mom said that you had a crush on him for years."

"*Honestly*, the rumor mill in this family."

"She said you had a crush on him for all your life." Minerva felt doubly guilty, because not only was she marrying the man that her sister had feelings for, her own feelings were a fabrication.

"Yes," Minerva said, her throat going dry. "It's why I always followed him around."

He was the one who had brought that up.

That was not why she'd followed him around. She had felt compelled to interact with him. To be near him. Like a person might stare at a big cat through the bars of a zoo cage.

He was wild and compelling, and it had never failed to call to something inside her. Though, she didn't know what to call that thing.

Maybe it was because nothing in Minerva was wild or compelling at all.

She was bookish, and she was a tomboy, and she was ever injuring herself while running around outside imagining she was various literary characters that she found between the pages of her books.

She'd been called a dreamer more than once. Someone who didn't connect well with the harshness of reality.

And so there was something about the darkness simmering beneath the surface of Dante's skin that she had always found wickedly interesting.

Like he was a dragon in folklore.

And that was down to her rather dreamy nature, as well.

It had nothing to do with him. And it certainly had nothing to do with feelings of any kind.

If she had any sort of feelings for him, it was that sharp, tangled-up gratitude over his helping mitigate the shame of her being rejected in front of an audience and then, of course, the way he was helping her now.

"It doesn't matter," Violet said. "I haven't really fancied him for ages. But he is handsome. You have to admit."

Minerva felt her face getting hot, and she wasn't sure why.

Violet shook her head and rolled her eyes. "Of course you already know. You've seen him naked."

The temperature in her face increased. She had not seen Dante naked. And she would not.

But surely her sister knew all about these things. Violet was so lovely and smooth. She did so well at parties, mingling with important, high-powered people everywhere she went. Her ability to harness her image and control a brand was renowned.

She imagined her sister was much more

sophisticated when it came to men than Minerva was.

Then, the average sixteen-year-old was slightly more sophisticated when it came to men.

Of course, no one could *ever* know that.

"Let's get you fixed up," Violet said.

And true to her word, Violet did fix Minerva up. Quite well, in point of fact.

And she had been right about the gold. It took her mousy brown hair and made it something else. It surprised Minerva that she had left her hair mostly unstyled. Letting it fall in waves down her back, though it seemed much glossier after her sister had sprayed something on it, and the gold leaf headband that she had woven into her hair made it all look very intentional, rather than that Minerva's hair sat somewhere between curled and straight, and she didn't know what to do with it.

The dress she was wearing made the most of her slight curves, and the plunging neckline looked elegant, and not trashy. A gift, Minerva supposed, of having a very small chest. If her more voluptuous sister had worn the dress, she would've looked stunning, but the effect would have been different.

"I love it," Minerva said, but her stomach

felt hollowed out, and her body felt unsteady. She lifted her hand to touch her hair and her sister caught it, examining her bare fingers.

"I do hope that Dante is planning on giving you a ring," Violet said.

"Oh," Minerva responded. "I hadn't even thought of it."

"You do want to marry him, don't you?"

"I need to," Minerva said. "Desperately."

"Good," Violet said.

Well, it hadn't been a lie, she did need to marry him. It just wasn't because of her emotions or anything like that.

Her sister had been kind to her, and rather than putting her in heels had chosen a pair of sparkling, pointed-toe flats that were actually quite pretty. They were also very comfortable. And made Minerva feel like less of a gangly, awkward deer than she might have if she had been up on stilts.

She left her sister's bedroom, nearly ready to go down to the party, when she ran into her mom coming up the stairs.

"I was just coming to fetch you," she said.

Elizabeth King was a stunningly beautiful woman, more along the lines of Violet and Maximus than Minerva.

They all looked a lot alike and there was no question of the fact that they were siblings, but there was something about the way her parents' features had rearranged themselves on both Violet and Maximus to be an even more pleasing configuration. And somehow, on Minerva it had always seemed wrong.

Her nose was similar to her mother's, but it was longer, more like her father's.

Her mother had a full upper lip, slightly more so than her lower, which gave her the brilliant look of a rather exquisite doll.

Minerva's was yet more imbalanced, her cheeks somehow looking round, rather than sculpted, in spite of the fact that Minerva didn't have an ounce of extra fat on her body, nor curves to speak of.

What was commanding height on Maximus was gangly on her.

Her mother's hair could be called a brilliant toffee, while Minerva's was more mouse-ish.

"I'm here," Minerva said.

"You look lovely," her mom said. "Are you ready?"

"Yes," Minerva said, suddenly feeling horrendously insecure. "Don't I look ready?"

"Of course you do," Elizabeth responded. "That isn't what I meant. I meant… You want this, don't you, Minerva? Because I will tell your father to call the whole thing off if you don't. I know that he got angry and he insisted that Dante do the right thing, but if you don't love Dante then this isn't the right thing."

Bless her mother, who only wanted her happiness, but of course this wasn't for Minerva. It wasn't about Minerva.

It was all right, she was used to that. Nothing in her life had ever truly been about her.

Every member of her family was a brilliant gem that shone brightly in their own right. Her mother was a former model and beauty queen. Violet modeled herself, and additionally was a business tycoon. Maximus had taken his share of their father's fortune and multiplied it exponentially. His face was famous, his business acumen renowned.

And her father...

*California King* had been the headline of business pages for years, along with the requisite mattress jokes. But Robert King was not a joke. He was one of the most highly successful manufacturers the world over. Managing to be both savvy and profitable, while maintaining a strict standard of treatment for workers.

Only Minerva was *nothing*.

And she had been content to be, in many ways. *Privileged* to be.

Because there had been no pressure for her

to go out and make something of herself in order to survive.

Her survival had always been a given. Because no King would be tossed out onto the streets if they failed to make a living for themselves.

Her survival had always been a given until Isabella. Until Carlo.

The one good thing about all of this was that at the very least she had discovered that when things were difficult she did possess the mettle to get through it.

"You don't have anything to worry about," she said to her mom. "I know what I'm doing."

Really, for the first time in her life she felt like she knew what she was doing. At least with a grander and broader purpose than simply trying to stay unnoticed.

And everything would be fine in the end. Because this would buy her time, it would keep her safe, and then she and Dante could be free of each other.

Her mother escorted her down the stairs, to the exquisitely decorated backyard.

Their home and the large courtyard overlooked the beach and the ocean. The family had private access, and the whole stretch of sand belonged to them.

There was a bonfire already going there,

and the sun had set, casting an orange glow that faded to purple in the sky, silhouetting the palm trees that lined the shore.

So many people had come, and she didn't know any of them.

She had friends from school, but most of them were out of the country still.

And, of course, poor Katie was gone.

Oddly, the fact that the place was littered with strangers, and faces that she only knew because she had seen them plastered on television screens and newspapers, hit home the point that she was doing the right thing.

That what she did she did for Isabella, and it was important.

Certainly of more significance than the rest of her life.

But it was the sight of Dante that unraveled something inside of her.

He was wearing a white shirt, the sleeves rolled up, and a pair of dark slacks that somehow made her very aware of the fact that his thighs were powerful.

Which she thought had to be the oddest observation in the history of observations.

"Glad you could join us, *cara mia*," he said.

"Of course you knew that Violet wouldn't allow me to show up until at least an hour after the party had started," she stated.

"Of course," he responded. "That seems an incredibly Violet perspective on things."

"One has to make an entrance. One cannot do that if they arrive early."

"Well, I had no idea I've been doing entrances wrong this entire time."

She studied him, his sculpted jaw, his imposing height and his broad shoulders. "Honestly, Dante, I imagine whatever time you arrive you create a spectacle."

"Thank you," he said, inclining his dark head.

"That was *not* a compliment," she said.

"I took it as one. Anyway, you must look happier to see me, Minerva," he said. "As you *are* madly in love with me. So madly in love with me that you decided to seduce me in an inebriated state, taking terrible advantage of me and my agency."

She rolled her eyes at his ridiculousness. "I had to say *something*. Otherwise my father was going to skin you alive."

"I believe the offer of marriage was sufficient. Though I appreciate your efforts to protect me." He said the last part so drily she could tell that he didn't mean it at all.

"Well, you're of no use to me if you're dead. You can't protect me then."

"I don't know. If Carlo believed that your

dad killed me because I had fathered your child…"

"Well, I don't want you dead," she said. "Not at the moment. Though—" she held a finger up "—I have arrived on a solution to your issue of divorce."

He narrowed dark eyes. "Have you?"

"Yes," she said brightly. "Obviously we'll get an annulment."

His dark eyes flicked up and down. "An annulment?"

"Yes! Because we won't consummate."

The look he treated her to could only be described as pitying. "Minerva, on what planet would anyone believe that?"

"You said yourself that you are not…attracted to women like me. I'm not offended by that. I'm not attracted to men like you." She patted his forearm, then removed her hand quickly when she found him disturbingly hot and firm. She cleared her throat. "Your tastes are public. So, no one will be surprised."

"Except the public, and your family for that matter, think that we had a child together."

"A fluke. And we will claim that there was no spark left once we married. And at that point Carlo won't be an issue. So it will be a mere blip in the headlines."

"Minerva, it would be a blip in the headlines if it were only you. But sadly, I am included in this, and I am more than a blip in any headline."

Minerva sighed heavily. His ego was such a massive yoke over his shoulders it was a miracle they were so straight and broad. They should be sagging beneath the weight.

Sadly, nothing on the man sagged.

"It *will* work," she insisted.

"So you think that your father will blithely allow me to leave you?"

"If we explain."

"Explain?"

"Once…" She looked around. "Once Carlo is no longer an issue we can explain everything to my family. And at that point he'll be so grateful he will likely allow you to continue on with your efforts in the company."

He looked at her as though she were a child, his expression nearly pitying. "It is not something we need to concern ourselves with."

"We simply need to concern ourselves with *not* consummating."

He looked at her for a long moment. "I will try to control myself."

The arid reply left her feeling scraped raw, and she trailed after him at the party rather angrily thereafter.

But of course she couldn't *look* angry.

She had to look pleasant.

It was very strange, acting the part of accessory to someone. She had never done it. And here she was, keeping position next to him, moving as he did, trying to mirror his body language, and facial expressions, so that they seemed as if they were in one accord, whether they were not.

By the time they had made their rounds, Minerva was famished, which was only adding to her mood.

Then Dante swept her aside, taking both of them out of the glow of the string of lights that went overhead.

"It's time to put on a show, *cara*."

"Show?"

"Yes," he said. "I have a ring for you."

"Oh," she replied.

"Look surprised," he instructed as he grabbed her hand and dragged her back beneath the lights.

"Of course I'll look surprised," she whispered. "I *am* surprised."

"Try to look *happy* too," he said.

She had no time to respond to that before he had turned toward their guests and, somehow, by his very motion commanded the attention of the crowd.

Minerva stretched her lips into a wide smile that she had a feeling fell flat around the corners.

"As this has come together very quickly, there is one aspect of our courtship that I have neglected. We have done a great many things out of order, Minerva and I."

This elicited light laughter from the crowd.

Of course, in the rather sophisticated culture of the rich and famous in Southern California, having a baby before marriage—or without marriage at all—was not considered out of order.

But no doubt the chuckles were in deference to the presumably more conservative culture Dante came from.

"And in all the activity I have neglected to give Minerva her ring. I will do so now."

He pulled a ring box out of his pocket, and he did not drop down to one knee. "I've made the request already, I think," he said, opening the box and presenting it to her. It was huge. A statement piece if ever there was one, and she herself was so very not a statement piece that it seemed shocking, and nearly vulgar.

But he didn't ask her, and instead was sliding the monumental rock onto her finger.

As if…

As if something so magnificent, something so glorious, should be there. On her thin, fine-boned hand that was not manicured or elegant or anything of the sort.

She recalled her school friends had once likened her hands to *claws*.

And there was Dante Fiori's ring.

On one of her *claws*.

Min swallowed hard, and when she looked up at him, he was gazing at her with sharp intent. It pierced her, made her feel like she couldn't breathe. And before she could do anything, say anything or decide how she might react, he was moving in toward her.

All that sharp intensity was focused on her, and somehow she could feel it gathering in her stomach, nearly painful.

He was so close they were breathing the same air.

And then, his mouth was on hers.

*His mouth.*

This, *she knew*, was not kissing.

It couldn't be.

She had been kissed before by that stranger in the club, and that hadn't been kissing either. Because it had been unpleasant and cold, and it made her want to run, rather than embrace the man giving it.

But this…

It was not romantic.

It was not gauzy and sweet, wrapped in warm summer breezes and crashing waves. Blooming flowers and other grand literary euphemisms.

It made something in her stomach twist hard. Made her feel like some creature was biting down on her windpipe. The feel of his lips against hers was so *real*. So very physical. They were warm, and firm, and as he took command of all things, he took command of her mouth.

Shifting her slightly so that she was fitted more firmly against him.

All in all, the kiss was not terribly long, and it was not terribly intimate, but when it was done she felt like she had been hollowed out, her hands shaking, her whole body shaking.

And he looked… As unreadable as ever. Utterly infuriating, that man. He was like a block of obsidian that could not and would not be disturbed, not by anything. Least of all by her.

He had just handed her a ring, and then he had pressed his mouth to hers and tilted her entire world on its axis.

And there he was. Like a guardian of the underworld, completely unbothered by the whole thing.

The audacity of the man.

He had just kissed her. And he hadn't had permission. She would badger him about it, but she had the distinct impression that he wouldn't care.

"Shall we go mingle, *cara mia*?"

He whispered that question in her ear, and he made it look as though there was an intimacy between them that there just wasn't.

*That is the entire point of all of this. Keep it together.*

But she was having difficulty keeping it together. Because he was very large and hard beside her, and because she had always liked the idea of creating an effect in him. When she had followed him about and pestered him when she was a girl, part of it was that she had enjoyed seeing if she could get a reaction.

But right now it was clear that he would always have the upper hand. She would never, ever be the one to get a superior reaction out of him. He would always be the one to create havoc in her.

Because that was what it was, wasn't it? Her chasing after him. He was affecting her. She had always imagined herself leading the charge in those interactions. But it wasn't true.

It was him. It always had been.

Even in this, even in her scheme, he had somehow managed to take charge.

It was demoralizing. Dispiriting.

In front of all these people, downright humiliating.

She felt red and sore and exposed somehow, and she couldn't pinpoint why.

"Smile," he whispered, bending down, his lips nearly touching her ear, a shiver winding down her spine.

And so she did.

She had to remember that this was for Isabella. It wasn't for her.

And her own discomfort had nothing to do with it.

For Isabella, she could do this. For Isabella she could do anything.

It wouldn't be forever.

She stared at his patrician profile. No. Whatever he said it would not be forever.

Dante Fiori might be used to running a business. He might be used to commanding women, manipulating them with his good looks and power. And maybe in the past he had had an effect on her behavior, as well.

But she knew now. Was unbearably conscious of it.

Minerva King might be the least famous

of her family. The least successful. And the least powerful.

But she was also stronger than anyone knew.

And in the end, that strength was going to carry her through.

# CHAPTER FOUR

IT WAS HIS wedding day. His secretary had informed him firmly on Friday that this was to be the happiest day of his life.

He'd done his best not to laugh at her. Because she was sincere and just because he didn't possess the ability to see the world in such a pure fashion didn't mean he had to destroy the illusions of others.

Dante had never been under the impression that this would be a joyous day for him. Rather, he had always known that it would be a calculated move that benefited him in some way.

But this… This was not what he'd envisioned.

They had put the wedding together very quickly, and Min had been lying low in the meantime, rarely leaving her parents' house, at his express command.

Though she had told him with great umbrage that she didn't need him to command a single thing because she was completely happy to hide until they had made things legal between them.

Security. That was all. Just added layers of security.

Dante was not a man who believed in taking unnecessary chances.

He was standing in the back room of a cathedral sanctuary with his future father-in-law and his future brother-in-law standing on either side of him.

He had not imagined that Robert and Maximus would be in that position. Had it been another scenario, he would have imagined they were offering support. As it was, he had a feeling they were making sure he didn't run away.

It was all a bit close and familial for his taste.

He would always appreciate what Robert King had done for him, and if he had a friend, Maximus King was the best one he possessed.

But the way that they were with each other, the ease that the family had with one another, had always made his skin itch.

He was not familiar with these sorts of dynamics. Not privy to the way families typically acted with one another. He didn't understand. He hadn't grown up with it.

If he had siblings, then he didn't know any of them. His father had never been part of his life, and his mother had died early, and even before then she hadn't exactly been the model of maternal care.

He wasn't angry about those things. It was simply life.

Life, in his estimation, was not fair, from conception.

You could be born into a family like the Kings, or you could be born into the streets of Rome as he had been.

You could have a father like Robert King, or a father like Isabella's who was threatening the life of her mother and trying to drag her into a criminal underworld that was no place for anyone, let alone a child.

These things were accidents of fate and there was no point railing against them.

There was only making decisions about what you would do with the things you were given.

Dante believed that firmly.

He had made the most of what he'd been given. He had been given a hand up, and he had taken hold of it.

But that didn't mean that he felt completely comfortable with his situation, or his position.

In some ways, he would have imagined that Maximus would be with him on his wedding day in this capacity. He just hadn't imagined he would also be related to the bride. And that was where the connections became uncomfortable.

"If you hurt my sister," Maximus said, smiling and clapping his large hand on Dante's shoulder, "I'll kill you myself."

There weren't many men who stood at eye level with Dante, but Maximus was one of them. With ice-blue eyes and blond hair, he was a Viking counterpart to Dante's fallen angel.

He would never have thought of something so fanciful, but when they had gone out together in the past, women had made such comments.

Which gave Maximus's threat a lot more weight. After all, Maximus had seen up close Dante's appetite for beautiful women, and he imagined that his friend's believing that such an appetite had spilled over onto his younger sister was something that was never going to sit easy with him.

In fact, Dante imagined the only reason

that he wasn't dead was that he had fathered a child—supposedly—with Minerva.

Had they simply been caught in a compromising position, he imagined that Maximus would have simply dispatched him on the spot.

"I believe it," Dante said, because he knew that was better than any empty promises that Maximus would have discarded.

And he *did* believe it.

They were friends, it was true, but they were not blood.

The King family was connected by blood.

Dante had no such connections. And it was fine by him.

"You have always been like a son to me," Robert said.

And Dante knew that the old man *thought* he meant it. But Maximus had never had to worry about whether or not he could have access to sharing his father's company.

Dante wasn't bitter about that. It was just a difference. One that he was ever aware of, even if Robert was not.

"I suppose we had better get things started," Dante said.

"Nothing will start on time," Robert responded, looking at his watch. "I believe Violet is in charge of hair and makeup?"

"Yes," Dante said. "I imagine she's also in charge of entrances."

"What?" Robert asked.

"Never mind."

They filed in from the back, and all of them took their places. Robert made his way back to where the bride was.

It hit Dante then that whatever differences between himself and Maximus, Robert was seeing to the double duty of being father of the groom and bride.

Had Dante been capable of feeling warmth over such a gesture, he would have, he was sure.

The crowd that filled the sanctuary, Dante knew, was not enthralled by any love story between himself and Minerva. No, they were hoping to gain the attention of either himself, Maximus, Robert or Violet.

It hit him that no one would be here for Minerva.

It was a strange thing to be bothered by. He had rarely given consideration to Minerva beyond cursory. But Minerva didn't possess anything that anyone might want.

He was under no illusions that anyone was here because they cared about Robert or Maximus or Violet.

They cared about what any of the aforementioned people might be able to do for them.

He wondered if that was how Minerva had been vulnerable to a man like Isabella's father. If she had been left vulnerable because of her position in the family.

As he had been thinking earlier, life was very much what you fashioned from what you were given. Minerva could have created anything.

As it was, she had created a baby with a dangerous man. And that had been her decision.

But not Isabella's.

And if he was being magnanimous in any way, then it was on her behalf, because he knew what it was to be a child hamstrung by his parents' poor decisions.

And yes, there was the matter of getting to have possession of King. That did matter to him.

What he had not expected was for Minerva to look quite so lovely last night. And for the kiss to send a jolt of electricity through his body.

The very strange thing was that Minerva's reaction was…unreadable.

She had been angry with him at some point during the evening.

She had not gone pliant, she had not melted against him, she had not responded at all.

Quite the opposite, she had been stiff. She had been still against his mouth, behaving like a woman who didn't know what to do.

He had done his best to seize control of it, to change the tenor of things, but she had not allowed it.

And he could not for the life of him figure out if it had been inexperience or disgust that caused her to react in such a way.

Mostly because he had never kissed a woman who found him *disgusting*.

But then, he had never kissed a woman for show.

What made him most irritated was the fact that he was not disgusted by her.

Minerva wasn't *beautiful*.

There was a prettiness to her. It was simply that she was also a bit plain, and he preferred something a bit gaudier. He had been raised, after all, with a prostitute for a mother. For the years when she'd been well, she'd been all hair, perfume and jewels, and it had been the same with her friends who had passed through their run-down apartment. His concept of beauty was a bit more bedecked.

She was also young. The younger sister of

his friends, and because of that she'd been firmly off-limits from moment one.

The fact that she had the power to effect a response was irritating in the extreme.

The bridal party began to come down the aisle, though it was a simple bridal party. Violet walking arm in arm with Maximus, who came to stand next to Dante. He flashed his friend a smile.

"I will kill you," he whispered, never breaking that smile. "I did mean it."

Dante said nothing. But a grin tugged at the corner of his mouth as he turned to face the doorway of the cathedral.

And suddenly there she was.

Her hair had been twisted and gathered up into a complicated style that was loose and sparkling, thanks to jewelry of some kind that had been woven in.

The dress itself was simple, soft, flowing fabric that seemed only barely there. It rested over her curves like a fine mist. With each step she took, the long billowing lilac fabric swirled around her.

Something had been applied to her cheeks that made them glow in the candlelight, her lips, pale and shimmering.

She had been made up, but it was still very much her. Even more so than it had been the night of their engagement party. And somehow it was as if it had uncovered the essential beauty that Minerva possessed. A beauty he had never seen before.

She was ethereal. Like a creature of the earth transformed into one of the sky.

A treasure that had been hiding only to be brought out and polished now.

When she looked up at him, her green eyes shone bright, and he could see that it was her. And suddenly, the Minerva that he knew every day blended with this one, and he knew that he would never be able to unsee the beauty, even if she were to revert back to the way she'd been before.

When they joined hands, a sly smile crossed her face. Anyone watching would be forgiven for mistaking it for intimacy.

"I'm glad you decided to follow through," she whispered.

"I would not abandon you," he said, offended by the assessment he might.

"No," she said, frowning. "Of course you wouldn't."

The priest began his solemn intonations and there was something about the way Minerva held herself, about the strange expression on her face that caused a response in the vicinity of Dante's heart.

He had to wonder if for Minerva, this was somewhat conflicting.

He should not feel sorry for her at all, given the fact that she was the one who had gotten them into this position in the first place.

She was the one who caused this, and if she didn't like the end result, that was her problem.

But he couldn't overlook the fact that she was softer than he was. That for her, marriage was never intended to be a cynical meeting of people who wanted to firm up business deals.

No, for Minerva it was never supposed to be that at all.

That she had gotten herself into this mess, and the fact that he had twisted it to suit him as well, wasn't something he was going to waste time feeling guilty about. He didn't waste time feeling guilty in general. It was a fruitless exercise. Just like wishing that a pauper had been born a prince.

Or that a street urchin from Rome had been born a King.

It did nothing to solve one's problems.

For him the vows were easy. But she hesitated over each promise she made, possibly because she was afraid of what would happen when she didn't keep them.

It hadn't been nice of him to make fun of her about not being able to divorce.

He had done a great many things the church wouldn't approve of. He was hardly going to start worrying over much about his eternal soul now.

At the end he could go to confession, take his penance and spend the last bit of his life atoning.

He was far too busy to atone now.

But, the question of the permanence of the marriage was a tricky one considering that it would impact his portion of ownership with King Corporation. He had a feeling that Robert King would take an even dimmer view of Dante divorcing his daughter than he did to Dante marrying her in the first place.

That was a considerable issue.

Though, she did have a point. If when it was all said and done, they were able to explain everything, then Dante would possibly be considered a hero when she told the tale. Something he wouldn't have asked for, but a possibility.

It wasn't as if he wanted to stay married to Minerva forever.

When it was finished, it was time for them to kiss again, and she shrunk away from him.

One thing was certain: he could not stay

married to a woman who shrunk away from his touch.

He wrapped his arms around her and she gasped slightly.

He didn't give her time to react. Because if he did, he feared that she was going to cause difficulty.

He crashed his lips down onto hers. Swallowing her gasp and parting her lips with his tongue.

He didn't know why, but he felt compelled to affect her. Perhaps because she had affected him, and it didn't seem right that she'd had nothing but a negative response to him. An unreadable response.

A nonresponse.

He had a kick in his gut the moment he related that desire to instigate a response from her with the way that she had followed him around when she was a young girl.

The way that she had always been trying to gain a response from him.

It was petty. And it was childish.

But he allowed his tongue to delve between her lips anyway.

And she tasted… Like sunshine. Spring. Something that was indefinably Minerva.

Still, she was frozen beneath him. Her

hands clutched at his shoulders, but they were motionless. Not impassioned in any way.

And when they parted, it was like yet another veil had been ripped from his eyes.

He could no longer see a girl.

But a woman.

That hint of fearsomeness that he had seen when she had defended Isabella shone through those green eyes now.

Not a hen. Not a mouse.

A tigress defending her cub.

He had misjudged her.

And for a man like Dante Fiori, this was a terrible sin. He was never a man to misjudge or underestimate an enemy, an adversary or a potential partner.

But he had misjudged Minerva.

He had looked at her, and he had seen all that she had shown the world, which was only a facet of what she was.

He wondered what Isabella's father had seen of her.

He couldn't help it. Was she a tigress for him?

He despised the other man.

They were presented to the guests, but he was not conscious of what was being said, or what was happening.

There was a ringing in his ears.

They charged down the aisle and into the waiting room where he assumed that Minerva had been before.

She went over to her purse, and diaper bag, and began to root around inside, pulling out her phone.

"Eager to check your social media?" he asked drily.

"No," she said. "I'm worried. Because our wedding is today, and I'm concerned that…" She went pale. "He texted me."

She handed the phone to Dante.

I feel that I should come to the reception so that I can have a look at the child and see if she is indeed mine.

"Well, he's not getting near you, or Isabella," Dante said. "And at this point, I think we should inform the police that you have been receiving unwanted attention from a stalker. Nothing more."

"Do you think?"

"He's organized crime, and he's not from here. But if he does set foot in the country, he will face legal recourse from the law here. That's important. We must make sure that we put barriers in his way. And in the meantime, you and I are going on our honeymoon early."

"We are?"

"Yes. We are. Somewhere where he won't find us."

"Where is that? Because he found me, and he found her."

"No offense, *cara*, but your family is quite conspicuous, and you are known to live here. Plus, he clearly has your mobile number."

"I didn't give it to him," she said. "I got a new phone the moment I set foot onto American soil again. I changed my number."

Dante swore. "Well, it's no matter. I own an island, but it is not in my name, and it's hidden by a shell company. No one knows about it, and he won't know where to look. There will be no way for him to discover our whereabouts, and I will be using private investigators to make sure I find ways to remove him as a danger to your safety."

Her eyes went round. "In what way will you remove him?"

Dante waved a hand. "That is not your concern."

"Dante… I don't want you to do anything illegal."

He chuckled, low and dark. "That ship has sailed, I'm afraid. Or do you not know how I met your father?"

Her shoulders narrowed. "I thought that was just… A story."

"It is a story that has been greatly watered down."

He saw himself then, a boy of fourteen, holding a handgun extended toward an older man, pressing it to his forehead.

His hands were shaking. He was sweating.

One of his mother's boyfriends had told him that if you were going to do this kind of thing, you couldn't flinch. You couldn't shake. And you certainly couldn't sweat.

Above all else you had to be willing to pull the trigger.

And as Dante looked into the calm, kind face of the man that he was about to rob, he knew that he could not pull the trigger.

"Lower the gun, son," the man said in soft, clumsy Italian.

It was the kindness that immobilized Dante, for he had never known anyone to look at him with anything other than resentment, disgust or pity.

Until Robert King.

"You really held my father up at gunpoint?"

"I did," he said. "Believe me, I have no concern for what might happen to a mafioso. Men like him… Well, they bring ruin everywhere they go. They most particularly have brought ruin to my country, my streets. To women like my mother. They are part of a system that operates on fear and oppression. He is doing it to you in this personal capacity, but I guarantee you he has done it to many in a broader sense. I will not have it. I will not." He reached out and touched her face, and he suddenly meant those words more than he had ever meant anything in his life. "Nothing bad will happen to you or to Isabella. I swear it."

He took her hand, and led her out of the vestibule, and they nearly ran into Elizabeth, who was cradling Isabella, and Robert.

"There has been a change of plans," Dante said. "It seems that Isabella has picked up a stalker from her time overseas. She is being threatened."

"By who?" Robert asked.

"A man called Carlo Falcone. He's from a crime family in Rome. Whatever he says, don't listen to him. He's insane, and he will use anything he can to try to manipulate you and the situation. We must notify the police that he intends to show up at the reception."

Robert's lip curled up into a sneer. "I'm more than able to handle him by myself."

"Can you handle the retribution that will

come if you dispatch him? It isn't the law I worry about, but the rest of the family."

That seemed to calm some of Robert's readiness for a shootout. "I don't want anyone in my family targeted by this man."

"No. So we're going to call for police presence at the reception, but I also want you to make sure that it gets out that Minerva and I have left. That we are not there. Have Violet post it to one of her social media accounts. I believe that he's tracking our movements this way. And also, if she would be so kind as to indicate we've gone on a honeymoon in Italy, that would be brilliant."

"But you won't be," Robert said.

"No. He will not be able to find us where we are going. I will be able to keep her and Isabella safe. You can trust me."

"I do," Robert said. "And that is not a statement I made lightly, Dante, and it is not a statement I would make to most men."

"You saved my life," Dante said. "With all that I am I will protect hers."

Robert nodded, and he took Minerva's hand, then he used one arm to scoop Isabella from Elizabeth's arms. He had never held the child before. He was surprised by the way that she felt. Warm, and like a feather.

A small little thing he could have cradled in the crook of his forearm.

"I will keep them both safe."

# CHAPTER FIVE

Minerva's head was spinning and she couldn't breathe. Didn't breathe in fact until Dante's private jet had lifted into the air. Only then did she believe that they might be safe.

Isabella was laid in a plush bassinet, and Minerva had no idea how Dante had managed to acquire it so quickly.

And in the time she spent wondering about that she found time to worry about photographs from the wedding. It was stupid.

But the headlines after their engagement party had been…

They hadn't been outright cruel, but they had included a photograph of her from four years ago.

Seventeen, with her face streaked by tears, and him so much taller and broader and outlandishly beautiful than she could ever hope to be.

She imagined that the implication of the

photo was he'd been involved with her even when she'd been scandalously young, but looking at it she knew no one would ever take that seriously.

He was Dante Fiori. She was… Minerva the Mouse.

The girl who was worth a date only so her class could get a look at her house. And she'd heard later he'd wanted to get a look up her sister's dress, as well.

Violet had laughed herself hoarse after hearing that and then had gotten a deadly look in her eye. And Minerva had known if she'd ever seen Bradley after that Violet would unman him with the sharp end of her tweezers.

But that was the thing.

Violet was the hero in that story. The object of beauty and the one so above the idiocy she could laugh and make threats.

Dante was the hero in the story.

Willing to dance with her in spite of the fact she was gangly and unattractive and sad.

She was the object of pity.

And she feared when her wedding photos were splashed across the media it would be the same story.

Sad, pitiable Minerva snags a man due to a faulty condom.

Just thinking about *Dante* and *condoms* made her get hot to the roots of her hair.

"There will be supplies for her already on the island, as well," he said casually as he poured himself a drink and settled back into the plush leather sofa.

Minerva curled more deeply into the chair she was seated on, leaning over Isabella and adjusting her blanket unnecessarily. "How?"

"There are people that work for the shell company. They will be gone by the time we get there. None of them will ever know who gave the instructions. Who actually owns the house. They won't see us."

"Why do you have something like this?"

"I bought it quite a while ago as a precaution. Because one never knows when one might need to escape."

"Dante, you're not involved in anything illegal *now*, are you?"

"No," he said. "But when a man comes from a background such as mine he learns to be paranoid."

"I suppose. And I never did learn to be paranoid enough. Not until now."

Everything in her felt jumbled up.

She would love to think more about the kiss that he had given her at the altar. One that had turned so...intimate. But she hadn't had time to think about it or parse the way that it had made her feel, not in the face of the threatening text that she had received from Carlo so soon after.

"It is only a small island," he said. "The only building on it is my home, and the rest is unspoiled white sand and jungle. I think you'll like it."

"At this point, I like anywhere I'll feel safe."

For the moment, they felt united.

For the moment.

Dante busied himself with work during the journey, and Minerva slept when Isabella did, and woke when she was fitful. She marked the hours in feedings and diaper changings.

Until finally, the plane began to descend.

There was a small runway on the island, clearly.

"Your pilot knows where we are," she said.

Dante acknowledged this with a nod of his head. "I do trust him."

"*How much* do you trust him?" she pressed.

He lifted a dark brow. "Enough to allow him to fly me fifty thousand feet over the ocean?"

"Yes, but in that case his fate is tied to yours."

"Oh, believe me, Minerva, his fate will always be tied to mine. Because should anyone betray us—and in this case, the only option would be him as he is the only person on earth who knows we are here—his fate would be in a precarious position indeed."

"You're filled with death threats of late."

"Well, as is your life. Therefore, I find the situation merits more of them than I would typically be meting out."

Minerva pondered this as they got their things together and disembarked. She suddenly found him to be something of a stranger.

She had always known that he was hard, but she had also felt safe goading him. Now he had kissed her, and that made him feel unpredictable. And wholly different from what she had imagined he was.

Then there was his willingness to threaten someone's personal safety.

He did so with ease and without compunction. And it made her wonder what kind of man he was on a day-to-day basis.

She knew whom he was when he was interacting with her family, but she was beginning to think that wasn't the measure of him.

And given that he had actually robbed her father at gunpoint, she did wonder if Robert and Maximus had a better idea of who he was than she did.

Or Violet. Or Elizabeth.

She wondered if the women in the family were entirely ignorant of that side of him.

"You're thinking so hard I can see smoke coming out of your ears, Min," he said.

She tapped her chin. "I'm just thinking about your ruthlessness."

He lifted a shoulder. "People often do."

"Well, I didn't know that. You always seemed like somewhat of a stern older brother to me." She wrinkled her nose. "Stern. Not dangerous."

"Ah," he said. "An easy mistake to make, I suppose. Though, I don't think anyone else in the world has ever made it."

"Well, they don't know you like I do." She frowned. "Like I *did*."

They got off the plane and there was a car parked just there, waiting for them. It was fitted with a base for Isabella's car seat, and as soon as she was safely secured they were on their way.

The landscape was beautiful, and desolate as he had said. Dense forestation on one side, and brilliant white sand on the other. And there, built into the craggy hillside overlooking the sea, was an intensely modern, modular home, white squares to match the sand with glass all around.

"Home," he said. "For a while yet."

"It's very wild," she said.

He chuckled. "Wild?"

"Do you know what it reminds me of? *Swiss Family Robinson*. More the film from the 1960s than the book, I suppose. But it's a very modern house sort of up in the trees in the jungle."

He nodded slowly. "I thought of that, as well."

She turned to look at him, feeling surprised. "Did you?"

"Yes. I quite liked that movie when I was young."

"Did you?"

"For a while I went to a free community day care center, and they had a few old films on VHS. *Swiss Family Robinson* was one of them. I always thought that would be a good life. Off on a remote island where no one could reach you. Where you didn't have to answer to anyone. And you could build whatever you wanted for yourself. Make whatever you desired. Resources from the land. Provided you weren't attacked by pirates, of course."

"I thought the same thing," she said. "But

then, I also thought that I wanted to live on a farm on Prince Edward Island. And that I might want to live in Atlanta in a grand mansion." She sighed. "I've been so many places because of books. My college travels were supposed to be… They were supposed to be my big adventure where I could be the heroine instead of simply reading about heroines."

"And you brought back an enemy."

"I did," she said mutely. "I wanted adventure, but not quite like this."

"Well, you can have an adventure here. I promise you it will be safe."

Something about that promise settled heavy and hot over her skin, and she tried to ignore it. It was very disconcerting, the way his words had the power to affect her. They shouldn't. Things should be the same between them. Their mouths touching a couple of times shouldn't have profoundly shifted the balance between them any more than vows that had no honesty behind them.

"You've gotten very quiet again," he said.

"I should think you would like me to be quiet."

"I find it unsettling. Because it's not normal."

"I've never been accused of being normal, Dante. You of all people should know that."

Their eyes met for a moment, and she had

the vague sense he could see something inside her she couldn't even see clearly herself.

"What possible attraction did a man like this have to you?" When he asked, the question was so rough and fierce it caught her off guard.

"What do you mean?"

"You don't seem like the kind of woman to be taken in easily, Min."

She sniffed loudly. "Who says it was easy?"

His expression tightened, even as he kept his gaze on the road. "He didn't force himself on you."

"No!" The denial came swift and fierce. She knew enough about Katie's story, and about what had attracted her to Carlo, that she could easily repeat it to Dante, but she found that she couldn't. She didn't want to talk about being seduced, not when she hadn't been. Nor would she take a trauma on herself that she hadn't experienced. So she thought it best just to change the subject. Deflect as best she could.

"It is impossible for me to say what the attraction to a man like him is." She placed each word carefully, as if it were a footstep in a minefield. "Once you know everything about his character, whatever might have been charming is lost. He's not a good man."

That much was true.

"And he is dangerous," she said, thinking of Katie again.

They drove up the house, and Minerva—who was used to a certain amount of grandeur—was utterly enthralled. Her family's opulence was like a mix of Tuscany and California. Ornate and lavish.

This was incredibly sleek and spare, but each detail was perfect. Everything about it looked solid, like the best version of itself.

It was—she thought—exquisitely Dante.

He was that sort of man. Not a spare ounce of body fat on him, muscular, honed. His suits cut to tailored perfection, sleek, dangerous lines. Nothing overshadowed him. Rather it became a part of him. Absorbed into his orbit.

This house was no different.

He moved to the back seat of the car and retrieved Isabella's car seat, his movements as casual as if he had been doing it for the past three months.

"You're very good at that," she said.

"Thank you," he returned, and she couldn't tell if he was genuinely thanking her, or if he was making fun of her. She could never tell with him.

He made quick work of showing her the rooms about the place, and when he showed her to the beautifully appointed nursery she nearly collapsed.

It was an oasis. And Isabella would be safe.

Her daughter would be safe.

Whether Isabella had come from her body or not was irrelevant.

Carlo was her father, and he had blood ties to her, and it didn't mean that he cared. It meant nothing.

What mattered was love.

Isabella had given Minerva a sense of purpose she'd never experienced before. And yes, it had come with extreme exhaustion, uncertainty and a niggling feeling that she might be doing something wrong.

But mostly it was…purpose that she hadn't found before.

She'd left home to study in Rome because at home she'd always felt lost. She hadn't had a clear sense of what she wanted to study and she'd switched classes around at an alarming rate. History. Art. Art history. Business—which she'd quit immediately because it had depressed her since she had felt she would have to compete with Violet of Maximus to make it relevant.

But with Isabella she felt focused. She felt…fulfilled.

She gave Isabella a bottle, changed her diaper, and yet again, the little girl was ready to nap. Minerva took the opportunity to explore the rest of the house. Her bedroom was beautiful. Stark white walls, a white marble floor with the plush marble throw over it. The bedding was also white and soft, with large windows overlooking the sea. And she found that when pushed, they slid open, and were actually doors that gave way and led to a path outside. As far as she could tell that path led to the beach, and she had every intention of exploring it later.

For now, she needed a bath.

She slipped into the en suite and found a large tub that was also white, and looked like a freestanding bowl. It appealed to the romance in her spirit, and she began to fill it as she went back into the bedroom and began to rummage around for clothes.

It was then she realized that none of these were her own.

But of course they weren't.

Dante had procured a wardrobe for her. As she looked at the pieces, she couldn't imagine which woman he had been dressing when he had selected them.

Of course, Dante hadn't had anything to do with it.

But for a moment it was… Interesting. To

entertain the idea that he looked at her and thought that she was the sort of woman who should wander around a place like this in a brief crop top, flowing pants and a sheer caftan. That she was the sort of woman who should wear many dresses in various bright colors and... A white bikini.

She hated wearing swimsuits, and she definitely didn't gravitate toward bikinis. Not when her sister often wore them in her signature purple, showing off her brilliant curves.

Minerva's curves were so slight she doubted she could even roll a penny down the slope of her breast.

She imagined herself in the swimsuit. If it got wet it might be somewhat see-through. She wondered what Dante would think of that.

The idea sent a sip of something forbidden through her body and she immediately turned away from it. She went back into the bathroom with the crop top, pants and caftan and stripped her clothes off, settling herself into the warm water. It was only there that she allowed herself to reflect on everything that had happened. The kiss...

She was submerged in warm water, and yet she felt her nipples pebble when she replayed it in her mind.

No. She wasn't going to think of it. It was shocking. She should be angry at him, because he had kissed her in a way that no one would expect a man to do in a church.

Then she began replaying what he'd said about *Swiss Family Robinson.*

And that had an even deeper effect on her. Something that turned deep inside her and made her feel something in her chest.

She liked that even less.

The kiss was safer.

She got out of the tub hastily, wrapping herself in a towel and exiting into the bedroom. It was then she realized that Isabella was crying. Panic slammed against her, and she began moving around frantically looking for her clothing, but before she could, the bedroom door swung open and Dante appeared, cradling her in his arms.

Min just stood there, clutching the towel to her chest. "I was on my way," she said.

"I don't know what to do with the baby," he said, his tone accusing. "Take her."

She wasn't thinking clearly, and she reached out, taking Isabella into her arms, in spite of the fact that she was only barely wrapped in a towel. "I should've gotten dressed first," she said.

Dante paused, and looked at her, his dark

eyes seeming to slowly register the scene in front of him.

"Neither thing is my problem. Handle it."

And with that he turned and walked out of the room, and she wondered where the caring man had gone who had told her about *Swiss Family Robinson*. Even the man who had issued death threats to the one who had indicated he might cause her harm was better than this one.

She didn't know why he was angry with her.

It was like he wasn't capable of holding a baby for a moment.

She sighed heavily and went over to the diaper bag in the corner of the room, hunting around for a pacifier. She popped one in Isabella's mouth, then took a blanket and spread it out as best she could with one free hand before setting her on the floor.

"I'm just going to get dressed," she said, keeping one eye on her the entire time. After that she saw her safely soothed, but she found that she could not soothe herself.

She was going to be stuck here with Dante for the foreseeable future. And she truly didn't know how she was going to survive.

She might be physically safe with him, but she didn't know what was happening inside her.

Didn't know what was happening inside him.

And like it or not, something about the vows that they had spoken had affected her. Had changed something in her.

What was a person to do when she found herself angrily married to her older brother's best friend and stranded on his private island?

*You know what one of your heroines would do...*

Minerva blinked, and pushed that thought aside.

It didn't matter what one of her heroines would do.

No matter what her dreams had been, she wasn't one of them. She never had been. And she never could be.

# CHAPTER SIX

ALREADY THINGS WERE not going according to Dante's plan. And Dante had very little experience of things not going according to his plans. He was not a man who often had to deal with defiance, whether it came from another person, or life. Not a man who had been put in a position where another human being might come into his sphere and create disorder.

Chaos.

His life had been utter and complete chaos when he was a child. From the time he was born until he had been swept off the streets, half-feral, and put into a private school by Robert King.

Dante had been in possession of some concerns about Robert. Mostly, he had been convinced that a man who offered such things to a boy must have nefarious intent for him.

Dante had done a lot of thinking about whether or not he cared.

Because the streets had visited vast amounts of atrocities onto him. And when you were lean, and hungry, you tended to have a very flexible idea of what you might be willing to do for your next meal.

With that in mind, he had decided to take Robert's deal, and he had come to the conclusion that depending on what the man might ask of him, he would either comply and take the education, take the money for the time being, or he would follow through with what he had originally intended to do. Robert had given the gun back, after all.

All of those thoughts seemed so wildly removed from who he was now, and the kind of life he lived.

But it all came back when the baby had been wailing wildly, and he hadn't known what to do.

And then, he had gone looking for Minerva, only to find her standing there in a towel.

Her shoulders were enticing.

Her hair had been up, falling damply around her face, and he had found it disconcerting in the extreme. And resentment had burned in his chest. For what he and Minerva both new was that Isabella was not his child.

And if she cried, she was not his responsibility. The responsibility was Minerva's.

And he would also like to speak to her about her responsibility when it came to not being an enticement.

Of course, he had no desire to admit to her that she was an enticement.

He ate dinner, and found himself at loose ends.

There was little work to be done, simply because he was not a man who was ever behind.

He took on work. More than he could handle, many would say, but he always managed to get it finished. And he was constantly being lectured on the fact that he should find a way to have more leisure time.

But for what?

He could never figure it out.

He went out when he felt like it. Oftentimes, there were business reasons to go out, connections to be made when he did. And then, if he managed to meet a woman in whose company he wished to spend the night, it was a pleasant diversion. But he didn't need more recreation time for that.

Often, words like that were spoken by

those who didn't know what it meant to be hungry.

Who had never once had to entertain the idea that it might be preferable to endure the physical abuse of an older man in order to feed oneself.

No, in Dante's world, work and money were king.

It was a wall that he was building between himself and what he had come from so high and so thick that nothing would ever be able to cross it.

Safety.

He suddenly heard a soft voice, and the sound of a baby, and he turned and saw Minerva, wearing pants and a top that showed her stomach, coming down the stairs. "I'm starving," she said. "What's for dinner?"

"I ate," he said.

The look of thunderous fury that crossed her delicate features would have been amusing if it hadn't been quite so dark. "You ate? Without me?"

"I was not under the impression that we were required to eat in tandem."

"But what am I supposed to do?" she asked in a fury. "I would have thought that you would eat with me. *On our wedding night.*"

He cast her a flat stare. "Minerva," he said.

"Don't tell me you were hoping for a more traditional wedding night."

Her mouth dropped open, then she shut it again. "Of course not. We mustn't consummate. Remember? Your Catholicism."

He huffed a laugh. "Thank you, for your dedicated concern to my Catholicism, but I promise you I have not forgotten it."

"Well."

"I wear it like a hair shirt every day."

"Fine," she said, her eyes green like beetles, and just as mean.

"Let's find you some food," he said. "I wouldn't want to get on the wrong end of you when you're hungry."

She followed him into the kitchen, and he opened up the fridge. He already knew that there was an elaborate charcuterie board in there, and some meals to be reheated. That was one of the issues with having staff off-site.

He did know how to cook for himself, but his skills were a bit crude, owing to the time in his life when he had to provide for himself.

Spaghetti with tomato sauce was all well and good for an eighteen-year-old going to university, but he had moved past that.

"You can start with cheese," he said, taking the platter and setting it out on the white marble countertop.

Minerva, clutching Isabella to her chest like she was a tiny shield, went over to the board and began picking at the offerings. She picked up a date, bit into it and closed her eyes, an obscene moan escaping her lips.

He gritted his teeth and turned away from that. "Fish or steak?"

"Steak," Minerva said. "Always steak. I haven't the use for fish."

"Well. I suppose that means you'll be consuming all the steak during our stay."

"I could give you a bite," she said.

"Oh, don't flatter me by offering me your castoffs, Minerva."

He took one of the meals out and began to heat the steak and vegetables in a pan for her.

She sat there, holding the baby with one arm and eating cheese with another.

"This really is very nice," she said.

"Oh, now your anger has subsided?"

"I don't know very many people who can stay angry while eating cheese," she said.

"You seem like someone who could," he said.

"I find that very flattering."

He had the distinct impression that she meant it.

He finished heating the food and set it out in front of her. He noted she was very comfortable being served.

She looked around. "Can you hold her?"

Several thoughts went through his mind all at once, careening around like a runaway train.

And he wondered for the first time—not just since this started, but in years—if he had miscalculated. He had assumed he could make a delineation between the public and private. Not have to handle anything to do with the child in private.

Clearly, Min thought different.

He had no experience with babies. He wanted no experience with babies. And, also, there was no way that he, Dante Fiori, could allow himself to be defeated by an infant.

Practicality dictated that Minerva needed both hands to eat. And that meant that he should hold the child while she did so.

"Give her to me," he said.

"You might want to work on your tone," she said, rising up from her seat and bringing Isabella over to him, depositing her into his arms. Then, she went and sat back down in front of her plate. The child was so light. She was barely a weight in his arms, and yet she was warm. She leaned against him, so trusting. So very... Fragile.

Minerva was busy eating, and he was pondering this. The baby's fragility.

How could adults leave small things such as this to fend for themselves? How could they ever put them in danger?

"I'll kill him," Dante said, his hand resting on the back of her downy head. "I will kill him for what he's put you through."

"Well, that's not something I expected," Minerva said, looking up from her plate.

"It is true, though. It is wrong, what he's done to you. And her. But mostly her."

"Well, thank you very much."

"We are adults, Minerva, and we must answer for our actions. A child like her has done nothing except be born into a broken world. She is helpless. She is dependent on the people around her to make decisions for her survival, her safety."

"I know," Minerva said. "And that's why I was willing to do whatever it took to keep her safe."

He nodded. "Of course. You would understand that."

"I do understand it. There was nothing to be done. I had to... Whatever the cost, Dante, I had to make sure that she would be protected."

Minerva ate in silence for a while, and then he shifted his hold on Isabella, who promptly made a sound like a very juicy hiccup and cast up her accounts on his shirt.

"Oh!" Minerva jumped up from her seat. "I'm sorry."

She reached out and grabbed hold of Isabella. And he looked down at his damp shirt. He gripped the hem and tugged it over his head. "I'll leave this for the staff when they come pick up the laundry."

"Staff?"

But her eyes were not on his face. Rather, they were resting in the center of his chest.

"Yes," he said. "We will make sure that we are not about when they come, but we will need to have supplies brought here, laundry dealt with, food replenished."

"Yes," she said, her eyes darting up, down and back and forth, but never going higher than his shoulders.

"Minerva," he said. "My eyes are up here."

And then she did look stunned. Her cheeks turning red.

Minerva was not unaffected by him. She was just very, very good at playing games.

He was shocked by this realization. But, now that he had his shirt off, he seemed to have reduced her mouthiness by 20 percent or so.

"I know where your eyes are," she snapped. "I believe your shirts are upstairs, if you want to find one."

"I'm perfectly comfortable. Aren't you comfortable?"

"I'm not," she said, growing edgy and pink. "But that's because it's a little bit warm in here. And... I might walk down to the beach."

He arched a brow. "Might you?"

"I might."

He wouldn't have imagined that a woman— a grown woman with a child—could be made so uncomfortable at the sight of him without a shirt.

He knew that women found his looks impacting. It was something he'd enjoyed the effects of for the past twenty years. But he was used to purring, coquettish glances. Touching. Flirting. Not...fear.

"There's cake," he said.

Min tilted her head. "At the beach?"

"Here," he clarified. "Chocolate cake, if you would like to stay for some. However, if you're indisposed..."

She sat, holding Isabella. "I will accept cake."

He chuckled, and went over to the other

side of the kitchen, procuring a slice of cake and setting it on a plate.

He liked this reversal of fortune.

Because it had been bothering him that Minerva had had an effect on him, and now the tables had turned.

For a brief moment he saw his own actions, his own satisfaction, clearly.

He was delighting in some kind of sensual victory over Maximus's little sister. A woman who had been—until a few days ago—as a child to him.

But hell, they were going to be stuck here in this place for God knew how long. He supposed he had to take his victories where he could get them. He held the plate out to her, and with great effort, she looked up at his eyes.

# CHAPTER SEVEN

SHE DIDN'T KNOW what was happening to her. She felt warm and flushed all over and she couldn't seem to do anything but stare at his chest.

She was trying to remember if she had ever seen Dante without a shirt before. She must have. At least when she was younger, and they went to the beach.

She was around shirtless men all the time. She lived in California. They had beachfront property.

She didn't know why this felt different, why it made her insides shiver, and why she felt overheated.

It had been strange to watch him hold Isabella, the way his powerful hands gripped her delicate body.

It made her so unbearably conscious of his strength, and the control that he utilized in unleashing it. And now he was offering her cake.

And the image he made, shirtless and extending that decadent treat to her, his muscles shifting and bunching…

He had hair on his body. Not enough to conceal his muscles, but just enough to make her unbearably aware of his testosterone.

And that prickling in her skin was back. That racing in her heart, that unbearable, unsettling feeling that made her feel as if she had to do something. Anything. To get his attention. To get him to notice her.

And with a sudden horror, she realized what that feeling was.

And it was a feeling she had for a very long time. For Dante.

No. No. *No.* She wouldn't acknowledge it. She couldn't. She could not… Would not…

She had never.

And suddenly, she realized the little lie that she had told her father, her mother, her sister, might not have been such a lie after all.

Had she had feelings for Dante all this time?

That something in her simply refused to make them into the shape of what they truly were?

It was as if in that glorious chest of his she could see clearly. The most absurd thought she ever had in her life, but it was true.

Years of following after him, trying to climb trees in his sphere so that he might say something about her daring, talking and talking and talking at him even though he was so patently disinterested.

But she had never allowed herself to call it what it was, because he was far too old, far too beautiful, and if he was going to choose a woman from her family...

It would have been Violet.

It never would have been her.

Ever.

But maybe that was the real reason why the kiss in the club in Rome had felt so disappointing.

Because the man wasn't Dante.

And maybe that was why she had shut down completely the two times Dante had kissed her.

Because it wasn't real.

Because it was all a farce that she had set up, and if she really did feel this way, if the burning intensity of that bright something in her chest really did mean that she... That she had a crush on him, then perhaps using his name, using him as a solution, the fact that he was the father of Isabella, as a solution to her problem was...

The very idea made her squirm. Surely her subconscious hadn't done that.

But then, her subconscious was apparently a straight-up hussy for Dante, and she had kept her actual conscious from acknowledging that somehow.

And now, shirtless and with cake, she couldn't ignore it. Couldn't deny it.

Couldn't help but identify the sharp, reckless heat that had cut through her seventeen-year-old body the moment he'd taken her up into his arms to shield her from censure, to shield her from the world, had been…

Desire.

She snatched the cake from his hand and then looked down at it resolutely.

"Something wrong, Minerva?"

"Nothing is wrong," she said.

He approached her, and tilted her face up. "Nothing is wrong?"

He had touched her before. He had touched her many times, and this time it burned. Because this time she knew. Knew that that little prickling sensation he left all over her skin when his fingers made contact with her wouldn't happen with any man. Knew that it wasn't static electricity or something else that she could easily dismiss.

It was Dante.

But more than that, it was her feelings for him.
"I'm fine," she repeated.

But he was far too close to her.

"Good to know."

And then he moved away from her, and she realized, with stunning humiliation, that he was playing with her.

That he had known that she had been powerless in the face—or rather, the chest—of his magnetism.

She gritted her teeth and dug into the cake with ferocity. "I am fine. And I don't need you to eat dinner with me. After all, you ate already. You clearly didn't want to share a meal with me, so why hang around pretending? Go wash your shirt."

But he didn't obey. Rather, he stood there, watching her eat cake. And she refused to get up. Refused to let him win. So she ate every last bite, and then cleaned up each remaining crumb. Then defiantly rose, carrying Isabella in one arm, and the plate in the other hand, and deposited it in the sink before going back up the stairs. "I think I will get Isabella and me set up to have a date on the beach tomorrow. I know that you're very busy and have lots of work to see to. But it's fine. We will be just fine without you."

She was grateful that her hands didn't start

shaking until she got back to the bedroom and closed the door firmly behind her.

Because she didn't want him to see just what he did to her.

It was beyond a cruel joke.

Because as Dante had said more than once, she was not the kind of woman who would ever turn the head of a man like him.

She was much happier when her brain had understood that, and buried her feelings for him, sparing her from any disappointment.

Now she just felt deflated and frightened and uncertain of how she was going to get through the next chunk of time.

# CHAPTER EIGHT

THERE WAS A crackling fire burning beneath his skin, and he found it unconscionable.

True to her word, Minerva had been scarce the entire day.

When he peeked into the nursery, he saw that a great many of Isabella's items were gone, and he thought that it might be true that she had tramped off to the beach intent on staying there for the day.

Which meant that he would simply stay in the house and work. As she had said.

Dante had never had difficulty burying himself in work. No, quite the contrary, he had always found it to be a great solace. Another brick in the wall. But today he was restless, and today he found he would rather be outdoors.

Not a thought he often had, considering there had been a time in his life when he had been forced to be outdoors twenty-four hours a day, for lack of home.

Not that he didn't enjoy the beach on occasion, but he had been rather fond of temperature control since his first experience of it.

Before he could think much about it, he had stripped his T-shirt and jeans off, and gone on the hunt for swim shorts. Once he had acquired those, he took hold of a light T-shirt and put it on before making his way down the path that led to the private beach.

The sight of Minerva and Isabella did something strange to his chest. It tangled things up in there. And he didn't like it.

Minerva was wearing a white bikini, and he had never seen so much of her skin. She also had on a wide-brimmed sunhat, and she and Isabella were beneath a cabana, staying out of the sun.

Minerva's skin was that golden California-girl tone, courtesy of a lifetime spent at the beach. She had no makeup on today, her hair a riotous tangle beneath the hat, and he was sure that she had been out in the waves at some point. Her curves were slight, but they were delectable, her midsection slim but strong, muscles visible in her stomach.

Her arms were the same, slim but toned, as were her legs.

Her breasts were small, but round and high. His hands would eclipse them completely.

The thought sent a slug of desire straight through him.

What a strange moment. Standing there, looking at her as though she were...an object of desire.

Minerva.

*Min.*

When she looked over at him, her eyes widened, and the corners of her mouth turned down. "What are you doing here?"

"I came to check on you. Because you've been gone all day."

"I told you we would be," Minerva said. "I could think of nothing better to do while feeling safe than come to the beach."

That made him feel slightly guilty for terrorizing her last night.

"Have you been afraid of him all this time?"

"I... Yes," she said. "I had hoped that escaping would make him feel further away, but I was just waiting. Waiting for him to figure it out."

"Figure what out?"

She blinked. "Nothing."

"I know what it's like. To feel afraid all the time."

His mind was cast back to whom he'd been. That boy on the streets.

That boy who had held a gun to Robert King's head.

"It's terrible," she said softly.

"It is," he agreed.

He felt unkind that he had given her a false sense of what would happen in their marriage in the future. And now that he recognized she was so pleasing physically, there really was no question of them getting an annulment.

"Minerva, I know what it is to be afraid. I lived my life without security on the streets of Rome."

"I've been to Rome, and I can honestly say that now that statement means a lot more to me," she said.

"I'm sure it does. It is a terrifying thing to have no control. Whether that be because of a lack of money, or because a person has decided to dismantle that. And when you figure out how to have power, you'll never go back. Not ever."

"I don't suppose."

"Then you will understand why there is no question of the two of us divorcing."

"What?"

"I'm solidifying this business deal with

your father, the best way that I can. And if I were to divorce you it would cause problems."

"We talked about this. About… You helping me. And how he surely won't be angry with you if he knows that what you did you simply did to keep me safe."

"To a certain point. It is about consolidating power, Minerva. In my life I have always imagined that I'm building a wall between myself now and my past. Whenever I can build it stronger, build it higher, I will. This is such an opportunity, and I will take it."

He was not asking her for anything untoward, not in his mind.

It wasn't as if she were an innocent. She had a child.

"I will give Isabella my name," he said. "She will be my daughter. I can adopt her, legally. All of this can be accomplished once we are certain you're safe. Everything I own will be hers someday. And I will be her father."

The words sent a strange surge through his chest. "There are many things about family I don't understand. And I won't. I have been in yours for a great many years, and still… The foundation that is built beneath us during our earliest years matters a great deal. And I know that more than most. I can't promise I'll be the best father, but I will be better than the one that biology gave her. And I will be better than my own."

She picked Isabella up, in a move he now absolutely recognized. "And what about as a husband?"

"I will be good to you. Have I ever not been?"

"But will you ever love me?"

"You said yourself, Minerva, you don't even like me very much. What do you care if I love you? You won't love me."

She bit her bottom lip. "Well, that's a pretty sad start to a marriage, don't you think?"

"No," he said. "I don't. The mutual interest of protecting your daughter, a desire to unite our family names… And you don't dislike me. Admit it."

"I will do no such thing," she sniffed. "You're old."

"Yes. I know. When I was a child I had to walk to the soup kitchen, in the snow, uphill both ways."

"Stop it," she said.

"I'm offering you security," he said. "I can offer you nothing that means more to me than that. Security is what I have built my entire new life on. And I will give it to you. You must understand what value that has to me. And with that I give you the greatest thing in my possession. It is better than love. Love is fickle and it breaks. Love destroys the moment that it malfunctions. I have seen it. My mother loved my father, and what did that get her? Years on the streets. Prostitution. She loved many men, and all they did was take from her. And that love that she felt for them gave them that power. It is a folly to love. Did you love Isabella's father?"

Her face took on a strange pallor. "No," she said. "I didn't."

"Well, then. I suppose there is no comparison for you to be had there. But by God, Minerva, you must know that what I would give you, what I would give her, is better than the potential of someday finding a relationship that could give you what? Will a man claim Isabella so wholly as his own? Or will he always make her feel second? Will he care so much about the interests of your family? As much as I do? Will he be able to keep you safe in the way that I have done?"

"And you'll do this… All for a business?"

There was something in her look that was beseeching, and he knew that she wanted another answer.

He had one. Much to his surprise.

"I see myself in Isabella. A vulnerable child. There is little outright good I have done in the world, but if I can spare her the realities of life, that harshness, until she must absolutely face it, then I will. I will be her wall against all that is behind her, all that would seek to harm her, and the brilliant future that she can have. I will be a man she can call father safely. I will not harm her."

Minerva's green eyes were glistening now. He knew that he had said the right thing.

"All right," she said, setting Isabella down on a blanket beneath the shade. "I agree. I'll be your wife. Really."

What shocked him most was the roaring in his ears. It took him a moment to realize that it wasn't the waves. That it was some kind of hot flood of triumph that was rallying through him like a river. He closed the distance between them, and pulled her into his arms, and then, he claimed her mouth for real.

Not because of their farce.

Not because there was an audience.

Because she was his wife.

And she was his.

# CHAPTER NINE

MINERVA FELT LIKE she had come down with a terrible fever. She was hot all over, shaking, and her stomach felt like it was tossing and turning.

He was kissing her.

And it was different than the kiss that had happened at the engagement party. Different than the kiss at their wedding.

It was different than anything.

And she feared that she might be too. That somehow, between the revelations of last night, and this moment when his mouth had met hers, and all the in-between—those moments when he had made such a rational case for her being his wife permanently, and she had created a web of justification inside herself and pulled each gossamer strand tight, hoping that it would act as a safety net when she inevitably fell.

And fall she was doing.

Hard. Fast.

Into this deep, dark sensual kiss that kicked against her and made a mockery of what she had thought the day of their engagement party.

That she had thought it was in a kiss. Not a real kiss. For, a real kiss was supposed to make her feel light and airy, was supposed to fill her with joy.

But the feelings that she had for Dante were so much more complicated than that. A series of complications, in fact. That could never be so simple as a fantasy realized. Would that they could be. No, it was nothing like she had imagined because, of course, she hadn't taken into account that kissing involved another person.

Which meant that the movements were not all hers. Which meant that she wasn't in charge of how firm it was, of how deep it was.

And because there was another person involved, it was physical.

He was in a misty vapor of her fantasies the way that it all materialized in her head when she was reading about a handsome heroic character that she might want to dream about.

Because Dante was real. Mortal. A man in the flesh, with hot skin and a pounding heart. With hard muscles and hard...

He pressed his hand to her lower back and drew her up against him. Hard.

Yes. All of him was hard.

He desired her. Whether or not it was because he was a man and he could desire whatever he chose at a given moment, or because he desired her specifically, she didn't know. But he did.

And that was... Intense and heady and frightening.

She also wanted to lean into it as much as she wanted to run from it. More than anything in the entire world. Why was nothing about this simple? Why wasn't it easy? Why did it feel world-ending and wonderful all at once?

When they parted, she knew.

She looked into his dark gaze and she knew that it was him.

*Dante.*

And she had no idea how she had come to be the one kissing him.

She, Minerva, who was nothing.

Not by comparison of her exceptional family. And certainly not in comparison with him.

She had done one vaguely heroic thing in her life, and that was take care of Isabella.

But then, she had to wonder if it was heroic at all, or if she had just been reacting.

Because what could you do when there was a little girl vulnerable and alone in the world, her mother was dead and the police were declining to investigate.

She could have allowed Isabella to go into foster care in Italy, but that would have only made her vulnerable to Carlo.

She would've bounced around and…

And Minerva would never have seen her again.

So Minerva had told the police that Isabella was her daughter.

And that was how it had continued.

Dante thought that she was at least interesting enough to have engaged in an affair with a mobster.

But she wasn't.

She had just been a witness to it, and that made her all the more bland.

She suddenly felt small and weak and trembling, and she hated herself for it.

"What's the matter?" He lifted his hand and dragged his thumb along her lower lip.

"Nothing," she said.

She lied because there was nothing else to do. She lied because all of this was a lie, so she might as well be one too.

"I think we had quite enough of the beach, don't you?"

"Have we?"

"Yes. You're my wife. And it's time to make that real."

"Oh… Well, it is real, in that it's legal."

"You know," he said, his voice lowering to a growl. "There were days when a marriage wasn't considered a marriage until it had been consummated."

"Right," she said. "Wasn't there some barbarous practice of hanging bloody sheets out the window to alert the nation of the purity of the bride?"

He chuckled. "Luckily," he said, "neither of us have to worry about your purity."

Her stomach fell.

"Luckily."

He bent down and picked up Isabella. With shaking hands, Minerva began to gather her things.

"Leave it," he said. "It will be dealt with later."

Min was half out of her mind by the time they tromped back up to the house, by the time Dante laid Isabella down in her crib and closed the door to the nursery behind him.

"Will she sleep?"

"She doesn't run on a schedule. She does what she does."

"But she is…due to sleep?" he asked.

If there was one thing that made Dante

seem a little bit flummoxed, it was Isabella. Babies in general. And truly, she had managed to destroy some of his composure with her impromptu announcement about his being the father of her baby. She supposed that on some level she should be triumphant in that.

She might be relatively boring, but she had caused Dante Fiori a moment's concern. Had made that patrician brow crease for but a few seconds before he had taken control of the entire endeavor.

So she was several steps ahead of the rest of the world.

Maybe that made her not so boring.

But then, he thought that she was not a virgin. Thought that she might know something about how to please a man, and on that score he was going to be very disappointed.

"Do you really want me?" Her voice was small, and she despised it.

"Minerva," he said, his voice rough and hard. "Of all the things to come out of this ridiculous ruse of yours, the most disturbing is that I cannot look at you as I once did. I was content to leave you in the category of child. My friend's younger sister, the daughter of my mentor, but you insist on making yourself unique and singular. A woman who belongs only to yourself, and now, to me. I don't have a choice."

"You don't have a choice in what?"

"Wanting you. It is damned inconvenient, and I was content to stay immune to you. How... How have you made it so that I'm not? It makes no sense."

"Because I'm not your type," she said, feeling breathless.

"Not at all," he said, advancing on her. "I like women with dramatic curves, who wear makeup and style their hair." He reached out and took a lock of her own hair between his thumb and forefinger, rubbing it absently.

"I like women who respond to my touch with enthusiasm and not trepidation. I definitely don't like women who tell the world I have fathered their children and force me into a fait accompli. And yet somehow... Here we are."

He wrapped his arm around her waist and pulled her against his chest.

And they were right back where they'd been on the beach.

He wasn't just kissing her, he was consuming her. And she didn't know where she began and he ended. Didn't know what she wanted from all of this. Except that all she wanted was for it to keep going. For it to never stop.

No, kissing wasn't what she had imagined it might be. It was more. It was everything. It was physical. It consumed her. It made her doubt everything she had ever believed about herself and gave birth to entirely new ideas there on the spot.

It was magic. Dark, chaotic magic that she didn't know how to contend with. His hands didn't stay still. They roamed over her body, exploring dips and hollows in her spine, her waist, beneath her breasts.

He wasn't touching her anywhere outrageously intimate, and yet it almost seemed more scandalous for it.

She had been held in a man's embrace only one other time. And he had gone straight for the obvious places, his hand beginning to move to her breast even as his other hand had already moved down to grab her bottom.

She knew all about those obvious things, and she had found them so base and obvious they had contributed to the utter turnoff of the entire situation.

But Dante managed to take something base and elevate it. To make it feel like high art rather than simple pornography. It bewitched her. Mesmerized her. Made her into something she didn't recognize. But maybe that was a good thing.

Because she had never been all that entranced by what she did recognize inside herself. But he made her feel new.

He made her feel beautiful. And perhaps this would make it so.

He continued to kiss her, continued to explore her in that innocuous way that didn't feel innocuous at all.

She breathed in deep, inhaling the scent of him, the sensation of him as his mouth continued to move over hers.

Were they really going to have sex?

Was she really going to lose her virginity to Dante Fiori?

Her husband.

For a moment she was convinced that she had escaped the real world and slipped in between the pages of a book.

Because this was something that would happen to one of her heroines, but not something that would happen to her. This deep, rich, exciting experience that was all tongue and teeth and glory.

The hands of the man whom she cherished most, no matter that she had tried to pretend she didn't.

The kiss was all fraught, endless glory, and she reveled in it.

Then, he picked her up, cradling her against

him as he carried her past her bedroom and toward his.

She hadn't set foot in Dante's bedroom.

No, quite the contrary, she had avoided it.

Hadn't wanted anything to do with that.

But she could see now that it was because she did want something to do with it that she had avoided it quite so studiously.

These revelations about herself were coming too fast and on the heels of physical sensations that were far too new for her to fully understand them.

Why did she avoid the things she wanted most? Why did she bury them?

Why did she think she couldn't have these things?

She didn't know. Except that everyone had been so shocked by the fact that Dante was the father of her baby, that he wanted to marry her, that she knew on some level they all thought it too. That it was an accepted truth about Minerva to an extent.

Even though they loved her. Even though they supported her.

She was not now, nor had she ever been, considered a great and wonderful beauty.

And she had decided that meant she couldn't have things.

Had decided it meant she shouldn't try.

Even the way that she had been made up for the engagement party and the wedding had made her uncomfortable because she knew that people would compare her with Violet. She didn't want it.

But Dante wanted her. He was spreading her out on his large bed, and staring down at her with dark, keen eyes.

Then he stood back and stripped his shirt off, as he'd done the day before.

But the day before she hadn't been about to touch him. Hadn't been about to...

"Now you don't have to pretend that you aren't looking," he said.

"I would never pretend," Minerva said. "I don't have the kind of capacity to play games that many do. I'm honest."

But that was a lie. She wasn't honest. Of course Dante believed that she had experience with men. And she didn't.

But she wasn't about to tell him. It made the whole situation that much more precarious, made her connection to Isabella so much more tenuous.

"Well, then let me return your honesty with the same," he said.

He leaned over, grabbed the hem of her top and jerked it up over her head. Her nipples beaded in the cool air, a blush warming her against the chill. No man had ever seen her like this, and that this perfect specimen of one was staring at her now was more than a little bit embarrassing. But he looked… Well, he looked as entranced as she felt. And it made her feel… Something. Something so deep and intense, it made her want to cry. Made her want to turn away from him and turn toward him all at the same time.

She began to shake as he lowered himself down onto the bed, stretching his body over her.

His lips were a whisper away from hers, and all she wanted was for him to taste her again.

Because when his mouth was on hers, she couldn't think quite so well. And not being able to think was a gift.

She wanted to be carried away in the fantasy. She craved a little bit more gauze, a little bit of protection from this hard, physical reality. But she didn't know if she was going to be able to get any.

Not with him. Not with him so hard and real and large above her. Not with her heart threatening to pound out of her chest.

With her breath eluding her lungs.

A smile tilted up the corner of his mouth. That smile was… Wicked.

And she realized that she had never seen Dante like this before.

She had always found him beautiful. Formidable.

A tiger safely contained in an enclosure. She knew that he would never turn that focus, all that brilliant, amber glory, on to her. Knew that his fangs would be reserved for other quarry.

He had only ever protected her. But in doing that he'd concealed the most powerful parts of himself. Had hidden the true danger from her.

Except, now it was all focused on her. Deeply. Intensely.

Now, the tiger was looking at her as if she was going to be his next meal.

And here she was, lying down wantonly to be consumed.

He pushed the shorts he was wearing, discarding them quickly, and her mouth dried. She had never seen a naked, aroused man.

And the very first thing she wanted to say was that there was no way he would fit. On the heels of that came the hysterical urge to laugh. Because of course he thought she had given birth. In which case the size of a man's penis would be the smallest of concerns to her.

Though, his penis could never be called a small concern.

Yet again, she had to fight back the hysterical urge to laugh. Because it was either that or cry.

Either that or give in to the fear that was gripping her chest. No, it wasn't fear. Because she didn't want to run away. It was something deeper than that. Something that scraped at a raw edge in her heart. That call to deep emotion inside her that she didn't want to deal with or acknowledge.

That she wanted him to look at her and see beautiful.

That she wanted to be wrapped in his arms and held close, close to his body, and more than that to his heart.

That for her, this would never be a simple business deal, nor would it ever be a defense against the terrifying things out in the world. That for her, this was about feeling.

That for her, this would always be about her connection to him.

Because she couldn't have chosen another man.

She wouldn't have been able to imagine herself with another man.

She never would have been able to say the things she did to another man.

Just like she didn't want to kiss another man on that dance floor in Rome.

Because it was Dante. It always had been. And it always would be.

And that made her want to hide.

First of all because she was sure that he would see that shining out from her eyes. But second of all because she was absolutely convinced that she was reaching the highest, most brilliant peak of her life at the age of twenty-one. That she would never be able to have more or better than this moment.

Because at the end of it they would have to contend with reality. With what remained.

And perhaps he would be able to tell she'd never done this before, and perhaps he wouldn't. Maybe the farce would be over, and maybe it would not.

But whether or not she would be able to keep it up was another question entirely. Because once he had joined his body to hers...

Well. She would be new. She would be different. And she didn't know what would be waiting on the other side.

He grabbed hold of the waistband of her swimsuit bottoms and dragged them down her legs, leaving her exposed to his hungry gaze.

Yet again, he moved his hands to a place she didn't expect.

He pressed them against her hips, slid them upward, and then finally did he move his thumbs over her nipples. Back and forth. Stoking the heat in her body. Stoking desire in her soul.

He kissed her neck as he teased her there, kissed his way down her chest, pulling one beaded nipple into his mouth and sucking hard. And it was as if her universe now originated from there. As if she was nothing beyond that bright, white-hot point of sensation where his mouth met her body. He kissed her ribs, her belly button. Continued down her body until he grabbed hold of her thighs, wrapping his arms around her and tugging her down toward his mouth. And yet again he defied her expectations. He didn't ease her in with the touch of his fingers. No. Instead, his first contact with her most intimate area was with his tongue, sliding across her slick folds. Then he took that sensitized bud between her legs and sucked it between his lips, teasing and tormenting her with the tip of his tongue. She gasped, her bottom bowing up off the bed, and he took advantage of that to move his hands around to cup her there.

And then he held her up in place as he continued to torment her. As he continued to lavish pleasure on her until she couldn't breathe.

Until she didn't know herself. He had transformed her into a begging, weeping creature of need.

And this was what she had always feared. Truly, deep in her heart, she had feared this. That she would be debased before him. That she wanted him so much would be revealed and so easily.

She wanted him. No woman twisting and sobbing in the arms of a man, on the verge of orgasm from a few strokes of his tongue over her most intimate flesh, could pretend that she didn't have feelings for him.

No woman could pretend that she was dispassionate when she wasn't horrified by such an act, but craved more. Reveled in the intimacy of it. In the intensity. And then, he added a finger to his pleasuring. Pressed one digit deep inside her before adding another.

She felt herself begin to stretch. She felt like she was going to fly apart. Like it was too much. Like this was too much. How would she ever be able to accommodate the rest of him if two fingers pushed the edges of reason for her body?

Except all she knew was that she wanted more. Whether or not she was convinced she could handle more.

She wanted him. She wanted him even if it

made no sense. She wanted him even if she would cry. Even if it would cause her pain.

What a strange thing. That a woman must want a man so much the first time that she would willingly submit herself to that pain. That invasion.

That a woman must have a physical marker of her virginity in a physical cost for losing it.

But she was willing. She was willing to pay the cost.

And when he made his way back up her body, as she was spent from her first climax and his mouth met hers, treating her to absolute evidence of her own need for him. Of the intensity of it.

And yet, she wasn't ashamed. To the contrary, she was spurred on.

Because she did want him. She couldn't pretend she didn't. And maybe that was the key.

Minerva had little to offer him. But she had herself. All the desire in the world. And the purity of her need for him was real.

She could give him that. And perhaps that was something he had never gotten from those practiced, beautiful socialites whom he was accustomed to.

An authenticity of need.

Maybe…

Maybe there was a gift in her innocence. In all that she was. Maybe that she had no skills or tricks or trinkets to offer him was a gift in and of itself.

"I'll go slow," he said, his voice rough.

And she realized that he intended to go slow because he thought she was only three months out from having given birth.

Not that she was a virgin.

But perhaps that would help.

When the thick, blunt head of him probed her untried flesh, she winced, and when he began to inch inside her she cried out. Gritting her teeth as he met the resistance that she knew signaled her inexperience.

And then, he had breached her. It hurt. Terribly.

And there was no way she could pretend it didn't. She cried out, and cursed herself as ten times the fool that she had ever thought for believing that she could hide this from him.

He began to withdraw and she panicked, grabbing hold of his rear end urging him back in.

"No," she said. "We have to. I need you."

He began to ease forward again, the effort it was taking him to go slow visible in the way the cords stood out on his neck.

"Please," she beseeched him.

And on a growl he thrust all the way home.

She had not been prepared. For the intensity of this. For the invasion of this.

For his rampant masculinity in the way that it would utterly and completely demolish her softness.

Her femininity.

For the fact that it was like a conquering.

But one she had surrendered to. Willingly. Joyously.

His dark eyes met hers, his expression that of a fierce warrior. His mouth moved, as though he was about to speak, and she stretched up, capturing the words with her lips, swallowing them. Because she didn't want to talk about anything right now. She didn't want to inhabit reality.

All she wanted was this.

For him to inhabit her. For him to take her and remake her, so that she was new. And maybe, maybe parts of him would become new too. Maybe they could do that for each other. Maybe.

He growled against her mouth, but he didn't try to speak to her again. Instead, he began to move.

Hard and fast, establishing a rhythm that left her breathless.

That carried them both up to the stars.

And when she shattered there up among

the heavenly bodies, she finally felt like she belonged.

Like she was beautiful.

Beautiful in his arms. Beautiful for him.

Crying out her pleasure with no shame at all.

And when he tipped over the edge, a roar of pleasure coming from deep inside him, she held him. While he shook. While he poured himself out inside her.

She had never felt so female. She had never felt so powerful. Wrapped around this hard, muscular body that might have been carved out of rock were it not for the heat that radiated off him.

Were it not for the way he breathed. Hard and jagged as though something had been broken inside him.

When it was finished, he rolled away, and looked at her. His eyes were unreadable. Unfathomable.

And she couldn't guess what he would say next.

But she also couldn't contain the lie inside her anymore.

Whether he had guessed or not.

Based on the expression there, she had a feeling that he didn't know what he might have guessed or not.

But she wouldn't make him guess. She

wouldn't make him speculate. There was no place for that with them.

"I didn't give birth to Isabella," she said.

And by the way the mountain moved, she could tell that he hadn't been close to guessing that at all.

# CHAPTER TEN

DANTE WAS STILL reeling from the ecstasy that he had found in Minerva's arms. He had been ready to lecture her on allowing him to hurt her while her body was still tender, and then she had dropped that bombshell on him. And it made him go back in time. Every moment, every kiss, every touch since they had embarked on this farce.

The moment that he had first entered her body and she had flinched.

It was impossible.

It couldn't be.

That she was not an innocent was one of the only reasons that he could have justified demanding that she become his wife in body as well as in name.

He had been certain that she had known exactly what he was demanding of her.

But she did not.

And while he didn't hold to medieval ideas

about virginity, and he was certainly not going to go hang a sheet out the window, it was about his age. His experience. The fact that he had swept her off the beach and taken her practically straight to bed without...

She had wanted it. He was certain of that.

But how could he be sure that she knew what she had wanted?

And how dare she lie to him?

Because he had been embroiled in this entire situation against his will, and apparently, Isabella was not her daughter.

Which begged the question... Who was the child?

And whom was Minerva actually hiding her from?

"Dammit," he said, moving to a sitting position. "Have you stolen this child?"

"No!" Minerva scrambled to a sitting position, clutching the sheets to her breasts. The entire left side of her body was still completely bare, and his eyes were drawn to that golden skin that he knew now was softer than he could have anticipated.

And he had no reason to be staring at her now. Not when he was looking at a traitor.

She had lied to him.

"Then explain this," he said. "Explain this entire thing. She's not your child?"

"Not biologically," Minerva said. "I said I didn't give birth to her. I didn't say I wasn't her mother."

"You adopted her?" he pressed.

"Not exactly. I lied. And everything… Everything to do with her birth was a disaster." She pressed her hands to her temples. "I have to start at the beginning."

"You had better."

"You know when I left for school I was planning on doing a new country each year, a new university. Right. Well, when I went to Rome I was rooming with a woman named Katie. She was also from the States. We didn't know each other before, but we became friends. She was very different from me."

Minerva clasped her hands in front of her and made a study of them. "I liked her. I was fascinated by her. Mostly because I'd never known anyone like her. I know everyone thinks that Maximus and Violet are wild because they go to parties all the time. But nobody as successful as they are isn't working most of the time."

Minerva lifted a shoulder. "I was studying, mostly. And Katie was in and out at all hours. Finally, I agreed to go out with her one night. We went to a club down in Rome. We met men."

A dark anger welled up in his chest. "But you didn't. You didn't have sex with him. You were a virgin."

He didn't know why now he felt the need to confirm that. And why the idea that this other man might have done something with her angered him.

"He kissed me once," Minerva said. "I didn't like it. I told him I wanted to leave. But Katie didn't want to leave, because she had met someone and she wanted to go home with him. I went back to our dorm by myself. The next morning, she came home, and she was in a good mood. She liked Carlo. She wanted to keep seeing him."

"And then what?"

"She started realizing he wasn't a good man. She tried to pull away. And it seemed to work. He seemed to lose interest. Then she changed. She started seeming more depressed than wild. That was when she told me she was pregnant. And we had to hide it from him. She said he was dangerous, and that was why she had left him. But like I said, it seemed as if he had lost interest in her. But he came to visit one day months later, and he saw that she was pregnant, and he said he wanted the baby. She told him no. We called the police. But…"

"Connections within crime families extend far. I know."

"We hoped that we were safe. After she had Isabella, she slid into a depression. Only two weeks after Isabella was born she started using drugs. I mean, she had always used them, but when she went out for the night. Not at home, and not during her pregnancy. But she was paranoid, and she was anxious, and she needed something to calm her down. I quit going to class too." She looked down at her hands. "I was so worried about her. I was so worried about Isabella."

She took a breath and forged on. "I took care of her, like she was my baby. It just… happened one day. I decided I couldn't do half. And since Katie couldn't do it at all, I just did. I fed her, clothed her, rocked her to sleep." She blinked hard. "One day I went out shopping with Isabella, and when I came back there were police at our apartment. Katie was… Her body was gone already. They said that she had died of a drug overdose. But I was afraid that wasn't true."

Min's eyes met his, and the green fire there was intense. "I will always be afraid that isn't true. That he wanted the baby. I told the police Isabella was mine. And then the very next day I packed up and I left Italy. I came back home with her. And then he found me. I wanted him to believe that Isabella was my baby. I wanted to… Cast doubt on it. Because I'm sure that he never paid enough attention to me to know whether or not I might have been pregnant. In fact, I doubt he ever would have recognized me no matter how many times he saw me. I'm plain, after all. But I think he found out who was rooming with her, and he began a search. I think he can't be certain that Isabella is his, and I'm counting on that. I was counting on you standing with me. Because I never slept with him either. So if… If I have a baby. If I have one with you…"

Helpless rage coursed through him, because what could he say? He had been lied to. But Minerva had been doing the very best she could.

There had been nothing else.

And he would never have suggested another plan. There was nothing else. She was correct in that. Claiming the child for her own was brilliant, and using him was brilliant in ways he hadn't understood.

"He doesn't believe you, though," he said.

"He doesn't know, though," she said. "I'm sure of that. He's not completely certain. I don't think he ever saw Isabella. I don't think he can be sure if Katie had the baby. Only that there was a baby in our apartment."

"But you know he wants her anyway."

"Yes. And if he does any test then he'll know for sure that she's his. I fear that if he did a test and found out she wasn't he would have simply…"

"He doesn't care for anyone or anything," Dante said. "Men like that don't. Men who don't value life don't value life of any sort."

"She's in danger. And so am I." Min swallowed hard. "I think he had her killed, Dante. I do. I can't prove it, and maybe the police covered it up. But what would he do to her? What would he expose her to? And me? Well, he'd just get rid of me, wouldn't he?"

"You didn't make that clear enough," Dante said. "I'm going to make sure he's dealt with."

"Please," Minerva said. "Please don't…"

"I'm not going to have them killed. But I am going to finance operations to destroy that crime family. And I think I have the connections in Rome to do it. It will all have to be done at once, and it will require money they likely don't possess. The problem is you have to get everyone within law enforcement on his payroll at the same time."

She nodded slowly. "Right and that… That's difficult."

He shook his head. "Difficult is coming up from the streets of Rome. Starting out the son of a prostitute and becoming a billionaire. That is difficult. This just takes the right moves at the right time, and the right amount of money. And it will be done."

He stared down at her, at his wife. He had made her his wife in truth, and he could never go back on it. Minerva was his wife, and her protection was his responsibility.

He had grown up on the streets among men like Carlo.

He knew that his father was likely a man quite like him.

And this was his opportunity to do more than simply build another brick in the wall of his own security.

But to knock down the wall that separated an organized crime family from justice.

And he would do it.

For Minerva. For Isabella.

For the boy whom he'd once been.

This was all he could do. At the end of the day, it was the only thing.

He would be a father who protected Isabella. A husband to protect Minerva.

God knew he didn't have anything else to offer.

# CHAPTER ELEVEN

TIME SEEMED TO move differently on the island. It went in a haze, long leisurely days, gourmet food and sunshine. And then at night Dante made love to her.

She had the sense that he was angry with her for the deception, but he also hadn't turned away from her. She half expected him to. After the revelation that she'd been a virgin, she had expected that he might find her... She didn't know.

But time and time again he showed her that he didn't find her to be a problem. That he was attracted to her. That he wanted her.

And she wondered why that still didn't feel like enough.

She had never imagined that a man like him would find her compelling in the first place. And he did. Shouldn't she be happy with that? Shouldn't she, the less attractive sister, be happy with the crumbs that she was being handed?

Well, it didn't really matter. Because what they had was what they had.

And on the island it was only the two of them anyway. And whatever insecurity she felt about taking this into the real world…

She didn't doubt Dante's commitment. Not in the least. He was a man who would keep his word, she was certain of that.

But what she was less certain of was his feelings. Those… Those were unknowable. Utterly and completely. Today, she had talked him out of simply working in the office and had badgered him down to the beach. Often, she and Isabella spent their time there alone. Dante was a workaholic, though she was exposed to enough billionaires to know that you didn't build empires without being married primarily to your job. But still, she felt lonely.

And then she had to wonder if she was being selfish. Because wasn't she with her dream man? How could she want anything more?

Isabella began to fuss where she was lying on the towel, and she turned to Dante. "Can you pick her up?"

He looked stiff.

"She's our daughter now," she said. "Yours as much as mine."

"Meaning not?" he asked, his tone hard.

She looked at him for a long moment, trying to gauge that statement. What it meant to him.

"No," she said, slowly. "Meaning she very much is."

"Blood matters," he said.

She narrowed her eyes and studied him. "Why do you think that?"

If he noticed her careful appraisal, he didn't acknowledge it. "Because."

"You think that blood is more important than caring for a child. That blood trumps love?"

"No. I don't suppose I thought of it that way."

"But you think it matters."

"Of course it does," he said. "After all, your father didn't offer the company to me, not until I was engaged to marry you."

"Did you expect him to?"

"He always says that I'm like a son to him," Dante said. "But it's not the same."

"It very much is," Minerva said. "He loves you."

"And I'm a brother to you?"

Her cheeks heated. "Of course you're not the same as my brother. But that's the problem. You never have been. Not to me. You too… Well, I hear tell that my brother's beautiful, and I suppose that I'm proud of him in that way that a sister is. But I don't see his beauty, not in that way. Yours I could never unsee."

"Did you really have a crush on me when you were young?"

"I'm still young," she sniffed. "And you're changing the subject."

"What, you want to turn the subject back to something that's upsetting you? I don't know very much about marriage, Minerva, but I know enough to know that I shouldn't aim to upset my wife."

"I was willing to put my life at risk for her," Minerva said. "I am willing to do that. I was willing to uproot my entire life for her. Tell me, do you think that that needs blood to be more intense? Is there anything more intense? I would fix everything in her life if I could. I would vanquish all of her enemies. All of them. I hate that she's been exposed to threats. I hate that someone would harm her. Please, tell me, Dante, if you think her biological father loves her more than I do."

"Enough," he said. "This is a useless fight. The concept of family… It's good she has you. That you're willing to do that. For my part, I offer what I can."

"They say blood is thicker than water," she said. "I know they say that. But in my opinion blood can be dangerous. Blood can stain. It is not about the blood in your veins. The heart pumps the blood, after all. Isn't the heart the most important thing?"

"No," he said. "The heart is not most important. It is your brain that will serve you well, Minerva. It is your brain that you need."

"Your brain?"

"Your brain is capable of great compassion. Of rationalizing what the safest and best thing is to do. Your brain was fully engaged, your sense of duty when it comes to humanity. To tell you the truth, I don't believe even blood creates a family."

"What holds my family together, then?" she asked.

He made an exasperated sound. "Your father has a strong sense of civic duty. Something that I will now employ, something I will pay back with Isabella."

"You think *civic duty* is what holds society together?" she asked incredulously. "That is the most depressing thing I have ever heard."

"Yes," he said. "I do."

"You think… Swiss Family Robinson survived and built a house on an island because of civic duty? Or did they... Did they put their hearts into it?"

"That's more than a clumsy metaphor and *Swiss Family Robinson* is fictional."

"We learn from fiction, don't we? To see ourselves? The world? Our hearts?"

"Our hearts want things that are bad for us, Minerva. Witness your friend and Carlo. Carlo is another prime example of people who have corrupt hearts. Tell me, what can we count on to guide us with evidence such as this?"

"Love," she said. And it was clear, simple and concise to her. That love was what separated these things. That love was what made people choose someone else over themselves. Time and time again.

"Love," he said, the word a sneer. "Do you know what my mother loved?" he said. "Drugs."

"I thought that your mother... I thought that she was a prostitute to help support you."

"She was a prostitute to help support her cocaine habit."

He looked out at the horizon. And there was something so bleak and desolate in his dark eyes that she felt wounded by it.

"Dante, I'm sure that she loved you."

He shook his head, his lip curling up into a sneer. "Do you want to know one of my most vivid memories of my mother?"

"Yes," she said, knowing for sure that she didn't, because she could sense that there was nothing but pain in his next words.

"One of my very first memories of my mother was on her last birthday. I was eight years old. But I already knew how to cook for myself. I already knew how to cook for us. I had taken the money that she kept in our cookie jar, and I took it to market. With that I bought all of this, and I bought cheese. I bought bread. Pasta. I bought a feast, because I wanted to celebrate her birthday. There was cake. We never had cake. But it was for her, so I felt that it was okay. And when she got home, do you know what she said to me?"

He looked at her, his dark gaze unwavering. "She said, *You stupid boy.* And then she slapped me across my face."

Minerva clutched at her chest, her heart nearly folding in on itself. "No," she whispered.

"Yes. She said that she was going to have to go out and earn more money on her back to buy what she really needed for her birthday. It wasn't dinner with me, just so you know. It was more of her drug. She loved that more than she ever loved me. She took care of me out of a sense of obligation, and this is where I come back to duty, because thank God she did. Otherwise, she might have left me somewhere to die. Instead…"

He cut off his words.

"Dante," she said. "I'm sorry. But you must know that's not… That's not how it's supposed to be. Not in a healthy family."

"Really? And tell me, Minerva, in your healthy family, how is your sense of who you are? How is your sense of self when compared to everyone else?"

"I can't help it I was born into a family of overachievers," she said.

"I suppose not. But I'm just saying. Your family is among the most loving I've ever known, and can you honestly tell me they haven't given you issues of some kind? Love doesn't erase all of the issues out there in the world."

"I never said it did," she said.

"No, but on some level I think you believe it might."

"Wouldn't it be a nice thing to believe?"

"I'm not sure where that would leave my life."

She nodded slowly. Then she rose up from where she was sitting and crossed to him, pressing her hand to his bare chest and stretching up on her toes, kissing him slowly. Usually when they came together, there was an urgency to it. He was extremely conscious of her inexperience, and it had taken her a while to figure out how she felt about that.

Because the first time he had been considerate, but he had treated her like she knew what she was doing.

He had a tendency now to treat her like glass.

But still, they didn't linger over these sorts of kisses.

He braced his hand against her hip and held her as they did, and she felt warmth flood her body. An ache. A need that went beyond sexual. And when they parted she looked into his eyes, and she tried to see something. Anything. Caring. A connection.

She couldn't read it. She couldn't read him.

"Dante, you can have whatever life you want. You're a billionaire."

A small smile touched his lips and he brushed his thumb over her cheekbone. "Do you get all your ideas from books, Minerva? Or have you lived any of your own life at all?"

The words were said softly enough, but they were designed to pierce her chest.

They were designed to reinforce the fact that she was younger. That whatever she thought or felt, it would never be right, not in his eyes, because he knew more, had experienced more.

It wasn't fair.

And he knew it.

She turned away from him and went back and picked Isabella up. "It's fine," she said. "And yes, Dante, I have experienced things in life. You know, the death threats. Making the choice to be a mother to Isabella. And when I made that choice, by the way, I didn't make it thinking that it would be temporary. Thinking that all he would do was offer her base protection over her life. I knew that I was giving myself to her. To this. Maybe I understand more things than you think."

It was only when she had reached the relative safety and sanity of the house that she realized he had succeeded in derailing the conversation, even if she was the one who had left it on a good parting shot.

He was uncomfortable talking about family.

And given what his mother had done to him, she did understand. But it had nothing to do with her or Isabella. And none of it did anything to soothe the longing inside her. For this to be real. He'd said that she was going to be his wife in truth, but he didn't mean it. Not in the way that she recognized it. He meant sex.

And the sex was lovely, she wouldn't pretend that it wasn't. But for her all it had done was open up a deeper desire inside her. It satisfied nothing.

Because there was only one aspect of them that was engaged in it. Or rather, one aspect of him. His body. Not his heart.

And she wanted...

She wanted it. His heart.

She was perilously close to being in love with her husband.

He saw her. Whether clothed or naked, on the beach or in the kitchen, their bedroom, he saw her. And she had spent a lifetime feeling very unseen.

He wanted her.

And most of all, he had pledged to protect her, and to protect Isabella.

He had been protecting her for years.

Picking her up when she scraped her knees. Rescuing her from humiliation on a dance floor.

Oh, yes, there was a lot to love about that man.

The realization made her gasp. Because she could think of nothing lonelier. Nothing sadder than a life spent loving someone passionately, pouring out your desire, your body, to them and getting a hollow facsimile in return.

She would love Isabella. And Isabella

would love her back. And Dante would be her father.

He was right… He was right that with him she would have something much better than Carlo. She wasn't being robbed of anything there.

And Dante could not withhold his heart from his daughter. Whatever he said, Minerva knew that. Isabella was a baby, and babies existed to be loved by those who cared for them. Those who were not violent criminals anyway. Which Dante was not.

*She* was another matter.

But she was always another matter.

And she had Isabella to consider, which meant she would have to remain another matter altogether.

And she would have to find a way to be fine with it.

Three mornings later Dante was informed that Carlo had been killed in a shootout with police. The members of his crime family, including the top boss, had all been taken into custody, as had three members of the police department who were on the payroll.

It was the largest such operation to be completed in years. Dante and his money were largely seen as being responsible.

But all Dante saw was an opportunity to get back to his real life. To get back to the real world.

And it was time.

He was tempted to forget himself here on this island with Minerva. Tempted to get lulled into a sense that life began and ended here. The white sand to the line of the crystal blue ocean.

The longer they were here, away from life, the easier it was to forget who he was. The easier it was to let Min fill his vision and forget that there was reality waiting for them both.

But he had work back in New York, and he had to see to those things. Had to remember who he was.

Minerva was in her room. It was strange to him that she had opted to keep her own bedroom, especially considering she slept in his bed every night. But her things were still in the white room by Isabella's. And she was holed up in there reading a book. He startled her when he pushed the door open. "Carlo is dead."

"He is?" She sat up, eyes wide, and there was a kind of glittering triumph in her expression. Then it softened. "You didn't…"

"I didn't. It happened when the police tried

to take him into custody. There was nothing for it. But either way. You're safe."

"Does that mean we're going home?"

"Yes," he said. "We're going home." She let out a whoop, which surprised him, and leaped across the space, into his arms.

He stood there, unmoving for a moment, and then wrapped his arms around her.

He never knew quite what to do with her.

"I thought you liked it here," he said.

She separated from him. "I do," she said, her cheeks turning pink. "But…"

"Yes. It's rather isolated."

"Yes. It's just… As beautiful as it's been, I miss normal life. Isabella deserves normal."

"Well, you did marry a billionaire. Normal may not exactly be in the cards."

She laughed and shook her head. "Fine. I'll take your normal."

She smiled, and it tugged something in his chest. "We'll leave immediately."

"I guess I should get packed…"

"No need. Everything will be waiting for us when we get to our home. And anything you need here will be sent."

"Oh."

"The pilot is already on his way."

They were in the sky only an hour later.

Minerva was beginning to seem agitated.

"Why are you picking at your fingernails?"

"I'm not," she said, pulling at her finger.

"You are." He put his hand over hers. "What are you doing?"

She stopped then. "Nothing."

"Something."

"We didn't discuss… Dante, I know that you have a terrible reputation for being a womanizer. And you… You treat me like I'm fragile. You treat me like you might break me when we're in bed."

He was taken aback by her frankness, but he let her go on.

"I don't know any kind of bedroom tricks. There are always magazine saying there are one hundred sex tips in there. I don't even think I know two." She wrinkled her nose. "Well, no. I do. I might know three. But even then, they're not very well developed. And it was one thing when we were on the island and there were no other women. But are you going to… Are you going to get tired of me?"

"We said vows," he said. "I will not violate them."

She wrinkled her nose. "That isn't answering my question."

"Didn't you want to know if I was going to be faithful?"

"Well, yes. But I also want to know if you're going to be *bored*."

"I can have the same concern, Minerva. You've only been with one man. How do I know that you won't get resentful of that fact? That you won't want to try someone different. To experience variety."

"I won't," she said.

"Very confident. All the confidence of the inexperienced."

"No," she said. "It's that I had opportunity in my life, and I didn't take it. It took me all this time to realize it was because of you. Because of how I felt about you. That I… That I was attracted to you."

"Right. But now you know what it is to be with me. Perhaps the mystery is gone."

"It was never about mystery," she said.

"How about we simply both promise each other fidelity."

"Okay," she said softly.

And he could tell that he had done something wrong, but he wasn't certain what.

It was clear he had done another thing wrong when the plane began to touch down several hours later and Minerva let out a gasp. "Where are we?"

"I told you, we are going home."

"This is not home. This is… Manhattan."

"I live in Manhattan," he said.

"I don't," she said. "I live in San Diego."

"Not anymore," he said, feeling irritated now.

"You just assume that home would be your home."

"And you assume that home would be yours."

"Well… Well…"

"And I am the one with the private jet, so really, I was the only one that wasn't making assumptions, but had charted a course. If I were you, I would have checked if I was uncertain."

"I was not uncertain!"

"Well, clearly you should have been."

She huffed inelegantly. "Dante, this isn't going to work if you just think you can run around making all the decisions for me."

"I didn't make a decision for you. You didn't ask what decision was being made."

"You're infuriating. Somehow, I forgot that on the island. It was all the kissing."

"Well. I am good at kissing, even though I am infuriating."

"I miss my *family*," she said.

He didn't know why, but that word family caught him in his chest just then.

But of course she did. She missed Robert and Maximus, Violet and Elizabeth.

They were her family.

They were her blood.

"We will go and visit," he said. "And I promise you I will look into buying a home there. But my business is largely conducted out of Manhattan, and that is where we will be."

"And when you join with my father?"

"I imagine it won't change. As long as he is running things on the West Coast, I will be of more use to him here."

"I don't want to live in New York," she said, frowning deeply.

"You have something against it?" He looked out the window at the gray. Gray sea. Gray skyline.

"Please," she said. "It snows here."

"It's not like snow is imminent," he said.

"It's so busy."

"Wait to pass judgment until you've seen our home."

She kept her peace, at his request, and she only stared wide-eyed out the car window as they drove through the streets of Manhattan heading toward his penthouse apartment.

Then, she continued to be silent as they migrated to the building and went up in the gold elevator that carried them to the very top of the high-rise.

"This does not seem like a very good place to raise a child," she said.

"We are not in the penthouse yet," he said.

"We're in the elevator. It's adjacent."

"You must reserve your opinion until you see it."

"I mustn't *do anything*," she said, sounding crabby.

"You know, *cara*," he said, "many people are afraid of me."

"I suppose those people don't have any experience of you dancing with them to spare you humiliation at a party."

"Your father clearly expected it."

She bared her teeth, and he would have been amused by her show of anger if he weren't…compelled. And he didn't know what he felt compelled to do or why. She reached into places inside of him and…did that thing that Min did.

She couldn't leave well enough alone, not ever.

"Fine, then," she said. "I suppose those people also don't have experience of them marrying them so that you can protect a baby."

"That isn't the only reason I married you."

"It isn't?"

"No. I did want a share in your father's business."

He knew that that was unkind. He knew

that it was the worst thing to say to her, and yet he'd said it anyway. Her entire frame sagged. But then, the doors to the elevator slid open and it revealed the grand penthouse. Dark, marble floors and a grand view of Central Park.

"Those windows don't open, do they?"

"No," he said.

"It's very strange being so high up."

"You act like a country mouse. You were raised in California."

"Yes. And San Diego is the city. But not like this. This is *The City*."

"Yes. That's why I like it." Perhaps *like* was a strong word, but he appreciated the way that New York effectively drowned out his thoughts and memories. It was like a comforting white noise that followed you everywhere you went. So busy, so consumed with its own self, that it left you little time to reflect.

"I won't like it," she said resolutely.

"You've been here many times, and you do like New York."

"To visit," she said. "I love to see the Christmas tree in Rockefeller Center. And I love tea. Everywhere. I love the museums. But I've never wanted to live here."

"Isn't it a shame, then," he said, drawing the words out, "that you married me?"

Furious eyes met his. "I'm beginning to think so."

A muscle in his cheek ticked. "Do you wish to keep your own room here?"

"Yes," she returned.

He gritted his teeth. "Fine. You will find it is the second door on the left, and I believe clothes have been moved in for you."

"You knew that I wanted my own room."

"You kept one on the island."

A strange wave passed between them, a question that she didn't ask, and one that he didn't press.

"I'm going into my office."

"Where is that? Which room?"

"Not an office here. I must go into the office. We were gone for so long, and before that I was already in San Diego. Everything has been handled in my absence, but I need to make an appearance."

"You just got here."

"Yes. But you are in New York. I'm sure that you can find something to occupy yourself."

The man he'd been on the island wasn't the man he was in truth, and the sooner Minerva learned that the better.

There was no place for tenderness or pity inside him.

No place for hope.

He knew that those things only brought about destruction. And he would never allow himself to be destroyed again.

And without a backward glance, Dante walked back out of the penthouse, leaving Isabella and Minerva behind him.

# CHAPTER TWELVE

THEY WERE IN a strange standoff that Minerva couldn't quite decode. She had slept in her bedroom for the last three nights, and he hadn't come to her. On the island sex was how they'd communicated. And maybe that wasn't healthy, but it had provided some sort of closeness at least.

This confirmed that her decision to ambush him about the sex on the plane was valid. She'd had the sense if she didn't say it there, she wouldn't have the chance.

Almost as if she knew that once they were in this great gray city it would all be changed.

It was.

And she was oppressed by the gray. Emotionally and all around them. Even the view of Central Park felt gray.

And maybe out of sheer stubbornness she had not gone out of the apartment to explore the city. He was right, it was New York and there were endless things to do. But Isabella was still small, and Minerva was conscious of the various illnesses that lurked out there on every park bench, handrail and shopping cart.

At least, that was what she told herself.

And she did not allow herself to think that maybe she was just being stubborn.

That she was refusing to accept her new life out of sheer spite. Because she didn't want to be in this.

And why? She wasn't entirely sure.

It wasn't like she hadn't left home before. She had. On her grand adventure to Rome—which had ended up containing a little bit of disaster.

She swallowed hard.

Mostly, she was a little bit grateful for this strange coolness between them.

It had allowed her some time to regroup.

On the island she had been convinced that she was in love with him. Or at least, mostly in love with him. Here, she could see that it had been a combination of sun and sex. Here, she could see that she was inexperienced, and was responding to him in that way.

That she had been afraid of leaving the island in part because she had known that it would affect a change in their relationship.

That losing the cocoon of intimacy that

had surrounded them there would thrust them back into the real world, and she would have to contend with the fact that marriage vows neither of them had particularly meant would not create an unbreakable bond.

Neither would they create feelings where they didn't exist. At least, not on his hand.

But it was fine. Because her feelings had been magnified.

She had to accept that she had a crush on Dante, and now that she was working it out she had a bit of clarity.

When he returned home that night, his expression was stern. "Three dresses are being sent, and the nanny will be here shortly."

"Nanny?"

"Yes. The nanny that you were using back in San Diego is on a plane on her way here. We have an engagement to go to tonight."

"We do?"

"Yes. A gala. As I didn't know if I would be back in the city I hadn't committed to it, but as it is, it's a connection that your father would very much like me to make. It is in the interest of King, and given that, it is important that you come with me."

"So, my father has been in touch with you? He hasn't been in touch with me." She could have easily been in touch with her family.

But she was in high avoidance mode. Feeling fragile and not wanting to deal with the realities of her family, now that she married and slept with Dante, and she didn't want to hear anything about the news reports on them either.

She wanted to hide in this apartment. And she wanted to be home.

She didn't make any sense even to herself.

And she was far too wrung out to care.

"We had business to discuss."

"Well. I'm glad to know business is so important." She felt wholly shunted off to the side, which wasn't fair at all. She didn't care.

"Minerva," he said. "Being my wife is a role. I apologize if you didn't realize that, but you took the vows. You needed me to fulfill my end of the brief, and I have done it. Additionally, I am acting as Isabella's father."

"You're not acting as her father. You are her father."

For the first time she was starting to worry he might not bond with her. She'd taken his reluctance as a typical reaction from a man who had no experience with babies. Now she was a bit concerned about the distance. Which was beginning to seem resolute.

"Fine," he said. "According to the paperwork that we will soon process, I am her father."

The distance in those words kicked against Minerva's heart. "Yes," she said drily.

"And you are my wife. What I need from a wife is someone to come to events on my arm and look appropriately adoring at me. I need you to help enhance my image. I most particularly need you to do this as I act on behalf of King. It would not do for me to be seeing to this business and having you looking dour beside me. You know what people would say."

"The truth? That it's a marriage of convenience?"

"It is a decidedly inconvenient marriage," he said. "And I would like it to be more convenient."

"It didn't seem so inconvenient to you when you had sex on tap."

"Who turned the tap off?"

"I was under the impression it was mutual."

She sniffed off to her room in a huff and fed Isabella. Then, when the dresses arrived, so did the nanny, and she was overjoyed to be reunited with the baby.

Minerva felt slightly annoyed by it, but she was happy that Isabella would be with someone familiar.

The dresses were beautiful. Far too beautiful for her. There was a note pinned to one of them. From Violet.

Minerva nearly burst into tears, and she picked up her phone and dialed her sister's number. "The dresses are wonderful," she said.

She couldn't put on a front, not now. She didn't have the strength to. Violet had breached her hiding place, and she couldn't be angry. She wanted to connect to someone too badly.

"What's wrong?" Violet asked.

"It's a disaster," Minerva said. "We're at each other's throats. He's not speaking to me hardly at all and he's not… Well, he's not anything and I miss him and I shouldn't. It's not fair! I didn't ask for this part of it!"

"I don't understand…"

The whole story came pouring out of Minerva. She didn't want secrets between herself and her sister. She desperately needed an ally, and whatever issues she had with Violet were her own. Her own smallness. Her own feelings of inadequacy.

"Wow," Violet said. "I mean… Minerva," she said. "That is the bravest thing I've ever heard of."

She sniffed, sitting on the edge of the bed, feeling worn down. Brave was the last thing she felt. "I don't know if I was very brave."

"Yes, you were. Why do you have such a hard time taking credit for the good things that you do?"

She picked at the velvet fabric on the duvet cover. "Because they're nothing. Nothing compared to the kind of things that you and Maximus do."

"I manufacture makeup," Violet said drily. "And I sell it very effectively. But I've never saved anyone's life." Minerva was distinctly uncomfortable with that statement.

"You're amazing," Minerva said. "Don't minimize it."

"We are talking about *you*," Violet said. "And you can't even handle a compliment when you're the topic of conversation."

"Vi," Minerva said. "You shouldn't have to talk yourself down to try and make me feel better."

"I'm not," Violet said. "Trust me, Minerva, my sense of self is pretty well developed. But you're clearly lacking in perspective."

"I just…" Min fell onto her back and gazed up at the ceiling. Even from this perspective the light seemed gray. "He doesn't love me. He never even slept with me. I mean…before all this started."

"You have now." It was more of a confirmation request than a question.

"Yes," Minerva admitted. "I did have feelings for him. I mean, like a crush. You remember what he did for me at Dad's party."

"Yes. When that snot-nosed Bradley called you an ugly duckling on the dance floor?"

"Yes. I... He rescued me. And I think in my head it became something. I hid it, deep down, but not far enough and when I needed help he was the one I thought of. I know that moment didn't make him...want me. But since then... We've been married, you know? I thought maybe he had some kind of attachment to me but I don't know if he has an attachment to anyone or anything."

"What about you?" Violet asked.

"What about me?"

"Do you feel something for him? I mean, more than your crush."

"Well... Who wouldn't?"

"A lot of people. He's quite difficult. That's why even though I also had a crush on him at one point I let it go a long time ago. I prefer men who are a little bit less...*hard*."

"He is hard. But I think he's good. He had a hard life, but he wants to do the right thing, in spite of the fact that I don't think anyone has ever shown him what the right thing is. Well, anyone except Dad. But he's convinced that he's not... Really a part of our family."

"Well, he is now. By marriage at the very least."

"That might be the only thing he really likes about me."

"I don't think so."

Unspoken between them was the truth that if he really wanted that, he would have married Violet. Not just because she was more beautiful, but she was older. It made more sense. In just about every way.

"Well. It's an asset. He really only agreed to the marriage because he wanted to help me. And now… We're married. So he's making the most of it. At least from a business standpoint."

"And you love him?" Violet pressed.

"No," she said, the denial kicking hard against her chest. "I'm not that silly. I'm not. I know that he's not ever going to feel that way about me. I think we can have a partnership, but I just have to figure it out…"

"You're not cut out for halfway, Minerva. That's your problem. You keep hiding yourself because you're afraid that you can't measure up to Maximus and me, but nobody ever asked you to. I'm not like Maximus. It would be easy for me to say that what I do is superficial. He bails people out of pretty terrible situations. And I'm sure that he would tell you sometimes he feels guilty about the people that he rehabilitates images for, since they oftentimes don't deserve it. But we do what we do, and we are who we are. Whoever you're destined to be... That's you. And you were never meant to live in shadows or to be quiet. And that's why you just... Shrink in on yourself altogether. Because if you speak out, you know it's going to be loud. And if you love, you know it's going to be big. That's good. It's not a bad thing."

Sure, it was easy for Violet to say. Minerva would be the one left with a fatally broken heart.

"You should wear the red dress," Violet said.

"Red?" Minerva questioned. "But I'll be so... Conspicuous."

"Be conspicuous, Min. You've been hiding in books, in the garden, behind that horrible mean-kid stuff that happened to you in high school. They don't get to decide who you are, you do. Isn't it time that you took center stage?"

"I have done that multiple times over the last few weeks," Minerva pointed out. "First of all at your product launch. Second of all at the engagement party, then at the wedding..."

"And you did it for Isabella. Do something for yourself. Is that so wrong?"

"Yes," Minerva said. "Because I'm not… I'm just me."

"Yes, you're just you. And you is pretty amazing. Be kinder to her."

"I am being kind to her. I'm hiding away from the potential broken heart."

"No. You're hiding away from life. You let all that stuff get in your head. You let yourself think that you were less than we are."

"I'm not as pretty."

"That's a lie. It's all about how you present yourself. And there's nothing wrong with being you. There's nothing wrong with not being flashy. I can't be anything else. I have to wander around with a pound of my product on my face all the time."

"I would look silly that way."

"Yes. You would. Not because you aren't beautiful, but because it isn't you. Different is fine. Different is good. But don't accept less."

"So what should I do? Put on the red dress and demand that he love me?" The very idea made her skin crawl.

She'd cared about a boy once, and she'd thought he'd cared too. Instead he'd humiliated her on a dance floor.

"Yes. Have you ever considered demanding that he love you? Because it might not be the worst thing in the world."

"Or it might be," Minerva said darkly.

"Or it might not be."

"I don't even know if I love him." But she was beginning to accept that that was a lie.

"Then I guess the question is… Are you going to stay with him even if you don't love him?" Violet asked.

"He can be Isabella's father…"

"So what? Set her aside for a second. Or, don't even set her aside. Would it be good for her to watch you live with someone you're miserable with? And who cares about Dad and Dante and their business thing? They can work that out on their own. It's not up to you, Minerva. If you love him, then you should demand more. If you don't love him, then you should demand more too."

"When did you become an expert on love?"

"I'm not." Violet's denial was vehement. "This isn't about knowing anything about love. But I do know a little bit about life. I know that if you are successful people are going to come after you, and it's easy to get caught up in trying to please everyone. No matter how independent and strong someone seems. You're caught up in this idea that you're not special, and I think because of that you work too hard to please everyone around you. And you don't work hard enough at pleasing yourself."

"The red dress?"

"Whatever makes you happy. Not what you think will make him happy, or even me happy. And not what you think you should wear. What do you want to wear?"

She got off the phone with her sister and she looked at the dresses again.

The red one.

She really did want to wear the red one. And why wasn't she wearing it? Because a boy had embarrassed her four years ago? Because she'd let the kids at school make her feel like she was ugly, like her family was the only interesting thing about her?

Because she'd chosen to get lost in the quiet nooks and crannies of her home when she was a child, lived in books, lived in her head, and then wondered why she felt left behind sometimes?

She wasn't like everyone else. But did that mean there was something wrong with her? Or did it just mean she was her?

Slowly, and with great care, she took the dress out of the bag and took it off the hanger.

She slid the glorious fabric over her body. It was slinky and perfect, molding to the curves that she had, making the most of her figure.

She worked on her hair, and her makeup, employing tips from videos that Violet had posted online.

She didn't do them quite like Violet. She did them like herself. And when she was finished, she felt...beautiful.

She felt like she was stepping out into the spotlight. Into something new and frightening. And she didn't know why it should seem that way. Because it wasn't as if any of this centered on her. Not really.

Except it felt like it did.

When she emerged in the living room, Dante was standing there looking beautiful in a suit, a crisp white shirt and a black jacket that conformed perfectly to his masculine physique. His dark eyes were unreadable, and passive as they took her in. "Are you ready?"

Her kneejerk response was to ask if she looked ready. To ask him why that was even a question. If there was something wrong with what she had chosen. But she knew that she looked amazing, and she didn't need to be insecure. She didn't need to question anything.

She lifted her head and squared her shoulders. "Yes," she said. "I'm ready."

# CHAPTER THIRTEEN

DANTE COULDN'T KEEP his eyes off Minerva. She was stunning in red. Her lips were the same crimson color to match, her eyeliner dark and winged. Her green eyes seemed like emeralds tonight. Had he ever thought that she was anything less than stunning? Had he ever thought that she was somehow the less beautiful King?

He couldn't even think of her as one of them, not now. She was set apart.

Glorious and otherworldly, because it all seemed transcendent of here and now. It wasn't just beauty for the eyes. He could breathe it in. Taste it. Feel it settle over his bones.

And yet, there was something about this beauty that felt like a challenge. It made him hesitant to touch her, and Dante was never hesitant.

But when they got out of the limo in front

of the museum where the gala was being held, he pressed his hand against her lower back, a show of possession before the two of them walked up the stairs and made their way into the venue.

He didn't need to check in at the door, because everyone recognized him by face alone. At first, he thought Minerva might shrink against his side, but instead she stood proud. And when he introduced her as his wife, the mother of his child, she smiled and shook hands with each person with extreme confidence.

He didn't know what had possessed her this evening, but it was doing a very fine job.

After a time, music began to play and the guests filtered out onto a dance floor. Minerva saw this, and her eyes went wide, then she blinked rapidly. He knew just what she was thinking of.

That night four years ago.

He had seen the whole thing. And he had lied to her when he'd said that her father put him up to anything.

He had watched that boy take her out onto the dance floor, lean in and whisper something in her ear. And then he had watched as she crumpled.

And he had taken pictures. Wrapped his

arm around her shoulder, taken a selfie with a tear-streaked Minerva and himself.

And that was when Dante had stepped in.

*"I have been waiting to dance with you all evening, Ms. King."*

And though he knew Minerva hadn't seen it, the boy had paled. And he had looked... Perhaps like he thought he had made a grave mistake.

She had felt slight and bony to him as he held her. Her body had changed quite a bit since then.

He had felt... Protective of her at that time. Like when he had helped her up off the ground when she had been much younger, her knee skinned.

He had always wanted to protect Minerva.

And now she had come into his sphere as his wife, and the fact of the matter was there was no way for him to protect her from himself.

But they were here.

And she was beautiful.

So they might as well dance.

"Would you like to dance with me? And no, before you ask, I have no designs to humiliate you."

A small smile touched her lips. "Okay. If you really want to."

He smiled in return, because he couldn't

help himself, and he took her out to the center of the dance floor, holding her close and spinning her. Then he drew her back to his chest. She looked up at him, the smile on her face brilliant.

It was a strange thing, to be with Minerva apart from the baby. Without her present as a clear and obvious reason why the two of them were together. Yes, they had spent time alone together, but it had all been in service of Isabella.

It had nothing to do with a farce. There was no reason for a farce anymore.

He could let them go. They would be safe.

For some reason, the idea filled him with a hollow kind of terror, and he couldn't account for why.

He drew her close, leaned in and whispered in her ear. "What did he say to you? That night at your father's party."

Her eyes went misty. "Do we have to talk about that?"

It still bothered her. It was hard for him to imagine that. He'd lived through poverty. Loss and pain. And it wasn't so much that he didn't think people like her—people who lived in comfort and relative ease—didn't also feel pain for the things in their lives. It was simply that of all the things he'd ever cared about, the good opinion of others wasn't often one of them.

Robert, he cared about his opinion because the man had changed his life.

But in general, he'd never... He'd been thrust into private school with boys who had been privileged and cosseted all their lives. They'd either found Dante to be a source of fascination, or something quite beneath them.

He hadn't care for either. But he hadn't cared about it, either.

He'd had trouble connecting. The only person who had ever mattered to him was Maximus. Their friendship had been unsteady at first, Maximus clearly not understanding why his father had ever cared much about the Roman urchin he'd pulled off the streets.

Eventually, slowly, rooming together at boarding school had brought them closer together. Dante had told Maximus about holding his father at gunpoint and he knew then it would either break their bond or solidify it forever.

Maximus had nodded and said: "You do what you have to, I guess."

And so, solidified their bond had been.

Whatever anyone else thought hadn't mattered. Minerva, though, was still clearly haunted by her humiliation.

Witnessing that had enraged him, and it bothered him she was still hurt.

That no man had stepped in to heal that wound.

*You're her husband. The only one she'll have.*

It was a profoundly depressing realization. For *her*.

Another man might have eased this pain already, but he had not. Suddenly he found that he did want it. More than anything.

"I want to know," he said.

"He… He just said that I was stupid if I thought he really wanted to be here with me. He just wanted to be at the party. Wanted to see the house. Being my date was a dare. What he really wanted was a chance to see my sister."

"I see," Dante said. "What is more beautiful? A ruby or an emerald?"

"I don't understand."

"What's more beautiful, a tropical island or a desolate mountain?"

"They're both beautiful," she said. "Just different."

He nodded slowly. "Exactly. There are some things you cannot compare, Minerva, because they are not alike. One is not less. You cannot compare yourself to Violet. She's beautiful. She's successful. I don't want her. I do want you," he said, his voice rough. "Because the truth of the matter is, whether an emerald or ruby are equal in beauty, or a tropical island or a mountaintop are both perfect in their natural splendor, there is always one that a man prefers. And it has nothing to do with how it looks, not really. But what calls to his soul. And in this case, to my body. That's you. I cannot explain it. But it is."

"You don't sound very happy about it."

"I'm not. I was very happy to go through my life never having been bewitched, Minerva, and finding myself held in thrall by a woman that I have known for more than half my life is a very strange thing. I am not sure how it happened. This is not the first time we danced, but it is not the same as that first time."

"But still, when the pictures get published in the paper I imagine the headlines will be the same."

"I don't think so," he said. "But even then, what do you believe about yourself? What you know to be true, or what a bunch of strangers say about you?"

"I don't know," she said. "But... I do like what you said about me. I suppose, even if I can't win with strangers, I can content myself to have nice things said by you. Does this mean that we are going to be... Nicer to each other again?"

"I hope I was never unkind to you."

"I felt lonely."

"I don't know how to be a husband," he said.

"You were doing a pretty good job a minute ago."

"The last thing I want in this world is to hurt you, Minerva. I have done my best to protect you when I could. I owe a great debt to your father for all that he did for me. I would never want to harm what was most precious to him."

"Is that the only reason you don't want to hurt me?"

"No," he confirmed. "But that doesn't mean I won't. You have to be careful with men like me."

"You keep saying that. But the man that you are for the rest of the world... He's not the man that I've seen."

"You have such faith in me, Min, and I fear it is misplaced."

"I don't think so," she said, smoothing her hand up his chest.

His body reacted. Violently.

He pushed her back, the motion reflexive. Like he'd been burned.

"Sorry," he said. "I see David Carmichael back there." Thankfully, that was true. "Your father wished for me to speak with him before we leave."

"Oh…okay."

He took her hand and led her from the dance floor and was summarily stopped by a floppy-haired blond man in a suit that looked intentionally askew. It took him a moment, but he recognized him.

Chad Rothschild. A spoiled asshole he knew from his years in boarding school. Someone who had been friends with Maximus until Dante. Then he'd made an ass of himself pretty routinely all the years since.

"Dante," he said. "What a surprise to see you here."

To see he wasn't back in the gutter, Dante imagined. Though Chad had to know he was not, as his reputation was legend. Chad's, on the other hand, consisted of many instances where he'd had to say, *But my father's a lawyer.*

"I don't see why it should be," Dante said. "This is, after all, where I do business. I am not sure what it is you do."

"Investments." A code for nothing. Chad's eyes flickered over Minerva. "Well, your ugly duckling certainly cleans up well."

"Excuse me?" Dante asked.

He felt Minerva begin to tremble then. "I'm teasing. But surely you've seen that old picture of the two of you. I have to hand it to you, you seemed quite chummy with Maximus in school. I had no idea you were messing with his sister."

Dante's lip curled. "I was not."

"If I were going to do that it would have been the other one."

"I'm sorry," Dante said. "Am I having a stroke? Are we back in boarding school?"

Chad kept on as if he hadn't heard the warning buried in each of the words Dante had just spoken. "She's not exactly the fabled beauty of the King clan, but I suppose if you have access to Robert King's millions and influence you're going to take what you can get. Though I thought that your own wealth exceeded that."

"My wealth is not in question. Neither is the beauty of my wife. I think it's apparent to all here that she is the most beautiful woman in the room."

"Undoubtedly, she is compelling," Chad said. "But I'm surprised you didn't marry her sister instead."

Dante saw red. And not just the red of Minerva's dress. A red haze of rage covered his vision. But Minerva's gentle hand on his arm stopped him.

"I appreciate that money is the only reason you can think that someone might marry you," Minerva said. "But that isn't the way it is for everyone. I care about Dante. We have a child together. I care about him more than anyone will likely care for you unless you do something to fix your repellent personality. Undoubtedly, someone will marry you for your money. But if I were you I would aim for more. It's quite sad."

And with her head held high, Minerva released her hold on Dante, and began to walk away. Dante went after her.

"What he said…"

"It's what people think," Minerva said.

"It doesn't matter what anyone thinks."

"No," she said. "It doesn't. Not really. It matters what I think. And the problem is that I believed the same thing for far too long."

He grabbed her arm and dragged her into a courtyard, away from the crowd. Away from prying eyes. And then he pinned her against the wall, his hand on her neck. "You incite me to madness," he growled. "No one else ever has. What he said… There is no reason for it. And he is wrong."

She touched his face. "But you didn't choose to marry me."

"Does that matter?"

"It always will to some people."

He arched his hips forward, letting her feel the effect that she had on him. "Does this feel like a choice to you?"

"No," she said. "I think even that you feel somewhat angrily."

He released his hold on her. Because she wasn't wrong. He hadn't chosen to feel what he did for her. It rearranged things inside him, and he didn't like it. He couldn't find where he had put his resolve, his reserve. He couldn't find himself at all. And he found it nearly unbearable. But it was no more unbearable than spending nights in separate rooms.

That he could truly no longer endure.

"We should leave," Dante said.

"Don't you have a business deal to make?"

"I will make it later. And I will make it without using you as a pawn. I will not subject you to more censure and speculation."

"Dante…"

"Your father will understand. And if he doesn't… Well. That's hardly my problem."

He had to get out of here. Before he did

something they would both regret. Either to Chad or to her.

He felt… At the end of himself. And he didn't know what Minerva had done to him to make him feel this way.

He had no way to correct course, because he couldn't understand where the wrong turn had come. Heart pounding, he grabbed her hand and made his way toward the exit. He sent his driver a text, and the limo met them outside.

"Drive around the block until I tell you to stop," Dante said.

When they tumbled into the back of the cab, he grabbed her, kissing her, hard and deep, pouring all of his anger, his frustration and confusion into the kiss.

He didn't do fear.

He didn't do confusion. He was above it. Beyond it. He had ascended in life, and he refused to be dragged back there. Certainly not at the delicate hands of Minerva.

He didn't need anyone.

He didn't need anything. He had learned long ago that he had to depend only on himself to survive. That he could not expect anything from anyone. Simply because he had received kindness from Robert King didn't mean that he could come to expect it from anyone else.

He didn't even take it for granted from Robert.

And then there was Minerva. For whom everything was so simple. Isabella had needed her, and so she had made herself available.

She claimed that she knew she didn't want another man, ever, in spite of the fact that she had no other experience of sex, and couldn't possibly understand what she might truly want in a few years.

No, for her everything was so straightforward. So simple.

And he wanted to...punish her for that. Something in him did.

So he kissed her. And it wasn't a kind kiss. Wasn't a nice kiss. Wasn't infused with the kind of gentleness that he had tried to inject into all the lovemaking on the island after he had discovered that she'd been a virgin their first time together.

Her dress was exquisite, beautiful. Off the shoulder and clinging to her curves just so. He tore it down, revealing her breasts, their gorgeous, rosy tips, to his inspection.

She was perfection, was Minerva, and that man who had dared to make commentary on her beauty deserved no thought from her.

Even in his anger, anger that was unwieldy and reserved for any target in his path right now, he could not deny her beauty.

Her beauty was the only thing that made sense.

Because nothing else did.

Nothing else felt like him.

On the heels of that thought came another one, far more disturbing.

That he wasn't sure exactly what him was.

A boy who had tried to throw a birthday party for his mother. A boy who had found her dead the next morning of an overdose and had held her body and cried for hours. Afraid to leave her. Afraid that if he didn't no one would ever come.

The boy who had held the gun to Robert King's head.

The one who had taken his education and transformed it into a billion-dollar industry.

The one who was here now in the back of the limousine with Minerva, kissing her as though she were oxygen and he would die without her.

None of it felt real.

Except her hands. Her mouth. The physical sensation of touching her, holding her.

That was real.

He wondered which piece of her was real.

The little girl who had run around on the estate and fallen out of trees, skinning her knees and terrifying her mother.

The dreamy teenager with her nose stuck in a book.

The brave tigress who had demanded marriage to protect her cub.

The woman in his arms now.

Were they all every piece of those things?

And how did they bring them together?

Was it even wise to do so?

All those questions burned away in his consciousness as Minerva kissed him back. As her hands went to his tie, loosening it and undoing the buttons there. He batted those hands away.

He leaned down, taking one pert nipple between his lips and sucking it in deep.

She gasped, arching against him. But she wouldn't hold still, and her hands were skimming over him. He grabbed hold of her arms and pinned them to her sides, holding her still as he continued to lavish attention on her breasts.

He had to have the control here. She couldn't.

"Dante… Your driver can't…"

"Soundproof," he said.

"You told him to drive until you asked him not to."

"Undoubtedly he knows," Dante said. "But why should I be ashamed? Why should I be ashamed that I can't keep my hands off you? That I need to have you now. That I cannot wait until we are safely ensconced in the penthouse."

He was asking himself that question as much as he was asking her.

"Why should I be ashamed of you?" he said, their eyes meeting. He pulled her dress down as far as he could, until he met resistance at her hips. Then he moved down her body, grabbing hold of the hem of her skirt and pushing it upward. He exposed her legs, grabbed the center of her panties and swept them aside, exposing the heart of her. "How could I ever be ashamed of you?"

He pressed his fingers down against her, spreading her wide, then leaning in to taste her. Deep and lavish and long.

She tasted like Minerva. Amazing how distinct that had become to him. Unmistakable. This woman.

This woman.

One who had known more versions of him than any other woman he had ever taken as a lover.

But she was more than a lover.

More than his friend's sister, that was for damn sure.

She was his *wife*.

He growled, his ministrations on her body intensifying, surging forward, his hands joining in with his mouth as he pleasured her. As he pushed her to new heights. As he kept at her until she cried out. Until she pulsed with pleasure, her orgasm crashing over her, causing her to shake and shudder out his name.

After that, he couldn't wait anymore. Couldn't wait to join himself to her. He needed her. And he didn't want to admit to need. It was anathema to him. This feeling in his chest. The sense that he no longer belonged to himself.

That somewhere along the line he had lost some of himself in her.

But he couldn't stop himself either.

No. All he could do was take control.

"Up here, sweetheart," he said, lifting her and then turning her so that she was facing away from him, her face to the window, to the cars that were passing them by.

"Dante..."

"No one can see," he said. "The windows are tinted."

"Oh," she said. And he wondered if that was what she was even asking him about. Or if there was something about this that bothered her.

It wasn't up to her.

"I'm going to take you like this," he said, his voice rough.

He undid the closure on his pants and freed himself, pressing the blunt head of his arousal to the entrance of her body. Sliding into her was like coming home. She was perfect. In this, they were perfect. This was right, it was good. Because she needed him. This wasn't simply his wild need. No, she was right there with him. And that made him feel powerful. That reminded him that he was the one in control. Not her.

He plunged into her, and she gasped, arching against him. And he gripped her hips, slamming her back against him. She whimpered, her face pressed against the window.

"Dante," she whispered.

Over and over she said his name as he drove himself home. Until she was sobbing his name. Until she couldn't control herself at all.

Until he felt like he had fixed some of what had gone wrong inside him.

He knew this. And he knew who he was.

This was only sex. That was all.

She was beautiful, so of course she appealed to him. But that was all. It was all.

He repeated that himself, over and over again. She might have been any beautiful woman.

But then she looked back over her shoulder and the light from the neon that flashed on the buildings outside illuminated her face. Those green eyes.

And he knew it could only be her. Minerva.

She began to shake. Her climax taking her over.

"Dante," she said, whispering his name one more time.

He clenched his teeth shut to keep from saying hers.

But his orgasm consumed him, grabbed him by the throat and shook him.

*Minerva.*

Her name echoed inside him, but he refused to give it voice. He refused. But the deep, physical need came for him all the same, and he was spent, destroyed in the aftermath of his release. Splintered.

Except he was coming to realize that the splinter wasn't new.

Something had broken in him indefinably when he was young. And he had no earthly idea what could be done about it. He had the feeling that the answer was contained somewhere in her. He rejected that. And he pulled away.

He was Dante Fiori. And whatever he wanted, he could have. Whatever he needed was contained inside himself. He did not need anyone else. Least of all his friend's little sister.

He straightened in the limo. "Fix your clothes," he said.

She looked at him with wide eyes, but she complied. Then he lowered the window between himself and the driver. "You can take us home now."

He felt very much like he had broken something. But he could not quite put his finger on what.

And he could not give a reason for why it bothered him at all.

# CHAPTER FOURTEEN

MINERVA HAD TAKEN herself to her bed and cried herself to sleep after she and Dante had gotten home.

She hadn't wanted him to be quite so careful with her sexually as he had begun to be, but she hadn't wanted that either.

It had been physically wonderful. It had left her feeling emotionally hollow.

He had used that position to distance her from him. And when she had looked behind her and established a connection with him, he had been very apparently angry.

She wrapped her arms around herself and looked out at Central Park. It was so cold outside.

She didn't actually know if it was cold. She hadn't checked. She hadn't been outside and she hadn't looked at anything to see what the temperature actually was.

But she assumed that it was. Because of all that gray.

Maybe the gray was inside her. Because if she stopped staring at it all like one big chunk, she could see the grass, she could see the trees.

But somehow, she couldn't feel them.

She was upset. And she supposed she didn't have anyone to blame but herself.

Last night had been a perfect opportunity for her to tell Dante how she felt.

After all, she hadn't hesitated to tell Chad how she felt.

But then, even though she had stood up for herself in the moment, she had also felt small when he had said those things. Because they echoed inside her.

Because they played at certain insecurities that she had no matter that she had put on a red dress. When it came to mothering Isabella, her confidence had grown.

When it came to other areas of herself… She was still a work in progress.

She sighed heavily, and went to check on Isabella, who was kicking happily in her crib.

She picked her up, and set her in a swing out in the living room so she could gaze out at the park too.

She had a feeling that Isabella didn't particularly care.

She should be happier. There was no threat on Isabella's life. The paperwork for the adoption was very nearly finished. Everything was easier because of Dante's money.

Her father had money, so it wasn't as though she didn't know that things were easier when you had it. It was just that Dante wielded his with authority and power, and even when it came to the workings of the upper class, Dante seemed to command a greater amount of attention than those around him.

He was one of those men. Legendary. Whispered about in every room he entered.

And she had been around him all her life.

He had a great impact on her, even with all that familiarity.

She almost felt sorry for women who hadn't had such long exposure to him.

He was devastating even with it.

Of course, it was more than just physical devastation that she experienced when she looked at him.

She was in the grips of soul-deep devastation. She had no idea what to do with it.

She sighed heavily and turned to the laptop that was sitting on the marble island that separated the kitchen from the living room.

She pulled up a homepage, and much to her surprise saw her face staring back at her from the society pages.

She had a triumphant smirk on her face, and she was standing in front of Dante, who was left slightly blurred.

*Fiori's New Wife Unleashes Fury at Gala*

She read on, and saw that the article described in great detail the way that she had flayed that ridiculous man the night before. The article concluded that she had been wrongly overlooked all this time, because she was clearly much more interesting than anyone had given her credit for.

She stared at the woman there in that picture. She looked strong. She looked confident.

Her phone buzzed and she looked down at it.

You wore the red.

Her sister Violet's text of triumph made something resonate in her chest.

She had.

And she had come out on top.

Except…

Still not with Dante.

Well. She was the only person that could fix that.

Minerva King had allowed herself to be leased for far too long.

It was finally time for her to do something for herself.

She made sure that Isabella was taken care of for the evening by her nanny, and she prepared dinner. Now all she had to do was wait for him to come home. She really hoped that he did.

It wasn't like he had ever not come home, but he sometimes did come home late.

She could have texted him, but she didn't want to.

Because she didn't want to…

Oh, there was no point trying to play it cool.

She had never done it, not once in her life. There was no point starting now.

She picked her phone up.

I made you dinner.

She waited. And waited for a response. Five interminable minutes went by without a response.

You didn't have to do that.

Obviously. Since I don't normally.

I'll be a little while yet.

Come home soon.

I have to finish some things.

Come home now.

She didn't get a response after that, and she paced around waiting.

Ten minutes later, the door to the penthouse opened. "I don't take orders."

She smiled and smoothed her hands over the tight, emerald green dress she was wearing. "Except, clearly you do take orders. Because here you are."

"A coincidence. I managed to finish everything on time. Why did you make dinner?"

"Because I wanted to… On our wedding night we didn't have dinner together. And I would like to have dinner together. It's different now that we're here. We are making a home together. The island was… Something else. It was removed from this. From reality. And here we are. Here we are together. This is our life. Isabella is going to legally be our daughter soon. Dante, I'm happy."

He raised his dark brows. "I'm glad."

"Are you?"

He lifted a shoulder. "I am as I ever am."

"What does that mean?"

"What did you fix?"

She noted he didn't answer, but she went ahead and let him redirect.

"Steak," she said. She waved her hand toward the table.

He cast a glance at it. "Let's eat."

They went over to the table, and Minerva scampered after him, moving to sit across from him. He was being as opaque and maddening as he'd been the night before.

They started to eat in silence. Minerva was feeling frustrated. But, she wasn't going to say anything. She had a feeling that he was doing all of this by design, she just couldn't work out why.

He seemed to enjoy dinner, and when it was done, she served dessert.

Chocolate lava cake.

She held it out to him, and her heart was pounding. It reminded her of that night on the island. When he had offered cake to her. When she had realized that more than the dessert was a temptation when it came to Dante. He didn't seem to remember that. Didn't seem to get the reference that was happening here at all.

Well. She could fix that.

She stood from her seat and unzipped her dress, letting the top fall down, then letting the rest of it fall along with it. Then she walked over to where he was sitting, completely naked except for her high heels.

"There is a second offering for dessert."

He looked up at her, and he pushed the cake into the center of the table. "I think I'll have that now," he said.

"Not yet," she said.

She leaned forward and unbuttoned his shirt, pushing it down his shoulders. He stood, and she began to work at the belt on his pants, pushing them down his legs. And then, she sank to her knees before him.

"Minerva," he said, his voice rough.

But she ignored the warning in his tone. Ignored it completely as she leaned forward and let her tongue dart out, tasting him. Taking him into her mouth.

He groaned, fisting her hair in his hand, holding her steady as she began to pleasure him.

Her position was submissive, to be sure,

but he was the one who was shaking beneath her attentions.

It was exhilarating. Doing to him what he'd done to her so many times. But she hadn't been brave enough to do this. Not before. Not because she didn't think she would like it but because she was afraid he would compare with other women and find her wanting. But she finally understood.

Experience didn't matter. Because no other woman could bring to the table what she did, here and now. It was their connection. And that was why he was afraid.

He was pulling away from her because everything in the two of them was drawing them to each other. There was no denying it. There was no escaping it. No matter what he thought. She curved her hand around his shaft, stroking him in time as she continued to pleasure him with her mouth.

"Minerva," he growled. "Enough." She did not obey. But then, he pulled on her hair, and she had no choice but to go with him.

She was suddenly embarrassed, because what they'd done was in a public part of the house, and while the nanny had been given instructions to stay in the nursery, there was still the possibility they could have been walked in on. Except... They hadn't been.

And she found it very difficult to care one way or another.

Dante picked her up, and began to carry her from the room, shucking the rest of his clothing as he went. The trail of clothes would be a clue if nothing else. But again, she couldn't find it in her to care.

He took her into his bedroom, the first time she had been there since they had returned from the island. And he set her in the middle of it, spreading her across the bedspread.

She parted her thighs for him, touching herself as she watched him, looked at his body while he stood there. At his proud masculinity, at the well-defined muscles.

"You're beautiful," she said.

She had nothing to hide. She felt free.

Joyful.

This was sex as it was meant to be. The exchange was more than just bodies. So much more.

He came down on the mattress with her, thrusting inside her body, and she gripped his shoulders.

"I love you," she whispered.

He growled, pulling out and slamming back home. "I love you," she said again, in case he hadn't heard her the first time.

He had heard.

But he was doing his best not to respond, she could tell.

So she said it. Over and over again until it blurred with whimpers of pleasure. Until she lost herself in it. In him.

Until she was certain that the feelings had come straight from her chest and wound themselves around the two of them, that it had joined in with the physical sensation. That it was a real and living entity in the room with them.

*Love.*

She loved him.

And she wanted him to love her back.

Wanted it, deserved it. Needed it.

If she wasn't ashamed. No. She wasn't ashamed.

And she didn't feel undeserving. She didn't. She deserved it all. Everything.

He flexed against her, his body hitting that sensitive bundle of nerves between her legs, and she cried out, pleasure breaking over her like a wave.

Love echoing in her like a storm.

"I love you," she said, one last time before he shook and shuttered and gave himself over to his release.

And when he pulled away, she knew what he was doing.

She knew already that he was going to try to run from this like he had tried to run before.

But he had been able to get as far as he had only because she hadn't challenged him. But she was going to challenge him now. Yes, she was. She was going to challenge him and she was going to demand what she wanted. Was going to demand everything she deserved.

"I love you," she said again.

"I don't know what you expect me to say to that."

"Well, I would like for you to say that you love me too."

"I can't," he said.

"Can't or won't?"

"It amounts to the same thing in this instance."

"No. It doesn't. Dante, I know that your childhood was difficult. I know that your mother hurt you. But this is different. We are a family. We can be different."

"No," he said, turning away from her. "That's enough, Minerva. I will care for you, I will take care of you and I will be faithful to you, but asking anything more of me is unnecessary."

"No," Minerva said. "It is not unnecessary. It is absolutely and utterly necessary. Because I have spent my entire life asking nothing.

Nothing of myself. Nothing of anyone else. I have never demanded that I get everything because I thought for some reason I didn't deserve it. I always felt like the small sparrow in a family filled with glorious peacocks. And I sank down into that role because I was afraid that if I wanted anything more I would be in pain for all of my life. I was afraid that if I asked for something more it would confirm what I believe secretly. That I couldn't have it. That for some reason I wasn't put together in such a way that I deserved it. But I know better now. I want this life, not just for Isabella, but for me. I want love because I deserve it. And so do you. We don't deserve anything less than everything, Dante, and there's no reason we shouldn't have it."

"There is every reason," he said. "Love is a lie. Love is just waiting for other things to come in and prove themselves more powerful. You know what is more powerful than love? Fear. Addiction. Poverty. These things can destroy love. They can defeat it. Trust me, I've seen it. I have no desire to have it again."

"You see examples of love all around you. All around you. There's no reason you shouldn't accept it for yourself. You know that what you're saying is a lie. If all these things exist in the world, why wouldn't you cling to love?"

"I don't want it," he said, turning back around again, grabbing hold of her arms and staring down at her with his fierce dark eyes. "I don't want you. Don't you understand that?"

"You don't… You don't want me?"

"I tried to pull away from you politely over the last few days. But it's become very clear to me that you don't actually understand what's happening between us. I thought that we needed this marriage, but we don't. There is no reason for the two of us to stay together. No reason at all. I don't need your father's money and Carlo is dead."

"It wasn't about me…"

"No. This is over. I will allow the adoption to continue with you and Isabella. I will withdraw my name."

"You're going to abandon Isabella?"

"It is for the best," he said. "I am no kind of father, and she no longer needs my protection."

"What about you? Don't you think she could possibly need you?"

"No. Nobody needs me. I have money, and I have power, and I wield it well. I wielded it to save you, but now that is over. This is done. We are done."

She sat there, utterly and completely devastated. And he began to collect his clothes. "I'm going back to the office," he said.

"No... Dante..."

"I will arrange for you to go back to San Diego tomorrow."

"I don't want to go back. This is my home."

"No," he said, his voice ragged. "Your home is with your family. And I am not your family."

And with that, he turned and walked out of the room, leaving her there with her heart broken in pieces around her feet.

She had asked for everything. In return, she had lost the biggest, brightest thing she'd ever dared reach for.

And all she could do was curl up in the center of his bed and cry.

# CHAPTER FIFTEEN

WHEN DANTE RETURNED from his trip into the office, he could hear a soft, plaintive voice. Wailing. He stood in the middle of the room, unsure of what to do.

His eyes were dry and his lungs felt bruised, and he didn't know how he was going to proceed.

With anything.

Minerva had said that she loved him, and there was something about that that had destroyed everything that he built, and told himself he'd built for the last two decades.

How? How had one small woman and a baby utterly and completely taken all that he believed about himself in the world and turned it upside down?

No one should have the power to do that to him, much less her.

And the baby was still crying. Where was she? Where was Minerva?

Isabella was not his daughter. And she wouldn't be.

He was going to put a stop to the paperwork that would make her his. Because it was the right thing to do. There was no other alternative. She wouldn't want him for a father anyway, and he would be an utterly useless one at that.

*He couldn't love.*

He couldn't. The baby was crying, and still Minerva wouldn't come. Neither did the nanny. He didn't understand what was happening.

He could go and get her. Wake one of them, as it was three in the morning and it was likely that they were asleep.

But he shouldn't have to.

It was an infant. Surely, he could handle whatever ailed her.

He charged into the room, and he stopped. He gazed down at her little, helpless body in the center of the crib, and everything inside him froze. She was just so... Small. Helpless. And he was brought again back to his childhood.

To the fact that his parents had created him, his mother had given him life, and had just...

He took a step closer to the crib. Slowly, he bent down, taking the tiny form into his arms and holding her close against his chest. He could hear his own breathing, ragged and intense above the sound of the little girl's crying.

He cradled the back of her downy head, and she rubbed her face against him.

"Are you hungry?"

Something about his voice made her startle, then still.

He didn't know how to make a bottle, but he damn sure could figure it out.

And in the kitchen with one arm, that was what he did, while he cradled her close.

He took her back into the nursery, and sat in the rocking chair, looking down at her as he fed her. And he had no idea how he had wound up here.

With an infant.

But she wouldn't be here. Not in his house. Not anymore. Because she and Minerva were leaving.

Something seized in his chest, and then he felt as if everything broke in half. Like a seismic shock had gone through his entire body. This child could destroy him.

As easily as Minerva could.

That became clear in the moment.

This weak, helpless thing held a power over him that he couldn't understand.

She opened her little mouth, one side of her

lip lifting higher than the other, and a small growl escaped her tiny body.

*His tiger cub.*

He was held in thrall just then. He couldn't look away. Couldn't pull away at all.

What was this feeling?

And more important, why did his mother not feel it for him?

Because one thing he knew for sure, feeling this on one side was absolutely the worst fate that could ever befall a man.

Because it didn't matter that his mother had been so distant, it didn't matter that she had hit him for throwing her birthday party. It didn't matter that she had overdosed and died and left him.

He had loved her still.

And no amount of telling himself he shouldn't, no amount of mourning could bring her back. It was pain. Utter, gut-wrenching pain. The kind that you didn't recover from.

And he would be damned if he ever gave anyone that kind of power over him ever again.

He couldn't.

It would be a blessing. That this was done now. Because Isabella would never remember him.

And someday, Minerva would find a man who could give her everything she wanted.

Already that thought hurt too much.

He laid Isabella down in the crib, comforted by the fact that she would have no memory of ever having held him.

But as he walked out of the room, he could still feel the impression of her tiny body cradled in his arms.

And he knew that he would never be able to forget.

# CHAPTER SIXTEEN

THANKFULLY, DANTE WAS not around when Minerva, the nanny and Isabella grimly loaded themselves onto his private plane and charted a course for San Diego.

She tried to hold her head high when she arrived at her parents' house, but the minute that she saw her mother she crumpled completely.

Her mother ushered her to sit down, and held her, and didn't say anything.

The entire story poured out of Minerva, all of it. The truth.

"But she will legally be yours?" her mother asked. "Soon?"

"Yes," she said. "Dante had all the paperwork processing. It's all over. But it's been... A nightmare. And we did everything we could to protect her. Everything we thought was right. I'm sorry that I didn't tell you. But..."

"Of course you didn't feel like you could chance anyone knowing," she said.

"I didn't. And it isn't because I didn't trust you…"

"You're her mother," Elizabeth said. "And you would do anything to protect her. Of course you did this. Of course."

Minerva nodded miserably and watched her mother hold Isabella.

"But he broke your heart?" Elizabeth asked.

"Yes," Minerva said. "He broke my heart. I don't know what to do about it. I don't know how I'm going to survive."

"You just will," Elizabeth said. "You will because you have her to live for."

"I just want to sit down and give up."

"But you won't do that either. It's okay to want to do that, as long as you don't."

"I just… I think it would've been fine if I hadn't demanded that he loved me. But I did. I demanded it because I thought… Don't I deserve it? Don't I deserve to have somebody love me?"

"Of course you do," her mother said.

"I know that I'm not beautiful like Violet, or successful. That I'm not magnetic like Maximus, and I'm definitely not a billionaire."

"What does that have to do with anything?"

"I just… They are exceptional."

"Minerva, you are now and always have been exceptionally you. Right down to this whole harebrained situation with the baby. You are utterly and uniquely yourself. And no one has ever been able to convince you to be anything but that. You're strong. And you're stubborn."

"No I'm not. I always just kind of… Go along with things."

"If you think that, then you don't even know yourself all that well."

"Well. Maybe I don't."

"Look at yourself. You stole this baby. You protected her with your life. You roped Dante into everything in spite of the fact that he is a terrifying and powerful man to most everyone else. Very few people would have dared to do what you did."

"I had to."

"Then you married him. Then you demanded that he love you. Love is not less. It's brave. You're very brave. That isn't something that can be taught. I'm proud of you, Minerva. Not just for everything you did before, not just for what you did with Isabella, but for how you handled Dante."

Minerva felt broken and easily wounded, but she forced a smile, and allowed a moment of happiness in.

"It's going to be all right," Elizabeth said.

"But what if it isn't?"

"Because Dante is a smart man. And you are an exceptional woman. I don't think he's actually going to let you get away."

"And if he does?"

"Then he's not a smart man. But you are still an exceptional woman."

Minerva thought about that all through the rest of the evening and as she laid Isabella down to sleep.

Her mother was trying to help, and she knew that. But in the back of her mind she wondered if fairy tales were for other girls.

For the bright, the exceptional, the beautiful.

Then she looked down at Isabella.

No.

Of course that wasn't true. Of course it wasn't...

It took her breath away how obvious it seemed all of a sudden as she looked down at her own daughter.

What she deserved in life had nothing to do with looks. Or money. Success. It had nothing to do with what a boy at a dance said about her. Had nothing to do with whether or not the kids at school liked her or thought she was pretty.

She had value all on her own.
And so did Minerva.
Whether Dante ever realized it or not.

# CHAPTER SEVENTEEN

"WHY IS MY sister back home?"

Dante looked up from his desk to see Maximus standing in his office doorway. No one should be standing in his office doorway. He paid his secretary well to keep that from happening. And Maximus really shouldn't be standing there.

"She missed her family," he said, keeping his expression neutral.

"Why is that?"

He pressed his hands on his desk and stood. "If you didn't know already that we're divorcing, then let me be the first to tell you. But I assume you did already."

"I didn't want to have to kill you, Dante, but I will."

"Maximus, I know you excelled in boxing at school, but I'm a street fighter. You're not going to kill me."

A dark glint shone in his friend's eyes and

Dante had the sense that he had gone too far. "Your mistake is always underestimating me, friend. You don't know everything that I could do to you."

"Whether you believe it or not, Minerva was in control of all of this. And her leaving... I asked her to go to protect her."

"My mom told me the whole story. I know Isabella isn't your baby. I had a hard time believing it in the beginning, I have to admit."

"So, she told you what Minerva did?"

Maximus nodded. "And if my sister wasn't crushed, I wouldn't be here. I would assume that you had done what you did to protect her, and now the deal was done but obviously something happened between the two of you."

Dante lifted a shoulder. "I won't lie to you. She was my wife."

"What happened to your Catholicism?"

"Tell me," Dante said, his temper fraying, "what would be the greatest sin? To divorce your sister or keep her with me for the rest of my life. You know me, Maximus. You know that I'm not...part of your world, not part of the one I came from. Not part of Min's or Isabella's. You know that I don't know how to... I don't know how to be part of a family. Not even yours."

"Your own choice, Dante. We've always wanted you to be part of us."

"And I don't know how to do it," Dante said, frustration eating at him. "Tell me. How should I be a good husband to Min? You don't know how to be a husband. What can you tell me?"

"Nothing about that. Though I had thought that you were a decent human being. My father opened his home to you and I called you brother. Was I wrong to do that?"

Dante had told himself he didn't care about much. But hearing his friend ask him if he was wrong to call him brother made something crumble inside him. The bit of heart, of humanity, he had left.

"If you care about Minerva at all..." Maximus continued.

"I do," he bit out. "I love her."

The words made the back of his neck prickle. Made sweat bead at his temples. He loved her. It was the thing he feared most because it was the one thing he could not control.

Not ever.

And he'd sworn he would never...

Minerva King.

She had been a girl when he'd first met her. How had she reached around inside him and changed him like this?

How had she become his dearest dream and greatest nightmare all at once?

"Then why are you doing this to the both of you? Go back to her."

His throat was dry. "I... I can't."

Maximus sighed heavily. "Please don't make me talk about feelings."

"*Dio.* Don't."

"You're forcing it. You're forcing me to."

"Can I stop you?"

"Quit being a jackass and go to my sister. Minerva is the kindest and most caring person I know. The kindest and most caring person I have ever known. If she loves you, you've done well for yourself, Dante."

"I never wanted to love another person again," he said.

"Well, what a tragedy. You found someone to love, who loves you very much in return. Some people would call that an unexpected gift. A lot like trying to rob a man at gunpoint only to get offered a chance at a new life. That was brave of you, to take that."

"Desperate," he said. "And I vowed I wouldn't be desperate again."

"Well, here you are I guess," Maximus said, looking around. "In all this glass and chrome. Not desperate at all. But meanwhile, across the country, there is a woman who loves you and a child who needs a father." He turned to go, then stopped. "And you know, the rest of us are fond of you too. My father reached out to you that day. Maybe it's time you reached back, brother."

And without another word, Maximus walked out of his office, as if he hadn't been there at all. And Dante was left with a burning sensation in his chest.

He loved her.

And she was not dead. She was not gone. And he...he had pushed her away because he had no earthly idea what else to do other than...

Accept it.

The idea filled him with dread. The idea of loving her, loving Isabella.

He looked around his office. His glass and chrome. This tower, surrounded by that wall he'd built for himself.

His security.

And suddenly it all meant nothing.

Suddenly it was not a protection, but a barrier. A barrier between himself and Minerva. Brick after brick, built to keep him safe. Built to keep him separate.

It could not endure.

Not anymore.

He loved her.

And it was a gift to a heart that had given up on loving ever again.

But most of all, she might still love him.

Him, a man from nothing. A man who knew nothing of how to love except getting slapped in the face for it.

She had loved him first. Before he knew how to show it or how to admit to himself that he loved her too.

But he couldn't stay safe. He couldn't stay on this side of the wall, not if he wanted her.

Suddenly it all seemed clear.

For love he would.

For Minerva, he had to. His girl, his *woman*. Who loved books and knew that his home had been patterned after *Swiss Family Robinson*. Who understood, somehow, these sharp, strange emotions inside himself that not even he understood.

He was done surviving.

He wanted to live.

# CHAPTER EIGHTEEN

IT HAD BEEN a week of feeling like her heart was beating with ground glass inside it, painful and sharp. Minerva was tired of it. Tired of herself. But she was also resolved.

She'd started trying to figure out what she wanted from her life too.

With the help of some of Violet's business consultants she'd begun feeling out what it would take to start job training for single mothers, with special focus on those recovering from addiction, depression, or any woman trying to escape an abusive relationship.

The KatiBella Foundation was on its way to becoming a reality, and Minerva was happy to know that she could honor her friend's memory that way.

And that she could honor her daughter, her inspiration for the foundation in the first place.

But she was still…

She missed him. She loved him. She hated that she did.

She felt utterly, thoroughly grown up. She felt old, in fact. She couldn't believe that just a few months ago she'd come home with Isabella. That only a year ago she'd been in Rome, an innocent university student without a care in the world.

She felt like she had a world of care on her shoulders now.

But she wouldn't change it.

No.

She was…changed. She was in love. And she loved Isabella. She was heartbroken, but she was stronger somehow even in that brokenness. She couldn't explain it, but it was true.

Isabella was asleep, and Minerva hadn't had any luck sleeping at all lately. Instead of even trying, she stole down to the beach and looked out at the waves.

The moon reflected on the water, the sound reverberating around her.

And her heart went tight in her chest.

She missed him.

She wanted to see this with him. To be on the beach with him again. Kiss him again.

She knew what it meant to want someone now. To love them.

She also knew beyond a shadow of a doubt that she hadn't been heartbroken four years ago at her father's party. She'd been wounded, but not heartbroken.

This didn't feel like shame. There was pride mixed in with it. It didn't feel like sadness, because it felt more brittle. More aged. Like it had maybe always been inside her. This sense of what it was like to not have Dante.

She hated him for teaching her this.

But she loved him for teaching her so many other things. Even when he wasn't here.

She put her hand on her stomach and watched the waves crash into shore, the whitecaps visible even in the darkness. He might have given her more than a broken heart, and she really had no idea what she would do if her period didn't start in the next couple of days.

"You'll be okay," she whispered to herself.

Because she would be. She had become the heroine, over the course of these weeks, these months. And because of that, she knew everything would be all right in the end.

"Min."

The sound of her name rose up above the waves, and she turned, her heart stalling out completely when she saw him standing there.

His face looked haggard in the moonlight. The hollows of his cheeks more pronounced, dark circles under his eyes that spoke of the same lack of sleep she had been experiencing.

"Dante."

For some reason, as Dante stood there on the beach staring at Minerva he felt more like that boy he'd been at fourteen, holding a gun he didn't want to use, his hands shaking, than he ever had in the intervening years since.

Perhaps it was because he was only standing there, with a heart pounding heavily in his chest that he didn't want to use.

But he had no choice.

After Maximus had come to see him, he had understood.

He had known beyond a shadow of a doubt that it was already too late to protect him. They had gotten under his skin, these two females who had moved into his home, his life.

Minerva, his tigress, and the tiger cub. Everything was upside down because of them.

Everything destroyed.

He had tried to make it right. He had gone back to work. He had tried to put another brick between himself and his past, but the problem was that the past had crashed through the wall and bled into his future.

It had made him turn Minerva away, and all he could think of was the incredible pain that had caused him. And then he thought he was going to have to build the wall again. In front of the time he spent with her. The nights making love. In front of those sun-drenched days on the private island.

In front of that night when he'd held Isabella in his arms and understood what it meant to be a father.

And he began to do that. Laying bricks. Over his heart, yet again. But he had realized that he didn't want to stop thinking about them, even if it hurt.

And so he was here. Because he didn't know where else to be.

"What are you doing here?"

"I'm here for you. I'm here to explain."

"It had better be a good explanation," she said, clenching and unclenching her hands into fists.

"I know," he said. "Minerva, it isn't that I don't believe in love. I do. But the problem is that I know what it's like to love someone who can't love you back. I know what it's like to be ill-used and abused and to not be able to let go. To want so badly for another person to care. She couldn't care. No matter how much I wanted my mother to care, she couldn't.

"And it broke me in ways that I can't begin to describe. Except to tell you that I was hollowed out by the time your father met me. I wanted to be ready to shoot him if I needed to get money, to get food. Instead, I found myself accepting his charity. And I thought to myself, *He's offering charity, he might well have disgraceful intentions for me*, and I thought that I could accept that too. I had lost my humanity somewhere in there. I... I lost my soul. Because I quit letting myself love.

"And even when I joined your family, it was the same. I told myself that I was different because I wasn't blood. I held Isabella the other night, and I knew blood had nothing to do with anything. It isn't because of him that I've been distant from your father. It's because of me. Because I never wanted to accept the gift that he offered me. This place in the family. Because I didn't want to need anyone or anything.

"I have been building walls ever since I escaped from Rome. Building walls between myself and the poverty that I had once. Because I thought they would keep me safe. Because I thought they would make it so I couldn't go back. But all they do is keep people out. People that you want. People that you need. And I can't live that way anymore. I can't. Because you showed me a better way. You showed me a better life.

"Minerva, I used to think of you as a mouse, but that isn't true at all. You're a tigress. You are brave and brilliant and you have taught me bravery. I'm sorry that I couldn't stand up and seize hold of it when I needed to. When you asked me to. But I want to do it now.

"Minerva, I am humbled by the gift that is you. You are the most brilliant woman who has ever been. Or ever will be. You are not second, you are first. It's only that my heart was blind. Because that's what it is when you take love away from yourself. You rob yourself of your senses. You make it so that you cannot truly see. But I see now. I see now because of you."

"Me?"

"Yes," he said. "You. You had to become a woman before I could have you, Min. And I… I should have waited until I became the man you deserved before I ever touched you."

"Dante," she said, flinging herself into his arms, wrapping them around his neck. And kissing him.

"That's it?" His voice was rough. "You're not even going to make me work for it?"

"We already worked for it. You already worked for it. And you know what? Even if you hadn't come to your senses, you taught me something. You taught me to demand everything."

"Good. Keep demanding it."

"I will. I will. Dante, you are the most brilliant man I have ever known. And I am really glad that I had to force you to marry me."

"I *want* to marry you again," he said.

"Really?"

"Yes. Not for spectators, not for show. I want to marry you again because I want to."

"Well. I'd like that."

"And then maybe this time your brother and father will want to kill me."

"Well..." she said. "They might."

"Why?"

She twisted her hands in front of her. "There is a small possibility that I might be a pregnant bride."

"What?"

"I'm late. And... We have been doing something that sometimes means..."

"Are you sure?"

"No. I'm not sure. If devastated broken hearts cause missed periods then that could be the problem. It's just that I think more likely it was pregnancy."

"But Isabella is only…"

"I know," she said.

"I'm going to be a father. Two children."

She laughed. "I know," she said. "Isn't that amazing?"

"I…"

His life flashed before his eyes. As if he was dying. Except he wasn't dying. He was living. And he saw himself, that boy in Rome with the shaking gun, angry and distrustful in private school, starting his first business endeavor, Minerva asking him to protect her. Him demanding she marry him.

All of it had brought him here. To this moment. There were no walls. And he was in no danger of going back. It was impossible. He had been afraid all this time that he might slip back into the slums by accident. But it had never been about the slums. They didn't matter at all. What mattered was this. The people in his life. And he would not lose that. He wouldn't lose them.

And he would never lose the love in his heart.

It had been said that Dante Fiori could condemn a man to any level of hell he chose with just the lift of his brow. That was a fabrication. But what was true was that Minerva

King could send him to heaven with just the touch of her lips to his.

"I love you," he said.

"I love you too," she said.

And he knew that he would never be alone again.

He had a family.

Not tied together by blood, but by love.

And that was the most powerful force of all.

# EPILOGUE

SHE WAS A pregnant bride. There was no denying that fact. But fortunately, they were technically already married.

Though, that did not stop her father from giving Dante an endless hard time. And it didn't stop her brother, Maximus, from giving him the evil eye, but then, Maximus hadn't stopped that at any point over the last few months.

Minerva wasn't put off by any of it. She was happy. The adoption for Isabella had gone through a couple of months earlier, and she and Dante were legally what they had already been in their hearts: her parents.

She was acting as their flower girl, even though Dante had to carry her down the aisle. And when the wedding was over, since the only guests were family and very close friends, when Minerva threw the bouquet, her sister, Violet, caught it, then stared at it like it was a live cockroach.

"Marriage might be coming for you," Minerva commented.

"Never," Violet said. "Though I like the colors in this bouquet. I could make a very nice makeup palette out of it. Use it as inspiration. I'll call it Minerva's Bouquet. The proceeds can go to KatiBella."

"That is the closest I will ever get to being a mogul," Minerva said.

"You could be one if you wanted to."

She put her hand on her stomach, and she looked at Dante, holding her daughter. "I'm everything that I want to be," she said.

"What's that?" Violet asked.

Minerva looked at her sister, her parents, her brother. Then again at her daughter and her husband.

"Loved."

And she was. For all her days.

\* \* \* \* \*

*Adored* The Scandal Behind
the Italian's Wedding—
*Millie Adams's dazzling debut for
Harlequin Presents?*

*Look out for her next story,
coming soon!*

ドナルド・R・キーオ

山岡洋一【訳】

# ビジネスで
# 失敗する人の
# 10の法則

*The Ten Commandments*
*for Business Failure*

日本経済新聞出版社

ビジネスで失敗する人の10の法則

The Ten Commandments for Business Failure
by
Donald R. Keough

世界全体に広がるコカ・コーラ・ファミリーを
過去、現在、未来に構成する無数の男女へ
本書を捧げる

# Contents

法則
11

仕事への熱意、人生への熱意を失う

198

ブックデザイン　守先正

# 序文

ウォーレン・バフェット

いつも信条にしてきた点だが、自分より優れた人物と付き合うようにたえず努力すべきだとわたしは考えている。そうすれば間違いなく、自分を高めていくことができる。そう考えて行動してきたので、結婚相手に恵まれたし、ドナルド・キーオという素晴らしい友人にも恵まれた。

ドン（ドナルド）・キーオと一緒にいると、上りのエスカレーターに乗っているように感じる。わたしという人間とわたしの仕事を楽観的にみてくれているので、もっと目標を高め、もっと自分を信じ、周囲の世界を信じるようになる。ドンと付き合っていると、いつも何かを学べる。信じがたいほど力のある経営指導者なのだ。優れた経営者がとりわけ偉大な成果をあげるとき、何かを自分で処理するのではない。周囲の人たちを動かして達成する。そしてドンは、世界中

9

のあらゆる性格の男女の気持ちをつかみ、この人が成功できるように支援しようと思ってもらえるのである。そういう事実をわたしはみてきた。

これはたぶん、状況を人間という側面から理解するのが、誰よりもうまいからだ。わたしの子供たちにたぶん、わたしより優れた助言を与えることができ、だから、子供たちに慕われている。同じことを友人と呼ぶ人全員に行っている。そして、友人の数はきわめて多い。

グレアム・グループという集まりがある。わたしの恩師であるベンジャミン・グレアムに因んでこう名付けており、二年に一度ぐらい会合を開く。ドン・キーオら、親しい友人が全員集まる。みな、ドンに基調講演をお願いしたいという。とくに熱心なのがビル・ゲイツで、毎回、ドン・キーオの話を聞きたがる。話がうまいし、学べることが多いからだ。ドンが一緒に行こうといえば、地獄への旅だって楽しめるだろう。

バークシャー・ハザウェイの取締役になってもらっているのは、安心して後を任せられる数少ない人のひとりだからだ。

ドン・キーオと知り合ったのはもう五十年以上前、オマハのファーナム街で向かいあった家に住んでいたときだ。当時はまだ、どちらも家族のために必死ではたらいている若者にすぎなかった。そのころに、ひとりはコカ・コーラ社の社長になり、もうひとりはバークシャー・ハ

ザウェイの経営者になると話したとすると、そのほら話を聞いた人はたぶん、ふたりともよほど金持ちの親がいないと大変だと思ったはずだ。

あるとき、わたしはドンの家に行き、一千ドルほど投資してくれないかと頼んだ。それはできないと断られた。当時ならわたし自身、わたしの頼みを断ったはずだ。

ドンとわたしの家族はほんとうに親しかった。子供たちはいつもどちらかの家で遊んでいた。

ドンの一家がヒューストンに引っ越したとき、子供たちはとてもつらい思いをしている。引っ越しの日は涙々で大変だった。

じつに面白い話がある。ドンの家とわたしの家から百メートルも離れていないところで、わたしのいまのビジネスパートナー、チャーリー・マンガーが育っているのだ。ドンはその後、ヒューストンからアトランタに移った。チャーリー・マンガーはロサンゼルスに移った。しかしやがて、親友として、パートナーとして再会しており、三人ともオマハの人間らしい面が色濃く残っている。いまではもちろん、オマハ出身だと胸をはる人がたくさんいる。

ドン・キーオがオマハを離れてからも、連絡は取り合っていた。ワシントンのアルファルファ・クラブの会合で会い、一度はホワイトハウスで会ったこともある。一九八四年にわたしがペプシを賞賛し、「できればチェリー・シロップが少し入っていればいい」と述べた新聞記事を読んで、ドンは翌日に新商品のチェリー・コークを送ってくれた。「神が与えた飲み物」を試飲

してほしいという言葉をつけて。飲んだ後、わたしは返事を書いた。「味覚テストの結果など信じないように。テストのことはあまり知らないが、この商品が売れることは分かる」

わたしはすぐにブランドを変更し、チェリー・コークをバークシャー・ハザウェイの公式の飲み物に指定した。

何年か後、わたしはコカ・コーラの株式を買いはじめたが、ドン・キーオには何もいわなかった。連絡していれば会社の弁護士にいわなければならないかもしれないし、その結果がどうなるかは、神のみぞ知るだと思ったからだ。ドンが困った立場になるのは望まなかった。やがてドンが電話してきて、たずねた。「コークの株式を買ってはいないだろうね」。買っているのはわたしだと答えた。そのとき、コカ・コーラ社の株式を七・七パーセントまで買い進めていたのだ。

これは簡単な決断だった。ドンが社長なのだから、なおさらだ。一九八八年に、同社は分別があり、正しい行動をとっていて、そのため、あきらかにきわめて価値が高い企業だとわたしは判断した。

コカ・コーラ社を代表する人物がひとりほしいというのであれば、それはドン・キーオだ。昔もいまも、ミスター・コークなのだ。たとえば、「汝の店を守れ。されば、店は汝を守るだろう」という教えだ。ドン・キーオは、ベンジャミン・フランクリンの教えを受け継いでいる。ドン・キー

12

オがやってきたことは基本的に、コカ・コーラ社が正しいと判断する行動をとるという点だ。

そしてドンは、自分が正しいと判断する行動をコカ・コーラ社がつねにとると信じている。

ドン・キーオの能力のなかでとくに優れている点は、問題の核心をずばりつかみ、官僚制のもやもやを切り裂けることだ。ものごとを単純にすることを原則としており、これはわたしにとっても原則である。

ハーバート・アレンがこう語っている。自分が知っている経営者のなかで、立候補すれば大統領になれたと思えるのは、ジャック・ウェルチとドン・キーオのふたりだけだと。わたしもそう思う。どちらも天性の聡明さをもっている。ふたりから学べる点は多い。

何十年にわたって付き合ってきたのだが、それでもわたしはドン・キーオに会うたびに、チェリー・コークを飲んだときのように爽快になる。いつも炭酸が抜けることがない。以前はコカ・コーラ社の取締役会で、いまではバークシャー・ハザウェイの取締役会で会っている。以前と同じように熱心だし、献身的だし、計画やエネルギー、アイデアがたっぷりあるし、夢をもつよう周囲をけしかけてもいる。本書で、キーオの独特の見方を多数の人たちが学べるようになったのは、ほんとうに喜ばしいことだ。

## はじめに

二十年以上前、コカ・コーラ社の社長だったころ、マイアミで開催される小売業の大規模な会議で基調講演を行うよう求められた。会議のテーマは「勝ち組に加わる」であり、事業で成功するための方法を話してほしいという。要するに、成功の秘訣を話すよう求められたわけだ。

ありがたい話だったが、事業で成功する方法についてなら、自分で実際に試したわけでもないのに、実証済みという触れ込みの助言を喜んで披露する講演者や著者がいくらでもいる。アメリカン・フットボールの元コーチや元経営者、心理学者、大学教授、説教師、占い師、成功のグルなどが講演や著書で、それぞれお得意の方法を並べている。どんなことにも良い部分はあるものだが、こうした助言の大部分は、煎じ詰めれば「一所懸命はたらく」「母親の教えを守る」という二点に尽きてしまう。何とも月並みで安易なのだ。わたしは企業経営に一生をかけてきたが、成功を保証できる法則や段階式の方法は、どんなことについてでも編み出せていない。まして、ビジネスのように、ダイナミックで変化が激しい分野では、成功の法則など開発

できていない。

たとえば指導力という点についていうなら、これまで研究しつくされてきたが、はっきりした結論はでていない。指導力の研究に専念してきた社会学の教授から、こういう話を聞いたことがある。それまでに教えた二千人近い学生のその後のキャリアを調べたが、指導力があるかどうかを判断するには、その人物に何人が従っているかをみる以外にないという結論に達したというのだ。

そこで、事業で勝利する方法について話すように求められたとき、わたしにはできないと答えるしかなかった。話せるのは、どういう方法をとれば負けるかということだけであり、わたしが示す方法を採用すれば、かなりの確率で負けることなら保証できるといった。

こうして引き受けた講演で話した内容が、長年のうちに改良を重ねて「事業を失敗に導く十の法則」になり、さらに長い年月をかけて、この短い本になった。本書は約六十年にわたる経験から導き出した教訓をまとめたものである。社会人としてのわたしの出発点になったのは一九四九年、ネブラスカ州オマハのWOWテレビに就職して、当時は新しいメディアだったテレビの世界に入ったときだ。

テレビ放送をはじめて経験したのは学生のときだ。わたしは海軍に入って第二次世界大戦に従軍し、戦後、復員兵援護法のもとでクレイトン大学に入った。法科大学院に進みたいという

漠然とした考えを抱きながら、人文科学を学び、哲学を専攻した。しかし、その後の何十年かに、哲学者の求人広告というのは一度も目にしたことがない。人間とは何か、宇宙のなかで人間はどのような位置を占めているのか、善と悪はどのような性格をもっているのか、人生の影と現実は何かといった点に関する大きな論争を学ぶのは楽しかった。経営大学院の卒業生ならと現実は何かといった点に関する大きな論争を学ぶのは楽しかった。経営大学院の卒業生なら

そんな「役に立たない」知識を小馬鹿にするだろうが、知られているかぎりの人類の歴史は、はるか昔の哲学者の考えが実現したり、ぶつかりあったりすることによるものだともいえる。

わたしはそのころ人間性に興味をもっていたので、弁論部に入り、即興演説を行い、やがて、演劇を行うようになった。そこでいわば「発見」されて、大学の医学部で行われた構内テレビ番組の司会役を仰せつかった。病気になった動物の手術の実況放送を、大教室におかれたテレビでみる催しであった。ところが実況は長くは続かなかった。手術をはじめて間もなく、動物は息絶えてしまい、別の動物を用意している間、何とか間を持たせようと四苦八苦することになったのだ。幸い、構内テレビだけの番組だったし、教室で番組をみていた人の数もたぶん、少なかった。わたしは、いまはやりの「リアリティ番組」の先駆者になったわけだ。このようにマスコミに興味をもっていたが、法律の講義もいくつか受け、夢中になれるかどうか試してみた。しかし結局はマスコミに興味が戻った。

学生のとき、メディア関連の奨学金を受けていた縁で、研修生としてWOWテレビではたら

く機会が得られた。運よく、初めての仕事として、プロ・チームによるアメリカン・フットボールの実況中継を行うことになった。シカゴより西では、はじめての実況中継だ。試合はナショナル・フットボール・リーグのプレシーズン戦で、オマハで行われたロサンゼルス・ラムズ対ニューヨーク・ジャイアンツであった。ラジオのスポーツ中継を担当するアナウンサーは、最新のメディアを少し調べただけですぐに断り、テレビのスポーツ中継なんて成功するわけがないと、相手かまわずいってまわった。

ラムズとジャイアンツの試合は、人生のハイライトにはならなかった。試合に使われたのは野球場を改造した競技場だ。放送席はバックネット裏の高い位置にあって、エンド・ゾーンから思い切り離れていた。照明も悪く、フィールドの半分しか見えない。助手がついていたが、酔っぱらっていて役に立たなかった。わたしの中継も正確だとはいえなかった。「ボールは一インチ・ライン上にあります」といってしまったほどだ。

この番組はテストであり、その年にはネブラスカ大学のアメリカン・フットボール・チーム、ハスカーのホーム・ゲームを中継することになっていた。ハスカーにはネブラスカ州民がこぞって熱狂するというのが常識になっている。当時は州内にテレビが数百台しかなかったのだが、それでもテレビ局経営陣の熱意はすさまじかった。テレビがすぐに、既存のすべてのメディアを圧倒すると信じていたのだ。この見方は正しかった。

ラムズ対ジャイアンツの試合では何とも冴えなかったが、それでもその年、ネブラスカ州での
ゲームをすべて担当することができた。小さな放送席に機材を運び入れるのを手伝わなけれ
ばならなかったが、その甲斐はあった。週に五十五ドルがもらえて、まるで王侯貴族になった
ようだったからだ。この給与で、「キーオのコーヒー・カウンター」という毎日のトークショー
も担当した。わたしの番組のすぐ後には、もっと楽しく、プロらしい番組が放送され、やはり
新たなメディアでキャリアの第一歩を踏み出したばかりの若者が司会をしていた。週給はやはり五十五ドルだった。後にショー
番組の司会者として有名になったジョニー・カーソンだ。週給はやはり五十五ドルだった。後にショー
ーソンは生涯の友人になった。

放送の仕事は面白かったが、トークショーのスポンサーだったパクストン＆ギャラガーズ・
バターナット・コーヒーがもっと高い七十五ドルの週給を提示して、誘ってくれた。同社は地
域の食品卸会社で、オマハに本社がある。この会社なら、収入は増えるし、出張が少なくなる。
わたしは結婚したばかりで、ミッキーとの新婚生活をもっと楽しめる。そこで一九五〇年の後
半に企業の世界に飛び込み、テレビの世界に戻ろうと考えることはなかった。

一九五八年に、ギルバート・スワンソンとクラーク・スワンソンが、成功を収めていたスワ
ンソン・フーズをキャンベル・スープに売却して得た資金を使って、大株主のギャラガー家か
ら同社を買収した。社名をバターナット・フーズに変え、大規模な事業拡張計画を立てていた。

これでビジネスの世界でのわたしの人生は、新たな章に入ることになる。これは余談だが、スワンソン兄弟が一九五〇年代にはじめて資産を築いたのは、ごく単純な商品と新たな冷凍技術を組み合わせて、当時の消費者が望んでいた二つの点を同時にかなえたからだ。もっとテレビをみたいという望みと、もっと簡単に料理できる食品がほしいという望みである。こうして、テレビをみながら夕食をとる習慣が生まれた。

クラーク・スワンソンが死んだ後、バターナット・フーズは売却され、わたしはもっと大きな新会社で新しい職を得ることになった。テキサス州ヒューストンのダンカン・フーズだ。経営者のチャールズ・ダンカンは後にコカ・コーラ社の社長になり、カーター政権で国防副長官とエネルギー長官を務めている。

その後、ダンカン・フーズはコカ・コーラ社に買収され、わたしは同社で三十年以上にわたってさまざまなポストにつき、世界でもっとも知名度の高いブランドを管理する仕事を続けた。そして一九八一年、ダンカンの後任として社長に就任した。わたしのキャリアのうちかなりの部分はコカ・コーラ社でのものだ。このため本書では、コカ・コーラ社という素晴らしい世界的な組織で起こったことをかなり取り上げる。

コカ・コーラ社の例を使うのは適切だといえる理由がある。きわめて多様で、多元的な会社なのだ。製造と小売店への流通に関与しているし、その小売店も露天商から大規模店舗まであ

るし、すべての人種、宗教、文化にわたる約二百の国で事業を展開している。コカ・コーラ社に勤務していたとき、わたしは各国の大統領や独裁者、大経営者、詩人、画家、映画スターに会ってきた。コカ・コーラのボトラーや、小売食品企業の経営者、消費者には、北極圏から南アメリカ南端のフエゴ島まで、中国本土からサハラ砂漠以南の無秩序な地域まで、世界のあらゆる地域で会ってきた。世界全体、人類全体を相手に事業を行っているといえる企業はないが、コカ・コーラ社はどの企業よりも、それに近い。

本書で、わたし自身の例など、コカ・コーラ社の経営者が失敗の罠に陥った例をいくつも紹介していくが、ほとんどの場合、すぐに間違いを是正し、比較的短期間で失敗から抜け出し、同社が生き残って繁栄していることを指摘しておきたい。二〇〇八年には新たな成長期に入っており、同社を指揮して素晴らしい実績をあげてきたネビル・イズデルが最高経営責任者（CEO）の地位を退き、ムーター・ケントが後任になった。ケントはきわめて優秀で、コカ・コーラのシステムと人びとに強い敬意を抱いている。

本論に入る前に、ロベルト・ゴイズエタとわたしの関係を説明しておこう。このふたりで、十二年にわたってコカ・コーラ社を経営してきた。どちらも同社に長く勤務し、友人であったが、一九八一年三月初めにゴイズエタが会長兼CEOに就任し、わたしが社長兼最高執行責任者（COO）になった。

ふたりの関係はめったにないほど密接であり、協力して大きな仕事に取り組むことになった。

ゴイズエタは、COOであり取締役でもあるわたしに、世界の二百を超える国でコカ・コーラ・システムを活気づかせるために、幅広い権限を与えてくれた。だが、誤解しないようにお願いしたい。わたしに大きな権限を委任する点では鷹揚だったが、CEOとしての最終的な責任は委任できないし、実際にも委任していない。ゴイズエタはわたしにとってボスであり、そして、アメリカの経営史を飾る有能な経営者のひとりである。一九八一年に就任したとき、コカ・コーラ社の株式時価総額は四十億ドルであった。一九九七年に亡くなったとき、一千四百五十億ドルになっていた。

わたしは十年以上前にコカ・コーラ社の職を辞した後、投資銀行のアレン&カンパニー社の会長として、経営の世界に関与してきた。こうした経歴を背景に、事業を失敗に導く十の法則を示し、同時に、これらの十の法則のうちひとつかふたつに注意深く従っていれば、事業に失敗するか、少なくとも破綻への坂道を勢いよく下ることになると保証する。事業の失敗はきわめて数が多い。アメリカの破産裁判所の統計によれば、二〇〇七年の一月から九月までで、二万百五十二社もの企業が倒産しているのだから。

なぜ失敗したかを説明してくれる自称経営専門家は多い。パワーポイントのスライドを大量に用意して、企業が倒産した理由を戦略面から詳細に説明する。顧客サービスが貧弱だった、

競争を過小評価した、供給連鎖（サプライ・チェーン）が混乱していた、間違った買収を行った、負債が過剰だった、などである。通常、どのような失敗があったかを、抽象的に説明していく。この会社はイノベーションに失敗した。この会社は創業者のビジョンを無視した。「この会社はこれこれのことをした。この会社はこれこれのことをしなかった」という。

しかし、会社というのは人間が考えた観念にすぎない。会社が何かに失敗するということは、実際にはない。失敗するのは個人だ。そして、少し調べていけば分かるはずだが、失敗はたいてい、戦略の間違いとして繰り返し指摘されてきた点にではなく（もちろん、典型的な間違いが何らかの形で揃っている場合もあるだろうが）、シェークスピアがいうように、われわれ自身、つまり会社を指導する経営者にある。会社は経営者個人の性格の産物であり、延長である。経営する人物の長く伸びた影なのだ。経営者はビジネスの舞台の主役だ。経営者が自分の弱点のために事業を間違った方向に導いたとき、事業は失敗への道を歩むのである。

本書で紹介する十の法則はどのような段階にあるどのような企業にも適用できるが、主に、ある程度の成功を収めた企業と経営者に役立つように考えてある。このため、これまでの実績がよいほど、これらの法則があてはまるようになっている。規模の大小を問わず、企業を経営する地位にあり、売上と利益で大きな成功を収めてきたのであれば、十分に注意するべきだ。

本書で示す法則のどれかに陥る危険があり、そうなっていれば失敗は間近に迫っている。

本書に描く失敗の法則は、とくに誰かを批判することを意図していないが、例として何人かの人をあげている。また、以下の十の法則は経営に関する見方を変える革命的なものなどではない。どれも常識だといえる。

失敗し破綻した事業の例をあげてみてほしい。どんな事業でもいい。最新のウィキノミクスに基づく事業でもいい。その事業を指導した経営者は、以下の法則にひとつならずあてはまっているとわたしは確信している。失敗への一歩を踏み出し、それを改めないとき、つぎの一歩へと進むことになる。

だからこの小論を戒めの書として読んでほしい。どれかにあてはまるようなら、注意する方がいい。失敗への道を歩んでおり、会社を道連れにすることになろう。

# 法則1 リスクをとるのを止める

人類のほとんどは、歴史のほとんどの期間、リスクを避ける姿勢をとりつづけてきた。狩猟採集民族は広範囲を移動していたと思うが、農業革命によって定住が可能になると、ほとんどの人は定住している。父親や母親、祖父や祖母と同じように生活していくことを選び、生まれ育った村から遠く離れた土地に行ってみようとはしなかった。そうしない理由は十分にあった。

村の外には、危険な世界が広がっている。昔の海図をみると、「未知の海域」と書かれた恐ろしげなところがある。ときには、「竜が生息」など、もっと恐ろしい警告が書かれていることもある。そんな海を航海するような危険なことをしようとする人がいるだろうか。

もちろん、そういう海に行った人も少しはいる。だがほとんどの人は生まれ育った土地から離れなかった。

リスクを冒せばさまざまなことが起こりうる。その大部分はたぶん、悪いこと

警戒しすぎる人は、
ほとんど何も達成できない
——フリードリヒ・フォン・シラー

　だろう。

　いまでも、サハラ砂漠以南のアフリカや、中東の一部、東南アジアの一部では、リスク回避の文化が強く、「これまでいつもやってきたことなのだから、これまでいつもやってきたとおりのことをしよう」という姿勢にとらわれている。これまでと同じように生活するサイクルが世代から世代へと受け継がれていき、極貧の家族や集団で受け継がれていくことも多い。

　これに対してアメリカは、そもそものはじめからリスクをとることで誕生している。新大陸を発見したコロンブス、イギリス人がはじめて定住したジェームズタウン、独立戦争を開始した第二回大陸会議、トマス・ジェファーソンが起草した見事な独立宣言など、リスクにつぐリスクのうえに築かれた国なのだ。アメリカ人の祖先は、リスクを恐れぬ人たち、屈強でへこたれない人たちであり、自分の命にいたるまで、あらゆるものを賭け、とんでもなく不利な条件を克服して生き残ってきた。ヘクター・セント・ジョン・ド・クレブクールは一七八二年にこう書いている。「ここではあらゆる民族の人が溶け合って、新

「アメリカ人は新しい人間である」

わたしの曾祖父、マイケル・キーオは一八四八年、まだ十八歳のときに故郷のアイルランドを離れ、たったひとりで当時、「つらい涙でできた海」と呼ばれていた大西洋をわたるリスクをとった。当時、大西洋航路の船内はすさまじかった。混雑し、鼠が走り、汚物が散乱し、病気が蔓延していた。船長は冷徹で、船客を積み荷として扱い、ほとんど世話をしなかった。航海の途中で死んだ船客は海に投げ込むか、最初の寄港地でおろした。カナダのケベック州グロス・イル島には、無数のアイルランド人移民が墓標もないまま葬られている。これ以上にひどい状態でアメリカにわたってきたのは、アフリカ人の奴隷しかない。

何とかたどりつけた移民も、アメリカが約束の地どころではなく、夜明けから夕暮れまでの重労働に耐えるしかない国であることに気づかされる。曾祖父がようやくみつけたのは、マサチューセッツ州ピッツフィールドの石切り場で石を運ぶ仕事であった。一日十六時間、刑務所より少しましといえるだけの仕事が続く。それでもこの重労働で、少しばかりの食料が手に入り、生活の心配はなくなった。すぐに結婚し、子供も生まれたので、ピッツフィールドに落ち着こうと考えても当然だった。

何かを達成できたとき、ごく小さなことにすぎなくても、これ以上リスクをとるのはやめて

27

おこうという誘惑にかられる。

これが人間の本性なのだ。これを得られた。せっかく得たものをふいにすることはない。山のあなたに何があるか、分かったものではない。行くことはない。

頭のなかでそういう声が響いていたのではないかと思う。ピッツフィールドでの知り合いのうち何人かもたぶん、忠告したはずだ。

「ここにいる方がいい。仕事があるのだから。石を運ぶのは立派な仕事だ。仕事がなくて困っている人がたくさんいるじゃないか」

しかし曾祖父は、苦しい重労働ではあっても安定した生活に安住するのではなく、牛車に乗り、大陸を半分横断してアイオワという僻地に行った。そうしてくれてほんとうによかったと思う。

祖父のジョン・キーオは、アイオワの農場を広げていき、毎年毎年、あらゆるリスクをとって作物を育て、ブリザードや砂嵐、蝗（いなご）の害と戦ってきた。祖父から聞いた話でよく覚えていることがある。農場には木がほとんどなかったので、週に一回、三十キロほどのところにあるロック・リバーまで何頭かの馬をつれて行き、木を切って貴重な燃料を手に入れていた。あるとき、斧を振り下ろした際に手元が狂って、つま先を切り落としてしまった。祖父はつま先を戻し、布でしばりつけ、そのまま仕事を続けたという。

28

つま先も足も、そして祖父も無事だった。抗生物質などなかった時代の話だ。

アメリカには、独特の遺伝子プールがある。アメリカ人のほとんどは、たいていの人が故郷に止まっていたときに、船に乗った人の子孫なのだ。アメリカにたどりつけなかった人も多い。

そして、大西洋か太平洋をわたる旅（あるいは山や平原や砂漠をこえる旅）で生き残った人も、信じがたいほどの重労働がいつまでも続く生活に耐えてきた。農場で、鉄道の建設現場で、いまでは想像もできないほど危険で汚い鉱山や工場で。一九〇〇年には、アメリカの家族は医療費の二倍近くを葬式に費やしている。そうしたなかで、何とか勝利を収めてきたのが、アメリカ人の祖先なのである。

こうした祖先が克服してきた困難と比較すれば、オフィスでの一日は、どんなに厳しい一日でも、公園を散歩するようなものだ。

しかし、生活が楽になり、豊かになり、快適になると、リスクをとるのを止めようという誘惑が強くなる。

これは、成功がもたらす大きな病のひとつだ。年齢が高くなるほど、この誘惑に負けやすくなる。年齢が高いといっても、六十歳になればという意味ではない。四十歳でもこの病にかかる。こう考えるのだ。「これまで苦労の連続だった。心配して夜も眠れないことが多かった。そろそろ、心配するのは誰かに任せよう。いまのままで満足だ」

起業家が自宅を担保にカネを借り、一切合財を賭けて新しいアイデアを試したり、まったく新しい産業をおこしたりするのは、リスクをとることのなかでも、もっとも難しい種類のものだともいえる。新規事業のうち、五分の四は失敗している。新製品のほとんどはテスト・マーケットの段階にも達しないし、この段階に達しても、成功を収めるのは十三分の一にすぎない。全米独立企業連盟研究財団の推計によれば、開業から五年たって営業を継続しているのは、従業員を雇用している企業では半分にすぎないし、その多くは赤字である。たしかに、容易ではない。

しかし、それと同じぐらい難しく、ときにはもっと難しいことがある。かなりの成功を収めているときにリスクをとること、そんな必要はないといえる事実が十分にあるときにリスクをとることである。今日、リスク評価にはかなりの時間と労力が費やされており、損失を被る統計的な確率から企業統治の規則に違反する可能性まで、さまざまな角度から評価が行われている。わたしはリスク評価の専門家ではない。わたしの経験からいうなら、新たなリスクやもっと大きなリスクをとる必要を考えるべきだという感覚、いま行動しなければ将来が危ういという感覚、さらには、せっかくの機会を逃してしまうという感覚だ、わたしはコカ・コーラ社にいたとき、事業がきわめて好調だと思えるといつも、まったく落ち着かない気分になった。ものごとはもっとよくなっているという感覚、現状に安住できない感覚であ

# 世界は満足できない人間のものだ
## ——オスカー・ワイルド

ロシア人がいうように、「ものごとがうまくいきすぎているのは、よくないこと」なのである。

たぶん、わたしの質問にいらだった人が少なくなかったはずだ。かなり頻繁に、経営幹部にこう質問していったからだ。「いつも同じことを聞いて申し訳ないが、何もかも好調なのはなぜなのか。いま心配しておけば、今後はその点を心配しなくてもよくなる部分はもっとないのか」

ロバート・ウッドラフはコカ・コーラ社の長老であり、現在の繁栄をもたらした第二の創業者だが、著名な劇作家オスカー・ワイルドの「世界は満足できない人間のものだ」という言葉が好きで、何度も引用していた。

コカ・コーラ社は一八八六年に設立された。一九三〇年には長く成功が続いていたのだが、それでもウッドラフは満足できなかった。まだ小規模だった国際事業を統合し、国際市場をさらに開拓したいと考えた。当然ながら、取締役会はそのような冒険に乗り出すには時期が悪すぎると判断した。一九二九年の株式市場大暴落から、まだ一年もたっていない。ドイツやイタリアや日本は軍備拡張に動いている。確実だといえる

のは、極端に不確実な状況であることだけだったのだ。

それで、どう動いたのだろうか。ウッドラフは個人の立場で巨大なリスクをとった。いまなら囂々たる非難を浴びるはずだ。しかしこれは、金融取引を規制する証券取引委員会（SEC）が設立される前の話だ。取締役会の承認を受けることなく、ニューヨークに行き、コカ・コーラ・エクスポート社を設立したのである。この思い切った決断がなければ、コカ・コーラ社がいまどうなっていたか、想像すらできない。世界の二百を超える国で事業を展開していることはなかったはずだ。

コカ・コーラ・エクスポート社は一九七三年ごろまで、ほぼ独立した企業として経営されていた。それまで四十三年間、国内事業の経営陣は国際事業の経営陣とはほとんど交流がなかった。ウッドラフは自分で選んだ人物に外国行きのチケットとある程度の資金をわたし、その国でコカ・コーラの事業をいつ、どのようにして築くかを各人が決めるまで、会うこともなかった。当時、国際的な通信は時間がかかったし、あてにならなかった。だから、国際事業は信頼に基づいて築くしかない。このときの方法が強力な先例になるとともに、国際事業の哲学が形成され、その後、長期にわたって使われることになる。

一九六四年に日本に行ったときのことをよく覚えている。ウッドラフに選ばれて日本事業の確立にあたっている幹部がいた。本社からは大量のメモや指令が送られてくるが、ざっと読む

32

だけで、ほとんどをゴミ箱に捨てていた。トップに信頼され、支援されており、それ以外の点は無視してもいいと分かっていたのである。

一九三〇年代にウッドラフはもうひとつ、おそらく国際事業の拡大より重要な点でもリスクをとっている。

大恐慌が一九三三年の底に向けて厳しさを増し、企業がつぎつぎに倒産し、株式市場が下落を続け、男性の労働力人口のうち四分の一が失業していた。ほとんどの専門家は、アメリカがふたたび繁栄する可能性は低いとみていた。ところがこの暗い状況のなかで、ウッドラフはコカ・コーラ社の広告予算を四百三十万ドルに増やしている。当時としては驚くほどの記録破りの金額だ。

この英断にはわれわれはみな感謝すべきだ。一九三〇年代の広告で、いまわれわれがみな知っていて、大好きなサンタクロースが登場したのだから。頬が赤く、太ったサンタクロースは、画家のハッドン・サンドブロムが制作し、毎年、クリスマスの時期に使われた広告がもとになっている。それまでのサンタクロースはかなり質素で、よい子にしていればクリスマス用に石炭をもってきてくれるというイメージであった。ウッドラフが何百万ドルもの資金を広告用に投じてリスクをとったお陰で、はるかに親切で、やさしく、愛されるサンタクロースが生まれた。

そして、コカ・コーラの売上は急増している。

これまで、じつに多くの優良企業が決定的な時期に重要なリスクをとらなかったために、打撃を受ける結果になっている。一時的に低迷しただけで後に回復した企業もあるが、転落して消えていった企業も多い。一九八〇年代だけでも、フォーチュン誌五百社のうち二百三十社が消えている。一九〇〇年代初めの大企業百社でみれば、いまでも生き残っているのはわずか十六社にすぎない。資本主義の霊園に、「リスクをとることなく死亡した企業ここに眠る」と書かれた墓碑がどれだけあることか。

おそらく、当初にリスクをとり、後にリスクをとらなかった企業の事例として、とくに劇的で、とくによく研究されてきたのはゼロックスだろう。同社には最大級の勝利と最大級の悲劇がどちらもある。

ゼロックスの歴史は一九〇六年にまでさかのぼる。当時の社名はハロイド社だった。ニューヨーク州ロチェスターに本社があり、写真印画紙の製造で成功を収めていた。設立から四十一年たった一九四七年、他社がみな見送った革命的なアイデアにかけて、大きなリスクをとった。ニューヨーク州クイーンズの無名の発明家、チェスター・カールソンが何年もかけて、「カーボン紙で十分だ」といわれ、「電子写真法」という新しい複写技術を売り込もうと努力してきた。IBMやゼネラル・エレクトリック（GE）など、二十を超える企業に断られつづけている。自分の発明をみせても、どの会社も「無関心を示すのに熱心だった」とカールソンは後に語っ

34

ている。

やがて、オハイオ州コロンバスのバッテル記念研究所と契約を結び、技術をさらに磨くことになった。ハロイド社はこの研究所で新技術を知り、カールソンの発明に基づくコピー機の開発と販売の権利を獲得した。オハイオ州立大学の古典語の教授が、ギリシャ語の「乾いた」と「書く」を意味する言葉を組み合わせて、「ゼログラフィー」という言葉をつくったといわれている。

わたしがはじめて訪問したとき、同社はハロイド・ゼロックスに社名を変更しており、中堅の地味な会社だった。見栄をはるようなところはまるでない。ロチェスターのオフィスは床がラバー・タイル張り、机も金属製で、技術者は胸のポケットにペンを何本もさし、真剣そのものと思えた。そして、みな生き生きとはたらいていて、熱心に仕事に取り組んでいるようだった。

一九五八年、カールソンのアイデアを取り入れてから十年以上たって、ベージュと茶色の飾り気のない機械が試作用のラインで組み立てられるようになった。世界ではじめての自動普通紙コピー機だ。一九五九年にゼロックス九一四として発売されると、たちまち大ヒットになり、全米のオフィスでカーボン紙は過ぎ去った時代の変わった遺物だとみられるようになった。そして「ゼロックス」という新しい名詞が世界中で使われるようになり、商標登録を担当した弁

理士には気の毒だが、「ゼロックスする」という動詞すら使われるようになった。

ゼロックス九一四は、世界でもとくに成功した工業製品になった。一九五九年から、生産を中止した七六年までに、二十万台以上が生産されている。現在では、アメリカの工業史を示す製品として、スミソニアン博物館に展示されている。

ゼロックスは十年以内に売上高が十億ドルを超えた。ひとつの技術に賭けてリスクをとった成果である。そしてその後、一時的に道に迷うことになる。リスクをとらなくなり、自社で開発された技術すら無視したからだ。

ゼロックスは本社をもっと魅力的なコネチカット州スタンフォードに移した。床はラバー・タイルではなくなり、分厚い絨毯になった。机も金属製ではなく、木製になった。本社に勤務するのは、大部分、「ボックス」の人間になった。ボックスを組み合わせたようなコピー機で育ち、豊かになったのであり、コピー機をもっともっと売ることが未来を切り開く方法だとみていた。

一九七〇年に、同社はカリフォルニア州パロアルトに研究所を開設した。七三年に、研究所でアルトのデモが行われた。世界ではじめての「パーソナル・コンピューター」だ。グラフィック用のモニターでアイコンを使い、画面上に複数の「ページ」を表示し、マウスと呼ぶ小さくかわいい器具を使う。

当時、ゼロックスは将来のライバルより、少なくとも五年は進んでいた。ところが本社の「ボックス」の人間はリスクをとらなかった。これは、前述のように、成功がもたらす大きな病のひとつだ。成功がもたらす病にはこれ以外に、満足と傲慢がある。何人もの技術者がパロアルト研究所を辞めてアップルやマイクロソフトに入っており、分厚い絨毯を敷き詰めたスタンフォード本社の経営陣は関心すら示さなかったと述べている。

一九九〇年代後半、ゼロックスはコピー機での主導的な地位を失い、損失を計上して、大規模なレイオフを発表した。二〇〇二年、SECは同社の不正会計と、何人かの経営幹部の証券詐欺を摘発した。しかし、ゼロックスはいまだ健在であり、新しい経営陣のもとで再建を進めている。

ゼロックスは誇り高い企業であり、技術革新を事業の基盤にしているのだが、コピー機という一種類の商品で完全な成功を収めていたことから、大陸の反対側にあるとはいえ、自社の研究所から新たな機会が飛び出してきたとき、リスクをとることがまったくできなかった。長期的に利益を生み出していくには、短期的にイノベーションが必要だという単純な真理を無視したのである。

もちろん、前進すれば失敗することがある。ウォルター・アイザックソンが書いたアインシュタインの素晴らしい伝記に、プリンストン大学での逸話が紹介されている。新しい研究室に

何が必要かと聞かれて、こう答えたという。机と椅子、紙と鉛筆、それに特大のゴミ箱がいる。

「大量に間違えて、捨てるから」というのだ。ビジネスの世界では、スティーブ・ジョブズがリサやパワー・マックキューブで失敗したのは意味があったといえるはずである。こうした冒険のためにアップルではきわめて創造的な社風が維持され、アイフォーンなどの大ヒット商品が登場したからだ。全米の経営大学院で、やってはならないことの事例研究では、典型的な失敗例としてエドセルやドーナツ盤レコード、ニュー・コークなどが取り上げられているが、これらの間違いすら、意味があったとも主張できる。これらの失敗は、後に経営陣の失態について教えてくれる貴重な教訓になっているが、要するにリスクをとってうまくいかなかった例なのである。

こうした計算違いは、その時点には高くついたとしても、事業を続けるためのコストの一部だ。ピーター・ドラッカーが五十年近く前に指摘しているように、会社の現在の資産を賭けて賢明にリスクをとり、将来に生き残れるようにすることこそ、経営陣の大きな仕事である。実際には、会社が間違いを犯さないとすれば、経営陣は高額の報酬にふさわしいほど、現状に満足できない姿勢をとっていないのではないかと思う。

ゼロックスは現状に満足できない姿勢はまったくとっていなかった。現状にまったく安住していると、リスクをとるのをやめたいという誘惑が強く

ていた。前述のように、現状に満足していると、リスクを

なり、ほとんど抵抗しがたいほどになる。そうなれば、失敗はほとんど避けがたくなる。

## 法則2 柔軟性をなくす

リスクをとらないことと柔軟性をなくすことは密接に関連しているが、微妙ながら重要な違いがある。ほんとうの意味で柔軟性がない頑固者は、リスクを避けようとしているわけではない。変化やイノベーションという点でリスクをとる機会があるのにためらっているわけではない。自分の流儀を確立していて、成功の法則に絶対の自信をもっているために、そもそも他の方法がみえなくなっているのである。コカ・コーラ社でそうなったことがある。

一九二〇年、コカ・コーラという商標の使用権をめぐって、最高裁判所までもつれこんでいた訴訟に決着がついた。オリバー・ウェンデル・ホームズ判事が、「ひとつの源泉から供給されるひとつの商品であり、社会によく知られている」として、コカ・コーラ社勝訴の判決を下したのだ。

# 現状は現状のままにしておきたい
## ——ヨギ・ベラ

コカ・コーラ社はこの言葉に感激して、聖書の言葉であるかのように扱った。教義のように受け入れ、必死に守るようになって、商品の源泉がただひとつであるという点を、商品そのものがひとつであるのと変わらないほど、重視するようになった。「あのコカ・コーラ」以外にコカ・コーラがあるとは、経営陣は考えられなくなった。そして経営陣が柔軟性を失って近視眼的になったのは、「あのコカ・コーラ」を、「例の緑の瓶に入ったコカ・コーラ」だと考えるようになったからだ。飲み物としてのコカ・コーラと瓶とは切り離せないとみるようになったのである。

もちろん、釣り鐘型のファウンテン・グラスも有名だったが、瓶とは違って、商標登録はされていない。

半世紀近くにわたって、広告ではかならず、瓶と飲料を一体のものとして扱っていた。アイゼンハワーからサンタクロースまで、みな緑の美しい瓶をつかんでいた。容器を変えるつもりはなく、変えることはできず、変えなかった。六オンス半（約百九十ミリリットル）の緑の瓶を使いつづけてきたのである。くびれのある六オンス半の緑の瓶こそ、神がさだめたコカ・コーラの販売方法、「ひとつの商品」なのであり、消費者

41

が何を望もうとも、神の意向にさからうわけにはいかないのだ。第二次世界大戦が終わるころ、経営陣はこの流儀にこだわりつづけていたので、事業の成長を止めかねないほどになっていた。

コカ・コーラはもともと、瓶で売られていたわけではない。一八八六年、アトランタのジェーコブズ薬局のジョン・S・ペンバートンという人物が、薬局のソーダ・ファウンテン用の商品として開発し、売り出した。その後もしばらく、カラメル色の原液に炭酸水をくわえ、グラスに入れてその場で飲んでもらう。その後もしばらく、同じ方法で販売されていた。コカ・コーラはいまでも、世界中のスポーツ・イベントの会場や劇場で、マクドナルドなど多数のファースト・フード店で、紙やプラスチックのコップに入れ、同じ方法で売られている。しかし、スーパーなどの小売店で瓶入りや缶入りの飲料として売られているものの方が、はるかに多い。

ペンバートンは一八八八年に亡くなり、新興企業だったコカ・コーラ社はエイサ・キャンドラーに引き継がれた。キャンドラーは事業をアメリカ南部一帯に拡大したが、薬局を通して売る方法は変えていない。十九世紀末には、炭酸飲料の瓶詰め技術はまだ十分に発達しておらず、瓶が爆発する事故も頻繁に起こるので、ときに危険でもあった。当然ながら、アトランタの事業を築いた創業者は、薬局のソーダ・ファウンテン以外に販路を拡大しても将来性があるとは考えなかった（リスクをとる理由はあるだろうか。第一の法則を参照）。

ところが一八九九年、テネシー州チャタヌーガの若手弁護士で、リスクをいとわないベンジ

ヤミン・トーマスとジョセフ・ホワイトヘッドが、キャンドラーに瓶詰めでの販売を提案し、リスクをすべて引き受けると申し出た。キャンドラーは瓶詰めに将来性があるとはみていなかったので、この提案に同意し、瓶詰めの権利をタダ同然の価格で売り渡すことにした。トーマスとホワイトヘッドは瓶詰めの無期限の権利をわずか一ドルで購入している。キャンドラーはもちろん、原液の権利を維持しており、この馬鹿げた計画が少しでも成功することがあれば、ボトラーに原液を販売して儲けられると考えていた。

ところが、瓶詰めは人気になった。一九〇五年には全米に二百を超える工場ができ、コカ・コーラは各種の店舗で売られるようになっている。とくに夏の暑い盛りには、食品店や雑貨店の店頭にトタン板でつくられた大きな水槽が置かれ、氷水のなかに各種のソフト・ドリンクを入れて、コカ・コーラもそのひとつとして売られるようになった。ルートビアや、ジンジャー・エールや、オレンジ・ジュースや、クリーム・ソーダなどがみな、同じ水槽に入れられていた。どれも八オンス（約二百四十ミリリットル）の標準的な瓶を使っているので、水槽の氷水のなかに手をつっこんで瓶をつかんでも、中身が何かは分からなかった。水のなかでラベルがはがれていれば、ますます分からなかった。

コカ・コーラ社は瓶による販売の可能性に気づきはじめていたので、ボトラーから要求を受けて、ルート・ガラス社にコカ・コーラのロゴが入った独特の瓶を設計するよう依頼した。さ

ペプシコーラは最高だ
十二オンスでたっぷり飲める
同じ五セント、量は倍
ペプシコーラを選ぼうよ
　　　──ペプシコーラのコマーシャル・ソング

　われば分かる瓶、氷水のなかにあるのをつかんだときに、すぐにそれと分かる瓶にするよう求めた。

　ルート・ガラス社は緑色のガラスを使った変わった形の瓶を提案した。砂時計のような形で、真ん中が膨らみ、くびれのある瓶だ。これがボトラーにも消費者にも好評で、大成功を収めた。そして、商品そのものと瓶とは一体だと考える人が多くなった。

　そして、前述のように、ここから問題が起こっている。

　ロバート・ウッドラフが世界事業を積極的に拡大していたころ、六オンス半の緑の瓶はすっかり定着し、ウッドラフも他の経営幹部も、他の容器で売る可能性を考えられなくなっていた。独特の瓶とコカ・コーラとは卵のようなものだとみていた。殻と中身は一体で切り離すことはできず、ひとつの商標をもったひとつの商品だというわけだ。

　一九三九年、ペプシコーラ社ではマーケティングの天才、ウォルター・マックが、素晴らしいコピーをつくった。「同

じ五セント、量は倍」というコピーだ。そして、十二オンス（約三百六十ミリリットル）の瓶でペプシを売るようになった。このコピーを大々的に使い、当時としては最大のヒットになったコマーシャル・ソングにのって、全米のラジオでも流されるようになった。

ペプシの売上は増加するようになった。

だが、コカ・コーラ社は動こうとしなかった。当時の社内では、ペプシコーラという名前すら使われていない。「模倣者」と呼ばれていた。

値段は同じ五セントで二倍の量が飲めるというわけで、模倣者の商品は戦後、アメリカの消費者の間で人気が高まっていった。冷蔵庫を買える人が増え、家庭で冷えた飲料を飲む人が多くなっていたのだ。一九四七年から五四年まで、ペプシの売上は二倍になり、コカ・コーラの売上は横ばいだった。それでも、コカ・コーラは競争相手を大きく引き離して第一位だったが、その差は縮小しており、最大の競争相手は勢いにのっていた。

だが、コカ・コーラ社の経営陣は頭が固かった。瓶を変更することなど考えもしない。それに、同じ値段で量が二倍なら、コストが高い砂糖を二倍使っていることになる。すぐに倒産すると考えた。

だが、倒産しなかった。

一九五五年になって、スーパーでの売上が急減したことから、頑固なコカ・コーラ社もつい

45

に気づいた。そして、新たに三種類の容器を加えた。キング・サイズの十オンス（約三百ミリリットル）。十二オンス、ファミリー・サイズの二十六オンス（約七百七十ミリリットル）である。

ボトラーの多くも柔軟性がなかった。

一九七四年、わたしがアメリカ事業の社長だったころ、ボトラーがコカ・コーラ社との契約更改に応じてくれることが、すべての関係者にとって生き残りに不可欠になっていた。ボトラーにとって、それが最善の道だったのだが、そうはみてくれないボトラーもいた。過去にしがみついて、動こうとしなかったのである。

コカ・コーラ社のボトラー制度は成功を収めていたが、時代後れになっていた。ボトラーの販売地域は十九世紀末から二十世紀初めにかけて決められ、馬車で日帰りできる距離に基づいている。販売地域の権利は変わらなかったが、大規模な小売チェーンはいくつものボトラーの販売地域にまたがって営業しているし、共通の価格を維持するのは難しくなっていった。一九六〇年代末になると、大規模な食品小売チェーンへの営業で問題が深刻になっている。だが、ボトラーの多くは売却や移転や合併に応じない。そして当時、ボトラーとの契約は無期限であった。ボトラーはそうとは気づかないうちに柔軟性を失い、その結果、自分たちの基盤であるシステムを徐々に弱めていたのである。

コカ・コーラ社がアメリカ国内の事業を続けていくには、値上げが不可欠だったが、ボトラーとの契約では値上げが禁じられていた。また、ボトラーの営業地域を小売チェーンの必要にあわせなければならなかった。このため、コカ・コーラ社はすべてのボトラーと契約を再交渉しなければならない。当時のルーク・スミス社長のもと、われわれは再交渉を開始した。

スミスとわたしは、すべてのボトラーのオーナーと話し合った。契約変更をいやがる人が少なくなかった。当時、関係者の間で語られていた話がある。ボトラーは今際の際に息子や娘に、「契約をいじらせてはいけない」というのだそうだ。そしてわれわれは、その契約をいじろうとしていたのである。

やがて、ボトラーの経営者のほとんどは、ここでやり方を変えなければ全員が共倒れになることに気づくようになった。世界でもっとも有名な商品、コカ・コーラは危険な状態になっており、コカ・コーラを救うためには全員が協力しなければならない。そして、われわれは協力した。

状況が変わったときに頑固に、それまでの流儀を守り通す。そうしていれば、失敗する。

かつてはイノベーションの先頭を走っていた企業が、頑なに柔軟な対応を拒否した例はいくらでもあって、数え切れない。誰でも知っているように、ハイテク企業の最上層部の人たちが自己満足に陥り、ご満悦の表情ですべてはうまくいっていると保証しあっているときに、事業

これが人間の悲劇だ。
状況は変わり、
人間は変わらない
——マキアヴェリ

がゆっくりと死に向かっていることが何度も起こってきた。

わたしは一九七〇年代から八〇年代半ばまで、IBMワール

ド・トレード南北アメリカの顧問委員会にくわわっている。当時、

同社ではすべてが素晴らしかった。売上高、利益、特許件数など、

どのような基準でみても、業界のリーダーであった。フォーチュ

ン誌五百社でも最高の企業だった。経営幹部は長い休暇をとる。

メインフレーム・コンピューターこそが輝く未来を築く製品であ

り、これまでもつねにそうであったように、今後もそうだと考え

られていた。そして長期にわたって、この見方は正しかった。一

九八〇年に同社は、九五年の売上高が二千五百億ドルを超えると

予想している。八四年には税引き後の利益が六十六億ドル弱にな

り、単一企業の利益としては過去最高になった。九年後の九三年

一月、IBMは単一企業としては過去最悪の約八十億ドルの損失

を計上すると発表した。

何が起こったのだろうか。IBMは完全に自分の流儀に固執す

るようになっていたのだ。コンピューターの世界で何が起こって

48

いるかは知っていたし、一九八一年にはパソコンを開発して成功を収めている。しかし、その将来性を信じてはいなかった。八七年の世界のパソコン販売台数は二十五万台以下になるという社内の予想を信じていた。八五年にはすでに百万台を超えていたのだが。IBMの経営幹部は、巨大なメインフレームの販売とサービスで世界を制覇してきた方法を信じていて、パソコンの販売方法がまったく違っていることを理解せず、理解しようとしなかった。軍の将軍がいつも前回の戦争に備えるように、IBMの経営陣はメインフレーム流の考え方を心から信じていたのである。

一九八〇年代を通して、わたしは何度も、コカ・コーラ社のさまざまなオフィスでパソコンの台数が増えていると指摘したが、同社の経営陣はいつも礼儀正しい笑顔をみせるだけで、とりあおうとはしなかった。IBMの経営陣は川岸にたって、川の流れを眺めているようだった。どれだけ長く眺めていても、川の流れが同じだということはない。いつも変化している。過去は下流にある。将来は上流にあり、機会や危険が訪れるかもしれない。だが、IBMの経営幹部は下流にばかり気をとられていた。収益性が高く美しいメインフレームが川を下って世界各地に運ばれていく様子をみて、悦にいっていたのである。

IBMのパソコンをめぐる物語の終わりを象徴するエピソードは、IBMのブランドだったシンクパッドが中国のノート・パソコン工場で生産されるようになり、レノボのブランドとし

49

て売られるようになったことだ。いうまでもなく、IBMは幸先のよいスタートを切っていただけに、悲しいことだ。いうまでもなく、IBMの業績は回復しているが、経営再建は容易ではなかった。

コンピューター産業の歴史は比較的浅く、短期間に大きく成長してきたが、創造的なイノベーションに基づいて設立されたものの、驚くほど急速に柔軟性を失った企業がかなり多い。こうした企業はIBMほど好運ではなく、生き残ることができなかった。

多くの人が伝説の名前として思い出す企業のひとつに、ディジタル・イクイップメント（DEC）がある（いまでは、知らなかったという人もいるだろうが）。一九五八年、マサチューセッツ工科大学出身のふたりの優秀な技術者、ケン・オルソンとハーラン・アンダーソンによって設立され、ピークになった八〇年代には世界第二位のコンピューター会社で、従業員は約十万人、技術力の高さを誇りにしていた。いち早くインターネットに接続した企業であり、総合的な検索エンジンの先駆けのひとつ、アルタビスタを開発している。社内には早くから電子メールがあり、電子メールの市場価値が認識されるようになったのは、はるか後になってからだ。要するに、DECは多数の分野で時代を先取りしていたのである。にもかかわらず経営が悪化していったのは、MP3型の個人用音楽再生ソフトの開発は、同社の研究所ではじまっている。

正しい方法はひとつしかないと信じこんでいたからだ。すべての点で「DEC中心主義」をつらぬき、独自技術にこだわった。同社の創業者はきわめて優秀だったが、コンピューター事業

で新たな主流になったオープン・システムの採用を拒否した。その結果、経営困難に陥って事業を切り売りすることになり、最後に残った事業も一九九八年に買収された。DECのロゴはその後も短期間、インドの情報技術会社に使われていたのだが。

柔軟性を失うのは、きわめて深刻な病である。

おそらく、この病の症状がとくに重くなった例としては、アメリカの文化を文字通り変えた天才、ヘンリー・フォードを筆頭にあげるべきだろう。

フォードがアメリカで第一位の資産家になったのは、自動車を発明したからではないし、大量生産方式を発明したからでもない。大量生産方式の改良を続けて、自動車を生産することに一生をかけたからだ。ヘンリー・フォードが天才だといえるのは、大量消費市場を直感的に理解していたからだ。コストを引き下げていけば、自動車が金持ちの道楽から大衆の輸送手段に変わることを、当時の誰よりも見抜いていた。そのために、ふたつのリスクをとっている。第一に、自動車一台当たりの利益を圧縮しつづけ、販売台数を増やせるようにした。第二に、一九一四年、自動車組み立て工場の労働者の平均日給が二・五ドル以下であったときに、五ドルという前代未聞の金額を支払うと発表した。

いまでは「生産消費者（プロシューマー）」という言葉がビジネスの世界で使われており、財やサービスを生産すると同時に消費する顧客を意味している。フォードはこの概念を一世紀近く前に予想してい

たのである。一日五ドルを支払うことで、フォードは一夜にして市場の規模を拡大した。自社の工場労働者が、製造している自動車を買えるようになったのだ。そしてそれ以上に重要な点として、不安定なことで有名だった工場労働者が、会社に忠誠心をもつようになった。当時、自動車業界の常識では、工場労働者の回転が速いのは避けがたいことだとされていた。フォードはこの常識が間違っていることを証明したのである。

ところが何年かの後には、これほど先見の明があった天才がまったく柔軟性を失い、経営が破綻寸前になっている。

ヘンリー・フォードはT型フォードについて、「買い手はどんな色でも選べる。黒でありさえすれば」と語ったといわれている。かなりの期間にわたって、これでよかった。だがやがて、人びとは黒のT型フォードに飽きてきた。一九二〇年代にもっと大きく、もっと速く、もっと美しく、明るい色の車に人びとが殺到するようになっても、ヘンリー・フォードはT型フォードにこだわりつづけた。一九〇八年からほとんど変わっていないこのモデルこそ、アメリカ人が望み、必要としているものであり、見方を変えるつもりはないと主張していたのだ。

当然ながら、シボレーやダッジなどの新興企業がフォードの市場を奪うようになり、圧倒的なシェアを誇った同社の地位を脅かすようになった。ついに、もっと理性的な経営幹部の主張が通り、ヘンリー・フォードも、もっとよい車をつくる必要があることを認めた。主力工場の

操業を六か月にわたって止めた後、一九二八年にA型フォードを発売して成功を収めた。しかし、ヘンリー・フォードが柔軟性を欠いていたために、同社は倒産寸前になり、競争相手に対する優位を失って、二度と回復できなくなっている。

もっと最近には、ゼネラル・モーターズ（GM）とフォードはともに、一九八〇年代と九〇年代に大型で燃費の悪いSUV（スポーツ・ユーティリティ・ビークル）に頼り続けたが、市場で最大手の地位を奪うようになったトヨタは、燃費のよいハイブリッド車を開発して成功している。北米トヨタ社長だったジム・プレスはこう語っている。「われわれはみな、同じ事実を知っていた。同じ調査結果をみていた。今後、燃料はもっと豊富になるのか、それとも不足するようになるのか。大気はきれいになっていくのか、汚くなっていくのか。社会の動きに合わせるために、早めにイノベーションを進めるのか。それとも現状にすがりついて手放さず、苦しい結末を迎えるのか」[*]

失敗の物語は企業によって、産業によってもちろん違っている。単純明快な場合も複雑な場合もある。いまの時点から振り返ってみればあきらかだが、二十世紀前半に繁栄していた製氷

[*] ジョージア工科大学コンピューター学部長、リチャード・デミロが二〇〇七年二月二十八日に行った講演、「殺人、饑餓、破局」に引用された言葉。

会社は、他の事業を探すしか方法がなかった。どれほど時代の流れに抵抗しても、電気冷蔵庫の普及で氷が売れなくなるのははっきりしていたのだから。それほど明確だとはいえないのは、三千社以上あった自転車製造会社の大部分が消えていった一方で、一部が自動車事業に転じて生き残り、ライト兄弟の例にみられるように、航空機製造会社になった企業すらあることだ。突出して柔軟性の高い人がいるのはたしかだ。

しかし、かつて業界で傑出した先駆者であった企業が消えていく理由について、実際のところ疑問の余地はない。モンゴメリー・ワードはカタログ販売を発明した企業だ。同社が行き詰まったのは、ひとりの経営者に柔軟性がなかったからである。

モンゴメリー・ワードは、頑固で柔軟性を欠いた弁護士、スーエル・エイブリーのために疲弊することになった。エイブリーは大恐慌の時代、他社が事業を拡大しているときにコストを厳しく削減し、同社を救っている。問題は、大恐慌時の心理を生涯にわたってもちつづけたことだ。「陰気なスーエル」と呼ばれていた。いつになっても、エイブリーのカレンダーは一九二九年のままであった。いつも、数日後には大暴落が起こりかねないと考えていたのである。

第二次世界大戦が終わって、ニューヨーク市近郊のレビットタウンなど、新興住宅街に若い夫婦が移り住むようになったとき、エイブリーは社会が豊かになった現実に気づかなかっただけではなかった。現実をみるのを拒否したのである。一九五〇年代半ばには、十代の子供たち

のお小遣いが、四〇年代の家族全体の可処分所得を上回るまでになっている。アメリカは豊かになり、年々さらに豊かになる道を歩んでいた。しかしエイブリーは頑なだった。戦後の経済ブームを示す事実が周囲にいくらでもあるのに、その事実を認めようとしなかった。投資や事業の拡大はまったく行おうとしない。そのため、戦後の十年間にライバルのシアーズが売上高を二倍に伸ばしたなかで、モンゴメリー・ワードの売上高は逆に十パーセント減少している。

モンゴメリー・ワードはいまでは独立企業としては存続していない。一方、柔軟性に欠けるエイブリーは、すぐにも厳しい不況がくるとの主張を変えないまま、死んでいった。自分の信じていることを信じ、意見を変えようとしなかった。そして、現実を知らせようとした部下を容赦なく解雇することで有名だった。

柔軟性をまったく欠いたために消えていった企業には、リパブリック・スチールもある。一九六〇年代、同社の主要な顧客のひとつは缶詰業界だったが、もっと軽く、輸送費が安いアルミ缶に切り替えはじめていた。当時、リパブリック・スチールは業績が好調で、資金がたっぷりあった。論理的に考えれば、みずからアルミ事業に参入するのが適切だと思えたし、当時であれば、巨額の資金を遊ばせていたのだから、それを使ってアルミ会社を買収するのは簡単だったはずだ。しかし同社の経営陣は柔軟性を欠いていたので、スチール缶を絶対に諦めないと発表した。アルミは「弱い金属」だと語り、あらゆる手段を使って缶詰市場を守るために戦っ

55

た。この戦いで結局、すべてを失うことになる。リパブリック・スチールはいまでは存続していない。

まったく愚かな頑固さの例として、テレビ産業の黎明期にハリウッドがとった姿勢を考えてみるのもいいだろう。わたしがオマハのWOWテレビで野暮ったいトーク・ショー番組を担当して四苦八苦していたころのことだ。強大で裕福なハリウッドは、生まれたばかりのこの産業をどう扱ったのだろうか。馬鹿にしきって、相手にしなかったのである。「ボードビルが死んで、その棺桶がテレビという小さな箱なんだってさ」というのが、当時のハリウッドではやった冗談だ。

大手スタジオは、こんなつまらない事業にはかかわりたくないと思っていた。ミルトン・バールみたいな昔のお笑い芸人の遊び場にしておけばいい。大きなスクリーンと映画にこそ将来があり、今後もその点に変わりはない。そう考えていたのだ。ハリウッドの主流はテレビとテレビ出演者を馬鹿にし、ケネディ政権の時代に連邦通信委員会のニュートン・ミノー委員長が「テレビは巨大な不毛地帯だ」と語ったとき、拍手を送っている。テレビをボイコットして、早く消えてくれるよう期待する動きすらとっている。アメリカ人はみなテレビが大好きになり、例外はハリウッドの人たちだけだったようだ。

もちろん、ハリウッドも結局はテレビを支持するしかなくなったのだが、当初に柔軟性に欠

ける動きをとったために、「映画関係者」と「テレビ関係者」との間に無用な対立が生まれ、と
きには同じ会社のなかですら対立しあうようになっている。そしていうまでもなく、絶好の機
会を活かすことができなかった。大手スタジオはテレビ業界の発展をもたらす原動力になれた
はずだが、実際にはせいぜいのところ傍観者の立場に止まり、最悪の場合には、ことあるごと
に妨害を試みる敵になったのである。

柔軟性を失ったときに何が起こるのか、とくに明確に示す例に航空業界がある。

一九三〇年代から四〇年代にかけて、科学技術の驚異によって交通の新しい時代がはじまっ
たことを何よりもよく示したのは、光り輝く航空機が要人を乗せて、ほんの何時間かで全米各
地を結ぶようになったことだろう。そして、革新的で素晴らしい旅行手段になっただけでなく、
間もなく斬新な方法で販売されるようにもなった。パン・アメリカン航空のホワン・トリップ
が「ツーリスト・クラス」を設けた。これで、航空旅行はもはや、映画の大スターやウォール
街の大物だけのものではなくなった。空の大量輸送の時代がはじまったのである。

このように大胆な動きではじまった航空業界はやがて、長期にわたって低迷するようになる。
航空機は大きくなり、速くなったが、事業のイノベーションは亀のように遅くなったのだ。何
十年もの間、政府の厳しい規制によって自由市場の荒波から守られたことで、航空業界の経営
者は起業家精神にあふれた実業家の性格を失ってしまった。柔軟性を失って硬直的になり、損

失が毎年ふくらむ状況になっても、事業の方法を変えることがなかった。同じ動きを何度も何度も繰り返し、同じように悲惨な決算を続け、繰り返し破産法の適用を受け、そのたびに経営の改善と事業効率の向上を約束してきた。業界にはこうした状況が続く原因として、連邦破産法の会社更生手続きのもとで事業を続けていくのが容易すぎる点を指摘する意見もある。たしかに航空事業は、公共の利益と民間の利益がからみあっている点で複雑な事業だ。だが、航空業界の経営陣は、たったひとつの戦略を引き出し、コストを削減することになっているように思える。従業員から賃金引き下げで譲歩を引き出し、コスト削減だけで収益性を回復することはできない。これは他の点で戦略を変えないかぎり、コスト削減だけで収益性を回復することはできない（わたしの経験からいうなら、常識であり、まったく正しい）。

そこに登場したのが破天荒な革新的起業家、ハーブ・ケレハーだ。ケレハーが設立した航空会社は、既存の航空会社と似ている点がひとつしかない。航空機で乗客を運ぶという点だ。それ以外のほとんどの点は変えている。まず、運航する航空機は一種類しかない。ボーイング七三七だけだ。これで航空機の整備が単純になり、合理化された。航空路線の設定の方法も変えた。座席の決め方も変えた。価格も変え、顧客層も変えた。その結果、どうなったか。サウスウエスト航空は、絶望的だとされて投資家の一部にも見放されていた航空業界で、利益を生み出しているのである（本書の執筆の時点には、サウスウエスト航空が黒字を維持できるかどう

58

# 意見を決して変えない人は、
## たまり水のようなものだ。
### 心が腐ってくる
——ウィリアム・ブレイク

か、疑問になっている。燃料費が高騰するなかで、コスト削減策をとらざるをえなくなっているからだ）。

だから、失敗したい点がある。柔軟性を否定すべきだ。しかし、明確にしておきたいのであれば、柔軟性自体に価値があるわけではないことだ。また、柔軟性をいいたてても、気の弱い経営者があれこれ迷うばかりで厳しい決断を下さないときの隠れ蓑にはならない。

柔軟性と適応力は、企業の指導者に不可欠な資質であり、管理能力や業務の能力、技術力といった個々の能力を超えるものである。柔軟性とは状況を調べ、必要に応じて、状況の変化にいち早く適応することであり、つねに深く考えることが不可欠だとわたしは信じている。要するに、ダーウィンがいう適者生存のカギになるのが柔軟性と適応力なのである。

なかには何世代にもわたって変化に抵抗できる組織もある。この点は認めよう。思い出すのは、ビング・クロスビーに出演してもらっていたころの話だ。クロスビーは間違いなく、その時代にとくに愛され、成功を収めたエンタテイナーだ。そして、ミニッツメイド

社の株式を保有していた。同社を買収した後、コカ・コーラ社は一九六〇年代後半、クロスビーにコマーシャル出演を依頼した。ゴルフをこよなく愛していたクロスビーはわれわれに、オーガスタ・ナショナル・ゴルフ・クラブの会員権を手に入れるよう依頼した。ロバート・ウッドラフが長年、同クラブに関係してきたことを知っていたからだ。

ウッドラフが依頼すると、クラブの帝王はこう答えた。「芸能人は会員にしない」

だが、企業はこのように風変わりな形で変化に抵抗することはできない。実際のところ、とりわけ頑迷な経営者でも、自分が柔軟性に欠ける人間だとはいわないはずだ。まず間違いなく、変化が必要だという考えに口先だけでも賛成し、自社がいかに変化を高く評価し、歓迎しているか、月並みな決まり文句を並べるはずである。しかし実際には、決まり切った現状に安住することになりやすい。なぜか。変化はどのような種類のものでも難しいからだ。自分自身の生活について考えてみるといい。別の町に引っ越すのは、じつに大変なことだ。

だが、企業の経営で柔軟性をなくす原因として、それ以上に大きな点は、つぎの法則に示されている点である。それは、柔軟性のなさの症状でもある。

## 法則3 部下を遠ざける

部下を遠ざけ、超然とした姿勢をとる。何とも魅力的だ。それに、何とも簡単だ。経営者として、部下を寄せ付けない状況をつくるために必要なことはそれほど多くない。まずは物理的な環境を整える。自分専用の安全な場所をつくる。物理的に隔絶した環境ほど、つまらない人間を遠ざけ、つまらないごたごたにわずらわされないようにするのに適した方法はない。だから、従業員が簡単には近づけない本社最上階に大きなオフィスを確保し、ドアを閉め切っておくべきだ。

ある派手なCEOについての話を聞いたことがある。本社ビルのなかに自分専用の宮殿をつくったという。同じ階には経営幹部のオフィスもあるが、フロアの半分がCEO専用になっていて、その奥に閉じこもっている。まず、分厚いガラスのドアで守られている。ドアを入ると

応接室になっていて、壇上に受付係がいて、その前に木製のドアがある。このドアの奥にCEOのオフィスがある。何とも奇抜で、奇妙なオフィスだ。ブラジルの派手な絵画が飾られ、ニューエージ風の音楽が流され、蝋燭が燃やされて、香料の香りがする。壁のひとつには、一面にテレビが並んでいる。CEOのエゴをまつる祭壇のような場所に入ったとき、中間管理職がどれほど圧迫感を感じるか、想像してみるといい。現場で起こった頭の痛い問題を報告する気持ちになるだろうか。入った瞬間に一言も口をきけなくなるはずだ。

自分専用の安全な場所をつくったら、そこを離れてはいけない。同じように安全な場所に閉じこもっている人に会いに行くときだけは例外だ。電話を自分でとるようなことをしてはいけない。絶対にいけない。コピー機がどこにあるのか、知ろうとしてはいけない。何よりもいけないのは、本社のなかを歩き回って、話をすることだ。わたしは本社ビルのなかを歩き回り、目についた部屋に立ち寄り、自己紹介をし、様子はどうなのか、何をしているのか、もっとよくする方法はないかと質問する。

もちろん、部下を遠ざけて、超然とした姿勢をとりたいのであれば、このようなことをしてはいけない。まったくの時間の無駄だ。話を聞けばかならず、日常業務の細々とした点が耳に入る。そんなことは知らない方がいい。従業員の名前を聞くだけでも無駄だ。従業員の名前を覚えようとしてはいけない。すぐに辞めてしまうかもしれない。そうなれば努力が無駄になる

62

（かつて、イギリスの変わった貴婦人の話を読んだことがある。使用人の名前を覚えようとせず、何回か代わった執事をみな、「執事」と呼んでいた。女中は「女中」と呼び、庭師は「庭師」と呼ぶのだそうだ。この貴婦人は部下を寄せ付けない点で、素晴らしいCEOになれる）。

超然とした態度を保ちたいCEOには気の毒だが、とくに成功を収めた経営者は正反対の姿勢をとってきている。事業を築き上げた伝説の経営者の多くは、社内のどの地位にいる従業員とも知り合い、心を通わせる能力がきわめて高いことが特徴のひとつになっている。たとえば、一九六〇年代から七〇年代にかけて、セスナ・エアクラフト社を築いたドウェイン・ウォレスは、カンザス州ウィチタの組み立てラインをよく歩き、約三千人の従業員全員の名前を知っているだけでなく、家族についてまで何かしら知っていたといわれている。このように事業の隅々まで把握し、従業員ひとりひとりと触れあうことは、もちろん、世界的に事業を展開する現在の大企業では不可能だ。しかし本社だけであれば、かなり規模が大きくても十分に可能だし、意味のある目標になる。もちろん、部下を遠ざけて、超然とした態度をとりたいのであれば、そんな努力をすることはない。

もっと部下を遠ざけたいのであれば、優秀なシェフを雇って、以下の推奨を厳格に守るといい。

昼食はかならず、ごく少数の側近とともに、経営者専用のダイニングでとる。あるCEOは

とくに傲慢で、この方法を厳しく守っている。毎日、昼食は本社最上階にあるダイニングで、少数の直属の部下だけととともにとる。階下の従業員の間で、そして株主の間で、不満が沸騰していても、大切な昼食を台なしにするようなことは許さない。この経営者は、利益を増やすことに成功しているのだが、長期的にみれば、その経営スタイルは従業員や顧客や株主を遠ざけたことで、好影響より悪影響の方が多かった。毎日、昼食をともにする経営幹部だけを遠ざけ、経営者が達成しようと努力している点を本心から信じていたのだとしても、常識的に考えれば、少数の味方だけでは結局、目標の達成には不十分だろう。

こうした傲然とした経営スタイルは通常、非生産的である。経営者がどのように従業員に対するかは重要なのだ。超然としていれば、従業員は遠ざかり、噂が噂をよぶ状況になり、ある程度の期間がたつと、反乱すら起こる。だが、失敗したいのであれば、これは最高の戦略だもっともっと部下を遠ざけて超然とした態度をとりたいのであれば、ゴマすりや太鼓持ちで周囲をかためるべきだ。自社の経営者がいかに素晴らしいかだけを考えるスタッフや助言者を雇うべきだ。仕事はそれだけでいい。

どんな点についても、真実をつかむのは困難になりうる。何段階もの管理者を経て報告されてくるのを待つしかなく、それぞれの管理者がそれぞれの見解にあう点だけを伝えようとする可能性があるからだ。だから、このような面倒はすべて避けるべきだ。自分で市場に足を運ぶ

ようなことはすべきではない。本社内の廊下すら歩くのは止める。情報はすべて、信頼するスタッフから入手する。できれば要約だけを提出させる。スタッフの仕事は、経営者に必要不可欠な情報だけを伝え、思い煩う必要のない点はフィルターにかけて伝えないようにすることなのだ。そして、鏡をみたときに、自分がどこからみても素晴らしい人物だというわけではないことが分かったとしても、あるいは、欠点をずばり指摘するわずらわしい配偶者がいるとしても、仕事の場で部下からそんな話を聞かされたいと思うだろうか。思うはずがないのであれば、部下を遠ざけておくべきだ。

取締役に怖がられるようにしておけば、超然としたスタイルをさらに強化できるし、おそらく、報酬も高くなる。社外取締役に関する規制が厳しくなっているなかでも、取締役がどのような人物であれ、CEOに感謝すべき理由を思い出させるのは難しくないはずだ。だが、注意しておくべき点がある。株主と各種政府機関は、経営者の報酬を業績に結びつけることに厳しい姿勢をとるようになっている。素晴らしい。何という間違いだろう。みじめなほど失敗しても、報酬面で失敗の責任をとらされることはないのだ。だから、まず最初に確認しておくべき点として、CEOとして実際の仕事をはじめる前に、会社の業績がどうなろうとも、たっぷりした報酬を受け取れるようにしておくべきだ。将来に批判される可能性をすべて取り除いてお

聞きたくないことを
聞きたいという人間は
めったにいない
　　——ディック・キャビット

自分の言葉や行動をほめてくれる
忠実な人ではなく、
自分の間違いを
親切にとがめてくれる人のことを
考えるべきだ
　　——ソクラテス

くのだ。
　こういう掲示を掲げておくべきだ。
ボスを怒らせるな。悪いニュースは伝
えるな。
　アドルフ・ヒトラーはこの点で達人
だった。秘書のマルティーン・ボルマ
ンは総統によいニュースだけを伝える
ようにすることを、すぐに学んだ。実
際のところ、どの組織にも通常、何ら
かの「よいニュース」はあるものだし、
それをボスに伝えて、昼食会に参加す
る側近グループにくわえてもらえるの
を期待する人がいるものだ。逆に、わ
たしの経験では、いつも偏執的に悪い
ニュースを求め、問題があればすぐに
経営陣に伝わり、素早く行動して悲惨

66

な結果になるのを防げるようにしておくのは、損のない方法である。

チャールズ・ケタリングは天才的な技術者で、ゼネラル・モーターズ（GM）の黄金時代を率いた経営幹部のひとりだが、「わたしに伝えるのは問題だけにしてほしい。よいニュースを聞くと、気力が衰える」と語った。わたしはここまで徹底した姿勢をとるかどうか分からないが、真実は単純である。定義上、組織の進歩はすべて、問題解決の努力から生まれるのであり、そしてもちろん、問題があることを知らなければ、問題の根源をみきわめることもできない。問題をみつけだして、解決のために努力しなければならない。

コカ・コーラ社の世界各地の事業所を訪問したとき、現地のマネジャーが空港で出迎え、コークが大成功を収めている顧客のところに連れて行ってくれることが多かった。しかしわたしは、そうしたリストに入っていない店舗を訪問したかったので、ときに車を止めて、目についた店舗に入ってみることがあった。また、一般の従業員と直接にじっくり話すことを求めた。「わたしはこんなことを考えている。どういうことを考えているか教えてくれないか」と話す。たいていは、率直な話が聞けたと思う。同じ問題点を何人もの従業員から聞くことが多かったからだ。

これは役立つ話だと思うが、第二次世界大戦のとき、ウィンストン・チャーチルは悪いニュースを自分に伝えることだけを任務とする特別の部門をつくっている。どんなことであれ、あ

デスクは、
世界を眺めるには
危険な場所だ
——ジョン・ル・カレ

りのままの事実を伝えるよう求めたのである。これに対してヒトラ
ーは、ぎりぎりまで戦争に勝っていると思い込んでいた。優れた指
導者になりたいのであれば、部下を遠ざけて批判を受け付けないよ
うにする誘惑に打ち勝つ方法を考えるべきだ。ボスの立場に立てば、
この誘惑がきわめて強くなるのだから。

部下が恐怖心をもつ環境をつくる。これはじつに簡単だ。雇用と
解雇の権限がある高い地位には、そういう環境が付随していて、気
がつかない間に部下に恐れられていることもある。バターナット・
コーヒーで、はじめて、何人かのセールスマンを管理する地位につ
いたときのことをよく覚えている。セールスマンは定期的に本社の
わたしのところに来て、各人の営業地域の状況について話し合うこ
とになっていた。営業実績がきわめてよいセールスマンがいた。ト
ップ・クラスの実績だったが、オマハの本社に来ない。いつも何か
理由をあげて行けないと連絡してくる。病気になった、顧客を至急
訪問しなければいけなくなった、車のエンジンがぶっこわれたなど
などである。

偶然、分かったのだが、このセールスマンは素晴らしい実績をあげているのに、わたしを恐れていたのである。本社に行き、エレベーターに乗って上司のオフィスに行くと考えただけで、怖くなっていた。そこで逆の方法をとることにし、こちらが出向いて、本人を車に乗せ、オマハの本社につれてきた。上司のわたしも、本社ビルも、恐れる理由がないことを実感してもらう必要があったのだ。このセールスマンはその後のキャリアで、大きな成功を収めている。

組織の環境という点で、創造力を刺激する緊張と、恐怖心が蔓延する状況とでは大きな違いがある。はたらきやすい環境をつくるのは簡単ではない。組織内のムードや気分を読み取る感性が必要だが、苦労する甲斐はある。フォーチュン誌の「はたらきがいのある会社」百社のリストでいつも上位にあげられている会社の多くが、株主にとってのリターンでもいつも上位に入っているのは偶然ではない。

これに対して恐怖の環境をつくるのは、努力らしい努力を必要としないので、経営者にとって魅力的に違いないと思う。何を理解する必要もなく、この環境をつくりだせる。怒鳴りつけ、癇癪玉を破裂させる。間違いをおかした部下を衆人環視のなかで叱りつける。恥をかかせる。悲しいことだが、こういうことをする経営幹部はいくらでもいる。そのうえ、部下に無茶な要求をしたり、手荒く扱うのを誇りにすらしている。二歳児のように振る舞う。乱暴な態度をとる。わたしの見方では、こういう態度をとるのは正当だといえるほど「創造的」な経営幹部は

ひとりもいない。ファッション雑誌の編集長であろうが、映画監督であろうが、企業再建の新星として売り出し中の経営者であろうが。悪い態度は悪い態度であり、弁解の余地はない。誰でも思わずかっとしたことはあるし、公正でない態度をとったこともある。だがそれは本来、恥じ入るべきことなのだ。もちろんときには逆に、それで短期的に成功する場合もあるし、マスコミにもてはやされる場合すらあることは否定できないのだが。

一九九〇年代初め、タフな企業再建の英雄があらわれたと、マスコミに頻繁にとりあげられた経営者がいた。アル・ダンロップであり、「チェーンソー・ダンロップ」と呼ばれ、「ピンストライプのランボー」を自認していた。従業員を大量に解雇し、あらゆる経費をぎりぎりまで削った。ビジネスウィーク誌によれば、自分こそアメリカで最高のCEOだと語ったという。

このほら話を信じた記者は少なくなかった。マスコミに大いにもちあげられた直後の一九九八年、ダンロップはサンビームという健全な企業を経営し、破綻させている。

部下を完全に遠ざけ、完全に超然とした態度をとりたいのであれば、あらゆる点で自分の功績を真っ先に主張するべきだ。何らかの点で功績を認められることがあれば、すべて自分の手柄だと主張する。何らかの点で非難されることがあれば、自分の責任はまったく認めない。何かよい点で自分の会社にスポット・ライトがあたった場合には、その中心に飛び移り、従業員や経営幹部など、自分を支えてくれた人たちはどこかの端に追いやっておく。功績を独り占め

70

した後、考えにくいことではあるが、自責の念を感じたのであれば、とくに苦労した幹部にクリスマス用のポインセチアか感謝祭用の七面鳥を贈れば、心が軽くなるだろう。あるいは、小さな水晶の文鎮に、相手の名前と「ありがとう」の一言、署名を彫って贈れば、感激してもらえるだろう。

スポット・ライトを独占すればかならず失敗すると保証することはできないが、従業員や幹部を完全に遠ざける一因になるのはたしかであり、そうなれば、大成功を収めるのは極端に難しくなる。

よく知っているか、ともにはたらいた経験のある経営者のなかで、とくに大きな成功を収めた人には、控えめな性格の人が多いことにわたしは気づいてきた。スポット・ライトを避けようとする人が多いのだ。ウォーレン・バフェットが毎年書いている株主への手紙を読めばすぐに気づく点だが、二段落目も終わらないうちにかならず、誰かを思いきり賞賛し、その功績をたたえる文章がある。アレン社のハーバート・A・アレンもそうで、自社のよいニュースがマスコミに取り上げられるときにはかならず、社内の誰かにスポット・ライトがあたるようにすることに熱心だ。何か問題があったとき、期待されたほどの業績をあげられなかったときには逆に、バフェットもアレンも舞台の中央に立って責任を負う。

超然とした態度をとりたい経営者への助言を続けよう。生活のどの部分でも、自分の意見に

賛成する人とだけ付き合う。できれば、他社のCEOだけと付き合うようにする。業界団体の会議や取締役会、加入するクラブや出席するパーティでは、意見があい、裕福な経営者を見つけ出す。経営者の知り合いに、アイデアや意見、政治に関する見方を聞き、そしてとり入れ、報酬の水準を聞く。わたしの経験からいうなら、知り合いの幅を広げるにはかなりの努力が必要だった。簡単なように思えて、じつは簡単ではないのだ。

オフィスのドアに重々しい肩書きが掲げられるようになると、違った意見をもつ人たちはかなり急速に離れていくものだ。だからわたしは、ジョン・ウッデンの話が大好きなのだ。カリフォルニア大学ロサンゼルス校のバスケットボール・チームを率いた著名なコーチだ。強い信念をもち、勝利を収めてきた。しかし、コーチに就任して十六年たったとき、全米大学選手権には毎年出場してきたが、一度も優勝できていなかった。一九六三年、ウッデンが高く評価するアシスタント・コーチ、ジェリー・ノーマンが、ウッデンの方法を何から何まで疑問視するようになった。反対意見を唱え、反乱の芽になりかねない状況になった。だが、ウッデンはノーマンの説得を受け入れ、戦術を事実上すべて変えることにした。その結果、翌年には全米大学選手権で優勝し、その後も十一年間に九回優勝している。ウッデンは後にこう語っている。

「人生で何をするにしても、自分の意見に反対して議論してくれる優秀な人物を周囲に集めるべきだ」

この点を理由のひとつに、経営は個人ではなくチームで行うべきだと、わたしは強く確信している。バークシャー・ハザウェイのウォーレン・バフェットとチャーリー・マンガー、キャピタル・シティーズのトム・マーフィーとダン・バーク、ディズニーのフランク・ウェルズとマイケル・アイズナーのように、チームを構成する複数の指導者が補完しあい、均衡しあっていれば、ひとりの欠点がべつの人の長所で相殺されることが多くなりうる。これに対して、圧倒的な力をもつひとりの経営者だけしか活躍できないようになっている場合、警戒した方がいい。そのひとりがどういう人物かでどういう会社なのかが決まり、そのひとりに問題があれば、会社の先行きは暗いからだ。

ひとりだけスポット・ライトの明るい光を浴び、周囲の人たちが目立たないようにしている経営者には、警戒すべきだ。

わたしはコカ・コーラで好運に恵まれていた。部下にはきわめて優秀な経営幹部が何人もいて、わたしが間違っていると思えば、そう指摘するのをためらわなかったからだ。それも、少々どころではなく、完全に間違っていると指摘してくれた。また、しっかりした秘書にも恵まれた。とても強い意志をもっていて、ときにわたしが書いた手紙を戻してくることがあった。じつに柔らかい笑みを浮かべ、魔法のような表現を使う。高校時代に校内新聞の編集者がよく使ったのと同じ表現だ。「ほんとうにこのままでだしていいのですか」。たいていはよくなかっ

73

た。これは電子メールにはない手紙の利点だ。考える時間がとれる。経営チームについては、後にもっと詳しく書く。

世界中の人がみな、自分と同じように生活していると考える。これも、超然とした態度をとるコツのひとつだ。ジョンソン政権の副大統領だったヒューバート・ハンフリーがかつて、こう提案した。連邦議会の議員や、政府高官はみな、週に一度は公共交通機関を利用して、庶民の生活に触れるべきだと。大企業経営者もそうすべきだ。「会社ではCEOでも、自宅ではゴミも出す」という古い言葉を思い出すのも一助になるだろう。

コカ・コーラ社の古参の一人から、こんな話を聞いたことがある。ニューイングランドの第三世代のボトラーに、貴族の家系の人がいる。たぶん、工場に足を踏み入れたことはないし、コークを飲んだことも何年もないはずだ。それでも自信満々で、日曜日の夕方近くにラジオでコマーシャルを流すのはおかしいのではないかといいだした。「日曜の午後には誰もラジオなんか聞いていない」というのだ。なぜか。「その時間には皆、ポロをやっている」。まったく超然としている。こうしていれば、いつも自分は最高だと考えていられるし、顧客や従業員、株主とはまったく接触しなくてもすむ。そして何よりもいいのは、その点に気づきもしないことだ。

第三の法則を厳格に守り、超然とした姿勢を保っていれば、自分の事業について何を知らな

いのかに気づくことはないし、そのうえ、自分が知っていることは正しいと完全に、本心から確信していられる。超然とした姿勢が極端になれば、神の特別の庇護を受けているという感覚すら生まれてくることが多い。ヘンリー・フォードやスーエル・エイブリーといった経営者や、ゼロックスやＩＢＭなど、大成功を収めた企業の経営幹部の多くは、自分の正しさを確信するようになっただけでなく、それ以上に致命的な点として、少なくともときおりは、自分が間違えることなどありえないと信じるようにすらなっている。企業の本社が発行する文書で、「われわれが間違えるはずがない、われわれは最高だ」と主張されるようになれば、よほど警戒すべきだ。その企業の経営者が自信満々になって、抵抗しがたいほど魅力的なつぎの法則を採用しようとしているからだ。

# 自分は無謬だと考える

何よりもまず、問題や間違いを認めてはいけない。何かが悪い方向に向かっていることが分かった場合、隠すか、それよりいいのは、完全な危機になるまで待って、外部要因によるものだと主張するか、誰か他人に責任を押し付ける。顧客は厄介なことが多い。何か問題が起こったとき、顧客に責任を押し付けることはつねに可能だ。

企業の年次報告書を読むと、驚くことが多い。とくに株主への手紙の部分には驚かされる。どれを読んでも、会社にとって悲惨な一年だったときですら、経営者の手紙はじつに巧みに、さまざまな原因を言い訳にしていることが多いのだ。為替相場の予想外の変動から、例年になく多かったハリケーン被害まで、さまざまな点が並べられている。たぶん、何度も読んだことがあるだろうが、どうしようもないものはどうしようもないと主張したいときの決まり文句が

使われている。「間違いが犯された」というのだ。壁が崩れ、天井が落ち、埃が舞っているといういうのに、その全体に責任を負う人物が明るくこう主張するのだ。「間違いが犯された」と。もちろん、「わたしによってではない」といいたいのである。

こういうものばかり読んでいると、ウォーレン・バフェットがバークシャー・ハザウェイ会長として毎年書いている有名な株主への手紙は、まったく新鮮に感じる。業績が前年より悪かったり、予想より悪かったりした年には、バフェットは「業績はよくなかった。これはわたしの責任だ」とすぐに認める。資本を巧みに配分して利益を獲得してきた点で、ほとんど並ぶもののないほど成功してきたにもかかわらず、自分が間違えるはずがないなどと主張することはない。たとえば一九九六年の株主への手紙では、USエアーへの投資でぶつかった問題を取り上げ、こう書いている。「別の状況で、友人に聞かれたことがある。『そんなに金持ちだというのだったら、頭が切れないのはなぜなんだ』。USエアーへの投資がみじめな状態になっているのをみて、この友人の言葉はもっともだと思われるかもしれない」

コカ・コーラ社にも、自分が間違えるはずがないと考える病を放置していたとき、何が起こるかを示す好例がある。

一九九九年、ベルギーで何人かの子供が体調を崩し、その前に飲んだコカ・コーラのためだと話した。コカ・コーラ社は少しばかり検討しただけで結論を下した。現地から何千キロも離

れた本社にいて、自社の商品に子供の病気の原因になるものは入っていないと考えた。何も問題はない。そうした点で、自社が間違えるはずがない。自社は無謬だと考えたのである。

子供たちは病気になったと考えた。親も子供が病気になったと考えた。医者も、子供たちはたしかに病気になったと考えた。だが、コカ・コーラ社の主要な幹部はそう考えなかった。

売上は急減し、いやになるほど時間をかけたすえ、コカ・コーラ社の経営陣はようやく、危機が起こったその日にとるべきだった行動をとらざるをえなくなった。問題の商品をすべて、商店の棚から引き揚げたのである。会社の経営陣が知るかぎり、コークはまったく汚染されていなかった。だが、世間の見方ははっきりしていた。この見方を否定する明確な証拠が示されないかぎり、見方が事実になる。問題は長引き、コカ・コーラ社の悪評判が広まる一方になった。

この結果、コカ・コーラ社の百二十年の歴史で最大の製品回収を行うことになった。傷ついた評判とイメージを回復するには、それから何か月もの期間がかかり、巨額の損失を被っている。評判とイメージはカネでは買えない。だから、命をかけて守るべきだ。諺にもあるように、「巨額の富より高い評判を選べ」なのだ。

シュリッツ・ビールはアメリカの醸造業界でとくに有名なブランドのひとつであった。覚えているだろうか。一九七五年にはバドワイザーにつぐ全米第二位であり、第一位の座を狙っていて、バドワイザーの経営陣は洗練されたマーケティングの能力に自信をもっていて、バドワイ

ザーを販売するアンハイザー・ブッシュの経営陣は頭が固いとみていた。競争相手よりも徹底して「マーケット・リサーチ」を行い、自分たちの方がはるかに頭がいいと自負するようになった。自分たちの方法は完璧で、間違えるはずがないと考えるようになってもいる。原料費を切り詰める方法をとったとき、醸造業界の伝統に反することになるとしても、何の問題もないとみていた。そしてしばらくは、素晴らしい方法だと思えた。

しばらくは、すべてが順調だった。

だがシュリッツは、その後も醸造工程に変更をくわえていった。醸造期間を短縮するために化学物質を使うようになり、ビールの品質に影響を与えるようになった。

ビールのようにごく一般的な商品でも、品質に対する信頼を失えば、すべてを失う。シュリッツ・ビールが禁じ手を使って原料費を切り詰めているという話が伝わるようになると、消費者の反応は厳しかった。ブランド・ロイヤリティが重要な意味をもつ事業で、シュリッツは消費者に見放されるようになったのだ。全米で第一位の座を争っていたシュリッツは、一九八〇年代半ばにはもはや、「ミルウォーキーを有名にしたビール」ではなくなっていた。市場から姿を消したのである。

われわれは何でも知っている、われわれは無謬だという態度を経営陣がとったために、多くの企業が現実を無視するようになり、機会を逃してきた。

ゼネラル・モーターズ（GM）は、時間と資金を費やしてラルフ・ネーダーを抑え込もうとしたために、評判に傷がついて、取り返しのつかない打撃を受けている。一九六五年、ネーダーは『どんなスピードでも自動車は危険だ』を出版し、自動車産業全体の安全への取り組みを批判した。とくに有名になった章で、シボレーの新しいリア・エンジン車、コルベアの安全性を取り上げている。GMの経営陣は、ネーダーら批判者に面会する方法もとれたし、業界の各社と協議して、リア・エンジン車全体の安全性を高めるためにネーダーに協力する可能性もとれたはずだ。しかしそうはせず、探偵を雇ってネーダーの身辺を調査し、プライバシーの侵害で訴えられる羽目になった。GMの経営陣はネーダーの批判を絶好の機会ととらえて、市民の安全を心から気遣っているというイメージを強化することもできたはずだが、この機会を逃して、GMは無謬だという見方を何が何でも守ろうとした。その結果、消費者の信用を失って、カネには換算できないほどの打撃を受けている。

前章でわたしは、部下にきわめて優秀な経営幹部が何人もいて好運だったと書いた。どの幹部も、わたしが経営者として無謬だといえないと考えれば、すぐに指摘してくれたからだ。なかでも重要な指摘を受けたのは、一九八九年にベルリンの壁が崩壊した直後だ。

失敗したければ、わたしと同じように行動すればいい。

わたしは西ドイツで現地事業の幹部との会議に出席し、本社国際事業部門の責任者でドイツ

人のクラウス・ハレも同席した。いつも通り、翌年の事業計画を検討したとき、ドイツの経営チームは大型のプロジェクトを提案した。五億ドルを超える資金を、民主化されたばかりの東ドイツに投資する計画であった。これだけの資金を投じれば、そのとき策定の過程にあった全社の予算が大きく狂うことになる。わたしはこの計画を拒否したが、そのときの姿勢は頑なで、ひどかったようだ。会議の後、ハレがわたしのところに来て、ドイツ事業の責任者が辞任したがっているという。

わたしはショックを受けた。なぜだ。

ハレはこう説明した。「意見を聞こうともしなかったからです。投資の大部分はドイツのボトラーが負担します。そもそも、東ドイツの可能性をご存じない。訪問したこともない。これが大きな機会になりうるかどうか検討するまでもなく、頭から拒否してしまった」

そして、こう助言した。「少なくとも、もう一度話すべきです。しかし、それ以上のことをするようお願いします。わたしと一緒に東ドイツに行き、現地を実際にみて、判断を下していただきたい」

そこで、東ドイツに行った。各地をまわった。そして、どこに行っても事業機会があることが分かった。わたしの見方は完全に変わった。そこで、関係者全員を集め、見方が狭く頑なだったと謝罪した。そして、東ドイツでいくつかの工場を買う計画をただちに決定した。

一か月後、スイスのダボス世界経済フォーラムで、わたしはコカ・コーラ・システムが東ドイツなどの東ヨーロッパ諸国に十億ドルを投資する計画を発表した。この計画は、コカ・コーラ社にとって、当時進めていた世界事業の新たな拡大を前進させるうえで、大きな転換点になったし、欧米の企業による旧ソ連圏への投資でも突破口になっている。コカ・コーラ社はボトリングと物流の事業、トラック、自動販売機に設備投資を行ったうえ、世界各地でそうなったように、経済開発の原動力になり、瓶や缶、箱、パレットの製造、印刷など、関連産業の開発を支える事業機会を生み出している。

コカ・コーラ社がやがて、東ドイツなどの東ヨーロッパ諸国で利益をあげるようになったことからも、快適な本社で報告書を読んでいるだけでは、ある国やある事業の状況を十分に理解することはできないといえる。ネビル・イズデルは二〇〇四年にコカ・コーラ本社に復帰してCEOに就任したとき、何ひとつ変更しないまま、当初の百日間を使って世界各地の事業を訪問し、従業員や顧客と話し合っている。この単純な真実をしつこいいほど強調しておきたい。何段階もの官僚組織のフィルターを通すので自分の目でみることがいかに役立つかを。そして、はなく、自社の従業員の意見を直接に聞くようにすれば、ほんとうに役立つのである。

マーケティングの機会があっても、それを活かすためには、現場で何が起こっているのか、どのようなトレンドがあるのか、事業を行っているそれぞれの場所で何が重要になっているの

かを知らなければならない。最善の情報源は自社の末端の従業員であり、各地の現場ではたらくチームである。経営方針や経営戦略は、上層部からの命令として現場に伝えられるだけであれば、失敗する運命にある。失敗する確率を高めたいのなら、自分の判断はいつも完全に正しく、間違っている可能性などないと主張すればいい。自分の知らない何かをひとつかふたつ、他人が知っている事実を否定すればいい。「確信は確実性を示す基準にはならない」というオリバー・ウェンデル・ホームズ判事の至言を無視すればいい。

失敗したいのであれば、無謬の指導者を装うといい。

そして、もっと派手に失敗したいのであれば、次の法則が最適だろう。

# 法則5 反則すれすれのところで戦う

わたしが三歳のとき、自宅が全焼した。一家はほとんどすべてを失った。どこかに移り住むしかなかったが、大恐慌がはじまっていた。父のレオはこのとき四十二歳、文字通り一から再出発するしかなかった。だが、生活を立て直すことができた。農場を離れ、アイオワ州スーシティに移り、地元の家畜市場で職を得た。家畜を集めて売買する大きな市場だ。父はここで腕を磨き、やがて地域でもとくに賢明な家畜商のひとりになっている。家畜をみて素早く評価する点で、神業のような能力を身につけたのである。何年かの後には、五十頭ほどの牛の群れをみただけで、平均体重を十ポンド（約四・五キロ）以内の誤差であてられるかどうか、カウボーイ・ハットを賭けないかと誰にでももちかけるようになった。わたしは十代のころ、夏休みに父のところではたらいていたが、賭けに応じた人をみたことはない。カウボーイ・ハットを

84

# 成功が長続きするのは
# 原則を曲げることなく
# 達成しているときだ
## ──ウォルター・クロンカイト

とられたことはなかったのではないかと思う。

だが父は、牛をみるたしかな目よりも、はるかに貴重なものをもっていた。詐欺師まがいが多い商売で、表裏のない誠実な人間だという確固とした評判を獲得していたのだ。ネブラスカ州西部やワイオミング州、サウスダコタ州の牧場主が有り金をはたき、ときには悪天候のなかで何か月もかけて牛を育て、貨車に乗せ、父に電話をかけて依頼する。「値段は任せるから、いちばんよい価格で買ってくれ」

牧場主はそうはいわないが、父を信頼しているのだ。この点でわたしは父にならいたいと願ってきた。信頼される人間になりたい。恐れられる人間ではない。愛される人間でもない。信頼される人間だ。まっすぐで誠実だと皆に信頼される人間、公正だと信頼される人間、正しい行動をとると信頼される人間である。

反則すれすれのところで勝負していれば、顧客や従業員に信頼されるとは思えない。そして、失敗する。

前述のように、ロバート・ウッドラフがコカ・コーラ社の世界

事業を構築するとき、信頼が基礎になっていた。信頼は当時もいまも、どのような事業にも不可欠な基礎だ。技術は進歩し、経営とマーケティングの新しい流行はつぎつぎにあらわれるが、すべての事業は煎じ詰めれば信頼の問題なのだ。商品は期待を裏切らないと消費者が信頼してくれる。経営陣は優秀だと投資家が信頼してくれる。経営陣は責務を果たすと従業員が信頼してくれる。これが基礎なのだ。

近年、優秀で精力的なのだが、何が正しく何が間違っているのかについて、しっかりした見方をもっていない人がかなり多いように思える。

Kマートとウォルマートはともに、一九六二年に設立されている。だがKマートは危険な道を歩み、二〇〇二年に倒産する結果になった。それまでの間、経営幹部が腐敗し、私腹を肥やしているという噂や主張が絶えなかった。そして実際にも、不動産を担当する経営幹部が贈賄罪で有罪判決を受けている。違法すれすれのところで勝負してきたのであり、ときには違法の部分に入ったと裁判所に判断される場合があった。

腐敗が広がっている一因は、社会全体が礼節を失い、倫理にもとる行動を許容するようになってきたことにある。いまは亡きダニエル・パトリック・モイニハン上院議員はかつて、これを「決定的な下方への逸脱」と呼んでいる。

一九六九年に有名な実験が行われた。行ったのはフィリップ・ジンバルドであり、スタンフ

86

ォード大学の心理学者だ。ナンバー・プレートを外し、ボンネットを開けた車を、一台はニュ
ーヨーク市のブロンクスに、もう一台はカリフォルニア州パロアルトに放置した。ブロンクス
では、車は何分もたたないうちに部品をとられ、壊されてしまった。

パロアルトではまったく違った状況になった。何も起こらなかったのである。一週間以上た
っても、車は無傷のままであった。そこである日、ジンバルドはハンマーで車の一部を破壊し
た。すぐに、通行人がハンマーを交替に使って、車を壊すようになり、数時間で車は完全に破
壊された。この実験から、犯罪の「割れ窓理論」が生まれた。割れた窓を放置しておくと、す
ぐに同じビルの残りの窓ガラスも割られるという見方だ。この理論によれば、割れた窓は「誰
も気に掛けていない。窓を割ったって、何も問題は起こらない。もっと割れ。問題はない」と
いうメッセージになるという。

ある意味で、数年前にはビジネスの世界にこれに似た状況があった。倫理面で小さな問題が
あっても、無視された。

腐敗が広がっている別の原因は、経営者がとんでもなく時間を使って、「市場」を成り立たせ
ている貴重な人たちのご機嫌をとるようになったことだ。貴重な人たちとは、ウォール街のア
ナリストだ。

コカ・コーラ社は設立から百二十年のほとんどにわたって、ウォール街とはあまり関係をも

たなかった。年次報告書は発行していたが、立派なものではない。わずか八ページのモノクロで、ティッシュ・ペーパーのような薄い紙を使い、写真はなかった。「知る必要があることはここに書いてある。読んでほしい」という態度だったのだ。

経営幹部がウォール街の人たちと話すことはめったになかった。広報部門は、経営幹部がマスコミで取り上げられるよう努力していたわけではない。取り上げられないようにすることを任務としていたのだ。スターは商品であって、CEOやCFOではないと考えられていた。

しかし、コカ・コーラ社でもほほどの企業でも、年次報告書はまったく違った意味をもつようになってきた。広報の手段になったのだ。会社の業績を報告するだけのものではなくなった。いまではほとんどの企業で、年次報告書はカラー印刷を何ページにもわたって使い、あらゆる人種、あらゆる宗教、あらゆる文化の人たちの写真を掲載している。そのうえ、メイン州の原生林を二ページ見開きの大きな写真で紹介したりしている。これほど紙を無駄遣いしても、切られずに残っている木があるようなのだ。美しい写真を満載した報告書のどこかに、決算報告の数値も書かれているというわけだ。

一九八二年に、史上最長の強気相場がはじまった。八七年に一時的に下げる場面もあったが、十八年間にわたって株式相場は上昇を続けた。その間に、多くの企業はアナリストを前庭に入れるようになり、やがて玄関に、台所に、そしてリビングに入れるようになる。そしてある朝、

目が覚めると、アナリストが隣に寝ていたということになった場合が多い。

アナリストはもはや、会社の事業を知るために来ているのではない。経営者と睦言をかわし、会社の指導部がとりうる行動をささやくために来ているのだ。

この大強気相場の前には、最高財務責任者（CFO）はどれほど創造的かで評価されることはなかった。頭が切れ、タフで、たいていはまったくのケチだった。基本的な責任は入金と出金が正しいかどうか、細かく確認することだ。金貨を扱っていれば、一枚ずつ噛んで、たしかに金(きん)かどうか確認したはずだ。経営者が喜ぶような話をもっていくとは考えられていなかった。事実を知らせるのがCFOの役割だったのだ。どんな点であれ、飾り立てて話したりはしない。CFOはCEOに真実を率直に伝えると期待できた。よいことも、悪いことも、よくも悪くもないことも。

しかし株価が勢いよく上昇するようになると、そして経営者がウォール街の人間を寝室に入れるようになると、CFOが率いる財務部門はゆっくりと、しかし確実に、プロフィット・センターになっていった。それも重要なプロフィット・センターに。「四半期の一株当たり利益が五セント足りない。あと五セント、どこかで探してくれ」と、あせったCEOが命じる。

やがてCFOは、会社の透明性と財務の健全性を守る裏方ではなくなった。何人ものCFOが、ビジネスの世界の大スターになった。そして、アナリストはウォール街の大スターになり、

投資銀行の業績を好調に保つうえで重要な役割を担うようになってきた。

株式を公開している企業がほぼすべて、ウォール街とつねに接触するようになり、短期的な業績を高めるよう、つねに要求されることになった。この要求はきわめて強いので、短期的な業績で目標を達成するよう求める圧力はほとんど逃れようがない。

かなりの経営者は「これは正しいことなのか」とは質問しなくなり、「これは合法なのか」と質問するようになった。こうなればあと一歩で、「これをやっても、ばれないか」と質問するようになる。

そうなった企業は、最後には悲劇になる。数値をごまかし、会計を操作する。そうやって負債を隠すか、利益をかさ上げするか、税金を避ける。なかにはこの三つを同時に行うものもいる。

こうした操作にかかわれば、最後には世間に非難され、刑務所に入る場合もある。CEOやCFOのなかには、経営者なのだから、社会を拘束している倫理や法律には縛られないと感じている人がいる。たとえば、ケーブル・テレビ大手のアデルフィア・コミュニケーションズでは、株式を上場した後も、創業者のジョン・リーガスと息子たちが同社を一族の私的な金庫のように扱っていた。エンロンやタイコなどの急成長企業が苦境に陥ったが、これら企業のCEOやCFOは株主や従業員を無視した経営を行っていた。

ほとんどの企業はルールにしたがって行動しており、第五の法則を取り入れていない。しかし、反則のラインすれすれのところで勝負している経営者も多く、ラインを踏んだり、ときにはラインをこえることもある。法律に違反して摘発された企業の数は多く、アルファベットでみて、Aのアデルフィアから Wのワールドコムまでにわたっている。残念なことだが、これら企業の不正が大々的に報道され、企業全体の評判にある程度傷がついた。不正をはたらいた経営者が派手なパーティを開き、政府高官や権力者やとびきりの美人と楽しんでいる様子をとった写真が、終わりがないと思えるほどつぎつぎにマスコミで報じられ、われわれ全員が傷ついている。

問題の別の側面として、有名人になることへの執着がある。これは現代社会でとくに不健全な面のひとつだ。一日二十四時間、テレビ・カメラがまわり、番組が放送されているいま、キャスターやレポーターはつねに新しい話題の人を探している。著名な経営者のなかにも、マスコミの要望に喜んで応じる人がいる。雑誌の表紙を飾りたい一心で、無理をする経営者もいる。

一財産を使って派手なパーティを開き、豪奢な家を建てる。

少しばかりでも重要な地位についた人は、注意した方がいい。マスコミが天まで届くかと思えるほどもちあげたり、本人にすれば考えにくいほど魅力的で優秀な人物だと褒め称えたりする。あるいは逆に、『クリスマス・キャロル』のスクルージも逃げ出すほどの悪人だと非難する。

管理者は
物事を正しく行うことに
関心をもつ。
指導者は
正しい行動をとることに
関心をもつ
——作者不明

わたしはコカ・コーラ社の社長に選ばれた直後に、経済関係の雑誌や新聞の記事に取り上げられたことがある。自分のことが書かれているとは思えないような記事になっていた。会社を救う白馬の騎士だと書かれるか、有名なピーターの法則の通りに、能力の限界を超えるところまで昇進した人物だと書かれるか、どちらかであった。

わたしは中西部の出身だ。故郷ではとくに裕福な農場主でも、自分の地位を隠そうと懸命になる。だから、大物ぶらないようにするのは、それほど難しくない。だが、有名人をもてはやす風潮に誘惑されて、倫理上、こえてはいけない一線をこえるようなことをしないよう、注意するべきだ。

アメリカでは、経済関係の大規模な不祥事が起こるたびに、規則がつくられてきたように思える。

債券と株式の売買を規制する試みが最初にとられたのは、一七九二年の暴落の後である。財務次官補だったウィリアム・デュアが倫理にもとる投機を行って、暴落の引き金になった。アメリカの初代財務長官、アレグザンダー・ハミルトンは清廉潔白な政治家だった。しかし、側近のデュアは、アメリカ人としてはじめて、インサイダー取引で有罪になった人物という不名誉な形で歴史に名を残すことになった。デュアが悪質な相場操縦を行ったことから、コーヒーハウスや歩道で取引していた証券トレーダーは、証券取引を集中して行う建物に移り、市場の管理と取引の記録の向上をはかった（こうしてニューヨーク証券取引所が設立された）。

十九世紀後半には、ユリシーズ・グラント政権の不祥事と、新興資本家による買い占めと競争を契機に、さらに規則がつくられ、反トラスト法が制定された。一九二〇年代初めには、ハーディン政権のティーポット・ドーム事件の後にさらに法律がつくられ、一九二九年の大暴落の後、大恐慌の時代にはさらに大量の法律が制定されている。その後の数十年にも、価格協定、不正入札、不公正競争などを規制しようと、大量の法規がつくられている。

だが、法律をいくら制定しても、人が倫理的になるわけではない。すでに七万一千ページにも及ぶ連邦法規があり、証券取引委員会（SEC）とニューヨーク証券取引所の規則があるなかで、エンロンの不正会計問題が起こっている。詐欺を禁じる法律は明確に規定されているが、二〇〇七年夏に住宅融資をめぐる問題があきらかになる前、インターネットのサイトで偽の身

分証明書類や、偽の給与明細書すら手に入れられるようになっていた。住宅融資を受けるのに必要だからだが、融資担当者はそういうごまかしが可能なだけでなく、かなりの確率で使われることを知っていたはずだ。いわゆるサブプライム危機は、じつにお粗末な判断の結果であり、一部は完全な犯罪行為の結果である。

本書を執筆しているいま、規制が強化されて、厳しすぎるという意見すらあるほどになっており、さらに、経営陣の過剰な報酬や疑わしい行動に対する世間の怒りが強まっているが、それでも、反則すれすれの行動をとっている経営者の話を聞くことがある。

これは理解しがたいことだ。わたしにいえるのは、こうした経営者は過去にもいまも、まったく現実離れしていて（第四の法則を参照）、人なら誰しももっている弱さ、本人ももっている弱さを理解できなくなっているということである。

わたしは第二次世界大戦末期に海軍に入り、とくに深刻な傷病兵を収容する病院に勤務することになった。手や足を失った将兵、視力や聴力を失った将兵、ショックで声がでなくなった将兵などである。軍の記録にはわたしが高校時代にスピーチの経験があることが書かれていたに違いない。発声障害に陥った将兵向けのリハビリ・センターに配属されたからだ。わたしは何の訓練も受けていなかったが、病院にいた本物の療法士からいくつかの方法を学び、ふたりで協力して工夫した結果、患者の会話能力の回復にそこそこ成功した。

患者の間には階級はない。兵や下士官も、士官も同じように扱う。リハビリを行うと、兵や下士官は必死に努力して完全に回復しようとするが、士官のなかには自分の能力に絶大の自信をもっていたために、まったく意気消沈して、みる影もない状態になる人もいた。この病院での経験のために、わたしはごく若いときから、人間の気高さと弱さを強く意識するようになった。気高さと弱さはかけ離れたものではない。人は立ち上がって偉大な仕事をすることがある。

そして、急速にどこまでも落ち込むことがある。

病院ではどこでもそうだが、軍の病院のように症状が深刻な患者が多い病院ではとくに、各人の違いよりも類似が目立つようになる。誰でも同じように必要とする点、同じように傷つきやすい点に注意するようになる。人は誰でも、ひっかけば血がでる。

イエズス会の聖職者で、優れた古生物学者のティヤール・ド・シャルダンは、「人が進化して未来を切り開いていくのは、すべての人たちとのつながりのなかでしかありえない」と述べている。ほんとうにそうだと思う。したがって、思いやりと敬意をもって他の人たちに接するのは、人として義務だというように止まらない。われわれ人類が生き残っていくために不可欠なのである。倫理を無視する人はしばらくの間、うまくいくことがありうるし、かなりの期間にわたってうまくいくこともある。しかし倫理感覚に欠け、謙虚さに欠けることから、いずれ失敗する。土台が腐っていれば、永続する強固な事業を築くことはできない。

わたしが誇りとしてきた点だが、コカ・コーラ社はつねに信頼に基づき、正しい行動をとることが絶対に必要だという信念に基づく企業文化をもってきた。

いまでも鮮明に覚えていることがある。一九七〇年代にNBCテレビが、移民労働者の窮状を伝えるドキュメンタリーを放送した。その番組で取り上げられた労働者の多くが人材派遣会社に雇われて、フロリダ州にあるミニッツメイドの果樹園ではたらいており、恐ろしいほど劣悪な環境で生活している場合もあることを知って、われわれは仰天した。当時のCEO、ポール・オースティンは、ルーク・スミス社長ら数人に現地を調査するよう命じた。わたしもその ひとりだった。移民労働者の生活環境はたしかに、まったくひどい場合が多かった。オースティンはこの問題を調査した上院委員会の公聴会で証言した。労働者の状況を具体的に指摘する質問を受けて、オースティンはそれが事実であることを認めたうえで、こう答えている。「状況はいわれる通りに悪いというに止まりません。上院議員が想像もできないほどひどいのです。問題を解決するたコカ・コーラ社は良心の問題として、この状況をまったく許容できません。問題を解決するために、最善を尽くします」

そして、実際に最善を尽くした。現地調査の結果に基づいて計画を立て、労働者の生活水準を全体的に引き上げていった。はじめに考えたのは、住宅の改善、果樹園までの輸送手段の改善、果樹を摘む作業に使う軍手の支給、果樹園での冷水の支給など、物質的な生活水準の向上

96

に必要なものを労働者に提供することであった。古い住宅はブルドーザーで撤去した。だがやがて、物質的な生活水準の向上だけでは不十分なことに気づいた。そこで、行動科学者のチームをフロリダに派遣し、人間的な生活の基本にかかわる問題に総合的に取り組む計画を立てることにした。この調査の結果に基づいて、診療所を開設し、社会福祉センターをつくって、保育、就学前児童の教育、成人教育を行うようになった。さらに、賃金と保険などの付加給付を引き上げている。また、地域の自治組織がつくられ、労働者が運営することになった。

農業労働組合が組織化に乗り出し、当初はある程度争議も起こったが、友好的に解決することができた。その後、果樹園の大部分が売却されるか、他の用途に転換されるまで、移民労働者との関係は良好だった。

オースティンが議会証言で語ったように、われわれは良心の問題として、移民労働者の悲惨な状況を許容できなかった。これは広報の問題ではない。正しい行動をとるという問題なのだ。資本主義体制に対する人びとの信認を維持するためには、上に立つ人間は道義心と良識をもっていなければならない。わたしが深く懸念している点だが、ラトガース大学の調査で、大学院のうち、経営大学院で学ぶ院生がもっとも人をだます可能性が高いとの結果がでている。最近では、いくつもの経営大学院で倫理の問題を扱うようになっており、「ビジネス倫理」と銘打ったコースをつくっていると報じられている。成功するよう期待したい。だが、そうしたコー

スで教えるのが、通常はビジネスの経験がない教員であれば、それほど効果はないだろう。実

社会では、倫理の問題は日常的に判断を迫られる。

わたしの父が倫理を学ぶ必要がなかったのはたしかだ。父は中西部の価値観のなかで育った。口にだした約束は証書と同じであり、握手は弁護士連中にとっての契約書と同じという価値観だ。父ならたぶん賛成しただろうが、ピーター・ドラッカーはビジネス倫理などありえないと語っている。あるのは、限定のつかない倫理だけだと。自分の生活のなかで、ビジネスと他の部分を分けることはできない。分野ごとに違った倫理や価値観をもっているのであれば、経営者とはいえない。テレビ・ドラマ『ザ・ソプラノズ——哀愁のマフィア』の主人公、トニー・ソプラノだ。

父はいつも、ぐっすり眠れるといっていた。「心にやましいところがなければ、雷がなろうと眠れる」という古い諺は正しいのではないかと思う。

# 法則6 考えるのに時間を使わない

いまの社会は技術に夢中になっている。全体としては、これはよいことだ。そのために生活が向上し、ときには驚くほど向上しているのだから。エジソンらの過去の発明家のお陰で電球が使える。いまの発明家のお陰で、信じがたいほど高速のコンピューターが使える。ジョージア工科大学コンピューター学部長、リチャード・デミロによれば、いまは技術革新のまったく新しい時代だという。世界は変わりつづけている。だから、本書で触れた技術も、読者が読むときには、かなりの部分が時代後れになっていると断言できる。

とはいえ、最新の技術を使えばこれこれのことができるというとき、かならずしもそれをするべきだとはいえない。最新技術を使っても生活が複雑になるばかりで、何かが目にみえてよくなるわけではない場合もある。それどころか逆に、はっきりと悪くなることもある。たとえ

> ほんとうに問題なのは、
> 機械が考えるかどうかではない。
> 人間が考えるかどうかだ
> ──バラス・フレデリック・スキナー

ば、わたしの車には七百十二ページのマニュアルがついている。カー・ラジオにはいくつものボタンやつまみがついているので、スイッチを入れるにも苦労し、スイッチを切るときもまた苦労する。厄介すぎるのだ。わたしにとって、夢のカー・ラジオはボタンが二つだけのものだ。ひとつはスイッチと音量調節に使う。もうひとつは選局用であり、それをまわすと、ナノ秒のうちに別の局に変わる。もう少しまわすと、また別の局になる。しかし、技術がそこまで発達するには、まだまだ時間がかかるのではないだろうか。

いうまでもなく、技術の発達にわれわれがみな夢中になっている分野として、筆頭にあげるべきはコミュニケーションである。キロバイトがメガバイトになり、ギガバイトになり、テラバイトになり、ペタバイト、エクサバイト、ゼタバイト、ヨタバイトになっていく。バイト数はどんどん増えていく。では、何のために増えていくのか。

「情報を増やすため」というのが答えだ。いまは情報の時代だと

いわれているほどなのだから。

だがこれは正しくない。情報の時代ではない。

データの時代なのだ。データは無限に入ってくる。一日二十四時間、週に七日間、休まず入ってくる。入ってくるデータは、量が増えつづけ、スピードがどんどん速くなり、その源泉もあらゆる方面に広がっている。ある推定によれば、世界全体で一日に六百億通の電子メールが送受信されているという。読者がこれを読むころには、何兆通かになっているだろう。それに電話がある。電話の通話数は、いまではとんでもない数値になり、どんな推定も無意味になっている。

われわれはみな、データを受信し、データを送信している。受け取ったデータにただちに反応して意識の流れを生み出し、新たなデータを発信する。まるで自動機械になったかのように、そして、何の評価もしないままに。どこにもいないように思えるのは、ドアを閉め、じっくり腰をすえ、ベルやチャイムをすべて切り、少しの時間をとって真剣に考えようとする人だ。

一九三二年に出版された『素晴らしい新世界』で、オルダス・ハックスリーはこう書いている。「いまでは、人はひとりになることがない。……われわれは人が孤独を嫌うようにし、孤独になるのを不可能にしている」

二〇〇六年と二〇〇七年に、経営幹部がとくに恐れていたことのひとつは、市場の暴落では

なかったし、それに似た大破局でもなかった。多機能携帯電話のブラックベリーを紛失するこ
とだった。このままでは、猫背でやぶにらみがアメリカ人の特徴になりかねない。いつも下を
向いて携帯を操作し、何かのニュースを、何でもいいからニュースを、あらゆるニュースを手
に入れようとしているのだから。

わたしにはまったく予想できないのだが、マイスペースやフェースブックなど、インターネ
ットのソーシャル・ネットワーク・サービスは長期的にみて、どのような影響を与えるのだろ
うか。きわめて大きな好影響を与えるかもしれない。そうなってほしいと思う。しかし、人間
関係の性格は変化しつづけているので、電子データに対する感覚に負担がかかりすぎるように
なるとともに、人間に対する感覚が鈍くなっている。他人との単純な付き合いが失われている
のである。子供たちすらそうだ。子供の多くは遊ぶときにも、ただ無邪気に遊んでいるわけで
はない。毎日の予定がつまっているので、友だちと遊ぶときは事前に時間を約束する。ふたりと
アポと同じように。そして、遊ぶ時間になっても、ふたりで話をするわけではない。仕事の
もそれぞれ、画面を見つめていたり、ハンドヘルドの小さな装置で遊んでいる。

パナソニックの雑誌広告に、車の後部座席に坐ってノート・パソコンのキーボードを叩いて
いる男性の写真がでていた。コピーにはこう書かれている。「並みのノート・パソコンではない。
運転手にビルの周りを何回か回らせている間に、電子メールを何通か送信できる」

こんな男の下ではたらいたらどのような思いをするか、想像できるだろうか。幸い、この男は実在しない。パナソニックの広告代理店が考えた虚構の人物にすぎない。

データ中毒になって、未処理のまま洪水のように流れ込んでくるデータに忙殺され、考える時間がとれなくなっている。この状態には、大きな問題が三つある。

## ①　受信箱ショックで犠牲になるもの

オフィスではたらいている人の多くは、「受信箱ショック」とも呼ばれる状態になっていて、やりきれないと訴えている。入ってくるデータが多すぎて、処理しきれなくなっているのだ。二〇〇六年のある調査によれば、会社員は平均して、一日に百三十三通の電子メールを受け取っている。それだけでなく、いくつもの通信手段で送られてくるデータを処理しなければならない。ファックスがあり、書類があり、会議に出席し、電話会議にも参加する。パワーポイントのプレゼンテーションがあり、動画レポートがある。電話がデスクの上で鳴り、ポケットの中で振動する。人間の神経系はふつう、これほど猛烈なペースと量で押し寄せてくる刺激を処理できるようにはできていない。

ある日、ブルームバーグのテレビをみていると、午後四時三十四分から三十五分までに、十

二の見出しが流された。画面にはそれ以外に、クレジット・ラインが二つ表示され、株価指数などの市場情報をまとめたボックスがあり、そして、生放送のコメントがつねに流されている。

これが一日中続く。毎日続く。かぎりなく言葉が流され、おしゃべりが流され、ノイズが流されている。

カナダ全土の大学教員を対象にした調査では、大量の情報と通信にたえずさらされてストレスを感じていると回答した人が四十二パーセント、情報通信技術のために研究に集中する能力が大幅に低下したと回答した人が五十八パーセントにのぼっている。また、いくつもの大学病院の医師が報告している点だが、電話では何かを熱心に伝えようとすると、つい大声になるので、喉を痛め、声がしゃがれる人が増えているという。

もちろん、こうしたことをすべて、楽々処理できるように思える人もいる。肉体的にも精神的にも、じつにタフな人だ。ストレスに苦しむどころか、ますます元気になり、金持ちになっていく。

何年か前、フォーチュン誌の記事にマイクロソフトのビル・ゲイツ会長について、こんなことが書かれていた。デスクのパソコンには三つのモニターがつながっていて、ひとつの画面から別の画面に、自由に行き来できるようになっている。第一の画面には、受け取った電子メールが表示されている。第二の画面には、いま書いている返信が表示されている。第三の画面に

はブラウザーが表示され、さまざまなサイトで情報を探し出せるようになっている。

ビル・ゲイツは電子通信技術の先駆者だ。天才であり、とくにデータを扱うことにかけては、まさに天才である。世界全体にわたって、社会にどれほど寄与したのかは、誰にも分からない。だが確かな点がある。遠く離れていた人びとを結びつけたことである。クリックすればすぐに接触できる距離に近づけたのだ。

しかしわれわれ凡人にとっては、情報通信技術のために、無駄な時間を省けて、いまやっていることに集中し、じっくりと考えられるようになるどころか、時間が圧縮されて、ストレスがたまるようになっている。オランダの社会学者、イダ・サベリスは「減圧」が必要だと語る。ダイバーが水深の深いところまで潜ったとき、浮上の途中で行わなければならないのが減圧だ。これと同じように、データのなかに深く潜ったとき、目の前の問題を深く考えて減圧する時間をとることが絶対に必要になるという。

データはいくら集めても、多すぎるということはありえないといわれている。しかし、これが間違いであることは、誰でも直感的に感じている。近くのドラッグストアで、歯磨き売り場の前に立ったことがあれば、何が問題なのかはすぐに分かる。コルゲートだけでも、十五種類か十六種類もの歯磨きがあり、それぞれ、歯の衛生、ホワイトニング、虫歯の予防などの点で少しずつ違った特徴がある。データが多すぎて、処理しきれない。

それ以上に大変なのは、新しい携帯電話機やテレビなど、少しでも技術がからむ商品を買うときだ。機種が多くて選択の幅が大きいのは素晴らしいが、大きすぎて迷うばかりになる。少なくとも、一部の人にとってはそうだ。

携帯電話機を買うとき、写真がとれる機能、音楽が保存できる機能、インターネットが使える機能、電子メールが送受信できる機能、テレビ番組が受信できる機能のうち、どれとどれがほしいのだろうか。どの機種を選ぶかを考えるとき、必要なデータはみな、すぐに入手できる。インターネットに無数にあるサイトに行くか、各地にいくらでもある販売店に行って親切な店員に聞けばいい。だが、知るべきことが多すぎて、判断が難しくなりかねない（頭のいい店員はこのことをよく知っている。だから、すぐに選択の幅を狭めようとする。ネクタイを十二本も見せられると、わたしは混乱する。三本だけ見せられれば、たいていは青いのを選ぶ）。

一九七〇年代前半に、心理学者がある実験を行った。競馬の予想屋にレースの結果を予想してもらうのだが、そのときに戦績や負担重量、血統など、提供する情報の量を変えていった。面白いのは、提供した情報がわずか五種類のときより、四十種類のときの方が、予想成績が悪かったことだ。じつにさまざまな状況で、情報が少ない方がよいというのは事実だ。

あらゆるものをあらゆるものと接続する世界的なネットワークは、すでに存在している。機械がたえず機械と対話している。グループがグループと結びつき、データを交換している。し

かし、生産的になるには、大量のものが構造をもっていなければならない。事業のネットワークは、建物などの物理的な構造がない場合もあるだろうが、ある時点で、何らかの種類の指針があって、すべての流れが正しい方向に、正しい目標に向けられるようにしなければならない。誰かが、あるいは何人かがまともに頭を使って、方向と目標を考えなければならない。誰かが、将来のビジョンをもっていなければならない。データだけでは役に立たない。データは矛盾していることも多い。社会の常識になっている見方と個人の判断とはまったく違うこともあるからだ。世論調査では、省エネ型の住宅がほしいと答える人も、実際に家を建てることになると、いまの三倍も面積がある家を喜んで建てる。

調査は重要だと思うが、調査ではその時点での状況を、ぼんやりと不完全な形で示すにすぎないとも思う。釣り鐘型の正規分布曲線からは、将来のビジョンをどう構築すべきかは分からない。市場調査では、今後、何が人びとの夢になるのかは分からない。将来のことは誰にも分からないからだ。ごく初期の自動車を開発した人たちが市場調査を行って、輸送について人びとが望む点を質問していれば、たぶん、「もっと速く走る馬がほしい」という答えになっていただろう。

失敗したいのであれば、考える時間をとらないようにするべきだ。成功したいのなら、考える時間をとるのはたぶん、各自の会社にとって、各自のキャる時間を十分にとるべきだ。考え

リアにとって、各自の人生にとって、最善の投資だ。

スティーブ・ベネットはゼネラル・エレクトリック（GE）で、あのジャック・ウェルチに鍛えられた経営幹部だが、インテュイット社のCEOに就任したとき、同社には十箇条の行動指針があった。ベネットはこのうち、ひとつの単語だけを変えている。九番目の指針「速く考え、速く行動する」を「賢明に考え、速く行動する」に変えたのである。インテュイットはそれまでも業績がよかった。ベネットのもとで、さらによくなった。考える時間をとるのは、ほんとうに重要なのだ。「人生には、速くすること以外に、やるべき点がたくさんある」とマハトマ・ガンジーは語っている。成功するには速く動けばいいというわけではない。しかし失敗するには、速く動くことだ。

## ② 未処理のデータは現実を隠しうる

二十世紀初め、量子力学の発達で物理学に革命が起こった。物理学を知らなくても、この革命の基本的な意味は分かるはずだ。世界のすべてを知るのは不可能であることをあきらかにしたのである。これがハイゼンベルグの不確定性原理であり、観察という行為によって観察したものが影響を受けるので、観察の結果が確実だとはいえないことを示した。比較的最近、ふた

# 困った問題を引き起こすのは、
# 誰でもよく知っていることではない。
# 困った問題は引き起こさない
# と思っていることだ
## ——マーク・トウェイン

（こう述べたのがマーク・トウェインではないことを知っているという人もいる。アーティマス・ウォードだという人、ラルフ・ウォルドー・エマーソンだという人、ウィル・ロジャーズだという人がいる。わたしはその誰でもないことを、たしかに知っている。叔父のバーンの言葉だ。叔父がこう述べたとき、わたしはその場にいたのだから）

りの物理学者が、不確定性原理もそれほど確実だとはいえないことをあきらかにしている。

だから、何かを「知っている」というとき、それがどこまで確実だといえるのか、慎重になった方がいい。

人はときに、みたいと思っているものをみることがある。現実をみるのではなく、現実を示すと考えるデータだけをみていることがある。現実を示していてほしいと考えるデータをみているにすぎない場合もある。

人間には、確認の罠と呼ばれる心理的な偏りがある。あらかじめ確立した見方を確認できる事実だけを探し、その見方が間違っている可能性を示す事実は探さないという偏りである。

エンロンはたくさんの人をだまし、社内の人間の多くもだまされたのは、自社の財務諸表に書かれていた内容について、じっくり考えてみようとしなかったからだ。それがほんとうだと信じたかったので、真実だとは考えにくい数値、理解できない数値をみても無視した。経済関係のマスコミも愚かだった。注目を集めるニュースを求めていて、かならずしも真実を求めているとはかぎらない。昔から何度も何度も、各種の贋作者や詐欺師が人の愚かさにつけこんできており、とりわけ優秀なはずの人すらだまされてきた。誰しも、ときには現実よりも夢を信じたがることをよく知っているからだ。

一九四〇年代後半、ペプシコーラが「同じ五セント、量は倍」で攻勢をかけていたとき、コカ・コーラ社の経営幹部は四半期の販売統計でケースを単位に使い、みずからを欺いていた。そして、販売数量をケース数でみれば、コークはペプシよりもはるかに多かった。唯一問題なのは、コカ・コーラの一ケースが六オンス半の瓶二十四本なのに対して、ペプシは十二オンス瓶二十四本だったことだ。誰も当然の質問をしなかった。「販売したケースの数でこれだけ差があるのに、差を縮められつづけているのはなぜなのか」。こう質問して現実をみるようになってようやく、コカ・コーラ社も大きな瓶を使うようになり、突破口が開かれた。

デトロイトの自動車会社も長年、お気に入りの販売統計だけに注目してみずからを欺き、世界の自動車産業の全体像を考えようとはしなかった。自社製品の品質についてすら、みずから

を欺いていた。品質の独自基準をつくり、品質を点数で示すシステムをつくって、点数が基準に近くなれば祝い合っていた。「できるかぎり最高の車をつくろう。そして改善を続けていこう」と考えたのだ。日本企業には独自基準はなかった。当然の方法だ。そして、賢明な方法だ。

わたしは、マーケティングと経営に関する研究には、極端に警戒するようになっている。もちろん、研究にはそれなりの価値があるのだが、不適切な変数を計測していることが多いし、計測した結果を評価しているのが不適切な人であることも多いと確信しているのだ。

コカ・コーラ社でその典型例だといえるのは、一九八五年の悪名高いニュー・コークの発売だ。製品名を示さずに二種類の飲料を飲んで比較してもらう味覚テストでは、甘みが濃い方が評価が高かった。この結果をみてわれわれは、コカ・コーラの甘みが足りないという間違った結論を引き出してしまった。

だが、こうしたテストでは、コカ・コーラという商品の全体像をまったくつかむことができない。全体的なイメージや文化的な背景は無視される。

当時、アメリカでペプシの販売数量が増えていた。そこでコカ・コーラ社の経営陣と、ボトラー業界の指導者は、スーパーマーケットでコークよりペプシの方が売れている理由を探し求めていた。アメリカ・コカ・コーラ社の経営陣も理由を探しはじめた。広告費や物流の問題でないのはたしかだ。問題は何か別の部分にあるはずだ。そうして行き着いたのが、百年近い伝

統のある商品そのものであった。調査担当者はこういう問いを立てた。何か具体的な違いを確認し是正できるだろうかと。そこで、二十万人を対象にした味覚テストを実施し、甘みの問題であることに疑問の余地はないと証明した。いうまでもなく、実際には甘みにまったく問題がないことが後にあきらかになる。だが、大量のデータで現実がみえなくなっていた。世界中の調査を集めて検討しても、正しい問いを立てていなければ、正しい結論は得られない。現実はまったく違っていたのだ。ニュー・コークという現実がみえなくなっていた。世界中のめることが必要だったのだ。ニュー・コークの発売で、皮肉なもので、この方向に前進することができたが、何とも痛い思いをして得た教訓であった。

予算計画でも、データの洪水が問題だ。アトランタのコカ・コーラ本社に勤める予算専門家は何年にもわたって、生データの洪水におぼれかかっていた。ほとんど役立たないデータが多いのだが、それでも毎年、同じデータを集め、社内の公式を使って処理していた。たとえば、「ファウンテン営業部門は昨年、Xドルを店舗内販促に支出した。したがって来年はXドルにYドルを足す必要があり、そのように予算を立てる」といった具合だ。予算の計画にあたって、全体像をみようとはしていなかった。

一九六〇年代末から七〇年代初めにかけて、ヒューストンにつくられて間もないコカ・コーラ社食品部門から、何人かがアトランタ本社に移っている。わたしもそのひとりだ。このとき

移った数人の強みは、外部から来たことだった。ものごとを違った角度から眺め、全体像をつかもうと努めた。少し距離をおいて問題をみていたのであり、事業全体について考えるために、時間をかけた。

この数人も、以前からの本社のひとたちと同じ家具をみていたのだが、ソファを動かせることを知っていた。

## ③　考える時間をとらないのは、要するに愚かであり、危険ですらある

クリミア戦争のバラクラバの戦いで、イギリス軍の軽騎兵旅団が壊滅した。軽騎兵が死の谷に突撃したのは、指揮官が立ち止まって考えようとしなかったからだ。兵士はみな、黙って命令に従った。兵士は自分で考えるようには求められていない。だが指揮官は考えるよう求められている。自明の理ではあるのだが、確認しておくべき点がある。戦争であれ、他のどの分野であれ、まともに前進するには、データを選り分けて、前回の経験に基づく結論に飛びつくようであってはならない。慎重に評価し、時間をかけて注意深く分析しなければならない。

考える時間をとるのは、贅沢でない。必要なことなのだ。ゲーテが語ったように、「行動するのは簡単であり、考えるのは難しい」のである。だが行動だけが重視されることが少なくない

軽騎兵隊、進めとの命令に
恐れ怖じけた兵士はいたか
誰かのへまだと分かっていたが
怖じけはしない
文句はいわず
理由は聞かず
死地に向かって突き進む
死の谷に向かう
六百人の軽騎兵
──アルフレッド・テニソン

し、実際にはそういう場合の方が多いといえるほどだ。理性に敬意を払いはするが、じつのところ、感情の虜になっている。人間は感情の生き物なのであり、何かの活動をはじめて事態が進み出したとき、興奮状態になって止めるのは難しくなる。意思決定にあたっては、集団願望に陥って、全員が目標を達成しようと熱心になるあまり、まともに考えられなくなることがある。

企業の合併・買収（M&A）の分野では、何億ドル、ときには何十億ドルもの案件で競争がはじまり、勢いがついてくると、参加者の間の対抗意識が前面にでてきて、戦いが白熱し（そう、まさに戦いになって）、何でもありの勝負になる。何が何でも勝たねばならないと考える。勝利は目の前にあ

るのだ。そうなると、積み上げた現金も、案件を裏付けるとされていた健全なはずの理由も、多数の利害関係者も、すべて問題ではなくなる。勝つことだけが目標になるのだ。「突き進むのだ、邪魔はさせない」と、とりわけ我の強い人物が叫ぶ。記者会見でスポットライトを浴びる夢があり、ウォール・ストリート・ジャーナル紙の一面トップを飾る夢があるのだ。魅力的な夢が実現すると思えば、金額を引き上げても十分に採算がとれると思い込む。占星術と変わらぬ程度の信頼性しかない予想であったとしても。ジョン・メイナード・ケインズがいう「血気」は、ほとんどの経営者が認めたがる以上に強力だ。

最近の悲惨な組み合わせをみてみるといい。ダイムラーとクライスラー、タイム・ワーナーとAOL、Kマートとシアーズ、クエーカー・オーツとスナップルなどだ。これらのM&Aがほんとうに実行されたことを、信じられるだろうか。満足できる結果にならないことは完全に予想できたのだが、当事者はみな案件の興奮に押し流されて、上から下まで誰も、結果がどうなるか、結果の結果がどうなるかを冷静に考え抜こうとしなかった。たしかに、さまざまな関係者が短期的に利益を得られることがいつも、こうした案件が実行される一因になる。だが、企業でどのような行動をとる場合にも、すべての利害関係者の生活と地位に長期的にどのような影響が及ぶかを、誰かがあらかじめ考えておかなければならない。

誰かが立ち止まって考えないかぎり、同じ間違いを何度も何度も繰り返すことになる。考え

る時間をとらないのは、失敗をもたらす確実な方法である。何らかの種類の失敗があれば、周囲を見回して責任を押し付けるか、言い訳をみつけるか、誰かを罰すればいい。そうすれば、立ち止まり、時間をかけて、失敗の原因をしっかりと分析することもなくなる。優れた病院では、定期的に病因死因検討会を開いて、自分たちの失敗について議論し、そこから学ぶようにしている。検討されるのは、生死にかかわる問題だ。企業のほとんどは、それに近いほど深刻な問題は扱っていない。それでも失敗があれば、技術の変更が思ったほど成功しなかった事例や、マーケティングの失敗例について考え、どこに問題があったのかをできるかぎり客観的に解明する絶好の機会になる。

経営陣はまともに仕事をしていれば、時々は失敗することがある。だが、もっと失敗したいのなら、間違いをひとつずつ検討し、分析するようなことは避けるべきだ。そうすれば、今後も同じ種類の間違いを何度も繰り返すことになる。

どうしても失敗したいのなら、考える時間をとらないことが不可欠だ。あるいは、そうしたいのであれば、誰かに考えさせることで、ほぼすべての責任をうまく回避することもできる。

これがつぎの法則である。

# 法則 7 〉 専門家と外部コンサルタントを全面的に信頼する

十代のころ、夏休みにスーシティの家畜市場ではたらいていたとき、何人もの家畜の売り手や買い手と知り合いになった。ある日そのひとりに、去勢していない雄牛の買い手になって仕事を手伝ってくれないかといわれた。こうした牛は一頭ずつ出荷され、市場のあちこちで売られている。繁殖用に役立たなくなったときに、食肉用に売られるからだ。しかしたいていの家畜商にとっては、広大な市場のあちこちを回って去勢していない雄牛を一頭ずつ買い集めていては、商売にならない。若くて元気なアルバイト生なら、市場内を走り回って貨車一両分の十五頭から二十頭を一日に買い集め、二十ドルほどのかなりの手数料を稼げる。

わたしを雇ってくれた家畜商はドイル・ハーモンであり、ミシガンのアメリカン・フットボール選手として有名なトミー・ハーモンの叔父にあたる人だ。最初の日の仕事が終わった後、

117

いくつかの疑問を知っている方が、
答えをすべて知っているよりいい
──ジェームズ・サーバー

ハーモンがやってきて、わたしが買った雄牛をみてまわった。かなりの数の牛は高く買いすぎていた。そこで、ハーモンが注意してくれた。「たくさんの家畜商に囲まれていて、おまえはうんと若いので、みな、お世辞をいったり、親切にしたり、気が散るようなことをいったりする」。そういって図を取り出して説明した。「牛のどこをみるべきかがこの図にみな書いてある。誰が何を話そうとも、この基本的なチェック項目から外れてはいけない」。そして最後に、ハーモンはこういった。「人ではなく、牛をよくみるんだ」

この単純明快な助言を、わたしはビジネスの世界で大切にしてきたし、投資銀行の世界にいるいまも大切にしている。いつも、どのような説明を受けても、商品そのものをみるように努めてきた。簡単ではないかと思えるかもしれないが、実際には簡単ではない。自分がどれほど優秀だと思っていても、一瞬でも牛から目を離し、人に注意を向けていると、まったく馬鹿げた企画に引き込まれかねない。第六の法則では、立ち止まって考えるようにしなければ失敗すると説明した。派手に失敗したいのであれば、さらに、お世辞に乗

る方法がある。どの分野にも、人当たりのいい詐欺師がいくらでもいて、お世辞を武器に売り込みをはかっている。

たぶん、そうした人物を詐欺師と呼ぶのは、少々気の毒かもしれない。ほとんどの人はマーケティングの専門知識、経営戦略、新事業の企画など、売り込んでいるものに誠実に取り組んでいる。それに、文句のつけようのない資格や経歴があり、絶対の権威者を自認していることも少なくない。また、難しい問題への明確な答えでしっかり武装しており、パワーポイントの見事なプレゼンテーションで示してくれる。そうした答えの多くは素晴らしく、問題はみあたらない。間違った問いに答えようとしていること以外には。

「人ではなく、牛をよくみろ」というのは、経営コンサルタントによる工夫をこらしたプレゼンテーションを頻繁にみせられるものにとって、じつによい助言だ。

コカ・コーラ社にいたとき、じつにたくさんの自称専門家が社内の従業員として、あるいは社外のコンサルタントとして、登場し、そして去っていった。ときには説得されて、しっかり判断すれば、あるいは直感的に、すべきでないと思った方針をとったこともある。人間は無謬ではないのだから、弱気になっていて判断を間違えることもある。

何年にもわたって、コンサルタントはコカ・コーラ社の経営陣に、事業を多角化する必要があると説いてきた。中核事業は炭酸飲料とジュースであり、将来に市場が変化したときに無防

備すぎる。中核事業に近いが、性格の違う事業の買収を考えるべきだという。そして、いくつもの企業を推奨してきた。そのうちのひとつに、素晴らしいワイン会社があった。そこで、コンサルタントの助言を受け入れ、その会社を買収した。

そのワイン会社が魅力的なことに疑問の余地はなかった。経営陣は優秀で、ワイン・スペクトラムという独立部門として活動した。コカ・コーラ社の経営幹部は、社内の夕食会やパーティのとき、テーブルにワインのボトルを並べて、喜んでいた。経営については本社の幹部はほとんど注意を払っていなかった。ペットを飼っているようなものだったのである。

そのとき、ロバート・ウッドラフは優に八十を超えていたが、社内での影響力は絶大であり、尊敬されていた。日常業務からは離れていたのだが、「わたしの会社」が参入したワイン事業の実態をみずから調査しようと考えた（ウッドラフにとって、コカ・コーラ社はいつになっても「わたしの会社」だった）。

そこで、主治医と何人かの友人を引き連れ、社有機に乗ってカリフォルニアに向かった。アトランタに戻ると、CEOのロベルト・ゴイズエタと昼食をとり、わたしも同席した。そのときの話の大筋は以下のようだったと記憶している。

ワイン事業は面白い。わたしはカリフォルニアに行って、葡萄園をみてきた。

葡萄の木を植えてから、収穫ができるようになるまで、五年か六年かかるようだ。その間、かなりの数の人が果樹の世話をし、天候に恵まれてよい葡萄が収穫できるよう祈っているいる。すべてが順調に進めばようやく、葡萄を収穫し、工場に運んで絞り、大きくてきわめて高価なステンレスのタンクに入れ、発酵させる。つぎに、高価なタンクからワインをたくさんの小さな樽に移す。これもやはり高価なフランスのオーク材でできている。樽は一個で五十五ドルする。ワインは小さく高価な樽でしばらく熟成させる。その間にワインの十五パーセントが蒸発して消える。

かなりの期間、熟成させたワインは、つぎにボトルに詰める。このとき、ボトルごとに税金を支払うが、その後も熟成のために貯蔵する。ボトルで何年か熟成させた後、すべてが順調で、そこそこのビンテージになったときにようやく、出荷して小売店の棚に並ぶようになる。棚には数百種類のワインが並んでいる。同じようなボトルのなかから、誰かが自社のワインを選んで買ってくれるのを、神に祈るしかない。

ところでわたしは、朝に瓶詰めして午後に売り、それもたいていは競合する商品がないところで売る事業で育ってきた。こういう種類の事業に参入したいものだ。

この話には、ゴイズエタもわたしも心を動かされた。コンサルタントはこれがいかに素晴ら

しい事業なのかを力説していたし、コカ・コーラ社はアメリカのワイン市場で、十一パーセントというかなりのシェアを握っていたのだが、この事業をもっと詳しく検討することにした。

そこで一九八一年初め、ゴイズエタとわたしは会社の指揮をとるようになって間もない時期に、ワイン・スペクトラムの経営幹部と会うことにした。

そこでワイン部門の幹部に、各自で一九九〇年までの投下資本利益率を予想して報告するよう求めた。その際には、九〇年までの間、経営判断がどれも完璧だと想定する。販売数量と利益は適正な範囲内で甘めに見積もる。こうした想定のもとでの予想を受け取った後に、ワイン事業を拡大するのか、手放すのかを決めると話した。ワイン事業を売却する場合にも、いまの経営陣が地位を維持できるようにするとも保証した。

ワイン事業の経営幹部はみな、同じ結論に達した。考えられるかぎり最善の結果になった場合でも、投下資本利益率が資本コストと同等かそれ以下になるとの結論である。報告書を読んで考えこんだ。ワイン事業をほんとうに継続したいのかと。

だが、継続したくないとすれば、どうすればいいのか。

いつも好運に恵まれるのはありがたいことであり、コカ・コーラ社は長年にわたって、好運だった。ワイン事業でまともな利益率を確保するにはどうすべきか、われわれには分からないという結論に達した直後に、シーグラムから打診があった。ワイン・スペクトラムに興味があ

るというのだ。そこで「渋々」交渉に応じ、両社にとって最善の取引が成立した。

牛から目を離していれば、かならず失敗する。現にわたしは失敗した。

アメリカ・コカ・コーラ社の経営幹部が本社経営陣にニュー・コークを提案してきたとき、われわれは説得されて、提案を真剣に考慮することにした。このとき、ゴイズエタとわたしはコンサルタントと専門家の意見を真剣に受け入れて、市場調査部門が行ったきわめて大量の味覚調査の結果をみれば、原液の配合を一新する根拠は十分にあると考えてしまった。何週間にもわたって検討し、論争し、議論した結果、われわれは計画を支持した。商品を変えるのが競争上、賢明な策だという意見に納得したのである。

それからが大変だった。さらに大量のテスト。さらに大量の専門家。フォーカス・グループ、試験販売、ランダム・サンプル調査もあった。どの調査でも、ニュー・コークがいつも勝者になった。ゴイズエタもわたしも、内心ではアメリカの伝統を象徴する商品を変えるべきではないと思っていたのだが、専門家が示す証拠にはうむをいわさぬ力があった。それに、意思決定の過程は、まさに、集団願望の典型になっていた。好むと好まざるとにかかわらず、集団による決定になっていった。ニュー・コークのアイデアは素晴らしく、疑問の余地なく正しいと考える人がきわめて多くなったからだ。ニュー・コークに勢いがつき、誰もこのお祭り騒ぎに水を差したいとは望まなくなった。CEOのゴイズエタも、社長のわたしも、懸念をもちつづけ

ながらも、劇的な変化をもたらす激しい潮流に巻き込まれていった。ゴイズエタとわたしは計画を百パーセント支持した。この大激変に関与したものはみな、ものすごいことが起こると予想して、みるからに興奮していた。

コカ・コーラ社は一九八五年四月と五月に、全米でニュー・コークを発売した。興奮を煽るために、街には楽団をくりだし、空にはアド・バルーンを浮かべ、その他、ありとあらゆる広告手段を総動員して、ニュー・コークの発売を後押しした。

何とも大きな騒ぎになった。世界の歴史のなかでみれば、ちっぽけな話にすぎないのだが、それでも当時、世界的な大ニュースになっている。

発表の直後から、アトランタの本社には抗議の電話が殺到するようになり、その数が増え続けて、回線が一杯になった。数週間の間に、四十万を超える電話と手紙が殺到し、すべてがニュー・コークに反対するものだった。ここで動揺してはいけない、方針を堅持すべきだと、専門家は助言した。

アイダホ州のある弁護士からの手紙は、ゴイズエタとわたしにあてられていた。「この手紙の下の欄に署名して返送していただけませんでしょうか。この手紙に大変な値段がつくようになるはずです。なにしろ、アメリカの経営史を代表する馬鹿な経営者ふたりがそろって署名した手紙になるのですから」。こういう手紙を受け取ると、鼻高々ではいられなくなる。ありがたい

ことだ。

アトランタ本社から遠く離れたシアトルでも、抗議者が集まっていた。アメリカ・オールド・コーク愛好者協会と名乗る団体がニュー・コーク反対のデモを呼びかけたところ、五千人が参加している。NBCの人気番組「トゥナイト・ショー」で司会者のジョニー・カーソンが、スポンジ・ケーキのトゥインキーズでも変更の計画があり、中にクリームではなく、ホウレン草を入れるのだそうですと発言する一幕もあった。

アメリカのボトラーはニュー・コークにとくに熱心だったのだが、そのうち何人かがゴルフもできないとこぼすようになった。地元のゴルフ場に行くと、知り合いの会員にニュー・コークへの怒りをぶつけられるというのだ。ボトラーの営業担当者は、小売店の店舗にニュー・コークが入るのを拒否するようになった。罵声を浴びることになるからだ。消費者はピックアップ・トラックでスーパーに行き、もとのコークを大量に買うようになった。集団ヒステリーの様相になってきた。この騒ぎは時間の問題で、すぐに収まる。ニュー・コークは大成功を収める。それに抗議が続いている間、コークがマスコミで取り上げられることになる。そう主張した。

それでも、市場調査の大家やマーケティングの専門家は冷静を装っていた。

七月後半、ゴイズエタとわたしは夫婦でモナコの近くにあるイタリアン・レストランに入った。世界の大手ボトラー、二十五社を集めた会議がモナコで開かれた直後のことだ。レストラ

ンのオーナーはわれわれがコカ・コーラ社のものだと聞いていて、席についた直後にテーブル
に近づいてきた。枝編みのバスケットをもち、赤いビロードの布をかぶせている。なかには最
上のテーブル・ワインが入っているに違いない。ところが、布をとったとき、あらわれたのは
コカ・コーラだった。「これは本物のコークです」と、危うい英語で誇らしげに語った。まるで、
めったにない古いコニャックであるかのように。マスコミが無料でコークを大々的に宣伝して
くれている時期ではあったが、これで目が覚めたともいえる。

しかし、方針を堅持するだけではいけないと悟ったのは、八十五歳のおばあさんと話したと
きだ。ロサンゼルスの老人施設から涙ながらに電話をかけてきた。わたしはそのときたまたま、
コール・センターを訪問していて、電話を受けた。「わたしのコークをとってしまうなんて」と
泣きながら訴えている。

「この前、コークを飲んだのはいつですか」

「そんなこと、覚えていません。たぶん、二十年か二十五年前です」

「だったら、なんでそんなに悲しんでおられるのですか」

「お若い方、わたしが若かったときの記念の品をもてあそんでいるのです。それだけは止めて
いただきたい。コークがわたしにとってどんな意味をもっているか、お分かりですか」

この話を聞いて、はっきり分かった。問題は味覚ではないし、マーケティングですらない。

あれだけの専門家、あれだけのデータはすべて、誤解のもとだったのだ。これは人びとの心の奥底の問題だ。ブランドは経営者や専門家の考えで決められるようなものではない。ブランドは、消費者ひとりひとりの心のなかにあるもので決まっている。コカ・コーラはいくつもの文化の無数の人に飲まれているので、コカ・コーラがどういうものなのかは、個々人で違っている。

これでようやく分かった。どれだけ巨額の資金をかけても、アメリカでニュー・コークを成功させることはできない。ゴイズエタも同じ結論に達した。アメリカの消費者は明確に、大きな声で主張している。コカ・コーラは自分たちの商品であり、自分たちに返してほしいと。われわれはこの主張に同意した。わたしはテレビ・カメラの前で、以前のコークを「コカ・コーラ・クラシック」として復活すると発表した。ABCテレビではそのとき、人気番組の「ゼネラル・ホスピタル」が放送されていたが、これを中断してアンカーのピーター・ジェニングズが登場し、コカ・コーラがもとの成分に戻るというニュースを伝えた。大手ネットワークとテレビ局は一斉に、ニュース番組でこれを伝えた。新聞は特大の大見出しでこのニュースを伝えた。

アメリカは興奮に包まれた。コカ・コーラ社には花束や感謝の手紙が大量に送られてきた。あのフランク・キャプラ監督の名作映画のような終幕だった。大企業が決定を下し、民衆が抗

議し、大企業が間違いを認め、民衆が勝利したのだ。消費者は競ってコカ・コーラを買い、売上は急増した。われわれの間違いを許してくれただけでなく、ますます好きになってくれたのである。政治家はこの件から教訓を得られるかもしれない。間違ったときには間違いを認め、無謬ではないことを認めるべきなのだ。アメリカの人びととはじつに寛大だ。

そのとき、われわれがこの状況に陥るときに一役買った専門家は姿を消し、もうつぎの会社のために一役買おうとしていた。

常識というものがないのだろうか。専門家のなかには、専門知識の間違いが繰り返し示されて、いくら何でももう信頼されないだろうと思える人もいる。

フィリップ・テトロックは世界政治に関する専門家の見方を調べてきた。「ソ連共産党が一九九三年にも権力を握りつづけていると予想した専門家、カナダは九七年までに解体すると予想した専門家、ネオ・ファシストが九四年までに南アフリカの政権を握ると予想した専門家、欧州連合（EU）の経済通貨同盟（EMU）が九七年までに崩壊すると予想した専門家、……湾岸危機が平和的に解決すると予想した専門家はそれぞれ、逆に予想した専門家より多かった」*。

こうした専門家は、自分の予想が八十パーセントの確率であたるとみていた。実際には四十五パーセントしか正しくなかった。硬貨を投げて予想した方がよかったわけだ。

だが、専門家の限界を何よりもよく示す点は、その後にある。これら予想の間違いが議論の

128

余地なく示された後に専門家がどういう姿勢をとったかをテトロックが調査したところ、状況の理解について確信が揺らいだ様子はなかったという。状況を考え直すのではなく、さまざまな言い逃れを並べていた。わたしの見方はほぼ正しかった、予想した通りにはなっていないが、間もなくそうなる、地震のようなまったく予想できない力がはたらいた、与えられたデータに基づくかぎり、予想は正しかった、云々かんぬん。

専門家は間違ってきた。何度も何度も、繰り返し間違ってきた。だが、反省するでもなく、企業に、そして政府に相変わらず顔をだし、何らかの新しい理論、何らかの予想、何らかの新しい専門用語、あるいは、何らかのアイデアの使い回しを売り込んでいる。

よくもまあ、つぎからつぎへとあらわれてくるものだ。X理論、Y理論、カオス、目標管理、TQM、ピーク・パフォーマンス、エンパワーメント、ダウンサイジング、ランピング・アップ、ランピング・ダウンなどなど。

専門家はたえず、「リエンジニアリング」を行っている。主に、言葉を対象にするリエンジニアリングだ。最近、従業員の「ディハイアリング」が必要だと力説している人がいた。

* Philip Tetlock, "Theory-driven Reasoning About Plausible Pasts and Probable Futures in World Politics," in Thomas Gilovich, Dale Griffin, and Daniel Kahneman, *Heuristics and Biases: The Psychology of Intuitive Judgement* (New York: Cambridge University Press, 2002)

たとえばマトリックス組織というのは何なのか。わたしが理解できたかぎり、マトリックス組織のお陰で、ひとりの従業員が、三人かことによるとそれ以上の数の上司のもとで仕事ができる利点を得られるようになったということのようだ。

インターネット・バブルがはじける直前に、「バーン・レート」という言葉を何度も聞いた。要するに、ベンチャー企業が誰か他人の金を使っていて、その金が二度と戻ってこないという意味の言葉だ。

どれも、何とも面白い現象だと笑っていられるのであればいい。だが実際には、専門家を崇めているために深刻な間違いに陥ることがあり、ときには間違いが広範囲に広がることもある。

たとえば、ジョン・メリウェザーとロング・ターム・キャピタル・マネジメント（LTCM）の例をみてみよう。

興奮の一九八〇年代、興奮の頂点にいたひとりがメリウェザーだ。ソロモン・ブラザーズの債券トレーダーを率いて、巨額の利益をあげていた。一九九四年、マイロン・ショールズとロバート・マートンというふたりのノーベル経済学賞受賞者をパートナーに迎えて、LTCMを設立した。いわゆるヘッジ・ファンドであり、ほぼ規制対象にならない投資ファンドだ。きわめて裕福な顧客から資金を集めて投資する。投資に使う素晴らしい理論は、ほとんど理解されていなかったが、高く評価されていた。間違えるはずがないとされていたからだ。そして当初

十月になった。あるインディアン部族の酋長が、今年の冬は厳しくなると予想した。そこで全員に薪を集めるよう指示した。念のためにアメリカ気象局に電話して、厳冬になるかどうかきいてみた。「長期予報では、厳冬になる可能性があるとされています」という答えだった。そこで酋長は念のために、もっと薪を集めるように指示した。一週間後にアメリカ気象局に電話すると、厳冬になるだろうという。そこで、薪になりそうな木片を残らず探すように指示した。二週間後、ふたたびアメリカ気象局に電話して、「この冬はたしかに厳冬になると断言できますか」と質問した。答えはこうだった。「絶対になります。インディアンが必死になって薪を集めていますから」

の三年間、運用成績は華々しく、ほとんど信じがたいほどであった。九八年には約九百億ドルを投資していたが、その大部分は借入で賄われていると。しかし、心配する人はいなかった。専門家が運用しており、間違えるはずはないと思われていたからだ。

LTCMが破綻寸前に陥ったとき、ニューヨーク連邦準備銀行が介入し、急遽つくられた債権者のコンソーシアムが救済することになった。同社が破綻すれば、市場は混乱し、数兆ドルもの金融商品に影響を与え、世界全体で金融市場の信認が揺さぶられかねなかったからだ。

LTCMは素晴らしい仕組みを作り上げ、すぐさま巨額の資金を集めることができたのだが、じつのところ、その仕組みは巨額を賭けるルーレット・ゲームのようなものでしかなかった。だが、人びとは専門家を信頼しようとするので、この馬鹿げた仕組みがウォール街でも飛び抜けて優秀な人たちに受け入れられたのである。

もっと最近では二〇〇七年に、金融市場が混乱した。市場が信頼していた統計モデルが、サブプライム・モーゲージ・ローンのリスクをとんでもなく過小評価していたからだ。「モデルの間違い」が原因だと説明されている。

実際には、モデルの間違いではない。間違ったのは人間である。誰でも常識がありさえすれば、適切な返済能力がない人に巨額のローンを貸し出すのではまともな事業にならないと予想できたはずだ。だが、金融市場の天才は、魔法の種を蒔きつづけてきた。そして、金のなる木

が育たないのをみて、誰もがあわてた。なんという愚かさだろう。

天才だと思える人は見方が狭く、知恵がない場合が少なくない。

大企業の経営ではとくにそうだ。経営は技であって、科学ではない。人間の行動を数量化し、

数式でとらえようとする経営幹部やコンサルタントには警戒すべきだ。コカ・コーラ社には、人間を数値としてとらえ

ようとする経営幹部やコンサルタントがたくさんいた。こうした人は成功していない。どんな

ものにも数値をあてはめることなど、できない相談なのだ。わたしの見方では、そういう人は

想像力に欠けているのである。

わたしはこれまで何度もぶつかってきたが、多くの専門家はひとつの企業を同じ業界の他企

業と比較し、業界平均に基づいて利益を最大限に高める計画を立案する。とんでもない間違い

だ。どの業界のどの企業も、他社と差別化し、何らかの点で独特の企業になるよう努力すべき

であり、平均に近づこうなどとしてはならない。わたしにとって、コカ・コーラ社は昔も今もコカ・コー

のひとつだなどと考えたことはない。わたしにとって、コカ・コーラ社が清涼飲料メーカー

ラ社なのであって、それ以外ではない。同業他社は社内の先輩が主張したような「模倣者」で

はない。コカ・コーラを販売していないだけのことだ。

わたしはコカ・コーラ社の社長として、じつにたくさんのマーケティングの天才や財務の天

才の話を聞いてきたが、結局のところ、経済学者のルードビッヒ・フォン・ミーゼズの言葉に

同意するようになった。「統計の数値は……繰り返すことがない過去の事例で何が起こったのかを教えてくれる」

もっとも、コンサルタントや外部の専門家に助言をあおぐのは、経営幹部がすでに決めた点について、お墨付きを得るためだけであることが少なくない。こうした幹部は自分の権威に不安を感じている。それで思い出すのは、クライスラー社の物語だ。創業者で指導者であったウォルター・P・クライスラーが死んだ後、経営幹部は不安にかられ、降霊会を開いてクライスラーにお伺いを立てようとしたという。クライスラーの霊が降りてきたかどうか、確たることはいえない。だが、降りてきていれば、おまえたちは全員クビだと叫んだのではないだろうか。

合併の後や、事業が不調のときなどにはリストラを行うのが一般的であり、そのとき経営幹部は従業員のレイオフという苦しい仕事に直面する。このとき、経営幹部が、犠牲になる従業員に誠実に、率直に対応するのではなく、外部のコンサルティング会社が立てた事業計画に書かれているので仕方がないのだと語ることがある。何とも臆病で卑怯な態度だと思う。新しい事業計画を実行するというのであれば、それは自分の子供のようなものだ。自分が責任を負わなければならない。それに、責任を負うのを避け、自分の権威を放棄して社外の専門家に頼るのであれば、事業計画をうまく実行することなどできないだろう。

わたしがいつも原則にしている点だが、悪いニュースを伝えるとき、とくに部下を解雇する

とき、電子メールやメモや電話を使ってはならない。心理的な影響が大きいことを伝えるとき

は、相手に会って、直接に伝える。

ジャック・ウェルチは、ゼネラル・エレクトリック（ＧＥ）の株主に宛てた最後の手紙で、

「自分の組織内の官僚制度を憎め」と助言している。そこでつぎの法則は官僚制度についてだ。

# 官僚組織を愛する

一九七三年に、わたしがヒューストンからアトランタのコカ・コーラ本社ビルに移って、執行副社長に就任したときのことだ。はじめて本社に出勤すると、長年の秘書、フローレンス・カリノウスキが泣いていた。数日前に先乗りして、わたしのオフィスを整えておくことになっていたのだが、まったくできなかったからだ。

なぜ、できなかったのか。

鉛筆すら手に入らなかったのだ。

それまで勤務していたヒューストンの食品部門は、規模が小さいし、組織も整っていなかった。鉛筆が必要になれば、同じ階の端にある備品・用品室に行けばいい。アトランタではそうはいかない。出庫依頼伝票に必要事項を記入して、提出してほしいといわれた。ところが伝票

は手元にないし、夕方になって伝票を支給する担当者はもう帰宅していた。これで我慢の限界を超えた。それまで二日間、本社の官僚機構と戦って、コピー機を用意し、電話をつなぎ、文房具を変更し、大きなファイル・キャビネットを手に入れ、その他もろもろのことを処理してきた。そして、最後には泣き出してしまったのだ。

「ここでは、何もできない。ホッチキスは仕方ないから自分で買ったのに、針すら手に入らないんですから」

今日の仕事は終わりにして、帰ってもらうことにした。そして、妻に電話し、仕事にならないので帰るから、早めに食事をして映画でも観に行こうと伝えた。

仕事がまったく進まないようにしたいのであれば、何よりもまず事務手続きを優先させるようにすべきだ。社内の官僚組織を大切にする。

ヨーロッパでは、「官僚制度」という言葉は十八世紀のどこかの時点に、フランスの経済関係の文書ではじめて使われるようになった。十九世紀から二十世紀初めにかけて、政治学者と社会学者が官僚制度の利点と欠点について盛んに論争している。すぐに予想できるように、欠点はたくさんある。スコットランドの気むずかしい批評家、トマス・カーライルは官僚制度について、「ヨーロッパ大陸の悪弊」と書いている。

だが、官僚制度はよいものであり、必要ですらあることを認識した人も多い。歴史的にみる

なら、大規模な組織を維持するには膨大な管理業務が必要になるので、まったく当然の方法として、官僚組織が発達してきたはずである。

原始的な部族社会では、指導者は個人としてのカリスマ性に基づいて、部族を率いることができたはずである。マオリ族の戦士のように、人一倍闘志があって目が輝いていれば、族長として、司令官として、仲間を率いることができる。しかし、社会がもっと複雑になると、カリスマ的なリーダーだけでは統率できなくなる。たとえば、古代中国の帝国や、古代エジプトの帝国、古代ローマの帝国は、何らかの官僚組織がなければ構築できなかっただろう。奴隷に対してすら、暴力だけでは細部にわたって命令できたはずがない。

二十世紀の初頭に、ドイツの社会学者、マックス・ウェーバーがこう指摘した。大規模な社会組織では長年のうちに階層的な権力構造が確立される。規則が文書で規定され、官僚が専門的な教育を受け、そして何よりも重要な点として、役職が作られて、正式な肩書きと権限が決められる。

人類の発明のうちとくに重要だと思えるのは、当然のこととして受け入れられているものだと思う。発明されて使われるようになると、当たり前のように思えるからだ。たとえば、何千年か前に通貨を発明したのは誰なのだろう。金や銀、貝殻やビーズなどの少量を使って、役立つものといつでも交換できるようにしたのだから、通貨は何とも偉大な発明だ（通貨について

は、後にも触れる）。

官僚制度の役職もじつに偉大な発明だと思う。

ウェーバーは官僚制度について、効率的ではあるが非人間的でロボットのようだという厳しい見方をとっていた。だが現代の社会では、複雑な組織が大量にあり、官僚制度の役職がなければ、動かなくなる。政府にも大企業にも、大量の役職がある。営業担当副社長、流通部長、人事部長などなどがあって、いずれも組織図に整然と配置されている。どの役職も長期的にみれば、人は代わっていくが、どの人もそれぞれの役職に決められた職務を果たして、組織全体の目標を達成するために努力する。じつに見事だ。人は代わっても、役職の機能は変わらない。

そうでなければ、権威の継続性は保てない。

わたしはコカ・コーラ社の社長だったとき、いつも話していたことがある。わたしがコカ・コーラの世界で何らかの権威か影響力をもっているとするなら、それはすべて、名刺に書かれているひとつの言葉によるものだ。それは、わたしの職務を示す「社長」という肩書きである。そして、この肩書きが重要なのは、そのすぐ下に「コカ・コーラ社」と書かれているわたしの名前ではない。名刺に書かれているのは、そのいちばん下に書かれているわたしの名前ではない。名刺に書かれていることのなかで、いちばん重要性が低いのが、わたしの名前だ。

これは冗談ではない。本気なのだ。

さらに、じつに整然とした形に作られた組織のために、個々人が創造性や生産性を発揮しにくくなってはならないとも思う。

個性、創造性、感情、熱意、想像力などの点で、各人がもつ力はきわめて大きい。組織のどの地位にある人も、これらを発揮できるようになっていなければならない。

複雑な大組織の指導者は、微妙なバランスをとらなければならない。規則や慣例をしっかりと定めて、すべての部分が適切に調和のとれた動きをするようにしなければならない。しかし長年のうちに、避けがたいと思える結果が生まれてくる。規則や慣例が一人歩きするようになり、それで達成しようとした目的よりも重視されるようになるのだ。硬直的で役に立たない儀式になり、組織の活力をそぐようになる。

こうした儀式を司る官僚は、命がけで儀式を守るようになる。少しでも変えれば、自分の力と権威が損なわれるからだ。官僚は徐々に、あらゆる進歩に抵抗し、失敗を保証する力だけをもつにすぎなくなり、往々にして実際に、その力だけを行使するようにもなる。

そして、官僚はいつも忙しくしている。社内の報告書やメモをつぎつぎに書く。オフィスにいつものファイル・キャビネットを並べて、大量の電子メールやメモを収める。夜遅く自宅に帰って、忙しくてたまらないとこぼす。だが、実際には一日中、生産的なことは何もしていな

い。そうした組織では、失敗は確実である。製紙業界によれば、数年前にアメリカ全体のオフィスのコピー機で、年に五千億枚を超えるコピーがとられている。昨年はどうだったかというと、専門家がいま必死に計算しているところだ。いったい、誰が誰のために、何のために、これだけのコピーをとっているのだろうか。電子メールの普及で紙は使わなくなると思っていたのだが。

（ゼロックスがどのような事業でいまの地位を築いたのか、考えてみるべきだ。）

わたしは若いころ、父親の家畜の仕事をみていたので、雄と雌の比率を適切に維持しておけば、家畜が増えていくことをよく知っている。官僚組織も同じように増殖する。仕組みは簡単だ。ひとりにマネジャーの肩書きを与える。一年半もすると、アシスタントがつく。アシスタントはすぐにジュニア・マネジャーになる。すると何が起こるか。その下にアシスタントがつく、この過程が繰り返されていく。

こうして階層が増えていくが、顧客から電話があっても、誰も席にいない。みな、会議中なのだ。会議があると、書類が増え、電子メールが増え、電話が増え、会議がまた増える。会議の準備のための会議すら開かれることが多い。会議は大きな官僚組織にとって、宗教儀式のようなものであり、官僚はきわめて信心深い。

ヒューストンにあるコカ・コーラ社食品部門に勤務していたとき、官僚組織はほとんどなか

った。ダンカン・フーズとミニッツメイドの合併でできた若い組織だった。責任者のチャールズ・ダンカンはスコットランド系であり、手強く、優秀で、質素な起業家だ。官僚制を嫌い、あらゆる手を使って、官僚組織を抑え込んだ。食品部門は、清掃係から社長までの間に五段階の階層があるような組織にはなっていなかった。素早く、効率的に動き、もうひとつ、収益性が高かったとも指摘しておきたい。

チャールズ・ダンカンは後にコカ・コーラ社の社長になり、カーター政権の閣僚になった。

アトランタに来て、アメリカの飲料部門でともにはたらくようにといってくれたとき、コカ・コーラ社の本社では何十年もの間、膨らんできた巨大な組織を合理化する必要があると語った。まさにそうだった。

アトランタに赴任した直後に、わたしの秘書は本社の巨大な官僚組織の壁にぶつかり、鉛筆も手に入らないと泣いていたわけだが、わたしはそれ以外にも、大きな官僚組織について学ぶようになった。何かを依頼したとき、「ノー」とはいわない。だが動かない。これこれのことをこれこれの期限までにやってほしいと依頼しても、その通りには動いてくれない。

アメリカ・コカ・コーラ社の本社に勤務するようになった後、エレベーターのうち一台で、カーペットがすり切れていることに気づいた。そこで、秘書のフローレンス・カリノウスキに、メンテナンス部門に電話してカーペットを交換するよう依頼してほしいと頼んだ。何か月かた

って、まだ交換していないねと秘書にいった。まだだが、メンテナンスを定期的に行っていて、カーペットの交換は予定に入っているということだった。

一年後、アメリカ・コカ・コーラ社の社長になったとき、エレベーターのカーペットがまだ交換されていないと指摘すると、すぐに交換することになっているという返事だった。二年後、アメリカ・コカ・コーラ社からコカ・コーラ社本社に移ったとき、エレベーターのカーペットはまだ交換されていなかった。メンテナンス部門は依頼を断ったことはない。「ノー」といわれたことは一度もない。ただ、カーペットは交換されない。

会社の前進をすべて止めたいのであれば、事務手続きを何よりも優先すればいい。官僚制度を愛することだ。

どの組織にも、業務のネックになっている部門があって、これも官僚制度の特徴のひとつだ。組織の最高幹部ですら、突き破ることはできない。この部分の番人を侮辱するようなことをすれば、業務の遂行にもっともっと時間をかけるようになるだけだ。何年か前、コピー・センターが最新のイノベーションだとされ、巨大な機械ですべてのコピーを行うようになったとき、同センターがまさにネックになって、オフィスの効率性が低下するようになった。センターの責任者が頑固な暴君になり、自分の権限と権威を振り回すようになったことが多い。コピーのように、じつに単純で簡単な業務すら、担当者のご機嫌をたえずとっておかないと進まなくなっ

た。

官僚組織にはどの部門にも似たような状況があって、組織内の小領主に逆らうことはできない。たとえば、旅行部門やオフィス用品部門の頭越しに行動すれば、後で仕返しをされることが多い。チケットやクリップを手に入れるという簡単なことであっても、これら部門に何かを依頼するときには、熾烈な戦いになる。比較的最近、ウォール・ストリート・ジャーナル紙のジャレド・サンドバーグが、こうしたオフィスの暴君についてコラムを書いている。ある購買マネジャーはどんなに小さなものにも依頼伝票を書くよう要求し、オフィス業務の障害になっている。依頼伝票を切らした秘書がこのマネジャーのところに行くと、「依頼伝票に記入して提出してください」といわれたという。

がちがちの官僚制が厄介なのは、みずからは生産的な仕事をほとんどしていないのに、他人の仕事をあきらかに妨げるからだ。官僚は自分の縄張りを守ることに必死になっているので、必要不可欠な情報の流れを遮り、会社が成功する機会を奪ってまで、自分の成功を追求する。

ビジネスのジャングルでは昔から、「他人の成功は自分の失敗」が掟になっているが、何段階もの階層がある官僚組織のなかでは、この掟が完全に通用している。血の臭いがただよっていると思えるほどだ。仲間と張り合うのは、人間の本性のひとつだ。しかし組織内の戦いは、問題がつまらないものであるほど、たいした結果を生まないものであるほど、生産性に打撃にな

る。

組織全体がガリバーのように、何百人ものリリパット人に縛り付けられているような状態になる。官僚制という名の新しいゲームがあるそうだ。全員が輪になって立ち、最初に動いたものが負けというのだ。

自社でとくに優秀な人材を失いたいのであれば、事務手続きを何よりも優先すればいい。官僚組織を愛することだ。

人事の専門家から聞いた話だが、中堅の幹部をひとり失うと、後任を探し出し、引きつけ、訓練するために、少なくとも辞めていった幹部の年間給与の二倍にあたる経費がかかるのだという。だからあきらかに、優秀な人材を失わないようにするのは、引き合うことなのだ。コカ・コーラ社では、ほとんどの企業がそうするように、とくに優秀な人材を維持するために努力した。世界全体で事業を展開している企業では、他社に引き抜きをかけられる幹部がでてくるのは避けがたい。だが、大切な従業員が不満をもっていることが分かると、迅速に動いて、その理由をみつけだし、状況を改善しようと努めた。ときには、気付くのが遅すぎて、何もできないうちに辞めていくこともあった。ときには、手の打ちようがないこともあった。

だが、わたしが経験から学んできた点だが、従業員が辞める理由としてあげるのは、給料が低いとか、仕事が難しいとかではないことが多い。官僚制をあげる人が少なくないのだ。組織

が官僚的なために仕事ができない。苛立ちがつのる。だが、前述の日本事業の幹部とは違って、本社から送られてくるメモや指令をゴミ箱に捨てるほどの勇気はない。

会社を辞める人に最後にインタビューを行うとき、なぜ辞めるのかという質問に対して、官僚的で息がつまりそうだからと答える人が少なくなかった。

大企業ではどこでも、大きな課題のひとつはつねに、不必要な官僚制をなくすことだ。コカ・コーラ社の社長だったとき、わたしはいつも高給取りの掃除夫を自認していた。わたしの仕事は、廊下をいつもきれいにしておき、とくに優秀な従業員が仕事ができるようにすることだ。顧客を獲得し、顧客に奉仕し、株主の価値を高めるのが、従業員の仕事である。

わたしはビジネスの世界に入って間もなく、そう驚くほどではない結論に達した。ビジネスとは要するに、既存の顧客にうまく奉仕し、新しい顧客を獲得することだという結論である。

販売しているのが自動車だろうが、化粧品だろうが、コンピューターだろうが、実際には顧客に奉仕する事業を行っているのである。とんでもなく珍しい事業を行っていて、たとえば油田火災の消火を専門にしているとしても、まずは油田消火の専門技術を売り込まなければ、仕事を依頼しようとはしてくれない。レッド・アデアはこの仕事をしていて、世界各地で売り込んできたことから、その名がブランドになって、油田火災の消火の代名詞になった。

コカ・コーラのブランドは、気持ちの良さ、楽しいひととき、さわやかさの代名詞になって

いる。「コークですべてがうまくいく」と広告で宣言しているのだから、コカ・コーラ社ではたらくものの仕事は、全員がすべての点でこの宣言の実現に全力をあげるようにすることにある。われわれが接触するすべての人が、コークでたしかにすべてがうまくいくと納得できるようにする。ボトラー・システムにかかってきた電話に応対する人から、会長室のスタッフまで、さらには取締役すらも、それぞれ役割に違いはあっても、実際の仕事はコカ・コーラを売ることである。

コカ・コーラ社で語り継がれてきた話がある。ウッドラフと法律顧問がどちらにとっても顔見知りの人ばかりの集まりに出席したときのことだ。集まりの途中で、ウッドラフが法律顧問に、会社でどういう仕事をしているか、皆に説明するよう求めた。法律顧問は一瞬もためらうことなく、こう答えた。「コカ・コーラを売る仕事をしています」

この点がわたしにとって、いつも最優先すべき任務であった。わたしはコカ・コーラ社の全体で、そして世界のコカ・コーラ・システム全体で、営業を最優先する強固な考え方を奨励した。どのような支出をする際にも、どのような部門をつくる際にも、どのようなプロジェクトを行う際にも、かならず基本的な問いに答えなければならない。顧客を獲得し、顧客に奉仕するのに役立つのかという問いである。この問いに対して、明確に力強く「イエス」と答えられない場合には、どのような支出でも、どのような取り組みでも止めなければならない。顧客に

関係のない五十のことを行うと決めれば、五十の官僚組織ができる。そこに属する人がきわめて優秀であっても、どのような形でも顧客に奉仕することはないのだから、そもそもするべきではない仕事をする結果になる。

多数の企業が道を見失っている。創業から間もないころは、質素で無駄がない。月曜日に送られてきた小切手を確認してから、火曜日に何に支出できるかを考える。事業で成功を収めるようになると、気が緩むようになり、失敗の種を蒔くことになる。厳しく支出を抑える姿勢は失われていく。アシスタントのアシスタントのアシスタントが増殖するようになって、すぐに会社は様変わりする。みな、互いに顔を見つめ合いながら、こう話すようになる。「どうしてここまで大きくなったのだろう。こんなにたくさんの人が本社にいて、いったい何をしているのだろう」。そうなるのだ。

デル・コンピューターは当初、じつに無駄のない筋肉質の会社であった。だが長年のうちに組織が大きくなり、管理階層が増えていった。収益性が低下し、パソコンで第一位の地位をヒューレット・パッカードに奪われた。このとき、創業者のマイケル・デルがCEOに復帰した。真っ先に行ったことのひとつが、全従業員への電子メールの発信だった。「当社には偉大な人たちがいる。……だが、新たな敵を社内に抱えることにもなった。それは官僚組織だ。資金を食い、会社の動きを遅くしている。官僚組織はわれわれがつくり、従業員を管理させたのであり、

148

委員会は、ひとりひとりでは何もできないが、集団としては、何もしてはならないという決定を下せる人たちの集まりである
　　　　——フレッド・アレン

われわれはこの問題を解決しなければならない」

官僚組織はそもそも、内部で衝突しあい、ぶつかりあうものなのだ。わたしはこうした不和を最小限に止めるために努力し、そのために、社内の誰であっても、わたしのオフィスに来て他の部門を批判するのを止めるよう求めてきた。批判の必要があれば、関係者全員が出席する会議で互いに相手の目をみながら批判するよう求めた。また、廊下でわたしを呼び止めて情報を伝えたり、質問したりするのを止めさせようとした。そんなことでは、トイレに行く途中での経営になってしまうと話したものだ。

トイレに行く途中で誰かに話しかけられ、「前からお話ししようと思っていたのですが」といわれると、わたしはこういって、話を聞かないようにしていた。「つぎの会議のときに話してくれないか」。会議の場で話せば、意見の対立を解消できるか、少なくとも打撃が大きくならないようにすることができる。

ウォーレン・バフェットによれば、バークシャー・ハザウェイがある企業を買収したとき、最初の一か月に五十四の委員会を廃止し、合計で月に延べ一万時間もの労働時間を節減したという。バフェットはいう。「企業にどれほど官僚組織がはびこるかは信じがたいほどだ。コストをほぼすべて顧客に転嫁できる企業では、とくに官僚組織が肥大化する」

ちなみに、バークシャー・ハザウェイは七十六の企業を傘下に収め、従業員は全体で二十三万二千人、年間の利益は百八十億ドルを超えている。本社にはわずか十九人しかいない。

ピーター・ドラッカーは六十年以上にわたって教育とコンサルティングを行い、三十以上の著作がある。一貫したテーマのひとつとして、優れた企業は従業員を細かく管理しようとはしないし、生活の隅々まで命令しようとはしないと指摘してきた。優れた企業は従業員を尊重し、会社に寄与するよう励まし、創造性を発揮するよう励ます。これに対してだめな企業は官僚制の何重もの管理階層で、従業員の創意を窒息させる。

ドラッカーは長く官僚制を批判してきたが、その頂点に位置するのが、「メールルームを売却せよ」と題した画期的な記事だ。一九八九年にウォール・ストリート・ジャーナル紙に掲載され、二〇〇五年の著書に収録されている。当時、大部分の企業は支援部門の効率性を高めようと努力していた。ところがドラッカーは、そうした業務を完全に外注して、なくす方がいいと提案した。ドラッカーはこう論じた。

社内のサービス・サポート部門は事実上の独占事業になっている。生産性を上げる理由はない。競争がないのだから。それどころか、生産性を上げないようにする理由が十分にある。企業でも官庁でも、組織では通常、それぞれの部門の価値と地位は、人数と予算で判断される。事務部門やメンテナンス部門、支援部門など、利益に直接に、計測可能な形で寄与するわけではない部門ではとくにそうだ。このため、これら業務で生産性を上げるのは、昇進と成功への道にはなりえない。

社内の支援部門が仕事の質が低いと批判されると、管理者は人員を増やして対応しようとする。外注先なら、仕事の質を高めると同時にコストを引き下げなければ、もっと優秀な競争相手に契約を奪われることを知っている。

外注によって組織の管理階層を減らし、無駄をなくしていくのは、企業経営の方法として効率的だし、革新的だともいえる。失敗したいのであれば、官僚制度を骨まで愛するべきだ。

最後に、官僚制の危険について、もうひとつ例をあげておこう。最悪の場合、成功を妨げるだけでなく、悲惨な失敗をもたらしかねない。

「ボブ、きみはどういう
仕事をしているんだ」
「何もしていません」
「ジョージ、きみはどういう
仕事をしているんだ」
「ボブの控えです」

　一九八六年一月二十八日、スペース・シャトルのチャ
レンジャーが打ち上げ直後に爆発し、乗組員七人が全員
死亡した。そのひとりはクリスタ・マコーリフであり、
アメリカ航空宇宙局（NASA）の宇宙教師計画で、教
師としてはじめての宇宙飛行士になった人だ。
　二〇〇三年二月一日、スペース・シャトルのコロンビ
アが大気圏への突入の際にテキサス州上空で空中分解
し、七人の乗組員が全員死亡した。
　二回の惨事はいずれも、技術的な欠陥が原因だとされ
ている。
　この惨事について、直接の知識をもたないものは、公
聴会や事後の分析であきらかになった情報に基づいて考
えるしかない。もちろん異論もあるだろうが、専門家の
多くは、この二回の事故で技術的な問題が惨事につなが
った一因が官僚組織の失敗にあるという点で、意見が一
致しているようだ。*どちらの場合にも、発射の決定を下

152

したのはNASAの官僚組織だ。これは何段階もの階層がある複雑な組織であり、科学界や国防総省、ホワイトハウス、議会など、多様な主人に同時に仕えようと努力している。さらに、部品やシステムを供給する多数の企業も、意思決定に関与する。

関係者の強い思いがこもった判断を下す過程に関与した経験があれば、きわめて多くの力がはたらいて、ときには冷静な見方が脇においやられることを知っているはずだ。わたしはいくつもの意思決定にかかわってきたし、とくにニュー・コークに関する意思決定に関与したので、NASAが意思決定にあたって、性格が似ている問題にぶつかったのではないかと思う。

もちろん、はるかに重大な結果をもたらす問題ではあるのだが。前述のように、関係者の興奮が強く、切迫感が強く、船頭が多いほど、官僚組織は意思決定にあたって、議論が暗礁に乗り上げるか、そうでなければ集団願望に陥る可能性が高くなる。ニュー・コークの場合がそうであったように、一部のM&A案件がそうであったように、誰も興奮に水を差そうとは考えなくなる。

そして、多段階の官僚組織のなかに対抗しあう部門がいくつもある場合、縄張り争いのために状況がさらに複雑になりうる。極端な場合、官僚組織がうまく機能しなくなって、実際には誰も水を差す力をもたなくなりうる。そうなれば、組織として、どのような点でも客観的な判

＊ Jeff Forrest, "The Challenger Shuttle Disaster: A Failure in Descision Support System and Human Factors Management," November 26, 1996.（二〇〇五年十月七日にDSSResources.COMで公表）。

断を下すことができなくなる。NASAについて伝えられた点をみていくと、責任が極端に分散していて、誰かが間違いをみつけてくれるだろうと誰もが考えるようになっていたようだ。そして、誰も問題をみつけなかった。惨事の後の議会証言によるなら、最終的に判断を下したのは最善の情報を握っている人ではなく、最大の権力を握っている人だったようだ。

ハリケーン「カトリーナ」による惨状は、官僚組織が機能不全に陥ったときにどうなるかを示す典型例だ。さまざまなレベルの官僚組織が完全に失敗し、人知れず被害を生み出し、人命が失われていった事例については、これまでに多数の本が書かれてきたし、今後も書かれていくだろう。

企業の官僚組織が機能しなくなったとき、そのコストは高くつき、解決は難しい。ものごとを整理するだけでも大量の時間が無駄になる。このためおそらく、仕事上の間違いが多くなるだろう。ほんの小さなことをしようとするだけでも、苛立ちがつのる結果になるからだ。そして、仕事上の間違いはコストがかかる。

人命にかかわる大きな判断を下す際に官僚組織の内部で対立が厳しくなっていると、悲惨な結果になりうる（NASAは最近の動きをみるかぎり、意思決定の過程を改善し、官僚組織の摩擦を減らす方法を見つけ出したようだ。連邦緊急事態管理庁も政策と手続きを簡素化し、管理階層を減らしたようだ）。

## 法則9　一貫性のないメッセージを送る

　一貫性のないメッセージや混乱したメッセージを従業員や顧客に送ると、競争力が損なわれ、失敗につながることになる。ジャック・ウェルチによれば、ゼネラル・エレクトリック（GE）のCEOに就任したとき、社内には一貫性のないメッセージが飛び交っていて、伝統のある部門がいくつも破綻寸前になっていたという。コカ・コーラ社でも一九七〇年代初め、メッセージが、控えめにいっても誤解を招く場面が少なくなかった。従業員やボトラーに対するものはとくにそういう問題が多かったし、顧客の小売店に対するものにすら、問題があった。とりわけ深刻だったのはファウンテン部門であり、この部門の幹部はいくつもの一貫性のないメッセージを送っていた。

155

メッセージで問題なのは、
たしかに相手に届いたと
錯覚することだ
——ジョージ・バーナード・ショー

「残さず食べないと、デザートはだしませんよ」と子供を叱る親のようなものだ。そう叱っても、本気ではない。食べ残しても、デザートはでてくる。

わたしが一九七三年、アトランタに移ってアメリカの飲料事業ではたらくようになったとき、ファウンテン部門は伝統のある部門として大切にされていた。何といっても、コカ・コーラ社の起源はアトランタのソーダ・ファウンテン事業にあるのだし、その後もマクドナルドからヤンキー・スタジアムまで、各種の店舗や施設でカップやグラスに入れた商品を販売し、毎年、順調に利益をあげてきたからだ。部門には七百人ほどの営業担当者がいて、顧客をまわっていた。チェーン店の本部を担当するものが何人かいた。大部分は個々の販売店を訪問して、コカ・コーラ社の商品の販売を支援していた。コカ・コーラ社が世界のファウンテン市場の最大手であることに、疑問の余地はなかった。

問題は……、じつのところ問題はいくつもあった。そして最大

156

の問題は、突然、赤字になったことだ。

まず、一九六〇年代後半に、ファウンテン部門が奇妙な割当制度をつくり、その年の各販売店の販売量に関する営業担当者の予想に基づいて、販売奨励金を支払うようにした。営業担当者のほとんどは根っから楽観的だ。問題は、営業担当者の予想に基づいて、各販売店が年初に奨励金の全額を受け取ることにあった。問題は、十二月になると、販売店の売上は予想を大幅に下回っていることがあきらかになる。

数学者でなくても分かることだが、奨励金を支払った後になって、それに見合う売上が実現しないのだから、粗利益は吹き飛んでしまう。また、販売店に対しても、社内でも、メッセージに一貫性が欠けることになる。

この変わった制度を維持していたうえ、原液の原料費が上昇していたなかで、コカ・コーラ社はそれを吸収しつづけていた。コカ・コーラ原液を小売店に売る際の価格を変更してはならないという規則が、石に刻まれているかのように思えていたからだ。長年の間にコストは上昇し、粗利益率は低下してきたが、当時の経営陣はこの問題に対処するのを拒否してきた。価格を引き上げれば事業が混乱し、競争相手の攻撃に負けると恐れていたのである。実際には、自社のコストが上昇しているとき、競争相手でもコストが上昇している。だから、競争相手が値上げに追随しないわけにはいかないはずだとわたしはみていた。

そのとき、チャールズ・ダンカンに要請されて、わたしはアトランタに移り、アメリカ・コカ・コーラ社のルーク・スミス社長の下ではたらくことになった。最初の任務は、ファウンテン部門の問題の解決であった。状況を調べていくと、値上げする以外に方法がないことがあきらかになった。ファウンテン部門の幹部がつぎつぎにわたしのところに来て、値上げできない理由を慎重な言い回しで説明してくれた。意見を聞き終わった後、ある金曜日に一ガロン当たり二十セントの値上げを決定した。

翌週月曜日、競争相手に殺される事態にはならなかった。競争相手はみな、追随して値上げしたのである。

この例をみると、ひとつの考え方が深く根をはって、動かせないと思われるようになりうることが分かる。わたしは外部から来たので、そこに長年いる人とは少し違った目で家具の配置を考えることができた。それで、ソファーを動かしたのである。動かしてみると、建物が倒れたりはしないことが分かったというわけだ。

通貨がいかに素晴らしい発明なのかについては、すでに触れた。わたしは長年、企業経営にたずさわるなかで、お金を実際の金額として理解する方法について考えてきた。通貨、お金というのは偉大な抽象概念であり、そのためにあらゆる商取引が可能になっている。だがわたしはいつも、抽象的な見方が極端になりすぎて、その背後にある現実がみえなくな

158

っていると心配していた。

一九七一年に、ヒューストンの食品部門にいたとき、気付いた点がある。従業員は大学を卒業し、人によっては経営大学院も卒業し、会社に入って四十年間、日常業務をこなしてきても、その間に一度も現金を扱わないことがありうるのだ。従業員への給与や、仕入れ先への代金や、メディアへの広告料や、広告代理店への報酬や、旅行代理店への代金などの支払いに、現金を使うことはない。本社では、スタッフ部門の幹部が扱うのは予算に書かれている数字だけである。これでは、実態がみえなくなる。抽象化がいきすぎて、何も意味しなくなった。

ラスベガスでは、台の上に現金が置かれたとき、ただちに対応してみえなくしなければ、担当者はクビになる。実際のお金を客が意識しないようにしているのであり、だからこそさまざまな色のチップを使っている。ギャンブルに興じている客は、無料の飲み物を受け取ると、五十ドルのチップを渡したりする。「五十ドル」だとは考えておらず、小さなチップ一枚だと考えているのだ。

アメリカの連邦政府は一日に平均七十四億ドルを支出している。だが、十億というのは、ほんとうにとんでもない数値だ。十億分前には、ローマ帝国のハドリアヌス皇帝が辺境の地に防壁を築いていた。十億時間前には、人類はまだ石器時代だった。十億日前には、人類は登場していない。

何十年か前、C・ノースコート・パーキンソンが有名な『パーキンソンの法則』で、巨額の予算にいくつもの零がついている数値が並んでいるのをみたとき、それが実際にどれほどの金額なのかを理解できる人はあまりいないと論じている。たいていの人が理解できるのははるかに小さな金額までであり、数百ドルから、せいぜいのところ数千ドルまでにすぎないという。

わたしはヒューストンの食品部門で、従業員が実際にどれほどの金額を支出しているのか、実感できるようにするにはどうすればいいかを考えていた。入金と出金を一ドルずつ実感できる方法である。あるとき、最高の方法を思いついた。実際にどれだけの金額かを考えるだけではだめだ、実際に現金を使えばいいのだと。

わたしは最高財務責任者（CFO）を呼んで、こう話した。来月の第一週に、すべての支払いを現金で行いたいのだがどうだろうと。誰か幹部がニューヨークに出張し、航空運賃が六百九十二ドルだというのなら、六百九十二ドルの紙幣で支払ってもらう。ニューヨーク・タイムズ紙の全面広告に一万九千四百八十五ドルを支払うのであれば、責任者が一万九千四百八十五ドルの紙幣で支払う。すべての代金を現金で支払うようにしたかった。すべてを、である。給与を現金で支払う。鉛筆を買うのであれば、現金で支払う。すべての取引に現金を使う。

食品部門は小規模ではない。だが、巨大企業ではない。それでも、ヒューストンのすべての銀行から集めても、小規模でない、この実験を行えるほどの現金はなかった。

もちろんこれは非常識きわまりないアイデアであって、実行に移すことはできなかった。だが、実行できていれば、面白い経験になって、従業員が予算に書かれている数字を扱うだけでなく、実際の金額を実感できるようになっただろう。

こういうわけで、お金というものの現実を劇的な形で実感できるようにすることはできなかったが、ファウンテン部門では少なくとも、金を稼ぐことの重要性を痛感させることができた。

ファウンテン部門には、一貫性のないメッセージの好例があった。長年の慣習で、業績がどれほどよくても悪くても、毎年冬に「営業会議」と称して、幹部と営業担当者の全員と配偶者をどこかの保養地に招待し、贅沢な祝賀会を開いていた。わたしが指揮をとるようになった年にも、営業会議が予定されていた。その年には部門で損失を計上する状況にあったのだが。

まさに、一貫性のないメッセージだ。「業績は悪くても問題ない。報奨を受け取れる」というわけだ。

そこで、いくつかの点を変える計画のひとつとして、業績が悪かった年には報奨を与えないことにした。その点を明確にするために、わたしはこう発表した。「今年の営業会議はシカゴで開催する。シカゴは素晴らしい都市だが、一月に観光客が集まる保養地ではない。会議はビジネス・ホテルで開く。二流のビジネス・ホテルだ。配偶者は招待しない。一部屋に二人ずつ泊まってもらう」

人生には
金より大切なものが
たくさんある。
そして、どれも金がかかる
──フレッド・アレン

（これも、往年のコメディアン、フレッド・アレンの言葉だ。
ハーバード大学経営大学院はアレンを招聘すべきだった）

わたしもそのホテルは敬遠したい。一月のシカゴは
もっと敬遠したい。しかし、稼いでいない金を使うわ
けにはいかない。そう伝えた。

メッセージは伝わった。

翌年、部門の売上と利益は大幅に増加し、ハワイで大
がかりな祝賀会を開いた。もちろん、配偶者も招待して。

その後、ファウンテン部門は毎年、利益をだしつづ
けている。

わたしにとってとくに恐ろしかった経験も、一貫性
のないメッセージの一例だといいうる。一九八五年、
わたしはジャマイカ政府からマーティン・ルーサー・
キング平和賞を贈られることになった、エドワード・
シアガ首相と、何人かの将軍が出席した。朝食のとき、
将軍が首相に何かをささやきつづけていた。最後に、
首相がわたしにささやいた。「講演の後、表で車に乗る
計画は変更します。お部屋で待っていただけますか」。

162

部屋に戻って眺めると、どの方角にも火の手があがっていて、デモ隊が叫んでいる。「この国でのコカ・コーラ社の事業について、わたしが知っておくべきことがありますか」とわたしは聞いた。「いやいや、ガソリン価格が上がったことに抗議しているだけです。しかし、万一ということもありますので、安全策をとります」。というわけで、みなヘリコプターに乗って、その場を離れた。

思い出すたびに、何とも皮肉な話だと思う。平和賞の授賞式の会場から、機関銃を構えたヘリコプターで脱出したのだから。

コカ・コーラ社では、一貫性のないメッセージという点で最大の問題は、世界のボトラー・システムに関するものだった。徐々に、世界の小売業界と歩調が合わなくなり、大規模な再編が必要になっていった。要するに、世界的に社会と経済が変化していくなかで、コカ・コーラ・システムが変化に追いつけなくなっていたのである。

この変化のうちかなりの部分は、技術の進歩によるものである。一九六二年七月十日、新しい通信衛星、テルスターを使って、大西洋を越えるテレビ中継がはじめて実現した。このときから、世界はどんどん小さくなっていった。

以前には、国によって服装が少しずつだが違い、歌う曲が違い、読む本が違い、人気のテレビ番組が違っていた。ところがある日、気付いてみると、誰もが同じ服を着て、同じ曲を歌い、同じ本を読み、同じテレビ番組をみていると思えるほどになっていた。アメリカ東北部のバン

ガーでも、インド南部のバンガロールでも、若者はみなリーバイスのジーンズにTシャツ、スニーカーだ。一九七〇年代にはロックとテレビのスポーツ中継で、それまでになかったほど世界がひとつになった。世界のどこに行っても、誰でもモハメッド・アリを知っている。一九七六年のモントリオール・オリンピックでは、十億人以上がテレビ中継をみている。料理にすら、世界のどこでも食べられているものがある。

このように世界が小さくなり、「グローバル化」が進んでいるなかでも、コカ・コーラ社は世界全体に広がる事業に、一貫性のないばらばらのメッセージを送るようになっていた。世界各地の事業を、ひとつのマーケティング方針、ひとつの全体的目標でまとめることができないようだった。世界がひとつになっていったとき、コカ・コーラ社はばらばらのままだったのだ。

「コカ・コーラ」という言葉は、世界中で知っている人の数が「OK」のつぎに多いともいわれているが、コカ・コーラ社自体は、世界の各国でかなり違った性格をもっていた。これが失敗の種になり、実を結びはじめていたのである。

こうなった主因は、国際事業の構築に使われた方法にあった。コカ・コーラの国際事業は何十年にもわたって、経営幹部を宣教師のように各地に派遣し、布教する形で進められてきた。各人に幹部は世界をそれぞれ違った目でみており、前述のように、ほぼ独立して動いていた。各人にはかなりの行動の自由が与えられていたが、その理由は単純であり、当時はそれ以外に世界事

164

業を築く方法がなかったのである。このため、地域によって事業開発の方法は違っていたし、

商品と会社のイメージも違っていた。違いがないのは、コカ・コーラの味、商標、容器、それにシ

ステムの情熱だけであり、このシステムによって大規模な世界事業がつくられていった。国や地

域による違いは、その市場を当初に開拓した個人の考え方に直接に起因することが少なくない。

たとえば、ビル・ベッカーという開拓者が中南米に赴任した。そこでみたのは、人口が多い

が、所得が低い世界だ。そこで、ベッカーは数量を重視して事業を計画した。メキシコとアメ

リカの国境を流れるリオ・グランデから南アメリカ最南端のパタゴニアまで、誰でも買える価

格でコカ・コーラを大量に販売した。このため、コカ・コーラ社はこの地域で、薄利多売の大

規模な事業を展開することになった。

ヨーロッパでは、マックス・キースという別の開拓者が、人口が少なく、所得水準がはるか

に高い市場に参入するために努力した。ジュースなどの各種飲料が普及していたので、コーク

を特別の飲み物と位置づけることにした。特別の機会に特別にだされる飲み物とされるように

したのである。このため、コカ・コーラ社はヨーロッパで、量は少ないが利益率の高い偉大な

事業を展開することになった。

これと同様に、アジアやアフリカ、中東の各国でも、コカ・コーラ社の事業はそれぞれ少し

ずつ違った構造で組み立てられている。ある国では、きわめて現代的で効率的な事業を展開し

ている。そして国によっては、ロバを使ってコークを市場に運んでいる場合もある。要するに、コカ・コーラ社の世界事業は多数の王国からなる不思議なモザイクのようになっていた。共通の商品と共通の品質基準によって結びつけられてはいるが、事業の他の側面では違いが大きく、全体の問題を議論しようとしても、話がかみ合わないほどになっていたのである。そして長い間、それで問題はなかった。

## ひとつのデザイン、ひとつのメッセージ、ひとつの売り方の必要

だが一九六〇年代になると、世界は急速に変わるようになった。七〇年代には、変化がさらに加速している。コカ・コーラのマーケティングはそれまで、ニューヨークのコカ・コーラ・エクスポート社が広告案を示すだけだったが、マクドナルドや大規模なスーパーマーケット・チェーンが世界的なマーケティングに力をいれているのに合わせて、活性化することが必要になっていた。缶や大きなボトルなど、新しい容器を使った商品を増やす必要もあった。また、このころに気付いた点がある。コカ・コーラ社の事業はいくつもの独立した企業が個々に行う形になっているのだが、消費者は世界のどこでも好みが似通うようになってきた。

一九七〇年代に、ポール・オースティン会長兼CEOがエクスポート社をニューヨークから

アトランタに移し、世界全体で事業の統一をはかるために、世界各国の幹部を集めた会議をそれまでより頻繁に開くようにした。だが、コカ・コーラ社の世界事業のように、国や地域によって企業文化に大きな違いがある場合、文化を変えていくのは容易ではない。

一九七〇年代半ば、アメリカでは景気が冷え込むとともにインフレ率が急騰していた。アメリカ国内では、ボトラーとの契約変更の交渉を行っていた。南アメリカでは政治の混乱で事業が打撃を受けていた。一方、ヨーロッパとアジアはこの時期、急速に変化している。そして、最大の競争相手であるペプシコ社はソ連で独占的な販売権を獲得した。コカ・コーラ社はイスラエルの企業にボトリングの営業権を与えていたため、アラブ諸国には入り込めなかった。ペプシコ社はマーケティング攻勢を再開していた。コカ・コーラ社の株価は大きく下がっていた。

要するに、コカ・コーラの世界は深刻な状況にあったのである。

## 古い秩序を刷新する必要

一九八一年、ロベルト・ゴイズエタとわたしが経営を引き継いだとき、コカ・コーラ社はいくつもの課題に直面していた。たとえば、会社のイメージを変えて事業を再活性化するために、何年も前から必要だと分かっていた新商品、ダイエット・コークをすぐにも発売することが不

可欠だった。だが、最大の課題は世界全体の組織の方向と目標を統一することであった。世界各地で長年、独立王国のように経営されてきた組織を揺さぶり、改革するのは危険だ。しかし、それを行わなければ、時代の動きに後れていたマーケティングを一新し、流通システムを効率化して、世界の顧客に奉仕することができない状況になっていた。

真っ先に取り組むべき点は、一貫性のなかったメッセージに一貫性をもたせ、関係者全員が新たな方針の正しさを納得できるようにすることであった。世界事業を担うそれぞれの組織はかなりの自主性を維持できるが、市場が国境を越えて一体になってきたのだから、コカ・コーラ社の事業も同じようにしなければならないのである。

バスケットボールのボストン・セルティックスを率いた伝説の名コーチ、レッド・アワーバックは、こう語っている。パスの失敗はパスした側の責任だ。「パスをする際に適切に合図を送っていれば、受け手はメッセージを受け取って、ぴったりの位置までぴったりのタイミングで走り、パスを受け取れたはずだ」というのである。これと同じで、このときの責任はわれわれ経営陣の側にあった。世界各地の事業を率いるリーダーが全員、コカ・コーラ社の事業が、そして各人の事業が変わらなければならないというメッセージを正しく受け取るようにしなければならない。

コカ・コーラの世界事業のリーダーが全員、世界各地からカリフォルニア州パームビーチに

集まり、会議に出席した。ロベルト・ゴイズエタは会議のはじめに、仰天するような提案を行った。「聖なる牛を毎日、一頭ずつ殺す」よう呼びかけたのである。会社をほぼ一から作り替えるには、それが必要だと語ったのだ。そして、単純明快な基本理念を紹介した。本社でかなり前から議論してきたものだ。要するに、国際事業の管理をアトランタの本社に一元化し、ひとつの目標に向けて事業を統合するとともに、それぞれの現地事業の強さと個性を維持する方針を掲げた。「グローバルに考え、ローカルに行動する」戦略が流行するようになるはるか以前に、われわれはこの戦略を実行して成功を収めていたのだ。

## もうひとつの一貫性のないメッセージ——会社の事業の性格について

コカ・コーラ社が事業を多角化する必要があるとみられていたことについては、すでに触れた。ワイン事業では、実現できるとされていた相乗効果が実際には実現できていないことが分かり、売却した。

これ以外にも多角化事業があり、利益をあげていたが、短期間のうちに売却している。映画事業である。

一九八二年一月、コカ・コーラ社はコロンビア映画の買収を発表した。ウォール街では買収

価格が高すぎるとされ、コカ・コーラ社の株価が十パーセント下がっている。ロベルト・ゴイズエタとわたしが大きな間違いを犯したと考えた人が多かったのだ。だがすぐに、コロンビア映画の買収はそれほど悪くはなかったと思えるようになる。『トッツィー』と『ガンジー』の二本が大ヒットになり、翌八三年には、われわれが予想した範囲の上限を五十パーセントも上回る利益をあげている。

その後数年間、コロンビア映画は国内事業の利益に貢献し、会社に刺激と興奮をもたらした。映画会社を買収し経営する決定は正しかったのである。映画会社の経営にかかわるのは楽しかった。この点に疑問の余地はない。それに、華々しいスターの世界でもある。＊しかし、飲料の世界事業が急速に拡大して売上と利益が伸びるようになると、コロンビア映画の売上と利益はそれほど多くないので、業績面でそれに頼る必要はなくなってきた。コカ・コーラ社の事業全体のなかでは比較的小さな部門だったが、それにしては経営陣が時間をかけ、たえず関心を向けておく必要があった。そして、コロンビア映画を傘下に抱えていることで、ほんとうに重要なことは何なのかについて、関係者全員に一貫性のないメッセージを送る結果になっていた。

それに、映画事業は業績の予想がつかないことで有名だ。事業の性格上、毎年、着実に利益をあげるというわけにはいかない。同社の買収にあたって助言してくれたハーバート・アレンは、はじめての交渉の際にこの点を強調しており、まったく正しい指摘であった。アレンの健

全な助言もあって、われわれは映画事業で成功を収めていたが、やがて、ゴイズエタとわたし
は会社の事業を基本に戻す必要があると判断した。

コロンビア映画はアレン社に依頼して売却することにし、買収の際に支払った金額を大きく
上回る価格で売却できた。

一貫性のないメッセージは打ち切る。われわれはテレビ会社ではないし、映画会社でもない。
飲料の世界事業を行う会社なのだ。これこそ、われわれが得意とする事業であり、社内の全員
が考えつづけてほしい事業である。

## ＩＢＭの例

ジョン・エイカーズがＩＢＭの指揮をとっていたとき、「新しいパラダイム」と称して、いつ
も強調していた点がある。顧客重視の姿勢、つまり、以前になかったほど顧客に近付き、顧客
に敏感になり、顧客の立場で考えることだ。

> ＊　もちろん、われわれ経営陣が華々しい有名人になったわけではない。『ガンジー』の公開の日、ロベル
> ト・ゴイズエタとわたしはリムジンで映画館の正面に乗り付け、フラッシュを浴びた。車を降りると、サ
> インを求める女性が駆け寄ってきたが、われわれの顔をみて引き返し、こう吐き捨てた。「誰も知らない
> 人じゃない」

この哲学を強調するために、一九八九年初め、エイカーズは世界各地ではたらくIBMの主要幹部をニューヨーク州アーモンクの本社に集め、大会議を開いた。大々的なイベントであり、さまざまな趣向をこらしていた。開催にあたって、エイカーズが演壇に立って、IBMにとって顧客がいかに大切かを強調した。新しいパラダイムの重要性を示すために、今回の会議のハイライトとして、コカ・コーラ社のキーオ社長に最初に講演していただくと語った。

午前の会議がはじまったとき、「キーオ氏を紹介する前に」といって、エイカーズはこう発言した。「全員にみてもらいたいものがある。本社で、どれほど徹底した議論を行って、顧客に優れたサービスを提供する方法を考え、顧客に尽くす姿勢を再確認しているか、全員に感じ取ってもらいたいからだ」。そして、ビデオを流した。エイカーズはじめ、本社の経営陣が上着をぬぎ、腕まくりをして、顧客と顧客サービスについて真剣に議論している様子を映していた。チャートやグラフが何枚もあり、プロの進行役がいて、新しいパラダイムの重要性を繰り返し強調していた。

わたしも出席者とともにビデオをみた。そのとき、嫌でも気付いた点があった。会議テーブルの上には、参加者ひとりひとりの前にペプシコーラの缶があった。顧客を大切にする方法について議論するなかで、その点については、誰も何もいわない。

そして、わたしが紹介された。わたしは招待いただいたことに感謝した後、素晴らしいビデ

オをもう一度流すようお願いした。そして、こう話した。

「われわれは、コカ・コーラ社がIBMにとって最大級の顧客のひとつであることを誇りに思っており、本日、ここに招待いただいたのもそのためだと考えます。ところが、このビデオを制作し、何度もチェックされたと思いますが、何人もの主要な経営幹部が出席した会議で、全員の前にはなんと、わたしの会社にとって最大のライバル、ペプシコーラの缶が置いてあるのです。この会議は文字通り、ここで終わりにしてもいいように思います。肝心要の点がこれで分かったのです。このビデオでは顧客を意識することの大切さを議論しているわけですが、顧客のひとり、しかもこの演壇の上にいる顧客のことは、誰も気付いていないようですから」

会議場は静まりかえり、凍り付いた。そして、歓声があがり拍手が起こった。メッセージは伝わったのだ。それから何年も、この話はIBMで語り継がれていったという。

その後、IBMははじめて外部からルー・ガースナーをCEOに招き、あらゆる点を見なおすようになった。独自技術の秘密を守るのではなく、他社にライセンスを供与するようになった。また、情報技術サービスを提供するようにもなった。ガースナーから経営を引き継いだサム・パルミサーノのもと、二〇〇六年には九百億ドルの売上高のうち半分以上を、一九九〇年にはなかった事業からあげるようになった。一貫性のないメッセージはなくなった。

## 法則 10 　将来を恐れる

ほとんどの人は将来について、慎重に警戒するのが賢明であることを知っている。警戒するのは悪いことではない。だが、事業にあたって、何ごとにも警戒して安全第一の方法をとっていれば、第一の法則で論じたように、失敗への道になる。

みていると、そういう場面に何度もぶつかる。終了が近くなると、アメリカン・フットボールの試合をみていると、そういう場面に何度もぶつかる。終了が近くなると、リードしている側のチームは安全策をとるようになり、リードを守ろうと慎重になる。そもそもリードできたのはある種のリスクをとったからなのだが、同じリスクをとろうとはしなくなる。そして終了間際になって逆転されて負けることが少なくない。

リスクをとるのを止めるのは、きわめてリスクの高いことなのだ。

しかし、それ以上に企業の力を弱める病がある。

# 恐ろしいのはフィルムを
# 現像するあの小さな暗室だ
## ——マイケル・プリチャード

恐れである。

将来を慎重に警戒することと、将来をともかく恐れることの間には、天地の開きがある。フランクリン・D・ローズベルト大統領が「われわれが恐れなければならないものはただひとつ、恐れそのものである」と語ったとき、わたしの両親はその意味を正確に理解している。あの大恐慌の一九三〇年代に、両親は大胆に動いた。実際のところ、両親の状況は最悪に近かった。しかし、恐れることなく行動している。アメリカという国を築いた人たちと同じように、何があっても希望を失わない楽観主義の姿勢をもっていた。

「アメリカ・ドリーム」という言葉が生まれたのは、じつに素晴らしいことだと思うのだが、一九三一年、失業者が街にあふれていたときであった。この年、歴史学者のジェームズ・トラスロー・アダムズが『アメリカの叙事詩』という壮大なタイトルの本ではじめて、この言葉を使った。「誰にとっても、生活がよくなり、豊かになり、充実したものになる、そうみられている国の夢」がアメリカン・ドリームだとアダムズは語っている。将来は間違いなく明るいと宣言する言葉な

のだ。

　いまでは、以前よりはるかに多くの人が、この夢をたしかに実現できるようになっているのだが、にもかかわらず、将来を考えてひたすら恐れている人がきわめて多い。リスクをとるのを恐れているだけではない。ほとんどあらゆることを恐れているのである。人生というものを恐れているのだ。これでは間違いなく失敗する。

　船長が「未知の海域」に迷い込むのを恐れていた時代は、はるかな昔になった。科学が発達したいまの時代に、産業が発達した欧米の社会に暮らしていて、将来をいつも恐れているのはまったく理に適っていない。しかし、失敗したいのであれば、これはよい方法だ。

　古代ギリシャの世界観では、神々が人間といちばん違う点は、ものごとがどう進んでいくのかを予見できることだとされていた。人間は、将来を知ることができない。古代ギリシャではそうだったし、いまでもそうだ。

　何日か後に何が起こるのかは、誰にも分からない。世界中の予言者に聞いても、最先端の大学にあるコンピューター・モデルをすべて使っても、明日の朝に太陽がたしかに昇ってくるとは断言できない。昇ってこないことだって、ありうる。おそらく昇ってくるだろうといえるにすぎない。絶対確実な知識は、誰ももっていない。

　知らないことを恐れる理由はいつもある。だが、知識が増え、ものごとの見方が科学的にな

ってきているので、恐れの対象は一般に減ってきている。たとえば重力のような自然の法則は変わらないと確信している。船や飛行機で、はるか遠くまで安全に旅行できると安心している。わたしが覚えている範囲でも、まず助からないとされていた病気が、いまではかなりの部分、かならず直ると思えるようになった。結核療養所や、小児麻痺病棟、ハンセン病療養所はほぼなくなった。要するに、われわれは将来に、ある程度自信をもって直面できるのである。少なくとも、フランクリン・D・ローズベルト大統領が恐れを払拭するよう呼びかけたときよりもはるかに自信をもって。

しかし人間は素直にはできていない。科学的方法を逆に使って、将来を大いに恐れるようになっている。将来が安泰で恐れるようなことがとくにないのであれば、恐れる対象を作り出すらする。へそ曲がりが高じて、コンピューターを駆使した高度な数学モデルを使い、何らかの種類の災難がどこかに、近くあらわれると喜びを感じる人が多いように思える。たとえば、南アメリカの小さな蜂を「殺し屋」蜜蜂と名付ける。鳥インフルエンザをめぐるパニックはどうだろう。雑誌や新聞、テレビのニュース番組が一斉にこの話題に飛びつき、ウイルスに感染した鳥のために、人類のかなりの部分が死亡する大惨事が近く起こると大騒ぎしている。暗くて恐ろしい未来を予想する予言者は、エレミヤからカッサンドラ、チキン・リトルまで、

いつの時代にもいたのだが、啓蒙主義の時代からはとくに、悲観的な予想の説得力が高まってきた。さまざまな科学者が科学的な方法や統計モデルを使って、暗い予想を発表するようになったからだ。こうした予想はしっかりした証拠だとされるもの、論理的な思考を発表するものに裏付けられているために、ますます恐ろしいと思えた。ぼさぼさ頭の予言者が何かの占いを行ってこの世の終わりがくると叫んでも、それほど怖くはない。怪しいものだと考えることができるからだ。だが科学者が反論できないように思えるデータを示して、同じように恐ろしい結論が証明されたと主張した場合、別の事実と統計をもっていないかぎり、反論するのは難しい。そして、一般の人はたいてい、事実も統計も集めてはいない。

## 二百年前から売られている恐怖の悲観論

悲観論が注目を集める産業として急成長するようになったのは、トマス・ロバート・マルサスが登場してからだ。マルサスはイギリスの農村の牧師であり、数学者、経済学者である。人口学の父だといわれることも多い。近代悲観論の父であるのは確かだ。

マルサスは一七九八年に出版された『人口論』で、人類の将来は暗いと予言した。人口の増加に食料供給の増加が追いつかなくなるのは避けられないからだという。そうした状況がすぐ

に、おそらくは百年以内にあらわれると考えていた。この避けがたい悲劇を食い止めるのは、悲劇そのものしかないともみていた。だから、マルサスの理論の信奉者は、アイルランドのジャガイモ飢饉を歓迎した。十九世紀半ばにアイルランドで主食のジャガイモが不作になり、厳しい飢饉が起こって、たとえばわたしの祖先はアメリカに移住したのだが、そのために人口過剰が自然に調整されるというわけだ。当時、インドでも繰り返し飢饉が起こっているが、ビクトリア朝時代の教養ある人たちは、敬虔な牧師であるマルサスが主張した恐ろしい数学法則を信じていれば、やはり傍観するのが正しいと考えた。

いまにいたるまで、マルサスは悲観産業の基礎になり、発想のもとになっている。暗い予言が実現していれば、わたしはとうに死んでいたはずだ。たとえばポール・R・エーリッヒは一九六八年の『人口爆弾』で、七〇年代に何億人もが餓死し、八〇年代には平均寿命が大幅に短くなると予想した。そうはならなかった。一九七二年には有名なローマ・クラブが『成長の限界』を発表し、九〇年代にはあらゆる種類の基本的な原材料が不足するようになると予想した。そうはならなかった。その後も二回ほど改訂版がだされているが、いずれも端から信用されなかった。資源の供給が横ばいに推移すると想定しているからである。これらの報告書では、技術の進歩による代替資源の発見や発明は基本的に無視されている。人間は羊の群れのようだと みているのである。たしかに羊なら、放っておけば放牧地の草を食べ尽くして、最後には草が

## 最悪ケースのシナリオは
## めったに実現しない
### ──作者不詳

なくなってしまう。だが、人間はラテン語で「知恵ある人」を意味す
るホモ・サピエンスという学名にもあるように、牧草を栽培する方法、
あるいは羊を別の放牧地に移す方法を考える。

だが、恐怖の予想はつぎつぎにあらわれてくる。たとえば、牧草を
栽培すると疑いもなく、生態系のある側面が不均衡になり、その点を
指摘する人がでてくる。気分転換にテレビをつける。すると、かの宇
宙物理学者、デルバート・ロバート博士が黄色いジャケットを着込み、
強風のなか、大きな波が押し寄せる海岸で熱弁をふるっている。殺人
的な嵐の脅威をご覧ください。この嵐でセーシェルは吹き飛びかねま
せん。嵐はいま、北北東ないしは西南西に進路をとって、海岸か海上
に向かっています。続報をお楽しみに。

わたしはこれまで何度も、世界の終わりがくるという話を聞かされ
てきた。一九七〇年代に世界は凍りつくと予想されていた。八〇年代
にはチェルノブイリの事故で世界の終わりまであと一歩になった。九
〇年代末にはいわゆる二〇〇〇年問題で、世界の終わりにさらに近づ
いたとされた。それ以外にも、リンゴの農薬で癌になる話、高圧線で

癌になる話、携帯電話で癌になる話、食品に使われる合成着色料で癌になる話、ダイエット飲料のタブに使われた人工甘味料のチクロで癌になる話を聞かされてきた。

一九七〇年にチクロ騒動が起こったとき、科学者の多くはチクロに発癌性があるとの主張に懐疑的だった。実験に使われたチクロの量が異様に多かったからだ。癌になったというマウスは、人間でいえば、チクロ入りの飲料を一日当たり七百本飲んだのと同じ量を投与されている。癌になる前におぼれ死ななかったのが不思議なほどだ。それでもチクロは使用禁止になり、サッカリンが代わりに使われることになった。

これほどいくつもの話を聞かされてきたのだから、どこかで飽きるようになり、悲観産業の将来に悲観するようにならないのだろうか。だが、そうはなっていないようだ。

## 失敗に注目する悲観主義

たぶん、メディアの性格を考えれば、これは避けがたいことなのだろう。テレビは悲観主義を勢いづける点で、マルサス以来の大きな力になっている。われわれはテレビを通して世界をみている。その場合、世界が実際よりよくみえることはない。

友人の建築家から聞いた話だが、世界一美しい建物でも醜くみせることは可能だという。カ

メラを使って、ある角度からある部分を拡大すれば、美しい部分が何とも醜悪だと思えるようになる。光り輝く超高層ビルが、都市の荒廃の象徴のようにみえるようになるというのである。

来る日も来る日も、世界のなかで失敗した部分だけに注目していれば、人生と将来についての見方はすべて、それによって形成される。わたしが大好きな詩の一節がある。ロバート・ルイス・スティーブンソンの詩だとされることもあるが、作者不詳とされることも多い。「ふたりの男が監獄の鉄格子から表を眺め、ひとりは泥があるだけといい、もうひとりは星がみえるという」。どのような姿勢をとるのか、上をみるのか下をみるのかで、世界はまるで違ってみえるのである。

報道機関は、よいニュースを伝えてもビジネスにならない。悪いニュースを伝えなければ、誰も関心を示してくれない。毎日、無数の車が事故も起こさず、安全に運転されている。素晴らしいことだがニュースにはならない。そのなかの十台を巻き込む多重衝突事故が起これば、大ニュースだ。

いまでは過去になかったほど、ニュースの大洪水に見舞われている。悪いことはあらゆるところで、四六時中起こっている。

インターネットとケーブル・テレビのニュース・チャンネルが一日二十四時間、週に七日、悪いニュースを流しているので、われわれはいまや、世界各地から伝えられる惨事の警告や惨

事の報道に首までつかっている。

それだけでなく、不安感を何倍にも高めている現象がある。マスコミが仕組んだ議論だ。どのような問題にもかならずふたつ、あるいはそれ以上の見方があると、われわれは信じこまされるようになってきている。反論の余地なく科学的に論証されている点ですらそうだ。いまの社会はただでさえ教養が不足しているというのに、テレビをつけると専門家気取りの愚か者が大声を張り上げ、さまざまな問題を論じている。こういう娯楽番組をみていると、どんな点も議論の余地があり、どんなことでも主張でき、どんな立場にもよい点と悪い点があるように思える。そして、証明する責任は何かを肯定する側にあるので、否定する側のほうがたいていは論争に勝っているように思える。世界は急速に破滅に向かっていると主張するほうがいつも簡単なのだ。そう主張する方が出演者にとっては楽しいし、視聴者にとっては不安感に刺激され、心を奪われやすい。

数十年前まで、ニュースは新聞で読むものだった。新聞は、大見出しがどれほど派手であっても、静かで落ち着いたメディアだ。ページをめくる音が安心感を与えるともいえるほどだ。やがてラジオでニュースを聞くようになったが、それでもいまのテレビのニュース番組とくらべればはるかに落ち着いていて、恐ろしいものではなかった。映画館で流されるニュース映画の方が正直なところ刺激が強く、第二次世界大戦での勝利を興奮して伝えたり、ハワード・ヒ

ユーズが開発した巨大な飛行艇のスプルース・グース、どこかの農家でとれた四百キロもある巨大カボチャといった楽しい話題を取り上げていた。

テレビのニュースは当初、かなり短かったし、気楽にみることができた。いまではそうはいかない。まったく些細な点についてすら、絶望的な気分になる。

人間はいつもスリルを求める一方で、安全にこだわるものなのだ。

いまではあちこちに警告のシールが貼られている。トースターには、風呂のなかに持ち込んで遊ばないようにという警告のシールが掲げられている。あるホテルに泊まったとき、こう書かれていた。「カリフォルニア州保健局は、この建物に健康を害する恐れのある建材が使われていると警告しています。ようこそ、マリオット・ホテルへ」

二〇〇七年に、おかしな警告ラベル・コンテストで最優秀賞を獲得したのは、小型トラクターに貼られていたもので、こう書かれていた。「危険、死を避けよ」

最近の子供たちをみてみるといい。朝起きてベッドから離れるとすぐに、ヘルメットをかぶらされているようにすら思える。車に乗れば、チャイルド・シートで厳重に保護する。がんじがらめにされて、転んで怪我をしないように、膝にはパッドをつける。肘にもパッドをつける。空を見上げることすらできない。

マイクル・クライトンが『恐怖の存在』でこんな話を書いている。ある日、ビールを飲むと

184

心筋が丈夫になるという記事を読み、同じ日に、ビールには発癌性があるという記事を読んで、飲むべきか飲まざるべきか、大いに悩むことになったという。

行き着く先はこうなる。クリス・グッドールは『低炭素生活の手引き』の著者であり、緑の党の論客として有名なイギリス人だが、何とも暗いニュースを伝えている。五キロほどの距離を歩いて買い物に行くと、車を使った場合より二酸化炭素の排出量が多くなるというのだ。歩くのに使ったエネルギーを補うために食べる量が多くなり、食品の生産には大量のエネルギーが使われているからだと説明する。要するに、地球温暖化を防ぐには、車を使わないという程度では意味がない。暗い部屋に坐り込み、テレビや冷蔵庫、エアコンのプラグをコンセントから引き抜き、何もせず、何も食べないようにするしかない。

## 過去の呪縛としての悲観論

ジョン・ボーグルは投資信託のバンガード・グループの創業者だが、「手こぎボート症候群」にかかっている人が多いと語っている。将来に向かって進んでいくときに、ボートのこぎ手のように、後ろを向いて、過去だけをみているというわけだ。

誰でも、ときには郷愁にひたりたくなる。時間は過去の苦い思い出を消し去る万能薬だ。歴

史のなかでとくにひどかった時代すら、時間が経てば輝かしく思えてくる。よいことを覚えていて、悪いことは忘れるのが人間の本性であり、記憶が失われていくのはありがたいことだ。

若い世代を疑いの目でみるのも、人間の本性だ。聖アウグスティヌスも、アリストテレスも、ホメロスも、古代アッシリア人すらも、若者が老人を尊敬しないと非難し、怠け者で、乱暴で、「古きよき昔」の人たちとはまるで違うと嘆いている。

こういう文章を読むと、大変だと思えてくる。「学校で学ぶ子供のうち、読んでいる言葉の意味を知っている子は十二人に一人もいない」。昨日書かれた文章のように思えるだろうが、実際にはアメリカ公教育の父と呼ばれるホラス・マンが一八三八年に書いたものだ。喜劇俳優のウィル・ロジャーズが五十年以上前に書いたように、「学校は昔ほどよくはなくなっているが、昔よりよかった時期は一度もない」のである。

ちょっとした郷愁にひたるのは、悪いことではない。だが、ボーグルのいう手こぎボートに惚れ込んでいて、過去を過去のものにすることができない人もいる。過去はある程度まで分かっているし、ある程度までは漠然と理解できている。だから、現在よりも安心できるし、将来よりはるかに安心できるという人がいる。そうした人は、悲観論を唱えるのが責務だとすら考えている。進歩は不可能であり、昔よりよくなったものは何もなく、今後よくなるものは何もないと、心底信じているからだ。将来を恐れているために失敗した例はいくらでもあり、恐れ

のウイルスはいつでも企業につきまとっている。

わたしはもちろん、現代の進歩の哲学を強く信じている。現代に生きるわれわれは、農民だった祖先の一生を繰り返すように運命づけられてはいない。過去百年に何が起こったのかをみてみよう。

一九〇〇年ごろ、アメリカ人の平均寿命は四十七年であった。当時、食べていたものはすべて有機食品だ。労働者の平均年収は四百ドルだ。当時の大統領はウィリアム・マッキンリーであり、一九〇一年に暗殺されている。当時のアメリカ社会は騒然としていたし、いまにいたるまでそうだ。だが、世界各地から移民が押し寄せていた。アメリカでなら、将来は豊かになり、充実したものになると信じていたからだ。

アメリカでは革命的な変化がいくつも起こっている。以前には絶対のもの、変化しないもの、絶望的なほど永遠に続くものとみられていた点が、いまでは様変わりしている。求人広告に「アイルランド人お断り」と書かれているのが普通だった時代があった。いまでは、アイルランド人はどこでも活躍している。

アフリカ系アメリカ人は裏口しか使えなかった時代があった。この壁は徐々に取り除かれてきた。ゆっくりと、しかし着実に、アフリカ系アメリカ人に開放される部分が増え、いまでは、アメリカでとりわけ重要な公職を狙うことも十分に可能だし、実際に重要な公職についている

人もいる。

女性もかつて、多数の職業や学校など、社会のかなりの部分から排除されていた。いまでは、大学全体でみても、医学、法律学、経営学の大学院でみても、入学者の半分以上が女性になっている。歩みは遅いものの、社会のなかでとくに頑ななな部分ですら、進歩してきている。こうした部分はときに、「伝統主義」と呼ばれることもあるが、友人でノートルダム大学学長を長く務めたセオドア・ヘスバーグ神父によれば、「反動的で救いがたい石頭」である。

娘のシェイラはノートルダム大学がはじめて女学生を受け入れたときに、そのひとりになっている。一九七二年のことであり、ヘスバーグ神父が当時としては革命的な決定を下し、一八四二年の創立以来の男子校という伝統を打ち破った。娘がはじめて大学のオリエンテーションに出席したときのことは、よく覚えている。学内ではまだ、女性の受け入れに反対する意見がかなり強く、先駆者になった女学生はもとより、その親も、うまくいくのかどうか、少々神経質になっていたからだ。

その日の行事はミサではじまった。百二十五人の女学生とその親はみな、大学がどのように対応するのか、心配そうにみつめていた。ヘスバーグ神父が長い銀髪と白い祭服をなびかせて祭壇に進んだ。神父はタイミングの感覚が鋭く、この最初の瞬間が新しい制度の正否を決めるうえで決定的であることを熟知していた。両手をあげ、有名な黄金のドームのいちばん上にあ

188

るマリア像を見上げて、こういった。「マリア様、あなたの娘をこの場所にお連れするのに百三
十年もの年月がかかったことを、お詫びします」
　信じがたい瞬間だった。わたしたちは親も子供もみな、楽観主義の光に包まれ、わたしたち
自身にも、大学にも、この国の女性の将来にも、強い希望を感じた。

## 恐れによる無気力状態としての悲観論

　故ジュリアン・サイモンは『究極の資源』を書いた経済学者で、マルサス流の陰鬱な見方を
批判することにキャリアの大半を費やし、以下のように警告している。

　生活が物質面で豊かになってきたのは、天の恵みによるものではない。わたしがその点
で満足感を伝えようとしているわけではないのは確かだ。究極の資源は人間、とくにしっ
かりした教育を受け、活気があり、将来に期待をかけ、自由を与えられた若者だ。そうし
た若者が自分の利益のために意志と想像力を発揮し、その結果としてかならず、残りの人
たちにも利益をもたらす。

ヘレン・ケラーは何年も前にお目にかかることができたが、かつて、こう述べている。「悲観論者が星の秘密を発見したことはないし、未知の土地に航海したことも、人間の精神に新たな地平を切り開いたこともない」

強い悲観論でとくに深刻な問題は、完全な無気力をもたらすことだ。暗い結果になるのを恐れるあまり、絶望して手をあげ、何もしなくなるのだ。将来を恐れていれば、将来に失敗するのは避けがたい。

アメリカ経済は一九四一年以降、一度もほんとうに深刻な不況には陥っていない。ところがさまざまな世論調査によれば、アメリカ人の多くはいつも、不況のただ中にあるかのように陰鬱である。

アメリカ経済の主要な産業が破滅するといわれたことが何度あったか、気付いているだろうか。アメリカの製造業は消滅したと専門家が主張したことは、過去二十五年に少なくとも十回以上ある。だがいまでも、製造業はチャールストンのロボット産業からシアトルの航空機産業まで、全米各地で高賃金の新たな職を生み出しつづけている。北部や東南部のもっと小規模な地域でも、製造業の新しい職が大量に生まれている。さらに、エネルギーを節約し、環境汚染を減らし、地球環境を改善する必要にこたえて、新しい産業が誕生している。

あるとき、経営大学院の二人の教授の訪問を受け、こう質問された。「世界的な事業経験に基

190

づいて、新規事業に有利なのはどのような時期だと考えますか。どういう条件が必要だと思いますか」

恐怖を売り歩く人たちの意見を信じるのであれば、どんなことでも、はじめるのに有利な時期などない。どの時期にも、何か問題がある。ビジネス・モデルにいつも穴があり、地面のすぐ下に埋められた地雷のような問題がいつもある。

だが、起業家がかならずもっている創造性を信じるのであれば、ほとんどどんな時期も有利だといえる。新規事業に必要な条件についていうなら、こう考えてみるといい。「人がいるだろうか。いるとすれば、何かを食べ、飲んでいるだろうか。何らかの経済活動が行われているだろうか。財やサービスの交換に使える手段はあるだろうか。以上の点が満たされていれば、事業をはじめるのによい場所だし、よい時期だ」

将来に楽観的であれば、忍耐強くなれる。コカ・コーラ社は長い歴史のなかで、しばらく完全に閉め出されていた地域があった。アラブ諸国のすべて、中国、インド、キューバだ。このうちキューバ以外の国では、事業を再開できた。キューバについても、いつでも取引をはじめられるようにしており、コカ・コーラ社の現在の経営陣は事業を再開できると予想しているはずである。

何らかの形で事業を指導する立場に立ちたいと考えているのであれば、楽観主義者でなければならない。

コカ・コーラ社での仕事がほんとうに楽しかった理由はここにある。一九三〇年代の大恐慌、第二次世界大戦など、アメリカが暗かった時期に、コカ・コーラはいつも生活のなかで明るい部分を代表してきた。何はさておき、コカ・コーラはよい知らせをもたらすものなのである。

こうした精神から、暗い年であった一九七四年に、われわれは広告の戦略を考えた。

それにしても、何という時期だっただろう。ニクソン大統領が有名なウォーターゲート事件に関与したとして弾劾され、辞任を余儀なくされた。中東の産油国はアメリカへの原油輸出を禁止した。アメリカ各地でガソリン不足が深刻な問題になった。アイルランド共和国軍（IRA）がロンドンとベルファストでテロ攻撃を起こし、ロンドンで最大のデパート、ハロッズすら攻撃された。アメリカ国内にもテロ組織があり、たとえばシンバイオニーズ解放軍と名乗る組織が新聞王の孫娘、パティ・ハーストを誘拐している。インドは原子爆弾を開発した。アメリカはまだベトナムから抜けだそうと苦闘していた。要するに、アメリカにとって多難な時期だった。

だからこそ、コカ・コーラが楽観主義の旗を高く掲げるには絶好の時期であった。当時のマ

ーケティング部長、アイク・ハーバートとわたしでこの点を議論し、広告代理店にアメリカが元気を取り戻せるようなテーマを考えるよう依頼した。広告代理店のクリエイティブ部門を率いていたのは、才能あふれるビル・バッカーであり、「上を向こう、アメリカ」と題して、気持ちを高揚させる素晴らしいコマーシャルを制作した。

この広告への反応は素晴らしかった。たくさんの消費者が、わざわざ時間をとってコカ・コーラ社に感謝の手紙を書いてくれた。コカ・コーラという特別な商品がアメリカ人の心理に特別の意味をもっていることを示したのである。コカ・コーラはアメリカのムードにささやかながらも影響を与える力をもっている。この力には責任が伴う。マーケティングにあたって、気分が暗くなることをしてはならないという責任である。いつも、将来は明るいという確信を示さなければならない。

　何らかの形で事業を指導する立場に立ちたいと考えているのであれば、合理的な楽観主義者でなければならない。

大量の悲観論者のなかに、たったひとり楽観主義者がいれば、全体が見違えるようになる。アリストテレスは紀元前四世紀に書いた『霊魂論』で、人間の感覚には視覚、嗅覚、聴覚、

味覚、触覚の五つがあると論じた。それ以来、人間には五感があるというのが定説になっている。だがわたしは、六つめの感覚があると信じている。ムードを読む感覚である。直感と呼んでもいいし、洞察力と呼んでもいいし、感受性と呼んでもいいが、成功を収める人はこの能力をもっている。偉大なマーケターはこれをもっている。偉大な政治家、偉大な企業経営者はこれをもっている。

その場、あるいは、その時代に主流になっているムードは何なのかを察知でき、ムードが悪ければ、それを変える方法を知っている。

かなり前、フィリピンでコカ・コーラのボトリング事業が不調になった。十九世紀末の米西戦争が終わって以来、いつも好調だったのだが、この時期に坂道を転げ落ちるような状況になったのである。ボトリング事業を行っていたのは地元のサンミゲル社であり、同社の経営陣がビール事業の拡大に経営資源を集中する方針をとって、清涼飲料事業を無視するようになった。一九八一年には、事業の状況が極端に悪くなり、コークはペプシの半分にまで売上が落ち込んでいる。

やがて、サンミゲルの経営陣がコカ・コーラ社の経営幹部のひとり、ジョン・ハンターの説得を受け入れて、共同事業契約のもと、コカ・コーラ社がボトリング事業の経営を引き受けることになった。

経営は引き受けたが、設備は何も変わらない。一万二千人の従業員も変わらない。変えたのは二つの点だけだ。まず、ジョン・ハンターをコカ・コーラ社フィリピン事業の責任者にした。オーストラリア出身で、コカ・コーラ社の日本事業と環太平洋事業を担当してきた経歴がある。つぎに、ネビル・イズデルをボトリング会社の日本事業の責任者にし、一万二千人の従業員を率いるようにした。アイルランド出身で、コカ・コーラ社の南アフリカ事業を担当し、一時期、オーストラリア事業を担当した経歴がある。

ふたりは協力して、フィリピンのボトリング会社を変革し、活気づける仕事に取りかかった。イズデルはボトリング会社の一万二千人の従業員を再活性化し、経営計画を確立して実行した。

当時、フィリピンでは政治が混乱していて、誰にとってもストレスが高まっていた。それに、競争相手が戦術と価格で攻撃的な姿勢を強めていた。ボトリング会社の経営者として、従業員の意見を聞いた結果、従業員の自己評価がきわめて低く、将来について、極端に悲観的で、恐れてすらいることに気付いたのだ。事業は基本的に変わっていない。しかし、ムードは悪かった。

イズデルは作業服を着て現場の作業にくわわり、決起集会を開いて従業員を勇気づけた。いつも工場内を歩き回り、従業員の名前を覚えて話しかけ、家族の話を聞いた。トラックに乗って商品を配送し、顧客と話し合った。イズデルには強い熱意があり、それを周囲に伝染させて

いく力がある。数値でとらえることはできないが、そういう人がいればすぐに分かる。これが指導力である。

一年間、ふたりは協力しあい、焦点を絞って活動し、業績を一転させた。コカ・コーラはペプシの二倍の売上をあげるまでになった。

ネビル・イズデルは、ボトリング会社の従業員を活性化するために何をしたのだろうか。従業員と心を通わせ、自分たちは競争相手よりも優れていると確信させたのである。そして、将来は明るいという見方を伝えた。楽観的な見方に強い熱意をもち、末端の清掃係からマニラで最大の顧客まで、全員に伝えていった。

ジョン・ハンターはその後、コカ・コーラ社の執行副社長になって国際事業を担当するようになった。同社を引退した後、シーグラムの国際事業の会長になっている。

ネビル・イズデルはその後、コカ・コーラ社のヨーロッパ事業責任者になり、最大級のボトリング会社の会長になった。そして最近まで、コカ・コーラ社の最高経営責任者（CEO）として、伝染性のある楽観主義を全社に伝えてきた。

悲観論者によれば、世界は混沌のなかで生まれ、それ以降、下り坂を下がりつづけているという。しかし人間生きていくには希望が欠かせない。明日があると考え、事業をはじめるのによい時期があると考え、結婚するのによい時期があると考え、夕陽の美しさに感嘆し、生き続

けていかなければならない。

失敗したいのであれば、将来を恐れるといい。成功したいのであれば、将来を楽観し、熱意

をもって将来に立ち向かうべきだ。

この点から、ちょっとしたおまけとして、十一番目の法則を示すことにする。

# 法則11 ⟩ 仕事への熱意、人生への熱意を失う

アメリカという国の核心は独立宣言にある短い句に表現されているというのが、わたしの父の意見だった。「生命、自由、そして幸福の追求」という句だ。父がとくに感心していたのは、「幸福の追求」の部分である。人生には生きるために必死にはたらくだけではない何かが必要だと、建国の父は信じていたのだ。パンだけでなく、バラも必要なのだ。

父はアイルランド系なので、人生の暗い面や悲しい面を経験してきたはずだ。だからこそますます、アメリカという国が誕生したとき、建国の原則のひとつとして「幸福」という言葉を使った大胆さ、信じがたいほどの楽観主義に感銘を受けていたのだろう。

なんと、「幸福」だというのだ。幸福とは何なのか、ほんとうの意味で知っている人はいない。

だがアメリカという国は、幸福が達成できるという確信に基づいてつくられているのである。

# 世界で偉大なものはすべて、
## 熱意がなければ達成できなかった
### ——ゲオルク・ビルヘルム・フリードリヒ・ヘーゲル

わたしは事業にかかわるキャリアのなかで、幸福とは何かについて、自分なりの考えをもっている。

こういう言葉がある。「何を愛しているかが分かれば、どういう人物なのかが分かる」という。まさにいいえて妙だと思う。愛という言葉はずいぶん古くから使われている。英語のラブの語源は、古代インドのサンスクリット語で欲求を意味する言葉だという。事業の世界では、幸福の大きな部分は、愛情をもって取り組めることを何でもいいから探しだし、それを行う方法を見つけ出すという心境になることだ。成功するには、毎朝起きて仕事に行くのが楽しくて仕方ないという心境になることだ。

ウォーレン・バフェットはこう語っている。「わたしは毎朝、タップ・ダンスを踊るようにして仕事に行く」。わたしも同じ意見だ。

仕事が楽しくなければいけないという意味ではない。そんなことを考えるのは、人材部門のよほどおかしな連中だけだ。みんな会社のためにがんばろうといい、クンバヤを歌おうという。だが、仕事というものは、本物の仕事であれば、きわめて厳しいことも多く、ときには心身ともに疲れ果てる。従業員を元気づけるとき、フィリピンでネビ

ル・イズデルが行ったのが好例だが、もっと仕事を楽しもうなどとはいわない。もっとよい仕事ができるのだから、もっとはたらこうと呼びかける。従業員は満足感を得るために、もっとよい仕事をしたいと望む。仕事が厳しければ、タップ・ダンスを踊るようにして仕事に行くようになる。その日の問題を解決しようという熱意こそが重要なのだ。

ほんとうに失敗したいのであれば、自分の仕事への熱意をなくすべきだ。タップ・ダンスにならないようにする。こう考えて満足する。「もう十分だ」「これは自分の仕事ではない」「どうでもいい」「もうすぐ引退するんだから」

そう考えている人がいることは、誰でも知っている。暗い顔をした無気力な人は、どの職場にもいる。悲惨な思いのなかに閉じこもり、何もかも暗いと嘆くばかりで、蝋燭に火をともそうとはしない。誰でもそういう人を知っている。人生に失敗した人だ。暮らし向きは悪くないかもしれないが、人生に失敗している。自分自身について、周囲の人たちについて、まったく低い期待しかもっていないのだから。

わたしが知っているかぎり、成功を収めている人はみな、自分の仕事に愛情をもっていて、きわめて熱心に取り組んでいる。経営者でも、政治家でも、芸術家でも、教師でも、医師でも、偉大な業績をあげている人はみな、自分の仕事に心から熱意を燃やしている。質問してみれば、他の仕事をすることなど想像すらできないと答えるだろう。少し度が過ぎるのではないかと思

えるほど、夢中になっているのである。

もちろん、いまや同じ職で同じ会社に引退まで勤める時代ではなくなっているので、情熱をもって仕事に取り組むという考え方が時代後れのように感じられることは理解している。数年もすれば、別の会社で別の仕事をしているのが当たり前になっているのに、情熱などもてるのだろうか。仕事に熱意を燃やして何になるというのか。そうみられている。

だが、だからこそ、仕事への情熱が重要なのだ。

わたしは本書の冒頭で、事業で勝利する確実な方法は知らないと書いた。ほんとうに知らないからだ。だが、自分の仕事に情熱をもつようにする方法についてなら、少し助言できることがある。情熱は育てられるものだと、わたしは強く確信している。

シェークスピアは「人間世界はことごとく舞台です」と書いた。

社会学者のアービング・ゴッフマンは大きな影響を与えた『行為と演技――日常生活における自己呈示』で、シェークスピアのこの言葉について詳しく論じ、人は何をするときにも、かならず何かの役で演技者にならなければならず、いくつもの役を演じ分けなければならないことも多いと述べている。店員は顧客のために演じる。ウェイターも客のために演じる。弁護士は依頼人のために、裁判のために、そして同僚のために演じる。医者は患者のために、同僚のために演じる。経営幹部は部下のために、上司のために演じる。

さまざまな演技で成功を収めるには、そのときの観客がどのような人物であっても、観客との感情的なつながりを確立することが重要だ。何を演技するときにも、演じているときに、自分の行っていることに心の底からの感情がこもるようにしなければならない。演じている自分自身をしっかり意識する。その時点の自分の役を理解する。

高校生のとき、ある科目が退屈だとこぼしたことがある。母はこうたしなめた。「退屈な科目などありません。退屈に思うのは、面白い理由を探し出そうとしないからです」

わたしは一生を通じて、さまざまな場面、さまざまな国で、そのときの状況に興味をもち、関係する人たちとの感情的なつながりを確立しようと、意識的に努力してきた。また、副次的な問題や雑音は無視して、そのときに対している相手の話を熱心に聞き、相手が伝えようとしている点が興味深い理由を見つけ出そうと、意識的に努力してきた。何秒かのうちに、相手の関心に共感できた。

不快な状況に直面したこともたくさんあり、できればそのときの課題を避けたいと思うことも少なくなかった。しかしそういうときにも状況をしっかりとみて、こう考えるようにした。「ここから何か、よい結果が生まれることはないだろうか。救いになる点は何だろうか。それを実現するために、わたしは何をすべきなのだろうか」。たいていは、よい点を見つけ出すことができた。見つけ出そうと努力したからだ。部下を解雇しなければならないのはたぶん、最悪の

202

仕事だろうが、そうしたときにも、相手にもっと適したキャリアかもっと適した会社を勧めるようにした。

そのときどきの仕事に熱心に取り組むのが、できるかぎり最善の結果をもたらすために不可欠だ。仕事の場で自分の心のなかにある情熱を育てようとするとき、もっとも簡単な方法は、自分の周囲の世界のうち、以下の四つの面に神経を集中させることだ。顧客、ブランド、同僚、そして自分の夢である。

## 顧客との感情的なつながりを確立する

自分の会社に対して、顧客が何を求め、何を期待し、何を望んでいるのかを、いつも、忘れないようにする。製品だろうか。サービスだろうか。楽しいひとときだろうか。助力や配慮、助言、専門知識だろうか。以上のすべてということもあるだろう。だがいつも最善を尽くし、顧客の立場にたって、自社が提供する何かにお金もあるだろう。顧客によって違うという場合もあるだろう。だがいつも最善を尽くし、顧客の立場にたって、自社が提供する何かにお金を支払ってくださる顧客の目線で考えるようにする。少し気を緩めると、個々の顧客を見失って、市場や市場セグメントなど、抽象的な概念だけで考えるようになる。市場セグメントというのは統計上の抽象的な概念にすぎず、実際には存在しない。実際にい

るのは人である。ひとりひとり個性のある人である。顧客を思い浮かべる。具体的な人を思い浮かべ、その人のためにその日、何をするのかを考える。わたしは長年、オフィスに一枚の写真を掲げていた。三十がらみの女性がショッピング・カートを押し、三歳ぐらいの子供が泣き叫んでいるので手をしっかりと握ってひっぱり、苦痛の表情を浮かべている。写真には「これが顧客だ」と書かれている。

コカ・コーラ社食品部門、後にコカ・コーラ本社に勤務していたとき、わたしはよくスーパーやファースト・フード店に立ち寄り、客の意見に耳をかたむけた。広告代理店は典型的な顧客像を示し、好みや生活スタイルについての統計データを大量にそろえてくれる。しかしわたしはそのときどきに、顧客の意見を直接に聞きたくなる。自分が奉仕したいと考えている人たちに、感情的なつながり、心からの愛着をもつことが必要だと感じる。その女性、その男性、その家族のことを気に掛けたいのだ。顧客が自社の商品で楽しいひとときをおくれるよう、わたしは心底望んでいる。

## ブランドとの感情的なつながりを確立する

わたしは自分が売っているものすべてに、愛情をもってきた。妻、子供、孫を除けば、これ

までの生涯にとくに強い熱情をもってきたのは、それを代表する名誉を与えられたブランドであった。当初の何十年かはコカ・コーラだったし、いまはアレン・ブランドとアレン社である。わたしはいつも成功を収めてきたわけではないが、それでもいつも、自分が扱うブランドを守り、強め、拡大していくよう望んできた。新しいブランドであれば、それを育て、強い基盤を作り上げるよう望んできた。

ブランドとブランド名は、事業でとりわけ強力な要因だ。ブランド力がなければ、どこにもある商品、ありきたりの商品を売っているにすぎない。どの会社でも市場に参入して、シェアを奪っていくことができる。強力なブランドがあれば、事業を守る武器になり、将来を築く基盤になる。ティッシュを売っているのであれば、多数の同業他社と同じ商品を売っているにすぎない。だが、クリネックスを売っているのなら、同業他社には対抗できない何かを提供できる。

強固なブランドに代わるものは何もない。この点は繰り返し繰り返し、さまざまな方法で確認されている。二〇〇七年に、ブランドの力がスタンフォード大学の研究で改めて示されている。牛乳、リンゴ・ジュース、人参といったごく普通の同じ商品を、包装だけ変えて被験者に味わってもらった。一方は何も印刷されていない白い紙を使い、他方はマクドナルドの有名なゴールデン・アーチが印刷された包装を使った。

結果がどうだったかは、いうまでもない。どの場合も、マクドナルドの包装を使った方が好まれた。人参すら、マクドナルドの包装を使ったものの方が美味しいとされた。

ブランドは魔法である。そして、その魔法を理解し、熱意をこめて保護する人が管理しているときに、ブランドは力を発揮する。法律事務所がブランドになっている。病院がブランドになっている。そしてアメリカという国は、まさにブランドである。ブランドは愛情をもって扱っていれば、消費者に熱心に支持される。そして、投資家にも強く支持されるのである。

シュリッツ・ビールのように粗末に扱っていると、ブランドは消滅し、会社まで消滅することになる。

## 同僚との感情的なつながりを確立する

「従業員は会社にとって、もっとも重要な資産である」。そう語る会社は多い。

つくづく好運だったと思うのだが、わたしがはたらいてきた会社では、この決まり文句に表現されている知恵をほんとうに大切にし、活かしてきた。いま所属しているアレン社は、独特の企業文化をもっており、ハーバート・アレンはかつてこれをこう表現した。「従業員にとっては福祉国家、経営幹部にとってはむき出しの資本主義」。アレンの優れた経営哲学のもと、従業

員は給与水準が高いうえ、ボーナスも多く、業績が好調だった年には十二か月分にもなる。し

かし、経営幹部にはセーフティ・ネットはない。各人が生み出した事業の収益のうち、決まっ

た比率を受け取るだけである。この仕組みはどの企業にも適用できるわけではないが、アレン

社ではみな満足しているようだ。定着率が高い点をみればそういえる。アレン社の企業文化で

は、従業員をほんとうに、会社にとってもっとも重要な資産として扱っている。理由は簡単で

ある。従業員がほんとうに、最重要の資産だからだ。

だが事実をみていくと、実際にそう考えている企業は、それほど多くないようだ。そう考え

ているのであれば、フォーチュン誌の「はたらきがいのある会社」のリストに入っているはず

だし、とくに優秀な人材が他社に流出することもないはずだ。

優秀な人材が辞めていく理由のひとつについてはすでに述べた。官僚組織で身動きができな

くなっていることである。

別の理由として、情熱をもって取り組めることが何もないという点があげられる。人事戦略

コンサルティング会社のタワーズ・ペリンが世界各国で実施した調査によれば、従業員の三十五

パーセントが、現在の職場に失望し、やる気をなくしていると回答している。

優秀な従業員にとって、収入と地位はたしかに重要だが、それ以上に重要なのは、熱意を燃

やして本気で取り組めるものに参加する機会だ。従業員の意欲を高める方法として、深い情熱

をもって全身全霊を傾けなければ達成できない課題を与えることに勝る方法はない。

一九〇七年、アーネスト・シャクルトンは南極大陸横断探検隊の隊員を集めようと、ロンドンのタイムズ紙に広告をだした。「求む男子。至難の旅。わずかな報酬。極寒。暗黒の長い日々。生還の保証なし。成功の暁には名誉と賞賛」。翌朝、少数の隊員に選ばれようと、新聞社には五千人が列をつくったといわれている。

ほとんどの人は何か意味のあることを達成したいという強い欲求、情熱をもっており、達成できる可能性が低くても情熱は失わない。難しいパズルを与えれば、必死になって解いてくれる。わたしの経験ではどの企業でも、意味のある課題を従業員に示し、それがいかに重要かを熱意をこめて説き、情熱と才能をどのように発揮すれば課題を達成できるかを説明すると、組織全体に電流のように興奮が伝わっていくものだ。

ひとつの部門での情熱は他の部門で情熱を燃え上がらせる。情熱は伝染し、新しいアイデアと新しい活力を生み出す。

## 自分の夢との感情的なつながりを確立する

夢は望んでいるだけでは夢のままだ。夢を自分が実現すると考え、実現できる人間になると

分別のある人は
世界に自分を合わせようとする。
分別のない人は
世界を自分に合わせようとする。
だから、進歩はすべて
分別のない人のお陰だ
──ジョージ・バーナード・ショー

決意し、実現したときにどうなるかを思い描こうにすれば、実現する可能性が高まる。人はみな、テイヤール・ド・シャルダンのいう「生成」の過程にある。進化の終点にある「オメガ点」、すべての力が人間に集中し、人間が完成に近づく点に向かっていくのである。人はみなオメガ点には到達できないが、重要なのはそこに向かって努力を続けていくことなのだ。

人はみな、いつかはいま行っていることから離れる。世界のなかでいま、自分がいる場所について考え、自分が離れるときにどうなっていることを望むかを考えてみる。

何年たっても、貴重な教訓を学ばない人がいる。人生には、あらゆるものを手に入れることより重要な点があるという教訓だ。キャリアを重ねていくなかで、ひとつの職についたとき、これが最後の職だ

と考え、与えられた仕事が何であれ、この職を離れるときには当初よりよい状態にするのだと決意するべきだ。

本書であげた法則はどれも、一貫して頑固に守っていれば、事業でかならず失敗すると断言できるものばかりである。

第十一の法則はそのなかでもとくに重要だ。情熱はアメリカン・ドリームを引き継ぎ拡大していくために不可欠だからだ。わたしは生涯にわたって、アメリカン・ドリームの恩恵を受けてきた。だから今後も何世代にもわたって、人びとが同じ恩恵を受けられるように望んでいる。

楽観主義と情熱は、指導力と社会の進歩という同じ織物の縦糸と横糸にあたる。失敗したいのであれば、こうした心理的な要因は無視すればいい。成功したいのであれば、こうした要因を活用して、自分がいる場を改善していくべきだ。

注意しておくべき点がある。情熱と楽観主義の旗を掲げていると、「現実主義者」を自称する皮肉屋に批判されることがあるが、それを恐れてはならない。だが、こうした批判を受け入れる前に、少し考えてみるべきだ。現実的になるというのは、安易な道を選んで、高い理想に向かうのを諦めるという意味ではないのかと。普通のものではない目標を目指しているとき、周囲の人たちはその目標をまだ理解できていないという場合もある。

ジャンヌ・ダルクは
みんなに笑われたが、
かまわず前進し、
目的を達成した
——グレーシー・アレン

　この地球上にはなんと、間違いを犯しやすい人間が六十億人以上もいるし、悲しくなるような欠陥がたくさんあるのだが、それでも素晴らしい場所だ。どこをみても、少しは改善できる部分がある。こういえば反対する人が多いが、世界中の人たちがもっとよい機会をもてるようにしていく点で、ビジネスが主要な手段のひとつだと、わたしはつねに信じてきた。そして、ビジネスの世界ではたらけるのは、ほんとうに名誉なことだとも信じてきた。この名誉には、責任が伴う。ものごとをもっとよくしていく責任である。わたしはコカ・コーラ社で好運な人生を送ってきており、その間に世界各地で以上の点をはっきりと示す例をみてきた。

　六百年ほど前、聖アウグスティヌスはこう論じている。「希望には美しい娘がふたりいる。その名は、怒りと勇気だ。ものごとが現状のようになっていることに対する怒り、そして、もののごとを本来の姿にする勇気である」

　子供や孫の世代に世界がもっとよくなっていることを望むの

であれば、信じることだ。ひとりの力で違いを生み出すことができると信じる。そして、自分がそのひとりになりうると信じる。

リスクをとるのを止め、柔軟性をなくし、部下を遠ざけ、自分は無謬だと考え、反則すれすれのところで戦い、考えるのに時間を使わず、外部の専門家を全面的に信頼し、官僚組織を愛し、一貫性のないメッセージを送り、将来を恐れていれば、かならず失敗する。

明るい面をみるなら、回復する方法がある。危険な徴候を見つけ、手遅れにならないうちに行動すれば、おそらく、これらの罠から、いくつもの罠からでも脱出できるだろう。これらの罠を避けるのが難しい時期は、誰にもあるし、どの企業にもある。これまでに書いてきたように、コカ・コーラ社の経営陣はわたしも含めて、これらの罠に陥る時期があった。しかし、長い期間にわたることはなかった。偉大な企業、優れた個人はみなそうだ。何が起ころうとも、失敗から抜け出せなくなることにはならない。ときに失敗するのだが、そこから抜け出す方法を見つけ出し、また前進する。

## 謝　辞

本というものは、ごく短い本でも、ひとりの力で完成するわけではない。過去二十五年間、わたしはふたりの仲間のお陰で、話す内容、書く内容を明確にし、まとめることができてきた。スピーチを行う機会が増え、対象とする人の範囲が広がっていった一九八一年、ジョン・ホワイトがスタッフになり、パートナーになって協力してくれるようになった。執筆の専門家であり、素晴らしい判断力をもっている。その後いまにいたるまで、いつも相談相手として、編集者として活躍してくれている。

デビッド・ブロムクイストはルネサンス型の教養人であり、同じ期間にわたって、わたしの考えやアイデアを取り上げ、論理立て、組織立てられるよう支援してくれた。わたしの考えが漠然としていたり、明確でなかったりしていれば、するどく批判し、わたしが話すか書く内容が対象とする人にふさわしいものになるようにしてくれた。

ニール・オーダウドはアイリッシュ・アメリカン・マガジン誌とアイリッシュ・ボイス誌の

共同創業者、発行人であり、北アイルランドの和平交渉で重要な役割を果たしてきた人物だが、わたしにとって長年の親友である。いかにもジャーナリストらしい調査を行って、わたしの祖先についてかなりの事実を発見してくれた。その内容は本書と他の出版物に記してある。

この小さな本が出版されたのは、ポートフォリオ社の創業者で発行人のエードリアン・ザックハイムが思い切った決定をしてくれたからである。担当編集者のコートニー・ヤングは適切で思慮深い質問をし、提案をして、原稿の質を大幅に高めてくれた。

アルフレッド・テニソンは「ユリシーズ」で、「わたしはこれまでに出会ったすべての人の一部だ」とうたっている。わたしの場合はまさにそうだと思う。子供のころには当然ながら、両親から大きな影響を受けた。母は音楽と絵画が大好きで、芸術と文学の面白さを教えてくれた。父は何度も苦境に陥りながらも、いつも将来への熱意をもちつづけ、事業の目標を達成し、誠実さこそが人生に価値があったかどうかを決める第一の基準だとみていた。

社会にでてからも、素晴らしい人たちに出会い、その下で、あるいは協力してはたらく機会を得てきた。パクストン＆ギャラガーのポール・ギャラガー、ギルバート・スワンソンとクラーク・スワンソン、チャールズ・ダンカン、ルーク・スミス、ポール・オースティン、ロベルト・ゴイズエタ、ハーバート・アレン、バリー・ディラー、ジャック・ウェルチ、ジミー・ウィリアムズらである。

コカ・コーラ社の長老、ロバート・W・ウッドラフはわたしを同社の家族の一員として受け入れてくれた。ウッドラフの晩年にともに時間を過ごせたのは、ほんとうに名誉なことであった。

ウォーレン・バフェットに出会ったのは一九六〇年、わたしがオマハで、バフェット家のすぐ向かいにある家を買ったときだ。それからの長く密接な付き合いは、それだけで一冊の本になるほどである。バークシャー・ハザウェイの取締役を務めているのは、ほんとうに名誉なことだと考えている。バフェットについて、世間で知られていないことを何かいえるだろうか。わたしにいえるのは、親しい友人、素晴らしい人物であり、いままさに脂がのりきっているこ とだ。ものごとを単純化する名人だ。複雑な経済理論や企業経営の問題を、聖書にでてくるようなたとえ話で説明し、簡単に理解できるようにしてくれる。万人があこがれるヒーローであり、わたしにとってもそうだ。

一九九三年四月十四日、わたしはコカ・コーラ社を引退した。翌日、アレン社の非常勤会長に就任するよう要請された。そう要請してくれたハーバート・アレンは、わたしがこれまで出会ったなかでも、とりわけ素晴らしい人物だ。機知と思慮をじつに巧みに組み合わせ、間違いには寛大で、社会がぶつかっている主要な問題に強い関心をもち、隠れた知識人である。わたしがアレン社にくわわったとき、たぶん、一年か二年だけとアレンは考えていたと思う。十四

年たって、わたしはまだアレン社にいる。わたしをおいてくれているのである。肩書きは大きいが、責任はそれほどなく、一族経営のこの会社で素晴らしい体験をしている。ハーバート・アレンと友人として、同僚として付き合い、息子たちや優れた幹部とともに仕事をするのはじつに楽しい。

誰でも一生のうちに、きわめて大きな影響を受ける人物に出会うことがある。わたしにとって、そういう人物にセオドア・ヘスバーグ神父がいる。九十歳になったいまはノートルダム大学の名誉学長である。神父はいくつもの分野で活躍してきた。神父であり、教育者であり、さまざまな公務につき、六人の大統領の相談相手であり、特別大使を三回務め、三十五年にわたってノートルダム大学学長を務め、ハーバード大学監督委員会の元委員長でもあり、もっとも多くの名誉学位を授与された人物である。タイム誌は、アメリカでとくに尊敬されている人物のひとりだとしている。わたしにとって、大切な友人であり、家族全員の相談相手である。

最後に、五十年以上にわたって素晴らしい人生の旅をともにしてきた妻のミッキーがいる。六人の子供とその配偶者、十八人の孫がいつも、わたしたち夫婦の生活に大きな喜びをもたらしている。全体として、ほんとうに素晴らしい人生だった、まあ、ある程度までは。

# 訳者あとがき

著者のドナルド・キーオは一九八一年から九三年までコカ・コーラ社の社長を務め、CEO のゴイズエタとともに、同社を繁栄に導いてきた経営者だ。同社を引退後、投資銀行のアレン&カンパニー社の会長を務めている。この経歴から想像されるのはたぶん、著名な経営大学院でMBAを取得し、コカ・コーラ社に入社して出世街道をまっしぐらに駆けてきたか、そうでなければ、著名なコンサルタント会社を経て、同社に引き抜かれたといった人物像だろう。

実際は、正反対とまではいえないにしろ、大きく違う。

第二次世界大戦中に海軍に入り、復員後に大学はでているが、専攻したのは哲学である。ネブラスカ州オマハのテレビ局で短期間、アナウンサーとして勤務した後、地元の食品会社に転職した。この会社が何回か買収され、やがてコカ・コーラ社に買収されたことで、同社に勤務するようになった。買収した側ではなく、買収された側の企業に勤務していたのだ。いってみれば、傍流の傍流から出発して、コカ・コーラ社全体の指揮をとるようになったのである。

若いころの経歴で目立つのは唯一、オマハでウォーレン・バフェットの向かいの家に住んでいて、親友になったことだけだろう。しかし、当時のバフェットはまだ、無名の投資家にすぎなかった。

この経歴から容易に想像がつくように、キーオは並みの経営者ではない。本書を読むと、そう痛感するはずだ。目から鼻へ抜けるような人物ではない。どの分野の専門家でもない。たぶん、茫洋とした常識人という印象だろうか。

本書の内容がまさにそうだ。アメリカを代表するどころか、世界を代表する企業の経営者だった立場で、事業に成功する方法は分からないとは、なかなかいえないものだと思う。そういいきってしまうのがキーオという経営者の凄さなのだろう。成功する方法は分からないが、失敗する方法なら分かるということで生まれたのが本書である。

成功の法則とやらを並べた本はいくらでもある。何しろ、成功の法則の本を書くのが成功の近道、とくに、金儲けの法則の本を書くのが金儲けの近道だという冗談があるほどなのだ。偉大な常識人である著者は、ビジネスのようにダイナミックで変化が激しい分野で、成功の法則など開発できていないという。そして、ビジネスの世界で数多く経験し、見聞きしてきた失敗例から導き出したのが、本書に書かれている失敗の法則である。

とはいっても、戦略上の失敗を扱っているのではない。会社の失敗ではなく、会社を指導す

る経営者個人の失敗に焦点を絞っている点に本書の特徴がある。とくに、大きな成功を収めたときに陥る罠を強調している。

コカ・コーラ社の失敗としてとくに有名なのは、たぶん、ニュー・コークだろう。この大失敗はキーオが社長だった時期のものなのだ。このとき、なぜ失敗したのか、みずからの失敗にどう対処したかが書かれている点が、本書の魅力のひとつだ。しかし、それだけではない。コカ・コーラ社や他社の経営者の失敗がつぎつぎに紹介されていく。多彩な具体例が本書の大きな魅力だ。そして、そこから得られる教訓を覚えやすい十の法則にまとめた点も。

ウォーレン・バフェットによる序文も、本書の魅力のひとつだ。長年の友人だから義理で書いたのだろうと思えるかもしれないが、そうではない。著者と本書を高く評価しているからこそ、推奨の言葉を書いたのだと思う。バークシャー・ハザウェイは本書を一千部買い、株主総会で配ったというのだから。

本書の原著は二〇〇八年の半ばに出版された。その後、金融市場が激震に見舞われ、景気が急激に冷え込むようになった。これまで巨額の利益をあげて成功を収めてきた企業がいくつも不振に陥り、経営が破綻した企業、政府の支援を受けてようやく生き残っている企業も少なくない。まさに、成功を収めたときの罠に陥ったのだろう。経済と社会が現在の苦境からどのように抜け出すのかは、まだ分からない。おそらく、大きな転機を迎えているのだろうが、新し

い方向はまだみえていない。こういう時期にこそ、本書のような戒めの書が役立つように思える。

本書の翻訳にあたっては、日本経済新聞出版社翻訳出版部の國分正哉部長と金東洋氏に大変お世話になった。また、いつものことながら、何人もの方にさまざまな助言をいただき、間違いを指摘していただき、質問に答えていただいた。この場を借りてお礼を申し上げたい。どんな仕事でもそうであるように、翻訳という仕事も、たくさんの方に支えられなければできないものだと痛感している。

二〇〇九年三月

山岡洋一

著訳者紹介 ─────────────────────────────

## ドナルド・R・キーオ（Donald R. Keough）

アレン＆カンパニー会長。1927年生まれ。コカ・コーラ元社長兼COO。ロベルト・ゴイズエタCEOと共に12年間にわたりコカ・コーラを経営し、世界200カ国以上のコカ・コーラ・システムを活性化させた。その後、投資銀行のアレン＆カンパニー会長を務めるほか、バークシャー・ハザウェイ、マクドナルド、ワシントンポスト、ハインツなど数多くの企業の取締役も務める。本書の序文を書いたウォーレン・バフェットとは長年の友人。

## 山岡洋一（やまおか・よういち）

翻訳家。1949年生まれ。主な訳書にアラン・グリーンスパン『波乱の時代』、アダム・スミス『国富論』、ジェームス・C・アベグレン『新・日本の経営』『日本の経営〈新訳版〉』、ジョセフ・S・ナイ『ソフト・パワー』（以上、日本経済新聞出版社）、ジェームズ・C・コリンズ＆ジェリー・I・ポラス『ビジョナリー・カンパニー』（日経BP社）などがある。

## ビジネスで失敗する人の10の法則

2009年4月20日　1版1刷
2009年6月25日　　　4刷

著　者　ドナルド・R・キーオ

訳　者　山　岡　洋　一

発行者　羽　土　　　力

発行所　日本経済新聞出版社

http://www.nikkeibook.com/
東京都千代田区大手町 1-9-5　〒 100-8066
電話　03-3270-0251

印刷・製本／中央精版印刷株式会社

Printed in Japan　ISBN978-4-532-31449-1

## グリーン革命（上・下）

温暖化、フラット化、人口過密化する世界

トーマス・フリードマン／伏見威蕃訳

● 各1900円

産業革命を超えるグリーン革命が始まった！ 温暖化、フラット化、人口過密化が進む「新世界」では、どのような経済活動、政治、生活が待っているのか。『フラット化する世界』の著者が世界の進むべき針路を示す！

## フラット化する世界【増補改訂版】（上・下）

経済の大転換と人間の未来

トーマス・フリードマン／伏見威蕃訳

● 各2000円

世界的ベストセラーがアップデート＆大幅加筆で登場！ 世界経済を呑みこむ「フラット化」という巨大な潮流に、個人はどうやって対応すべきかを示す新章が追加され、さらに結論部分も最新事例をとりいれて全面改稿。

## スターバックスを世界一にするために守り続けてきた大切な原則

ハワード・ビーハー、ジャネット・ゴールドシュタイン／関美和訳

● 1500円

信頼を大切にする、挑戦を怖れない、夢を大切にする、一人ひとりを個人として扱う……。全世界にスタバを広めた著者が「人を大事にする」という信念を軸に世界一へと上り詰めた軌跡と10個の大切な「原則」を明かす。

## コーチングの神様が教える「できる人」の法則

マーシャル・ゴールドスミス、マーク・ライター／斎藤聖美訳

● 1800円

有能な人ほど抱えている「20の悪い癖」とは何か？ なぜ、それを捨てないと出世できないのか？ ジャック・ウェルチもコーチした著者が、優秀な人材を「さらに伸ばす」方法を初公開。全米ベストセラー第1位！

## さあ、才能（じぶん）に目覚めよう

あなたの5つの強みを見出し、活かす

マーカス・バッキンガム、ドナルド・O・クリフトン／田口俊樹訳

● 1600円

知識や技能のように簡単には得られない才能こそあなたの「最強の武器」だ。200万人のインタビュー調査から導き出された34個の強みから、自分の強みを探し出そう。それをビジネスに活かしたとき、革命が起こる！

● 価格はすべて税別です